A TEXT BOOK OF

WIRELESS NETWORKS

(Elective IV)

FOR

SEMESTER - II

FINAL YEAR (BE) DEGREE COURSE IN
ELECTRONICS AND TELECOMMUNICATION ENGINEERING

According to New Revised Syllabus of
Savitribai Phule Pune University, Pune.
(2012 Pattern)

Dr. G R PATIL

Ph. D (E & TC),
Associate Professor, E & TC Engg. Department,
Army Institute of Technology,
Dighi, Pune

NIRALI PRAKASHAN
ADVANCEMENT OF KNOWLEDGE

N 3731

WIRELESS NETWORKS (B.E. E&TC SEM. II)　　　　　ISBN 978-93-5164-890-1

Second Edition　　:　　January 2017

©　　:　　Author

Published By :

NIRALI PRAKASHAN

Abhyudaya Pragati, 1312, Shivaji Nagar,

Off J.M. Road, PUNE – 411005

Tel - (020) 25512336/37/39, Fax - (020) 25511379

Email : niralipune@pragationline.com

☞ **DISTRIBUTION CENTRES**

PUNE

Nirali Prakashan　:　119, Budhwar Peth, Jogeshwari Mandir Lane, Pune 411002, Maharashtra
Tel : (020) 2445 2044, 66022708, Fax : (020) 2445 1538
Email : bookorder@pragationline.com, niralilocal@pragationline.com

Nirali Prakashan　:　S. No. 28/27, Dhyari, Near Pari Company, Pune 411041
Tel : (020) 24690204 Fax : (020) 24690316
Email : dhyari@pragationline.com, bookorder@pragationline.com

MUMBAI

Nirali Prakashan　:　385, S.V.P. Road, Rasdhara Co-op. Hsg. Society Ltd.,
Girgaum, Mumbai 400004, Maharashtra
Tel : (022) 2385 6339 / 2386 9976, Fax : (022) 2386 9976
Email : niralimumbai@pragationline.com

☞ **DISTRIBUTION BRANCHES**

JALGAON

Nirali Prakashan　:　34, V. V. Golani Market, Navi Peth, Jalgaon 425001,
Maharashtra, Tel : (0257) 222 0395, Mob : 94234 91860

KOLHAPUR

Nirali Prakashan　:　New Mahadvar Road, Kedar Plaza, 1st Floor Opp. IDBI Bank
Kolhapur 416 012, Maharashtra. Mob : 9850046155

NAGPUR

Pratibha Book Distributors　:　Above Maratha Mandir, Shop No. 3, First Floor,
Rani Jhanshi Square, Sitabuldi, Nagpur 440012, Maharashtra
Tel : (0712) 254 7129

DELHI

Nirali Prakashan　:　4593/21, Basement, Aggarwal Lane 15, Ansari Road, Daryaganj
Near Times of India Building, New Delhi 110002
Mob : 08505972553

BENGALURU

Pragati Book House　:　House No. 1, Sanjeevappa Lane, Avenue Road Cross,
Opp. Rice Church, Bengaluru – 560002.
Tel : (080) 64513344, 64513355,Mob : 9880582331, 9845021552
Email:bharatsavla@yahoo.com

CHENNAI

Pragati Books　:　9/1, Montieth Road, Behind Taas Mahal, Egmore,
Chennai 600008 Tamil Nadu, Tel : (044) 6518 3535,
Mob : 94440 01782 / 98450 21552 / 98805 82331,
Email : bharatsavla@yahoo.com

niralipune@pragationline.com　|　www.pragationline.com

Also find us on 🇫 www.facebook.com/niralibooks

PREFACE TO THE SECOND EDITION

I am glad and excited to announce that the First Edition of this book received an overwhelming response from the engineering student community, compelling me to release its Second Edition within a very short period of time.

This New Edition has been updated with including all University Question Papers In Sem. February 2016, End Sem. May 2016 and November 2016.

Special care has been taken to maintain high degree of accuracy in the theory and numericals throughout the book.

I take this opportunity to express my sincere thanks to Dineshbhai Furia of Nirali Prakashan, a reputed pioneer in the publication field. My special thanks to Jignesh Furia for their effective cooperation and great care in bringing out this revised edition. I also appreciate the efforts of M. P. Munde and the entire staff of Engineering Books Deptt. of Nirali Prakashan namely Mrs. Deepali Lachake (Co-ordinator) for bringing this book to the students in a timely manner.

I sincerely hope that this "Second Edition" will also be warmly received by all concerned as in the past.

Valuable suggestions from my esteemed readers to improve the book are most welcome and highly appreciated.

Pune   **Author**

PREFACE TO THE FIRST EDITION

It gives me great pleasure to bring out the book on **"Wireless Networks"**. This book is strictly written as per the New Revised Syllabus of Savitribai Phule Pune University, (2012 Pattern) for the students of final year Degree Course in Electronics and Telecommunication Engineering.

This book is as per New Revised Examination Scheme which has been implemented from this academic year. According to this, In-Semester Examination carries 30 Marks over first three Units and End-Semester Examination carries 70 Marks over entire syllabus of which is first three units will carry 20 Marks and Units 4, 5, and 6 will carry 50 Marks.

I have given **Sample Question Paper for In-Semester Examination (30 Marks) and End-Semester Examination (70 Marks) in this book for the practice.**

I have tried to provide the best possible material in simple and lucid language to the students preparing for degree course. The subject is divided into Six Units and each unit is explained thoroughly with diagrams. So, I am sure that, this book will fulfill all needs of the subject. Sufficient numbers of questions are also included at the end of each unit for the revision of the subject.

I would like to express my gratitude to the many people who saw me through this book; to all those who provided support for this book.

I am very thankful to the management of our respective institutes for their continuous support and encouragement.

Above all, I want to thank my family members and friends, who supported and encouraged me in spite of all the time it took me away from them. It was a long and difficult journey for them.

I am gratefully acknowledge co-operation from **Shri. Dineshbhai Furia, Shri. Jignesh Furia, Mrs. Nirali Verma**, **Shri. M.P. Munde** and **Mrs. Deepali Lachake** (Co-ordinator) of **Nirali Prakashan.**

Despite the best efforts taken by author, it is possible that some unintentional errors might have taken place. Author would gratefully acknowledge if any of these is pointed out. Suggestions and comments for further improvement of this book will be gratefully received and acknowledged from the students, teachers and others.

January 2016   **Author**

SYLLABUS

Unit I : Introduction to Wireless Networks   7L

Introduction, Technology and service trends of Emerging Wireless technologies, The Amazing Growth of Mobile Communications, A Little History, Mobile Communications Fundamentals, Mobile Data, Wi-Fi, Bluetooth, Cable Systems, Wireless Migration Options, Harmonization Process.

Unit II: Wi-Fi and Next Generation WLAN   7L

Wi-Fi (802.11), 802.11 Standards, Wi-Fi Protocols, Frequency Allocation, Modulation and Coding Schemes, Network Architecture, Typical Wi-Fi Configurations, Security, 802.11 Services, Hot Spots, Virtual Private Networks (VPNs), Mobile VPN, VPN Types, Wi-Fi Integration with 3G/4G, Benefits of Convergence of Wi-Fi and Wireless Mobile.

Unit III: Third Generation Mobile Services   6L

Introduction, Universal Mobile Telecommunications Service (UMTS), UMTS Services, The UMTS Air Interface, Overview of the 3GPP Release 1999 Network Architecture, Overview of the 3GPP Release 4 Network Architecture, Overview of the 3GPP Release 5, All-IP Network Architecture, Overview CDMA2000, TD-CDMA, TD-SCDMA, Commonality among WCDMA, CDMA2000, TD-CDMA, and TD-SCDMA

Unit IV : LTE   8L

LTE Ecosystem, Standards, Radio Spectrum, LTE Architecture, User Equipment (UE), Enhanced Node B (eNodeB), Core Network (EPC), Radio Channel Components, TD-LTE, Multiple Input Multiple Output, LTE Scheduler, Carrier Aggregation, Cell Search, Cell Reselection, Attach and Default Bearer Activation, Handover (X2, S1, Inter-MME), Self-Organizing Networks (SONs), Relay Cells, Heterogeneous Network (HetNET), Remote Radio Heads (RRH), VoLTE, LTE Advanced

Unit V : WiMAX   6L

Introduction, Standards, Generic WiMAX Architecture, Core Network, Radio Network, WiMAX Spectrum, Modulation, Channel Structure, Mixed Mode, Interference Mitigation Techniques, Frequency Planning, Features and Applications, Security, QoS, Profiles, Origination, Handover, Femto and SON

Unit VI : VoIP   7L

Why VoIP?, The Basics of IP Transport, VoIP Challenges, H.323, The Session Initiation Protocol (SIP), Distributed Architecture and Media Gateway Control, VoIP and SS7, VoIP Quality of Service.

CONTENTS

Unit - I

INTRODUCTION TO WIRELESS NETWORKS

1.1 INTRODUCTION

- Wireless networks are networks of equipment that are not connected by any cable. The equipment include a mobile, computer, connecting devices like switch routers etc.
- The wireless networks allow users to avoid the use of cables or wires. The cable or wires are costly and make the network more complicated to install and maintain.
- In a wireless networks the connection between equipment is established using radio waves.
- The wireless networks have disadvantage of reduced data rates due to attenuation and fading as compared to wired networks.
- Wireless networks provide internet access or data and voice communication to mobile devices. They also allow networks to extend beyond the range of their wired connections.

The various types of wireless networks are :

- (i) Wireless Local Area Networks (WLAN)
- (ii) Wireless Metropolitan Area Networks (WMAN)
- (iii) Wireless Wide Area Networks (WWAN)
- (iv) Wireless Personal Area Networks (WPAN)

- Following table 1.1 gives summary of these wireless networks :

Table 1.1

Network Type Standards	WPAN	WLAN	WMAN	WWAN
	Bluetooth (802.15) CT-2 DECT, PACS	HiperLAN2 802.11a 802.11b 802.11g 802.11n 802.11ac	WiMAX 802.16	1G, 2G, 2.5G, 3G, 4G...
Range	<10 m	<100 m	<100 km	>10 km very long

...Conti.

Speed	< 1 Mbps	1 Mbps to 6 Gbps	1 to 74 Mbps	9.6 kbps to 12 Mbps
Application	Device to device data transfer	Small enterprise and home networks Wi-Fi	Wireless network on large scale	Mobile communication Access to smart phones mobile phone.

- Let us take brief review and history of these wireless networks and technologies.

1.2 THE AMAZING GROWTH OF MOBILE COMMUNICATIONS

- The growth of mobile communication in the past two to three decades is phenomenal. It has changed the way the world was communicating earlier.

- The earlier communication was voice-centric only. Now, everything is communicated in digital format.

- This is facilitated multimedia communication at the fingertips of user who is on the move. The number of mobile subscribers is growing day by day and it is surpassing the number of fixed network subscribers.

- In the past three decades the wireless and mobile communication has evolved steadily through various generations of technologies viz. 1G, 2G, 2.5G, 4G and 5G. Today, in India the 3G and 4G mobile systems deployed.

- It is necessary to understand how these technologies have evolved over the years in order to understand the 3G and 4G systems.

1.3 A LITTLE HISTORY

- **1920s:** Use of radio telephony on experimental basis in USA. It was only suited for marine communication.

- **1930s:** Battlefield communication using Frequency modulation (FM).

- **1940s:** Mobile telephony service was available in some big cities. These systems were having limited capacity and commercially non-viable.

1.3.1 First-Generation Systems

- **1978:** First trail implementation of Advanced Mobile Phone Service(AMPS)in Chicago. Frequency band used was 800 MHz.

- **1979:** The commercial launch of AMPS in Japan.

- **1981:** Launch of Nordic Mobile Telephony (NMT) in European countries (Sweden, Norway, Denmark, and Finland). Frequency band used was 450 MHz. Later on NMT900 operating in 900 MHz band was implemented.

- **1983:** The commercial launch of AMPS in Chicago. It was also implemented in other cities the USA.

- **1985:** A modified version of AMPS called Total Access Communications System (TACS) was launched in UK. It operated in 900MHz band.

1985 onwards many other countries followed.

AMPS, NMT, TACS were successful first generation mobile systems. Their drawback was they were analog systems and had limited capacity and did not have add on services and security features. As number of subscribers started growing, they failed to cater to their requirements.

1.3.2 Second-Generation Mobile Systems

- The second-generation mobile systems are digital hence they have increased capacity, greater security against fraud, and more advanced services.

- Many variants of second generation systems exist. Following are the major variants of the second-generation technologies:

  (i) Global System for Mobile communications (GSM).

  (ii) Interim Standard 136 (IS-136) TDMA,

  (iii) IS-95 CDMA.

GSM

- As seen earlier, of Nordic Mobile Telephony (NMT) was the first generation system deployed in some European countries. There were other analog systems existing in other European countries. These systems were analog and incompatible with each other.

- In 1982, the Conference on European Posts and Telecommunications (CEPT) started developing a digital system to be used across all European countries.

- A group called (in French) Group Spéciale Mobile (GSM) was established to formulate the necessary technical work involved in developing this new digital standard.

- Further impetus was given to the GSM project when in 1989 the responsibility was passed to the newly formed European Telecommunications Standards Institute (ETSI).

- Under the auspices of ETSI the specification took place. It provided functional and interface descriptions for each of the functional entities defined in the system.

- The aim was to provide sufficient guidance for manufacturers that equipment from different manufacturers would be interoperable, while not stopping innovation. Thus the vision of a pan-European network was fast becoming a reality. However this took place before any networks went live.

- The aim to launch GSM by 1991 proved to be a target that was too tough to meet. Terminals started to become available in mid-1992 and the real launch took place in the latter part of that year. With such a new service many were sceptical as the analogue systems were still in widespread use.

- Nevertheless by the end of 1993 GSM had attracted over a million subscribers and there were 25 roaming agreements in place. The growth continued and the next million subscribers were soon attracted. This represented a major milestone in cellular telecommunications history.

- Originally it had been intended that GSM would operate on frequencies in the 900 MHz cellular band. In September 1993, the British operator Mercury One-to-One launched a network.

- Term DCS 1800 it operated at frequencies in a new 1800 MHz band. By adopting new frequencies new operators and further competition was introduced into the market apart from allowing additional spectrum to be used and further increasing the overall capacity.

- This trend was followed in many countries, and soon the term DCS 1800 was dropped in favor of calling it GSM as it was purely the same cellular technology but operating on a different frequency band.

- In view of the higher frequency used the distances the signals travelled was slightly shorter but this was compensated for by additional base stations.

- In the USA as well as a portion of spectrum at 1900 MHz was allocated for cellular usage in 1994. The licensing body, the FCC, did not legislate which technology should be used, and accordingly this enabled GSM to gain a foothold in the US market. This system was known as PCS 1900 (Personal Communication System).

- The summary of GSM history is given below :

  - **1982:** Groupe Speciale Mobile established to develop the pan-European cellular mobile system standards.

  - **1985:** Basic list of recommendations to be generated by the group was adopted.

  - **1986:** Field tests undertaken to prove which techniques should be adopted for the new system.

  - **1987:** TDMA approach adopted as the main access method for GSM. Frequency division is also used between channels, but time division each individual frequency channel. Also in this year the Initial Memorandum of Understanding was signed by telecommunication operators from 12 member countries.

  - **1988:** GSM system validation undertaken

  - **1989:** ETSI, European telecommunications Standards Institute takes on responsibility for managing the GSM standards.

  - **1990:** Phase 1 of the GSM specifications released.

- **1991:** Commercial launch of the GSM service.
- **1993:** Coverage of main roads GSM services start outside Europe.
- **1995:** Phase 2 of the GSM specifications released.
- **2004:** GSM subscriptions reach 1 billion. Announcement made at 3GSM in Cannes.

IS-54B and IS-136

- The second generation mobile systems in North America used Time-Division Multiplexing (TDM) as against the frequency division multiplexing of first generation systems. There are two standards of these TDMA systems IS-54B and IS-136.

- Three users share a 30 kHz bandwidth by splitting a 30 kHz carrier into 3 time slots. TDMA was first specified as a standard in EIA/TIA Interim Standard 54 (IS-54 also known as digital AMPS or DAMPS). IS-136, an evolved version of IS-54, is the United States standard for TDMA for both the cellular (850 MHz) and PCS (1.9 GHz) spectrums. Unlike IS-54, IS-136 utilizes time division multiplexing for both voice and control channel transmissions.

- Note that IS-54B involves digital voice channels only and still uses analog control channels. Thus, although it may offer increased capacity and some other advantages, the fact that the control channel is analog does limit the number of services that can be offered. For this reason, among others, the next obvious step was to make the control channels also digital. This step took place in 1994 with the development of IS-136, a system that includes digital control channels and digital voice channels.

- Today, AMPS, IS-54B, and IS-136 are all in service. AMPS and IS-54B operate only in the 800-MHz band, whereas IS-136 can be found both in the 800 MHz band and in the 1900-MHz band, at least in North America. The 1900-MHz band in North America is allocated to Personal Communications Service (PCS), which can be described as a family of second-generation mobile communications services.

IS-95 CDMA

- The idea for using the form of modulation known as Direct Sequence Spread Spectrum (DSSS) for a multiple access system for mobile telecommunications came from a California based company called Qualcomm in the 1980s. Previously DSSS had been mainly used for military or covert communications systems as the transmissions were hard to detect, jam and eavesdrop.

- The system involved multiplying the required data with another data stream with a much higher data rate, known as a spreading code, this widened the bandwidth required for the transmission, spreading it over a wide frequency band.

- Only when the original spreading code was used in the reconstruction of the data, would the original information be reconstituted.

- It was reasoned that by having different spreading codes, a multiple access system could be created for use in a mobile phone system.

- In order to prove that the new system was viable a consortium was set up and Qualcomm was joined by US network operators Nynex and Ameritech to develop the first experimental Code Division Multiple Access (CDMA) system.

- Later the team was expanded as Motorola and AT and T (now Lucent) joined to bring their resources to speed development. As a result the new standard was published as IS-95A in 1995 under the auspices of the Cellular Telecommunications Industry Association (CTIA) and the Telecommunications Industry Association (TIA).

- As part of the development of CDMA an organisation called the CDMA Development Group (CDG) was formed from the founding network and manufacturers. Its purpose to promote CDMA and evolve the technology and standards, although today most of the standards work is carried out by 3GPP2.

- It then took a further three years before Hutchison Telecom became the first organisation to launch a system.

- The IS-95 system was widely deployed in North America, and the Asia Pacific region, but there were also networks in South America, Africa, and the Middle East as well as some in Eastern Europe. In North America, IS-95 CDMA has been deployed in the 800-MHz band, and a variation known as J-STD-008 has been deployed in the 1900-MHz band.

- With the success of the initial IS-95 format, improvements were made and the standard was upgraded to IS95B. The main improvement was that this provided for an increased data rate of 115 kbps as data traffic was starting to be carried.

- The basic CDMA system was later further improved and evolved into a 3G system carrying much higher data rates and introducing new improvements.

- The 3G migration of IS-95 was given the brand name cdma2000, and was available in a variety of flavours including CDMA2000 1x, CDMA2000 1x ev-do (evolution data only or data optimised) and another version was termed CDMA2000 1x ev-dv (evolution data and voice), although this version was never seriously deployed.

1.3.3 Baseband Spread Spectrum System

- Fig. 1.1 shows an idealized model of a baseband spread spectrum system.

- The message signal occupied a bandwidth far in excess of the minimum bandwidth necessary to transmit it. This provides protection against jamming waveforms.

- Data sequence d(t) modulates a wide-band PN sequence c(t) by applying both these sequences to a product modulator. Thus, if data sequence d(t) is narrowband and PN sequence c(t) is wideband, product signal q(t) will have a spectrum same as the PN sequence.

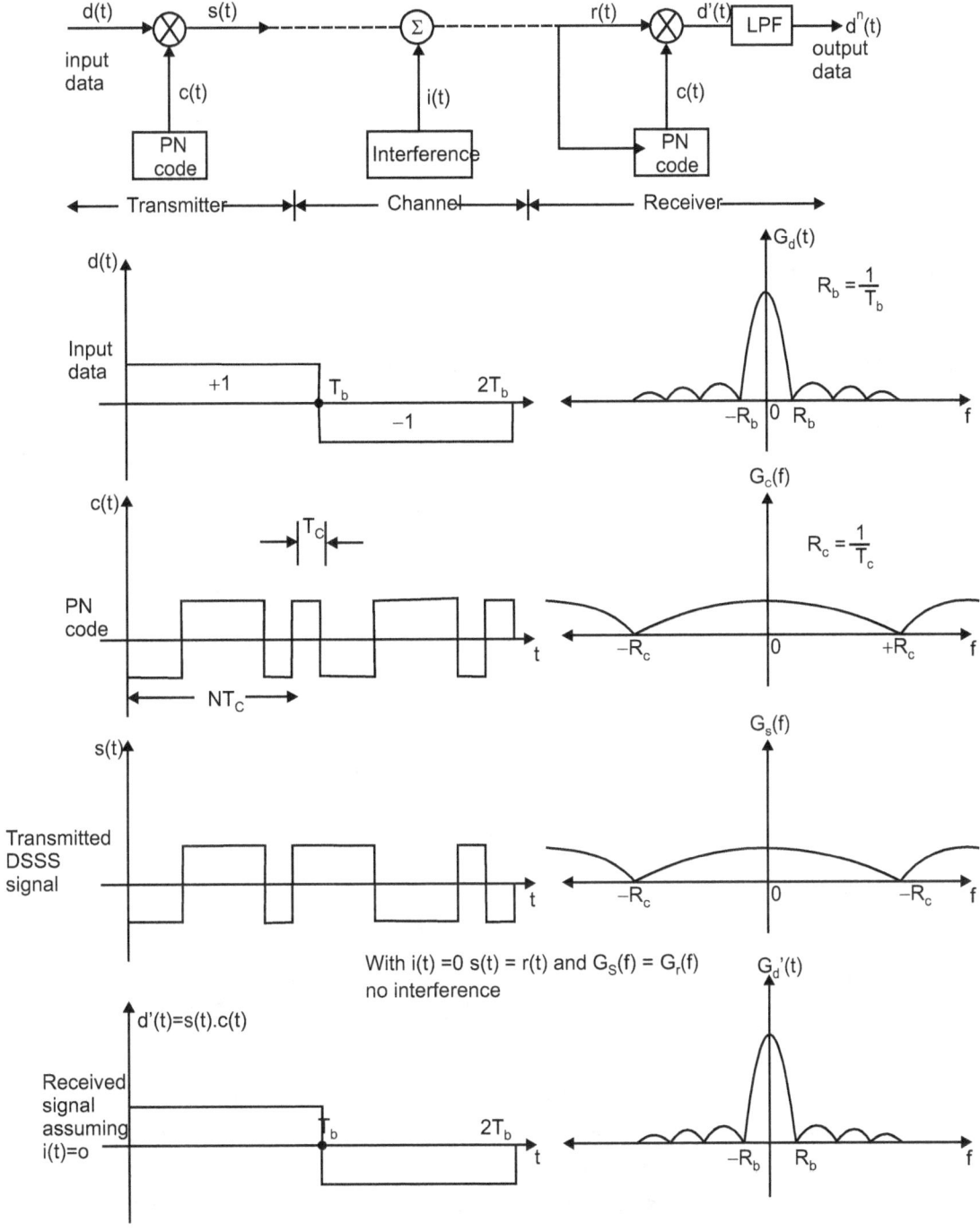

Fig. 1.1 : A baseband spread spectrum system

- The transmitted signal s(t) = d(t) c(t) gets added with the channel interference signal i(t). Thus, the received signal at the receiver side is,

$$r(t) = s(t) + i(t)$$
$$= d(t)\, c(t) + i(t) \qquad \qquad \ldots(1.1)$$

- The receiver consists of a multiplier followed by a low pass filter. The received signal m(t) is multiplied by an exact replica of the PN sequence that was used at the transmitter. The demodulated signal is therefore given as,

$$d'(t) = c(t) \cdot r(t)$$
$$= c^2(t)\, d(t) + c(t)\, i(t) \qquad \qquad \ldots(1.2)$$

Both the sequences c(t) and d(t) are represented in the polar form. Hence, $c^2(t) = 1$.

$$\therefore \qquad \qquad \hat{d}\,(t) = d(t) + c(t)\, i(t) \qquad \qquad \ldots(1.3)$$

The interference signal gets widened as it is multiplied by the spreading code c(t). Hence, when d(t) passes through the LPF, data signal d(t) can easily be recovered. The effect of i(t) is considerably mitigated at the receiver output.

- Now let us see the effect of interference and how the DSS system takes case of it.
- We will consider how cases of interference viz narrowband and wideband.
- If narrowband interference is added in the channel, it gets added to the spreaded transmitted spectrum as shown in Fig. 1.2

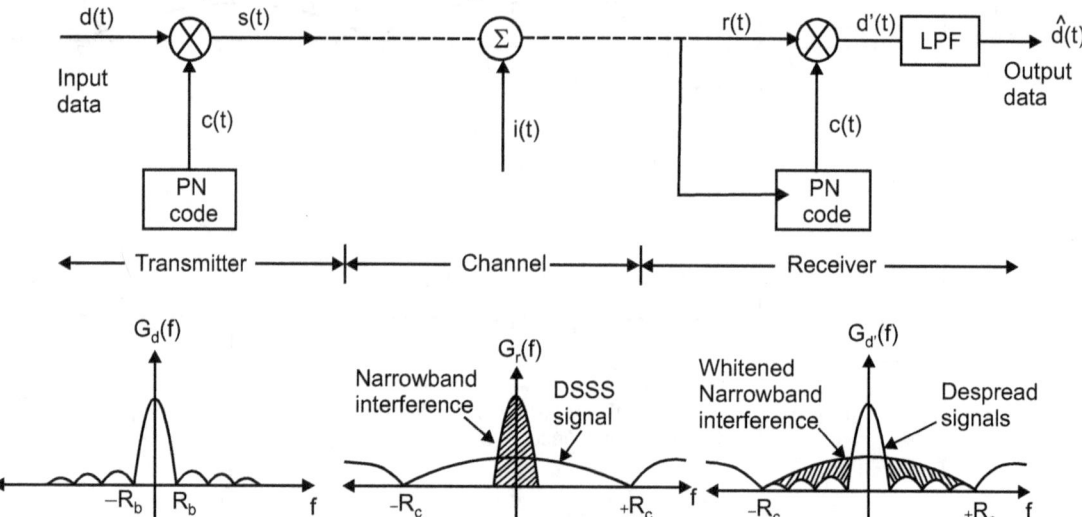

Fig. 1.2 : DSSS system with narrowband interference (whitened)

- At the receiver, the narrowband interference gets spreaded (whitened) in frequency domain as it gets multiplied by PN code where as the DSSS signal gets despreaded. The low pass filtering eliminates most of the energy of the interfering signal passing only the original message signal to the output.
- Now consider the case of wideband interference which can originate due to multiple users or Gaussian noise as shown in Fig. 1.3.

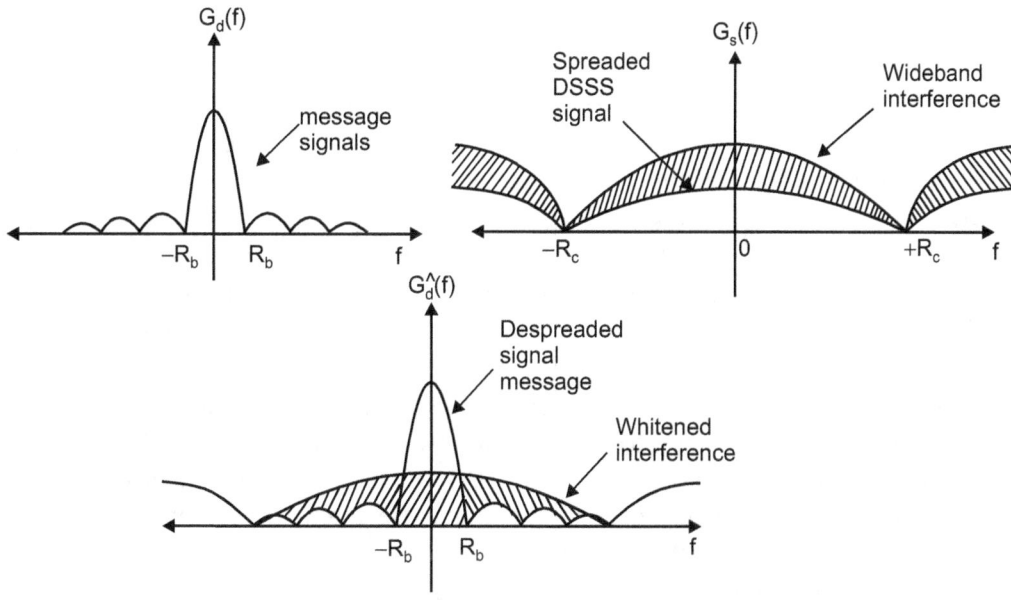

Fig. 1.3 : Spectra of DSSS with wideband interference

- At the receiver the wideband interference gets spreaded (whitened) due to PN code where as the DSSS signal gets despreaded. The low pass filtering eliminates the high frequency components of interference. Thus at the output the signal energy is more than the interference. Hence the spread spectrum technique is useful in combatting interference from other users.

- It can be seen that, spreading of the signal depends on chip rate $R_c = \dfrac{1}{T_c}$. Higher the chip rate, better will be performance of the system because the interference signal will be whitened properly. The ratio $\dfrac{T_b}{T_c} = \dfrac{R_c}{R_b}$ is called Processing Gain (PG). More is PG, better will be the system's immunity to interference.

1.3.4 The Path to Third-Generation Technology

- AMPS, NMT, TACS were successful First Generation (1G) mobile systems. Their drawback was they were analog systems and had limited capacity and did not have add on services and security features. Second-generation systems are designed to address all these issues. Systems such as IS-95, GSM, and IS-136 are much more secure, and they also offer higher capacity and more calling features.

- The voice centric and not well-suited to data communications. There was need for data centric services due to Internet, electronic commerce, and multimedia communications.

- Mid to end of the nineties the standardization of Third Generation (3G) mobile communications systems took place in several regions around the world. These are common to all of them focus on CDMA based technologies.
- To ensure equipment compatibility and to increase working efficiency, initiatives were made to create a single forum for WCDMA standardization.
- These initiatives resulted in the creation of the Third Generation (3G) Partnership Project (3GPP) in December 1998. Standardization organizations firstly involved were ARIB (Japan), ETSI (Europe), TTA (Korea), TTC (Japan) and T1P1 (USA). In 1999, also CWTS (China) joined 3GPP. The technical work in 3GPP was started early 1999 with the aim of having a common specification ready by the end of 1999.
- 3GPP stands for 3rd Generation Partnership Project, (3GPP) is a collaboration agreement, established in December 1998, to ensure a worldwide acceptance of 3G W-CDMA/UMTS standards. It is a partnership of 6 regional SDOs (Standard Development Organization). These SDOs take 3GPP specifications and transpose them to regional (Europe, North America, Korea, Japan, China) standards.
- ITU references the regional standards as IMT-2000.
- The International Telecommunications Union (ITU) defined the key requirements for International Mobile Telecommunications 2000 services more commonly known as 3G or IMT 2000

Following are the 3G Requirements:

- When the mobile system 2G syppose to improved system capacity, backward compatibility with 2G, multimedia support and high speed packet data meeting the following criteria :
    - 2 Mbps in fixed or in-building environments.
    - 384 kbps in pedestrian or urban environments.
    - 144 kbps in wide area mobile environments.
    - Variable data rates in large geographic area systems (satellite).
- The IMT-2000 effort within the ITU has led to a number of recommendations. These recommendations address areas such as user bandwidth (144 kbps for mobile service and up to 2 Mbps for fixed service), richness of service offerings (multimedia services), and flexibility (networks that can support small or large numbers of subscribers). The recommendations also specify that IMT-2000 should operate in the 2-GHz band. In general, however, the ITU recommendations are mainly a set of requirements and do not specify the detailed technical solutions to meet the requirements. To address the technical solutions, the ITU has solicited technical proposals from interested organizations and then selected/approved some of those proposals. In 1998, numerous air-interface technical proposals were submitted. These were reviewed by the ITU, which in 1999 selected five technologies for terrestrial service (non-satellite-based). The five technologies are:
    1. Wideband CDMA (WCDMA).
    2. CDMA2000 (an evolution of IS-95 CDMA).

3. TDD-CDMA (Time Division–CDMA [TD-CDMA] and Time Division-Synchronous CDMA [TD-SCDMA]).

4. UWC-136 (an evolution of IS-136).

5. DECT.

- These technologies represent the foundation for a suite of advanced mobile multimedia communications services and are starting to be deployed across the globe. TD-CDMA since has been defined as both TD-CDMA and TD-SCDMA.

- UWC-136 has not seen commercialization and has been abandoned as a viable technology alternative.

- This unit deals with four of those technologies WCDMA, CDMA2000, TD-CDMA, and TD-SCDMA.

1.3.5 4G and Beyond

- Third-Generation (3G) systems were successful in providing data-centric communication with number of features. They provided higher data rates, add on services, security, inter-operability etc. The future advancement in wireless access technology is Fourth Generation (4G). 4G wireless access is defined under IMT-2000 Advanced and is usually referred to as Long Term Evolution (LTE); however, a later version of WiMAX and HSPA are also classified as 4G. It is based on Internet Protocol (IP). It allows seamless mobility between 3G wireless networks and fixed wireless.

- 4G is the future technology for mobile and wireless communications. 4G deployments are approximately expected to be around the year 2010 to 2015. It will be the successor of 3G network technology.

- The basic voice is drive force for the Second Generation (2G) mobile communication, whereas video and television services are the chief factor for 3G.

- 4G low cost and high speed data are the dominant driver. High degree of personalization, application ubiquity and synchronization between user appliances are also the driven forces. The evolution to 4G from 3G will be driven by the services that offer better quality in multimedia, voice and sound.

- Personalization will be improved with greater bandwidth and sophistication in large quantity of information. Convergence with other network service will come through high session data rate.

- The impact on the network capacity is expected to be significant.

- Video communication is facing many challenges now. 4G wireless networks will provide many features to handle this. It will provide the end-users more opportunities and flexibilities in accessing video and multimedia contents.

- It accommodates radio access systems via flexible core IP network, resulting in a very high data rate, and enhancing the video applications. It provides better quality of service and security supports to the end users, and enhances the user experiences and privacy for multimedia applications.

- The applications of video and services would bring in a large volume of data transmission onto the wireless network. This is going to be a potential challenge for the 4G systems.

- Now a day it is quite interesting to note that the new mobile phones, specially the smart phones, are not just the simple phone but much more than that. They are a little mobile PC and functions more or less like that.

- They includes a keyboard rendered on a touch screen, provide user friendly graphical user interfaces, provide internet services, web browsing, email connecting, local wireless fidelity connectivity, built in camera, high quality music player capability, and small media management besides phone call functionalities.

- However, there are many features that some smart mobile do not support yet. This includes mobile television support to receive live programmes, multi user networked three- dimension games, realistic 3D scene rendering and high definition visuals.

- The lack of these functions are due to computational capabilities and power constraints of the mobile devices, available bandwidth and transmission efficiency of the wireless network, universal access capability of the infrastructure, and the compression and error control efficiency of video and graphics data.

- Mobile phones are moving faster to provide the user the same or even better experience than the personal computer, but there is long way ahead. From a mobile communication point of view, it is expected to have a higher data transmission rate as comparable to wire line network.

- The service and support for seamless connectivity and access to any application regardless of device and location. The expectation of mobile communication is the key feature of 4G. It is going to describe the next complete evolution in wireless communication.

- To provide a comprehensive IP solution where multimedia services can be delivered to the user on an 'anywhere anytime' basis with a satisfactory data rate and high security. The current 3G wireless infrastructure is not able to achieve this demand.

- The International Telecommunication Union (ITU) is working on the standard and targets for the commercial deployment of 4G system in the year 2010-2015 time frame. ITU defined IMT advanced as the successor of IMT-2000 or 3G.

- The advantage of 4G over 3G is listed in table 1.2 below. It is obvious that 4G has much more system improvement over 3G. This improvement is not only in bandwidth and capacity, but it also appears in coverage, latency, mobility and security.

Parameters	3G	4G
Architecture	WAN	W-LAN and WAN
Information type secondary	Voice is prime, data secondary	Converged data and multimedia services
Data rate	384 kbps – 2 Mbps	100 Mbps (moving), 1Gbps (standing)
Frequency	18 – 2.4 GHz	2 -8 GHz
Class of switching	Both circuit and packet	Only packet
Multiple access technology	CDMA	OFDMA
Broadcast	Not supported	Supported
Quality of Service (QoS)	Less supported	Supported

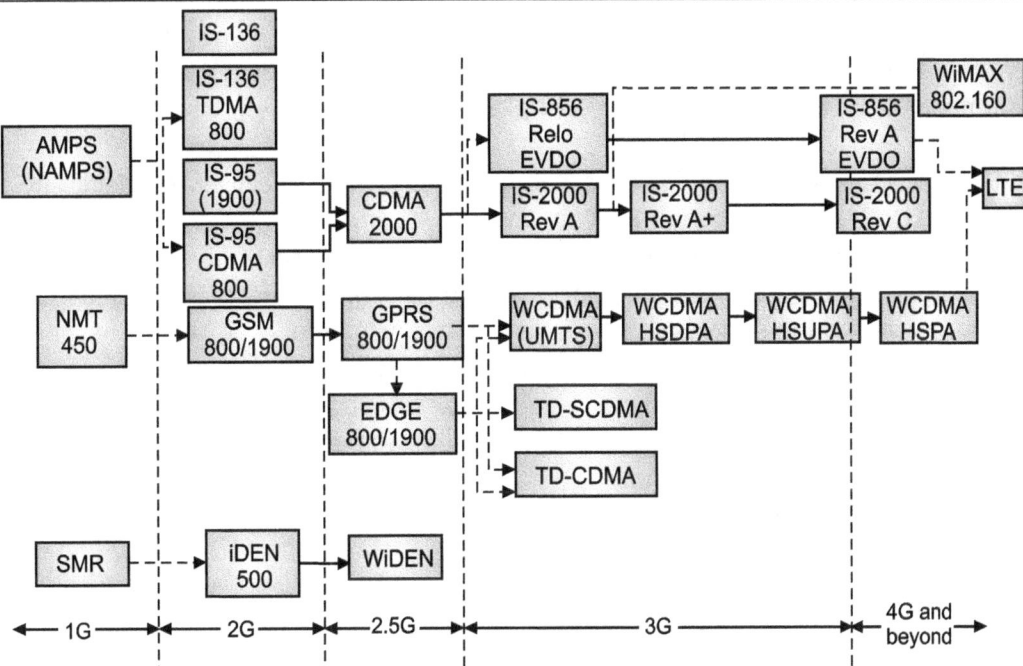

Fig. 1.4 : 4G and beyond access technology

To further help in how 4G maps to 3G and future Gs, the following data are provided:

- 3G- IMT-2000 specification (CDMA, WCDMA, WiMAX, TD-SCDMA).

- 4G- IMT-2000 Advanced (LTE, WiMAX, HSPA).

- 5G- Not defined however LTE Advanced is referenced as 5G, 6G and beyond not defined at this moment.

1.3.6 Next-Generation Wireless (NGW)

- The Next-Generation Wireless (NGW) system is an all packet-based system as compared to circuit switched 3G and previous generation systems.
- This allows wireless operator provide support services and applications desired by the end users instead of providing services and applications based on the underlying wireless transmission technologies.
- In an NGW system the core network is designed to be independent of the radio access network.
- This is possible since the NGW architecture is designed with the goal of supporting packet-switched traffic with seamless mobility, Quality of Service (QoS), and minimal latency.
- NGW systems are meant to provide seamless mobility for end users utilizing different radio access technologies and services.
- Unlike previously mobile wireless networks, they have been based on a circuit-switch design meant to support voice communications. Specifically, previously wireless networks were designed in a hierarchical approach where nodes like a Base-Station Controller (BSC) or Radio Network Controller (RNC) were an aggregation point in the network.
- In previous mobile wireless networks, packet networks were effectively overlaid onto the existing circuit switched–based wireless networks.
- NGW systems have come about due to the prevalence of packet traffic resulting in the need to switch from a circuit to a packet-based network architecture and is needed to properly transport the increasing packet data that is being sent over wireless networks.
- NGW fosters a packet network architecture which is a flat network that removes the hierarchical approach toward network topology. Specifically, a NGW system is packet-based, transport technology agnostic, and utilizes a flat architecture. As NGW system is packet-based it is able to support:
  - Multimedia services.
  - Voice and data simultaneous transport.
  - Quality-of-service enabled services.
  - Independent of the RF and physical transport technologies.
  - Heterogeneous networks.
  - Mobility.
  - Ubiquitous provisioning of services to end users.

1.4 MOBILE COMMUNICATIONS FUNDAMENTALS

- The cellular concept was developed and introduced by the Bell Laboratories in the early 1970's. The principle of cellular systems is to divide a large geographic service area into cells with diameter from 2 to 50 km, each of which is allocated a number of Radio Frequency (RF) channels.

- Transmitters in each adjacent cell operate on different frequencies to avoid interference.
- As the demand grows in a given area, cells can be split to accommodate the additional traffic. Cells that are sufficiently far apart can reuse the same set of frequencies without causing co-channel interference.
- Fig. 1.5 illustrate an idealized view of a cellular mobile system, where cells are depicted as cells using the same RF channels.
- Within each cell is a base station, which contains the radio transmission and reception equipment. It is the base station that provides the radio communication for those mobile phones that happen to be within the cell.
- The coverage area of a given cell depends on a number of factors, such as the transmit power of the base station, the transmit power of mobile, the height of the base-station antennas, and the topology of the landscape.

Advantages of Cell Structures:
- Higher capacity, higher number of users.
- Less transmission power needed.
- More robust, decentralized.
- Base station deals with interference, transmission area etc.

Problems:
- Fixed network needed for the base stations.
- Handover (changing from one cell to another) necessary.
- Interference with other cells.

Fixed Frequency Assignment:
- Certain frequencies are assigned to a certain cell.
- Problem: different traffic load in different cells.

Dynamic Frequency Assignment:
- Base station chooses frequencies depending on the frequencies already used in neighbor cells.
- More capacity in cells with more traffic.
- Assignment can also be based on interference measurements.

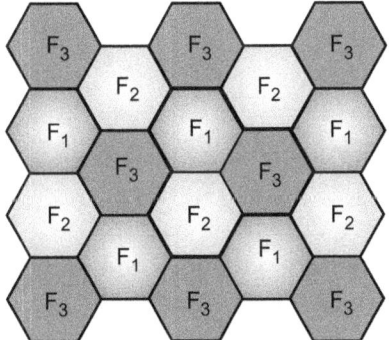

Fig. 1.5 : Cellular system

Cell: Why Hexagon?

- In reality the cell is an irregular shaped circle, for design convenience and as a first order approximation, it is assumed to be regular polygons
- The hexagon is used for two reasons:

  A hexagonal layout requires fewer cells, therefore, fewer transmission site.
- Less expensive compared to square and triangular cells.
- Irregular cell shape leads to inefficient use of the spectrum because of inability to reuse frequency on account of cochannel interference uneconomical deployment of equipment, requiring relocation from one cell site to another

Specific radio frequencies are allocated within each cell in a manner that depends on the technology in question. In most systems, a number of individual frequencies are allocated to a given cell, and those same frequencies are reused in other cells that are sufficiently far away to avoid interference. With CDMA, EVDO, WCDMA, HSPA, and LTE, however, the same frequency can be reused in every cell. Although the scheme shown in Fig. 1.5 is certainly feasible and is sometimes implemented, it is common to sectorize the cells, as shown in Fig. 1.6. In this approach, the base-station equipment for a number of cells is collocated at the edge of those cells, and directional antennas are used to provide coverage over the area of each cell (as opposed to omnidirectional antennas in the case where the base station is located at the center of a cell). Sectorized arrangements with up to six sectors are known, but the most common configuration is three sectors per base station in urban areas, with two sectors per base station along highways.

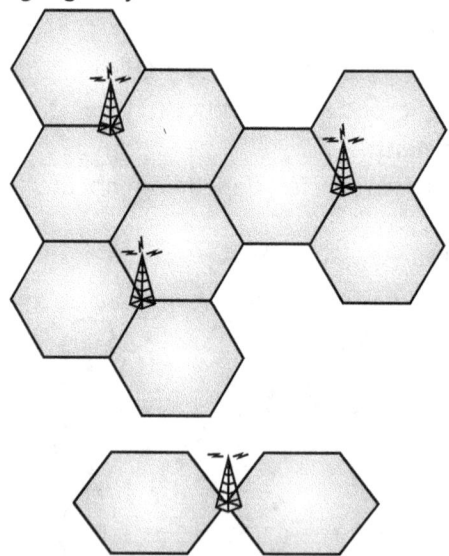

Fig. 1.6 : Typical sectorized cell sites (3 and 2 sector configuration)

- It is necessary that the base stations be connected to a switching network and for that network to be connected to other networks, such as the Public Switched Telephone

Network (PSTN), in order for calls to be made to and from mobile subscribers. Furthermore, it is necessary for information about the mobile subscribers to be stored in a particular place on the network.

- Given that different subscribers may have different services and features, the network must know which services and features apply to each subscriber in order to handle calls appropriately.

- For example, a given subscriber may be prohibited from making international calls.

- It should be the subscriber attempt to make an international call, the network must disallow that call based on the subscriber's service profile.

1.4.1 Basic Network Architecture

- The network forms the heart of any cellular telephone system.

- The cellular network fulfils many requirements. Not only does the cellular network enable calls to be routed to and from the mobile phones as well as enabling calls to be maintained as the cell phone moves from one cell to another, but it also enables other essential operations such as access to the network, billing, security and much more.

- To fulfil all these requirements the cellular network comprises many elements, each having its own function to complete.

- Fig. 1.7 shows a typical (although very basic) mobile communications network of the units within the cellular network, the BTS provides the direct communication with the mobile phones.

- There may be a small number of base stations then linked to a base station controller. This unit acts as a small centre to route calls to the required base station, and it also makes some decisions about which of the base station is best suited to a particular call.

- The links between the BTS and the BSC may use either land lines of even microwave links.

- The BTS antenna towers also support a small microwave dish antenna used for the link to the BSC. The BSC is often co-located with a BTS.

- The BSC interfaces with the Mobile Switching Centre (MCS). The MSC, also known in some circles as the Mobile Telephone Switching Office (MTSO), is the switch that manages the setup and teardown of calls to and from mobile subscribers.

- The MSC contains many of the features and functions found in a standard PSTN switch. It also contains, however, a number of functions that is specific to mobile communications.

- For example, the BSC functionality may be contained within the MSC in certain systems, particularly in First-Generation (1G) systems. Even if the BSC functionality is not contained within the MSC, the MSC still must interact with a number of BSCs over an interface that is not found in other types of networks.

- Furthermore, the MSC must contain a logic of its own to deal with the fact that the subscribers are mobile.

- Part of this logic involves an interface to one or more Home Location Registers(HLRs), where subscriber-specific data are held.

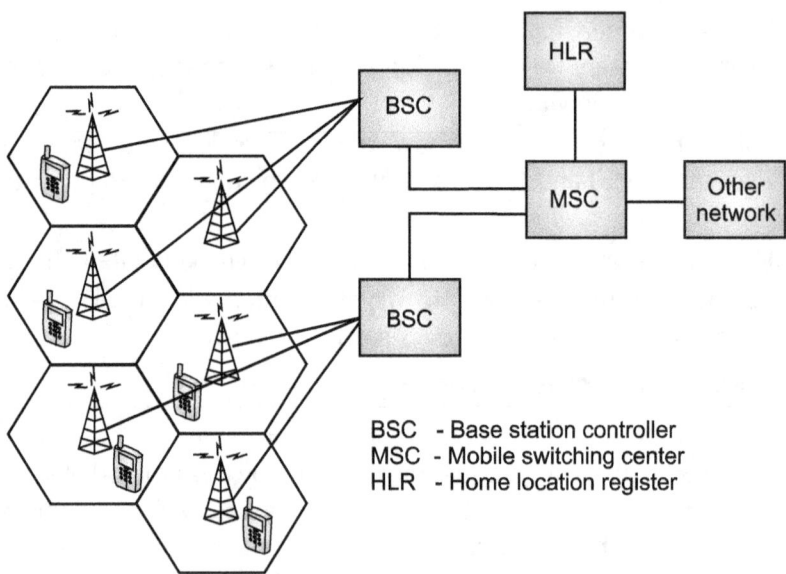

Fig. 1.7 : Basic mobile network architecture

1.4.2 Air-Interface Access Techniques

- There are a variety of different ways of controlling the two way passage of information using two transmitters.

- They range in complexity from the simplest systems requiring the least complex circuitry and providing more basic performance, to more complex systems providing higher levels of performance.

- However each scheme has its own advantages and disadvantages.

- **Simplex:** Although the definition of simplex is not always clear the ANSI (American National Standards Institute) definition for a simplex transmission, is one that can only occur in one direction. One example of this may be a broadcast system. Occasionally, simplex may refer to a half duplex scheme as described below.

- **Half Duplex:** This is a duplex scheme whereby communication is possible in two directions, but communication is only possible in one direction at a time. If one transmitter is transmitting, the other one must wait until the first stops before transmitting. This form of communication is used for walkie-talkies, CB, etc. It may also be referred to as simplex, in some circumstances although exact definitions can be contradictory at times.

- **Full Duplex:** Full duplex, which is sometimes referred to simply as duplex is a scheme whereby transmissions may be sent in both directions simultaneously. However it sis till necessary for the transmissions to be separated in some way to enable the receivers to receive signals at the same time as transmissions are being made. There are two ways of achieving this. One is to use frequency separation (frequency division duplex, FDD, and the other is to use time, Time Division Duplex, (TDD).

The two schemes are both widely used. Some cellular systems use TDD while others use FDD. Some standards also allow for the use of either as both FDD and TDD have their own advantages and disadvantages.

The air interface consists of an access method coupled with a protocol method. The access method involves the use of either Frequency-Division Duplex (FDD) or Time-Division Duplex (TDD), with each having its own advantages and/or disadvantages. The protocol method uses FDMA, TDMA, and/or CDMA.

FDD

- Frequency Division Duplex, FDD, uses the idea that the transmission and reception of signals are achieved simultaneously using two different frequencies. Using FDD it is possible to transmit and receive signals simultaneously as the receiver is not tuned to the same frequency as the transmitter as shown in Fig. 1.8.

- For the FDD scheme to operate satisfactorily, it is necessary that the frequency, i.e. channel separation between the transmission and reception frequencies must be sufficient to enable the receiver not to be unduly affected by the transmitter signal.

- This is known as the guard band.

- Receiver blocking is an important issue with FDD schemes, and often highly selective filters may be required.

- For cellular systems using FDD, filters are required within the base station and also the handset to ensure sufficient isolation of the transmitter signal without desensitising the receiver.

- While cost is not such a significant driver for the base stations, placing a filter into the handsets is more of an issue.

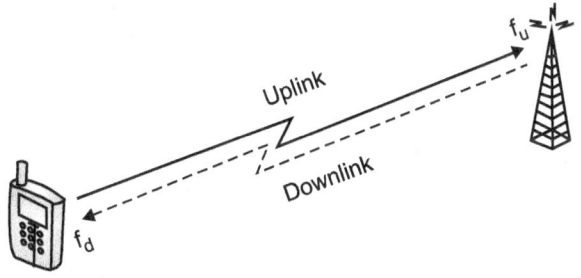

Fig. 1.8 : FDD system

- The channels f_d and f_u normally are spaced a distance apart for isolation purposes. The FDD system uses dedicated channels for uplink and downlink communication. Fig. 1.9 illustrates how the uplink and downlink channels are paired.

- The specific frequency band, channel size, and technology depend on the particular system.

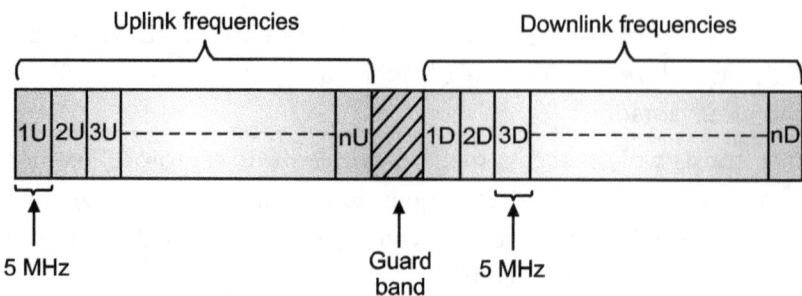

Fig. 1.9 : FDD spectrum-allocation

TDD

- The other system uses only a single frequency and it shares the channel between transmission and reception, spacing them apart by multiplexing the two signals on a time basis.

- Time Division Duplex, TDD, is used with data transmissions (data or digitized voice), transmitting a short burst of data in each direction. As the transmission periods are relatively short no time delay is noticed on voice transmissions resulting from the time delays introduced by using TDD.

- While FDD transmissions require a guard band between the transmitter and receiver frequencies, TDD schemes require a guard time or guard interval between transmission and reception.

- This must be sufficient to allow the signals travelling from the remote transmitter to arrive before a transmission is started and the receiver inhibited. Although this delay is relatively short, when changing between transmission and reception many times a second, even a small guard time can reduce the efficiency of the system as a percentage of the time must be used for the guard interval.

- For systems communicating over short distances, e.g. up to a mile or so the guard interval is normally small and acceptable. For greater distances it may become an issue.

The guard interval required for TDD will comprise two main elements:

- A time allowance for the propagation delay for any transmissions from the remote transmitter to arrive at the receiver. This will depend upon the distances involved, but it takes 3.3 μs to travel a kilometre, 5.4 μs to travel 1 mile.

- A time allowance for the transmitter receiver to change from receive to transmit. Switching speeds can vary considerably between equipments but can take a few microseconds.

- As a result, TDD is not normally suitable for use over long distances as the guard time increases and the channel efficiency falls. Also transmit receive switching must be fast.

- It is often found that traffic in both directions is not balanced. Typically there is more data travelling in the downlink direction of a cellular telecommunications system. This means that, ideally, the capacity should be greater in the downlink direction. Using a TDD system it is possible to change the capacity in either direction relatively easily by changing the number of time slots allocated to each direction. Often, this is dynamically configurable so it can be altered to match the demand.

- A further aspect to be noted with TDD transmissions is the aspect of latency. As data may not be able to be routed immediately onto a transmission as a result of the time multiplexing between transmit and receive, there will be a small delay between the data being generated and it being actually transmitted. Typically this may be a few milliseconds dependent upon the frame times, but in some applications it may be of interest, although for normal digitized speak, there would be no noticeable delay.

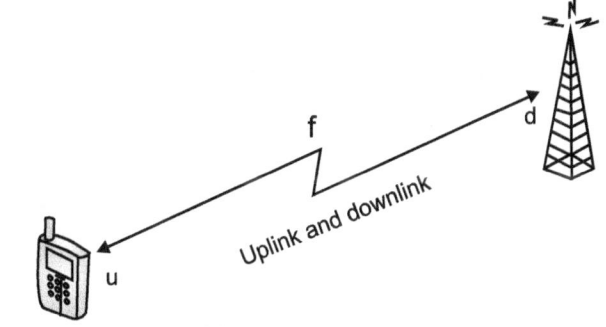

Fig. 1.10 : TDD system

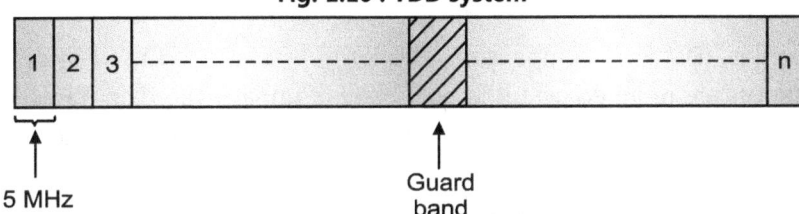

Fig. 1.11 : TDD spectrum-allocation

- Both TDD and FDD have their advantages and each can be used to advantage in different circumstances. Before deciding on a particular type of duplex scheme, it is necessary to analyse the advantages and disadvantages of each. An FDD TDD comparison will then determine the best option.

- **Use of Spectrum**

TDD: Uses only a single frequency for transmission and reception.

FDD: Requires one channel for transmission and another for reception. Spectral efficiency may not be as good.

Unbalanced Traffic

- It is possible to easily adjust the capacity in either direction by changing the number of slots dedicated to either direction. This can be achieved dynamically within the protocols of the system.

- Capacity in either direction can only be made by re-allocating channels. This is not normally easy to achieve as allocations are made by regulators specifically for uplink or downlink with sufficient spacing, and are normally balanced providing the same capacity in either direction.

Distance

It is normally suited to small distances as guard time increases with distance as signal propagation time increases and this needs to be accommodated. Signals take 3.3 µs to travel a kilometre and 5.4 µs to travel 1 mile.

Does not have a problem with small or large distances.

Latency

A small degree of additional latency may be added as a result of the TDD multiplexing.

FDD introduces no additional time delays and latency as channels are always "open".

Equipment Costs

- No major additional equipment costs required as transmit-receive switching is cheap to effect.

- Filters are normally required to prevent the transmitter block and de-sensitising the receiver. These costs can be a cost driver in items such as cellular handsets where volumes are high.

- In view of this TDD FDD comparison, TDD systems are often used in scenarios where short distances are required, with the possibility of unbalanced data traffic. FDD schemes are better over greater distances and where the traffic is balanced, i.e. similar in both directions.

- Both TDD and FDD duplex schemes have their own advantages and disadvantages. Accordingly they are used in different applications, or in different areas where the advantages of TDD and FDD can be used to the greatest advantage. In view of the advantages of unbalanced uplinks and downlinks in short range cellular and wireless applications, TDD solutions are finding an increasing number of applications, while FDD systems are still in widespread use where the there are different requirements.

1.4.3 Multiple Access Techniques

- Multiple access schemes are used to allow many simultaneous users to use the same fixed bandwidth radio spectrum. In any radio system, the bandwidth that is allocated to it is always limited.

- For mobile phone systems the total bandwidth is typically 50 MHz, which is split in half to provide the forward and reverse links of the system.

- Sharing of the spectrum is required in order increase the user capacity of any wireless network.

- FDMA, TDMA and CDMA are the three major methods of sharing the available bandwidth to multiple users in wireless system. There are many extensions, and hybrid techniques for these methods, such as OFDM, and hybrid TDMA and FDMA systems.

- However, an understanding of the three major methods is required for understanding of any extensions to these methods.

(A) Frequency-Division Multiple Access (FDMA)

- For systems using Frequency Division Multiple Access (FDMA), the available bandwidth is subdivided into a number of narrower band channels.

- Each user is allocated a unique frequency band in which to transmit and receive on. During a call, no other user can use the same frequency band.

- Each user is allocated a forward link channel (from the base station to the mobile phone) and a reverse channel (back to the base station), each being a single way link.

- The transmitted signal on each of the channels is continuous allowing analog transmissions.

- The channel bandwidth used in most FDMA systems is typically low (30 kHz) as each channel only needs to support a single user.

- FDMA is used as the primary subdivision of large allocated frequency bands and is used as part of most multi-channel systems. Fig. 1.12 shows the FDMA scheme.

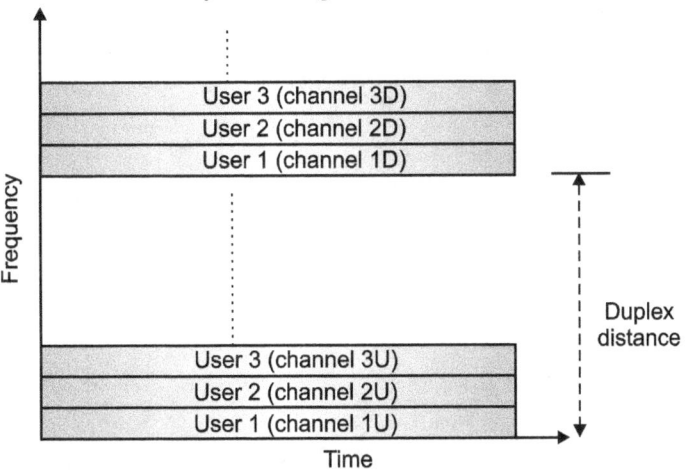

Fig. 1.12 : FDMA scheme

(B) Time-Division Multiple Access (TDMA)

- Time Division Multiple Access (TDMA) divides the available spectrum into multiple time slots, by giving each user a time slot in which they can transmit or receive.

- Fig. 1.13 shows how the time slots are provided to users in a round robin fashion, with each user being allotted one time slot per frame.

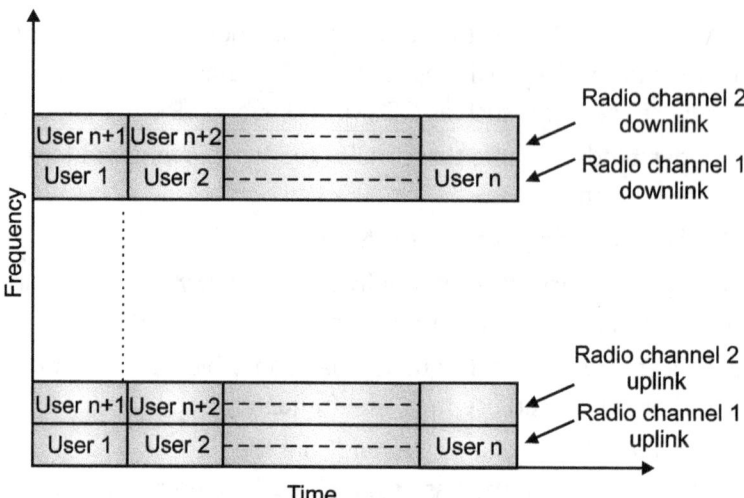

Fig. 1.13 : TDMA scheme

- TDMA systems transmit data in a buffer and burst method, thus the transmission of each channel is non-continuous.

- The input data to be transmitted is buffered over the previous frame and burst transmitted at a higher rate during the time slot for the channel.

- TDMA can not send analog signals directly due to the buffering required, thus is only used for transmitting digital data.

- TDMA can suffer from multipath effects as the transmission rate is generally very high, resulting in significant inter-symbol interference.

- TDMA is normally used in conjunction with FDMA to subdivide the total available bandwidth into several channels.

- To reduce the number of users per channel allowing a lower data rate to be used. This helps reduce the effect of delay spread on the transmission. Fig. 1.13 shows the use of TDMA with FDMA.

- Each channel based on FDMA, is further subdivided using TDMA, so that several users can transmit of the one channel.

- This type of transmission technique is used by most digital second generation mobile phone systems.

- For GSM, the total allocated bandwidth of 25 MHz is divided into 125, 200kHz channels using FDMA. These channels are then subdivided further by using TDMA so that each 200 kHz channel allows 8-16 users.

(C) Code-Division Multiple Access (CDMA)

- Code Division Multiple Access (CDMA) is a spread spectrum technique that uses neither frequency channels nor time slots. With CDMA, the narrow band message (typically digitised voice data) is multiplied by a large bandwidth signal that is a pseudo random noise code (PN code).

- All users in a CDMA system use the same frequency band and transmit simultaneously. The transmitted signal is recovered by correlating the received signal with the PN code used by the transmitter. Fig. 1.14 shows the general use of the spectrum using CDMA.

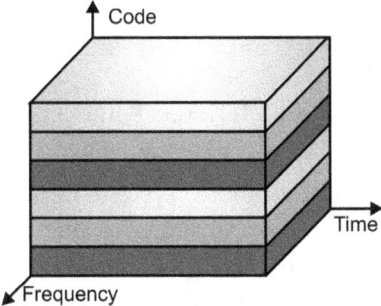

Fig. 1.14: CDMA scheme

- TDMA systems have a very well-defined capacity limit. A set number of channels and a set number of time slots exist per channel. Once all time slots are occupied, the system has reached capacity.

- CDMA is somewhat different with CDMA, the capacity is limited by the amount of noise in the system.

- Each additional user is added, the total interference increases, and it becomes harder and harder to extract a given user's unique sequence from the sequences of all the other users.

- Eventually, the noise floor reaches a level where the inclusion of additional users significantly impedes the system's capability to filter out the transmission of each user. At this point, the system has reached capacity.

- Although it is possible to model this capacity limit mathematically, exact modeling can prove a little difficult because the noise in the system depends on such factors as the transmission power of each individual mobile device, thermal noise, and the use of discontinuous transmission. By making certain reasonable assumptions in the design phase, however, it is possible to design a CDMA system that provides relatively high capacity without significant quality degradation.

- CDMA2000, WCDMA, and TD-CDMA are widely deployed CDMA systems for mobile communications, with TD-SCDMA on to be available commercially. All four protocols are use CDMA, with CDMA2000 and WCDMA being FDD-based and TD-CDMA and TD-SCDMA being TDD-based.

- For example, CDMA2000 uses a channel bandwidth of 1.23 MHz and is an FDD system. The bandwidth is 1.23 MHz means that the total system bandwidth (typically 10, 20, or 30 MHz) can accommodate several CDMA RF channels.

- Therefore, like TDMA, IS-95 CDMA also uses FDMA to some degree. In other words, within a given cell, more than one RF channel may be available to system users. More detail on the other CDMA protocols.

- A significant advantage of any CDMA-based system is the fact that it practically eliminates frequency planning.

- Other systems are very sensitive to interference, meaning that a given frequency can be reused only in another cell that is sufficiently far away to avoid interference.

- In a commercial mobile communications system network, cells are constantly being added, or capacity is being added to existing cells, and each such change must be done without causing undue interference.

- If interference is likely to be introduced, then retuning part of the network is required.

- Such retuning is needed frequently and returning can be an expensive effort. CDMA, however, is designed to deal with interference, and it allows a given RF carrier to be reused in every cell.

- Therefore, there is no need to worry about retuning the network when a new cell is added.

(D) Orthogonal Frequency Division Multiplexing (OFDM)

- Orthogonal Frequency Division Multiplexing (OFDM) is a multicarrier transmission technique, which divides the available spectrum into many carriers, each one being modulated by a low rate data stream.

- OFDM is similar to FDMA in that the multiple user access is achieved by subdividing the available bandwidth into multiple channels, which are then allocated to users.

- However, OFDM uses the spectrum much more efficiently by spacing the channels much closer together.

- This is achieved by making all the carriers orthogonal to one another, preventing interference between the closely spaced carriers.

- In FDMA each user is typically allocated a single channel, which is used to transmit all the user information.

- The bandwidth of each channel is typically 10 kHz to 30 kHz for voice communications.

- However, the minimum required bandwidth for speech is only 3 kHz. The allocated bandwidth is made wider then the minimum amount required to prevent channels from interfering with one another.

- This extra bandwidth is to allow for signals from neighbouring channels to be filtered out, and to allow for any drift in the centre frequency of the transmitter or receiver.

- In a typical system up to 50% of the total spectrum is wasted due to the extra spacing between channels. This problem becomes worse as the channel bandwidth becomes narrow, and the frequency band increases.

- TDMA overcomes this problem by using wider bandwidth channels, which are used by several users. Multiple users access the same channel by transmitting in their data in time slots.

- Thus, low data rate users can be combined together to transmit in a single channel that has a bandwidth sufficient so that the spectrum can be used efficiently.

- However, two main problems with TDMA. There is an overhead associated with the change over between users due to time slotting on the channel. A change over time must be allocated to allow for any tolerance in the start time of each user, due to propagation delay variations and synchronization errors.

- This limits the number of users that can be sent efficiently in each channel. In that, the symbol rate of each channel is high (as the channel handles the information from multiple users) resulting problems with multipath delay spread.

- The problems with both FDMA and TDMA. OFDM splits the available bandwidth into many narrow band channels (typically 100 to 8000).

- The carriers for each channel are made orthogonal to one another, allowing them to be spaced very close together, with no overhead as in the FDMA example. Because of this there is no great need for users to be time multiplex as in TDMA, thus there is no overhead associated with switching between users.

- The orthogonality of the carriers means that each carrier has an integer number of cycles over a symbol period. Due to this, the spectrum of each carrier has a null at the centre frequency of each of the other carriers in the system.

- This results in no interference between the carriers, allowing then to be spaced as close as possible. This problem overcomes of overhead carrier spacing in FDMA is required.

- Each carrier in an OFDM signal has a very narrow bandwidth (i.e. 1 kHz), thus the resulting symbol rate is low. This results in the signal having a high tolerance to multipath delay spread, as the delay spread must be very long to cause significant Inter-Symbol Interference (ISI) (e.g. > 100 msec).

- The OFDM is used in all the recent technologies such as Wi-Fi, ADSL, WiMAX, HiperMAN, LTE etc..

- OFDM can be used over many different media such as radio spectrum, Coaxial cable, twisted pair cable, Fiber optic cable.

- OFDM divides the data stream into smaller parallel streams of data, as shown in Fig. 1.15. OFDM, the smaller parallel data streams are each sent on a different channel and different frequency.

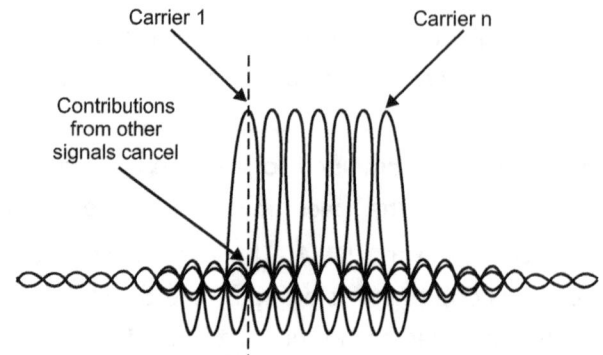

Fig. 1.15 : OFDM spectrum

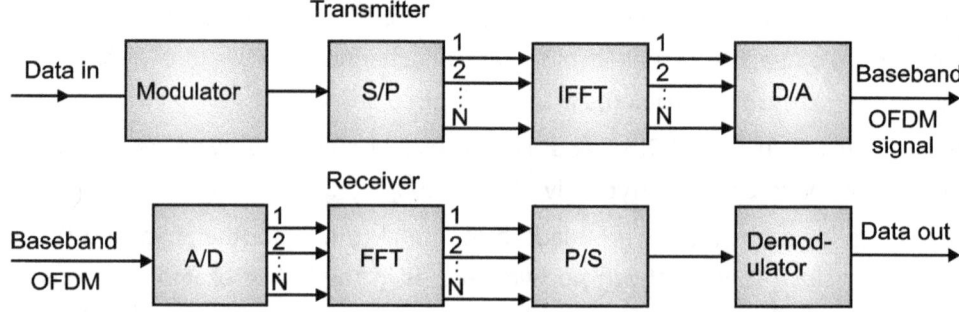

Fig. 1.16 : OFDM system

Advantages of OFDM

- Improve the spectrum efficiency bits per second per hertz, or bps/Hz.
- Multipath and fading resiliency.
- Improve the signal-to-noise ratio.
- Dynamic bandwidth allocation.
- Data rates can be changed base.
- RF environment.
- Services required.
- By subscriber.
- Spread spectrum.
- OFDM has the ability to reject impulse noise.
- OFDM spreads energy of an impulse noise over transmitted burst.

Disadvantages of OFDM

- High Peak-to-Average Power Ratio (PAPR).
- Transmitter amplifier complexity.
- Battery power consumption by mobile device.

An OFDM channel is divided into subchannels or subcarriers as follows :

- Less than the channel bandwidth.

- Experiences flat fading.
- Inter Symbol Interference is reduced.

To make OFDM work, all the subcarriers need to be orthogonal to each other and allow subcarriers to overlap without increasing ISI.

1.4.4 Roaming

- A wireless communications network a mobile communications network, it is essential to have some more attributes apart from air access interface. The user should be able to move freely without distribution of the communication link. The location of a subscriber is required to be tracked.
- Roaming is a term used to providing connectivity to the user in a location in which the user has moved to other than his home location. The term roaming was originally coined in GSM but also used in CDMA technology.
- The standard definition of roaming is "the ability for a cellular customer to automatically make and receive voice calls, send and receive data, or access other services, including home data services, when travelling outside the geographical coverage area of the home network, by means of using a visited network".
- This can be done by using a communication terminal or else just by using the subscriber identity in the visited network. Roaming is technically supported by mobility management, authentication, authorization and billing procedures.
- The roaming is carried out as below :
  (i) When a subscriber initially switches on his or her mobile phone, the device itself sends a registration message to the local MSC. This message includes a unique identification for the subscriber.
  (ii) Based on this identification, the MSC is able to identify the HLR to which the subscriber belongs, and the MSC sends a registration message to the HLR to inform the HLR of the MSC that now serves the subscriber.
  (iii) The HLR then sends a registration cancellation message to the MSC that previously served the subscriber (if any) and then sends a confirmation to the new serving MSC.
- In the initial periods of mobile communication, the protocol between the visited MSC and home MSC was not specified hence roaming was supported between them only when they have systems from same vendor. Hence roaming was not common,
- In North America, the problem was a standard known as IS-41 was used to address this issue. It is enhanced over the years. IS-41 is used for roaming in AMPS systems, IS-136 systems, and IS-95 systems.
- In Europe, a major effort was applied to ensuring that the problem was addressed in 2G technology specifically GSM. The protocol specified for GSM is known as the GSM Mobile Application Part (MAP). IS-41, GSM MAP also has been enhanced over the years.
- The term MAP is not specific to GSM. It refers to any mobility-specific protocol that operates at layer 7 of the Open Systems Interconnection (OSI) seven-layer stack. Given that IS-41 also operates at layer 7, the term MAP is also applicable to IS-41.

1.4.5 Handoff/Handover

- In cellular telecommunications, the term handover or handoff refers to the process of transferring an ongoing call or data session from one channel connected to the core network to another.
- The term handoff typically is used with AMPS, IS-136, and IS-95, whereas handover is used in GSM. The two terms are synonymous.
- Handoff usually means that a subscriber travels from one cell to another while engaged in a call and that the call is maintained during the transition (ideally without the subscriber noticing any change).
- In general, handoff means that the subscriber is transitioned from one radio channel (and/or time slot) to another.
- Depending on the two cells, the handoff can be between two sectors on the same base station, between two BSCs, between two MSCs belonging to the same operator, or even between two networks. (Note that internetwork handoff is not supported in some systems, often mainly for billing reasons.)
- It is also possible to hand off a call between two channels in the same cell. This could occur when a given channel in a cell is experiencing interference that is affecting the communications quality. In such a case, the subscriber would be moved to another frequency that is subject to less interference. A handoff scenario is depicted in Fig. 1.17.

Handoff in Wireless Mobile Networks

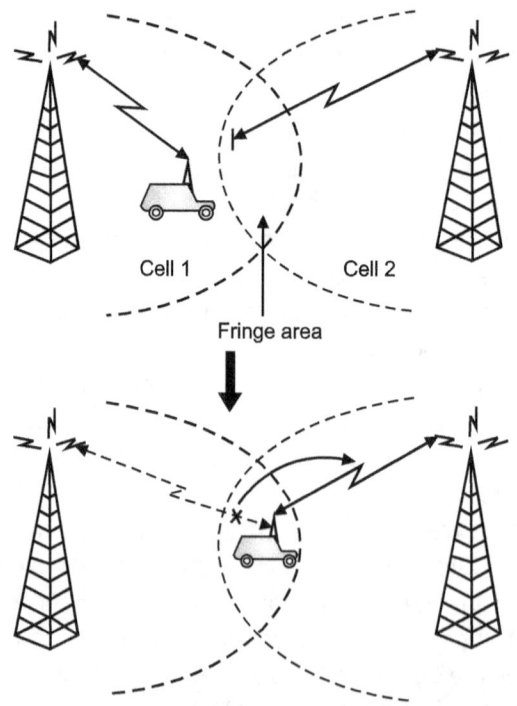

Fig. 1.17 : Hard handoff between the MS and BSs

- There are two types of handoffs:

    (i) Network-controlled handoff.

    (ii) Mobile-assisted handover .

- The decision of handoff is controlled by the network. When the signal strength of the signal received from a mobile device falls below a threshold value in a cell, the nearby cells are asked to perform the signal strength measurement of that device. The cell which records a better signal strength, allocates a channel by the subscriber.

- The network then instructs the mobile device to switch over to the new channel.

- This is known as a network-controlled handoff because the network determines when and how a handoff is to occur.

- When the mobile device controls the handoff, it is known as Mobile-Assisted Handover (MAHO). It is used in recent mobile communication systems.

- The mobile device periodically measures both signal strength and signal quality, and it sends these reports to the network.

- The analysis of these reports is done by the network to decide whether a handoff is required or not.

- If handoff is required, network reserves a channel on the new cell and sends an instruction to the mobile device to switch to that channel.

1.5 MOBILE DATA

- The need of mobile data is created because of following reasons:

    (i) The need to extend the corporate local-area network (LAN),

    (ii) Surf the Internet for information,

    (iii) Use Voice over Internet Protocol (VoIP) or

    (iv) Perform an IP-to-IP call (PTT).

- The mobile data are vertical i.e. every user's specific data requirements are different. For example, one user may require it for internet browsing whereas another user may want it for VoIP. Hence the mobile data concept becomes complicated.

- Cellular Data Packet Data (CDPD) is one of the examples that the wireless industry needs to always remember. CDPD was an excellent packet network that rivals many of the current wireless data offerings and was available close to a decade prior to 2.5G/3G.

- There are many mobile data technologies, but focus requires exclusion and wireless mobility for cellular/PCS is the focus. The key platforms used for 2G, 2.5G, and 3G wireless mobility are listed in Table 1.3.

Table 1.3 : Wireless Mobility Data

2G Technology	Data Capability	Spectrum Required	Comment
GSM	9.6 or 14.4 kbps	200 kHz	Circuit-switched data
IS-136	9.6 kbps	30 kHz	Circuit-switched data
IDEN	9.6 kbps	25 kHz	Circuit-switched data
CDMA	9.6/14.4 kbps	1.25 MHz	Circuit-switched data
(IS-95A/J-STD-008)	64 bps (IS-95B)		
HSCSD	28.8/56 kbps	200 kHz	Circuit/packet data
GPRS	128 kbps	200 kHz	Circuit/packet data
Edge	384 kbps	200 kHz	Circuit/packet data
CDMA2000-1XRTT	144 kbps	1.25 MHz	Circuit/packet data
3G Technology	**Data Capability**	**Spectrum Required**	**Comment**
WCDMA	144 kbps vehicular 384 kbps outdoors 2 Mbps indoors	5 MHz	Packet data
CDMA2000-EVDO/EVDV	144 kbps vehicular 384 kbps outdoors 2 Mbps indoors	1.25 MHz	Packet data
TD-CDMA	144 kbps vehicular 384 kbps outdoors 2 Mbps indoors	5 MHz	Packet data
TD-SCDMA	144 kbps vehicular 384 kbps outdoors 2 Mbps indoors	1.6 MHz	Packet data

- In above table 1.3, WCDMA enhancements are referred to as High Speed Downlink Packet Access (HSDPA) and High Speed Uplink Packet Access (HSUPA).
- Both HSDPA an HSUPA are enchancements to WCDMA facilitating greater throughput.
- CDMA2000 reference to EVDO and EVDV also is an enchancement to the original CDMA2000 data rates. Both WCDMA and CDMA2000 and its subsequent.

- In addition to the previous topics mentioned, the most obvious missing component to the data offering is Wi-Fi, WiMAX, WiMAN, cable, and Digital Subscriber Line (DSL) systems, which part of the technology the fixed-data-offering capability that can complement the mobile data portfolio when the subscriber is more stationary.
- Harmonization of IMT-2000 technologies with WiMAX and Wi-Fi all through the use of IP.
- **Note :** That CDMA, GSM, EVDO, HSPA, and LTE are 3GPP and 3GPP2 standards while Wi-Fi and WiMAX fall under the IEEE 802 standards.

1.6 Wi-Fi

- Wi-Fi is a wireless LAN protocol based on the IEEE 802.11 standards and is a standard feature in all laptops and wireless handsets for mobility. Wi-Fi operates in both licensed and unlicensed spectrums. However, the licensed spectrum is set aside for public safety. The unlicensed spectrum for Wi-Fi involves the ISM (2.4 GHz) and UNII (5.8 GHz) bands.
- There are multiple protocols for Wi-Fi that are in play right now and they are:
  - 802.11 b/g (ISM),
  - 802.11 a (UNII),
  - 802.11 n (ISM/UNII),
  - 802.11 g (ISM/UNII).
- However, Wi-Fi is not classified as a Wireless Mobile Broadband Network and is meant for small coverage areas.

Wi-Fi Advantages and Disadvantages :

- Some of the advantages include the ability to establish a wireless LAN that eliminates cabling requirements. Wi-Fi is an established standard and is universally accepted. What is important for wireless mobility networks is that Wi-Fi is an excellent broadband traffic offload platform.
- However, some disadvantages with Wi-Fi are its limited coverage from access point, security, and the use of unlicensed spectrum.
- Table 1.4 provides a high-level overview of some of Wi-Fi attributes.

Table 1.4 : Wi-Fi Attributes

Function	802.11b	802.11g	802.11a	802.11n
Maximum Data Rate	11 Mbps	54 Mbps	54 Mbps	540 Mbps
Number of non-overlapping channels	3	3	11	11/3
Frequency Allocation Band	2.4 GHz ISM	2.4 GHz ISM	5 GHz UNII 2.4 GHz ISM	5 GHz UNII 2.4 GHz ISM
Modulation/Coding	CCK, HR/DSSS HR/DSS/short HRDSSS/PBCC	OFDM	OFDM	OFDM

1.7 BLUETOOTH

- Bluetooth is used to connect various devices such as mobile phones, PDA's, laptops, PCs, LCD Projectors etc. wirelessly. The information can be exchanged using this connectivity. It operates in the ISM band (2.4 G Hz).
- Bluetooth is defined under IEEE 802.15 specifications. Most of the handheld devices are equipped with Bluetooth.
- There are various versions of Bluetooth specified as Bluetooth 1.0, 1.2, 2.0, 2.1, 3.0, 4.0 and 4.1. The Bluetooth 1.0 is basic version and the higher versions have increased throughput and better functionality.
- Bluetooth is a transport layer protocol. It offers following advantages:

  (i) The range of Bluetooth connection is 10m to 100 m.

  (ii) It does not require Line-of-Sight (LOS) for establishing communication

  (iii) It has omnidirectional antenna pattern hence there is no need for orientation.

  (iv) It supports ISO- and asynchronous services, because of which TCP/IP protocols can be implemented./

  (v) Bluetooth is different from Wi-Fi because it is meant to be a LAN extension providing connectivity with end-user devices not requiring high bandwidth.

  (vi) Bluetooth is also able to coexist with Wi-Fi in the same frequency band.

- Bluetooth uses frequency hopping where the frequency of transmission is changed using PN sequence.The modulation schemes used in Bluetooth are as below:

(i) All versions support Gaussian Frequency Shift Keying (GFSK) which provide data rates of 1 Mbps

(ii) Versions 2 and 3 support Phase Shift Keying (PSK) providing data rates of 2 and 3 Mbps

- Bluetooth spectrum has 79 channels as shown in Fig. 1.18. Each channel has a bandwidth of 1MHz. At the beginning and end of the spectrum there are guard-bands.

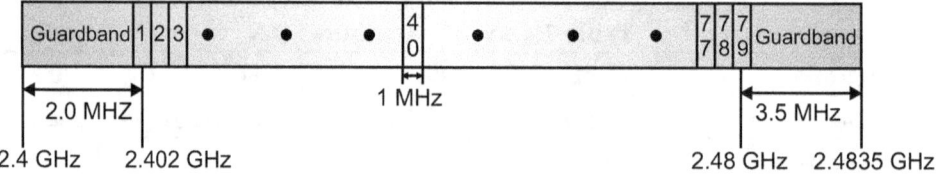

Fig. 1.18 : Bluetooth spectrum

1.8 CABLE SYSTEMS

- The television cable system is present in every house. The broadband service can be provided through cable modems.
- The data services are delivered via a cable modem that meets the Data Over Cable Service Interface Specification (DOCSIS).

- DOCSIS is an interface specification for cable modems enabling broadband to be delivered over a cable television network.

- The DOCSIS interface specification enables a cable television system to offer high-speed IP data between the subscriber location and the cable operator's head end.

- DOCSIS technology provides significant new value for cable operators and consumers of broadband services including:

- The cable modem IS typically, connected to a two-way cable RF path over a low-split hybrid fiber/coaxial (HFC) cable system that uses fixed-wire facilities, unlike the radio counterpart, Because OF it uses a fixed medium, downlink or downstream data rates of between 27 and 36 Mbps are possible using a radio channel that is 50 MHz wide and operating around 750 MHz.

- The uplink or upstream data rate is between 320 kbps and 10 Mbps over an uplink radio channel that is between 5 and 42 MHz.

- The common issue facing all broadband providers is the quality of their underlying transport layer. The quality of the cable plant itself dictates the services that effectively can be offered.

- The issue of quality of the cable plant is driven primarily by the number of drops that occur on any cable leg, which has a direct impact on the ingress noise problem that limits the ability of the cable plant to provide high-speed two-way communication.

- Since most of the information flow is from the head end to the subscriber, the system does not have to support symmetric bandwidth.

- An HFC network has the capability of providing two-way communication for both voice and data besides the video service offering.

- The primary access method is physical medium, where the connection made to the subscriber at the end of the line is via coaxial cable. For increased distance and performance enhancements, fiber optic cables often can be and are part of the cable network topology.

1.9 WIRELESS MIGRATION OPTIONS

- The various technology platforms were briefly discussed in previous sections. The existing wireless operators today, regardless of the frequency band or existing technology deployed. They are making very fundamental decisions as to which direction they will take in the 3G/4G evolution.

- The decision on fundamental technology and how it will interface with legacy systems will define a company's position in the marketplace for years to come.

- Some existing operators and new entrants are letting the technology platform be defined by the local regulator, thereby eliminating the platform decision. However, the majority of operators need to determine which platform they will use.

- Since the platforms to pick from use different access technologies, they are by default not directly compatible.

- The use of different access technologies for the realization of 3G also introduces several interesting issues related to the migration from 2G to 3G.

- The migration path from 2G to 3G is referred to as 2.5G and involves an interim position for data services that are more advanced than 2G but not as robust as the 3G data services.

- Additionally, the decision for which 4G technology to implement and the associated legacy network migration or interoperability.

- The business plan as well as the spectrum portfolio of the wireless operator directly influence the migration options that are truely available.

- Some of the migration strategies for an existing operator involve:
  - Overlay,
  - Spectrum segmentation.

- The 3G overlay approach typically involves implementing the 2.5G technology over the existing 2G system and then implementing 3G as either an overlay or in a separate part of the RF spectrum they are allocated, that is, spectrum segmentation.

- The 4G overlay approach involves deploying 4G in a separate frequency band, then legacy systems, and then migrating legacy systems.

- The overlay or spectrum segmentation naturally depends on the technology platform that is currently being used, to 2G or 3G, the spectrum available, the existing capacity constraints, and marketing.

- Marketing is involved with the decision because of the impact on the existing subscriber base and services that are envisioned to be offered.

- The plethora of technical options available the need to have a strong business plan is essential and this should provide the fundamental input to determine just what and how will implement 4G or any wireless technology with the legacy network.

- The decisions are rather straight forward, involving upgrading portions of the existing technology platforms that are currently deployed.

- Other operators have to make a decision as to which technology to use because they either are building a new system or have not migrated to a 4G platform, using only 2G or 3G networks.

1.10 HARMONIZATION PROCESS

- Harmonization refers to the vision and objective of the IMT-2000 and IMT Advanced specifications that enable the various technology platforms that are defined in that specification to interact with each other.

- True harmonization relative to the capability of a wireless system is based on having subscriber unit that operate in a radio access technology agnostic mode, commonly referred to as software-definable radios.

- Operating in a radio access technology agnostic mode would enable subscribers to achieve connectivity anywhere there is RF coverage.

- However, the access infrastructure that is able to support this is a goal, but not one that will exist in the near future.

QUESTIONS

1. Define wireless networks. What are various types of wireless networks based on the range ?

2. What are various 2G Mobile systems ? Write features of any one of them.

3. What is spread spectrum system? Draw block diagram of the DSSS transmitter and receiver.

4. Explain spreading and dispreading of spectrum in a DSSS system.

5. What were the requirements of 3G systems?

6. What are the features of 3G mobile systems which made it data centric ?

7. What are features of 4G mobile systems?

8. Compare 3G and 4G systems.

9. What are features of Next Generation Wireless (NGW) systems ?

10. What are advantages of cell structures in cellular systems ?

11. What are disadvantages of cell structures in cellular systems ?

12. What is sectored cell structure ? Explain.

13. Draw basic network architecture of mobile system.

14. What is FDD ? Explain.
15. What is TDD ? Explain.
16. Compare FDD and TDD.
17. What are various multiple access techniques ? Explain any one of them.
18. What is OFDM ? How it is spectrally efficient.
19. Draw the block diagram of OFDM system to explain how it works.
20. What is roaming and how it is handled ?
21. What is need of mobile data ?
22. Write a advantages and disadvantages of Wi-Fi.
23. Write in brief features of Bluetooth.
24. What is DOCSIS ?
25. What is harmonization process ?

Wi-Fi AND NEXT GENERATION WIRELESS LAN

2.1 INTRODUCTION

- Wi-Fi is the name of a popular wireless networking technology that uses radio waves to provide wireless high–speed Internet and network connections.
- The Wi-Fi Alliance, the organization that owns the Wi-Fi registered trademark term specifically defines Wi-Fi as any "wireless local area network (WLAN) products that are based on the Institute of Electrical and Electronics Engineers' (IEEE) 802.11 standards."
- Initially, Wi-Fi was used in place of only the 2.4 GHz 802.11b standard, however the Wi-Fi Alliance has expanded the generic use of the Wi-Fi term to include any type of network or WLAN product based on any of the 802.11 standards, including 802.11b, 802.11a, dual–band and so on, in an attempt to stop confusion about wireless LAN interoperability.
- Wireless connectivity for computers is now well established and virtually all new laptops contain a Wi-Fi capability. Not only that the mobile devices are also benefited by Wi-Fi which is providing wireless data connectivity to mobile users. Bluetooth and Ultrawide Band (UWB) also provides wireless data connectivity.
- This unit discusses Wi-Fi as the leading unlicensed broadband access technology.

2.2 Wi-Fi (IEEE 802.11)

- Wi-Fi is a wireless LAN based on the 802.11 standards. It is a wireless access method used to connect devices to either a LAN or the Internet via a wireless connection. Wireless LAN architecture is composed of different components which help in establishing the local area network between different operating systems.
- These components are very essential for Wi-Fi architecture:
  (a) Access point
  (b) Clients
  (c) Bridge

(a) Access Points

- A special type of routing device that is used to transmit the data between wired and wireless networking device is called as AP.
- It is often connected with the help of wired devices such as Ethernet. It only transmits or transfers the data between wireless LAN and wired network by using infra structure mode of network.

- One access point can only support a small group of networks and works more efficiently.
- It is operated less than hundred feet. It is denoted by AP.

Access point has the following characteristics:

- Provides Wireless Access for Wireless Adaptors (CPE)
- Provides Authentication for wireless adaptors
- Provides in some cases access to a wired LAN
- Is a hot spot
- Contains all the functions of wireless adaptors
- Can operate in a trusted or untrusted mode
- Can be combined with other APs

(b) Clients

Any kind of device such as personal computers, Note books, or any kind of mobile devices which are inter linked with wireless network area referred as a client of wireless LAN architecture.

(c) Wireless Adapters (CPE) / Bridge

- A special type of connectors which is used to establish connections between wired network devices such as Ethernet and different wireless networks such as wireless LAN. It is called as bridge.
- It acts as a point of control in wireless LAN architecture.
- Wireless Adaptor (CPE) has the following characteristics:
  - Wireless adaptor provides radio access between AP and other Wi-Fi CPE.
  - Wireless adaptors can be integrated into an appliance.
  - Wireless adaptors can be external to an appliance (USB, Express Card, PCMCIA, etc.).

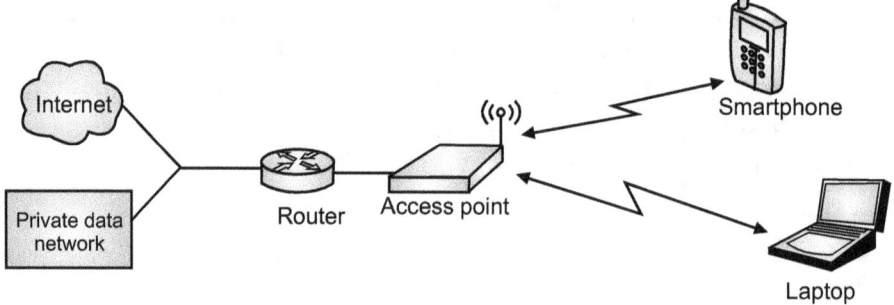

Fig. 2.1 : Wi-Fi components.

- As expected, Wi-Fi like any wireless access technology, has many advantages and disadvantages:

Advantages of Wi-Fi

- Now that we've covered the basics of the technology, let's check out some of the advantages Wi-Fi has over its wireless (and wired) competition.

(i) Unparalleled Mobility and Flexibility

- If have ever installed a multi–room stereo and had to run wires through a wall, you know the amount of time and effort it requires, not to mention the permanence of your installation.
- If you want to move the receiver to another room, the wiring has to be completely redone, and the holes patched.
- Thanks to Wi-Fi, users are no longer confined by the cords that link their devices, enabling new levels of connectivity without sacrificing function or design options. Products like network music players use Wi-Fi technology to wirelessly stream your music to speakers located throughout your house.
- Some systems are different than others, but typically you can listen to the same, or different music in each room, play music from your computer or other devices attached to the network, and even listen to Internet radio.

(ii) Quick, easy Setup

- Setting up a wireless network may sound like a daunting task, but it's actually a pretty straightforward process.
- Wi-Fi networks don't require professional installation, and, best of all, there are no holes to drill or wires to run through walls.
- Many new routers are "plug–and–play," meaning you just connect them to a power outlet, plug in an Ethernet cord, and voila your network has been created.
- Unfortunately, wireless security doesn't automatically configure itself, so it's important to remember to enable it via a personal computer once a connection to the wireless network has been established. (We'll touch on this topic more in–depth in the limitations section.)

(iii) Fast Data Transfer Rates

- With transfer speeds around 150 megabits (Mb) per second (18.75 megabytes), 802.11n is currently the fastest commercially available Wi-Fi protocol on the market. It's more than capable of handling the demands of streaming high–definition TV signals, as well as CD–quality audio.
- For information about the kinds of services you can stream through your TV, check out our article on Enjoying the Internet on your TV.

(iv) Wireless LAN

It is used to establish wireless LAN

(v) Established Standards

- The 802.11 standard id established and widely accepted and incorporated in number of devices.

Limitations of Wi-Fi

- So far we've covered some of the advantages offered by Wi-Fi wireless technology, but there are some limitations that must be addressed as well. Security and interference are the main issues with current Wi-Fi standards.

(i) Limited Range
- It has very small range of 100m.

(ii) Security Concerns
- Though typically very easy to set up, securing your Wi-Fi network requires a bit more effort. Wi-Fi access points do not come with encryption straight out of the box; you have to do it from your computer once the network is up and running.
- An unsecured wireless network is susceptible to attacks from hackers, potentially giving them access to all of the information stored by the devices on your network.
- In addition, "friendly," yet unauthorized computers will also be able to connect to your network, occupying the bandwidth and hindering overall network performance.

(iii) Interference from other Devices /Unlicensed Frequency
- Wi-Fi transmissions take place primarily within the 2.4 GHz spectrum, making them susceptible to interference from Bluetooth wireless enabled devices, cordless telephones, microwave ovens, baby monitors, and other household devices. The farther your Wi-Fi devices are located from these known interferences and the closer they are to one another the more robust your signal will be, so keep that in mind during setup.
- If you live in an apartment complex or in close proximity to your neighbors, their wireless network can also be a source of interference.
- Some newer routers automatically select the channel with the least amount of interference, ensuring that you get the best possible connection.
- Wi-Fi equipment costs for the end device as well as the infrastructure, APs, is relatively inexpensive, unlike its 2.5G/3G and 4G counterparts. Service is easy to deploy and affordable. Additionally, the Wireless Ethernet Compatibility Alliance (WECA) provides a certification process for all 802.11 components in order to ensure that the AP and CPE from multiple vendors can interoperate with each other.
- However, as always the real issue regarding ease of deployment and affordability is that it depends on the objective or service offering. For instance, if Wi-Fi is deployed for a home network for linking a computer or computers to the Internet then the low cost and ease of installation is real.
- But if the Wi-Fi network is to support more than the home usage and provide ubiquitous access to public and private packet data networks, i.e. the Internet and corporate LANs, then the cost and installation concerns take on another level of complexity.
- Add in the component of wireless mobile services and the decisions that need to be made, and then it becomes daunting.
- They are daunting because not all services are the same and you need to have prior knowledge of what you want to do before selecting the access method.
- Some of the key issues that need to be addressed or factored into the decision process are
  - Coverage
  - Roaming
  - Backhaul

- Security
- Device

- The coverage question comes down to a simple question: where are you going to use the service and how is it going to be used? If it is desired to have medical data available to visiting RNs for a large metropolitan area, then the use of Wi-Fi by itself will need to be augmented by a 2.5G/3G, 4G system.
- However, if the objective is to have coverage in the visiting conference area, then a stand–alone Wi-Fi system could be used.
- The roaming issue that needs to be answered is akin to the issue of coverage.
- It is desired to have the workforce use different Wi-Fi networks or hot spots that may or may not be integrated into a 2.5G/3G, 4G network. 802.11, however, elevates some of the roaming issue with multiple APs in different locations due to the ability to broadcast a common Service Set Identifier (SSID) establishing an Extended Service Set (ESS).
- The issue of backhaul is important from a wireless service provider's aspect as well as the end user.
- The service provider needs to determine and support the requisite backhaul transport level to ensure the service offered, at the defined data rate, is achievable and can be sustained via wireless or wired connections.
- However, if the Wi-Fi AP is a corporate LAN or a hot spot then best effort service may be the desired service level.
- As mentioned previously, wireless operators are basically compelled to try and off–load heavy data traffic onto another RAN to preserve or better utilize the RAN for less bandwidth intensive services or make them available for true mobility needs.
- Fig. 2.2 and 2.3 illustrates where Wi-Fi plays in the wireless access scheme.

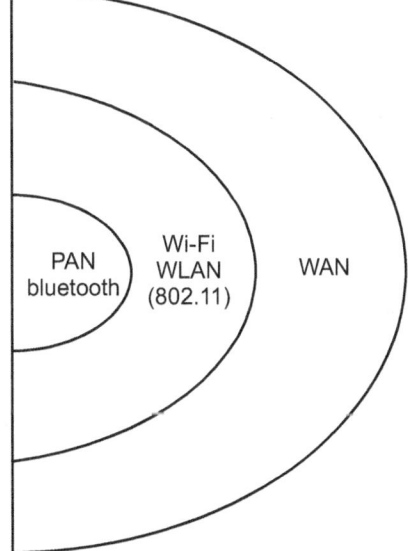

Fig. 2.2 : WAN, WLAN, PAN

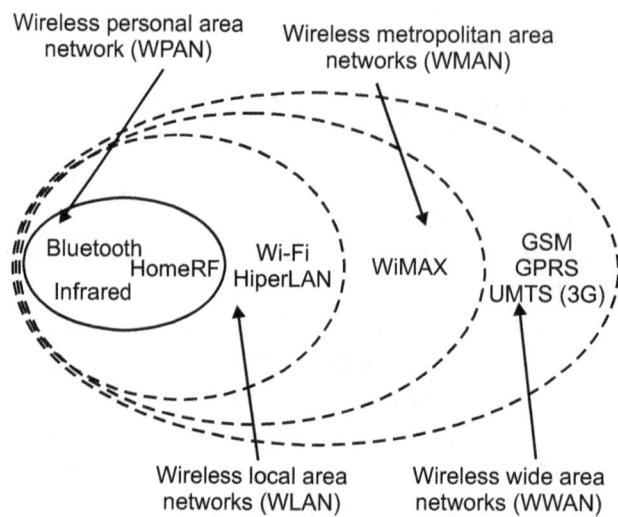

Fig. 2.3 : Range of wireless networks

- There are numerous standards that make up 802.11 with the most popular being referred to as Wi-Fi. This Unit objective is to provide an overview of the various flavors of 802.10. In addition, this unit will introduce and better define the interaction of 802.11 and wireless mobility.

- The convergence of 802.11 with wireless mobility has been described as the real "killer application." The killer application for mobility is that it will truly allow the subscriber to take advantage of all the applications available on the World Wide Web (WWW) while at the office or home office or on the road at some unknown location, provided, of course, that there is coverage. The issue of security and provisioning to make this a reality is not a trivial matter if true transparency is desired with the intranet of a company by its sales and support staff.

- It is not intended to present a detailed definition of the 802.11 specifications, since they can be found in the appropriate IEEE side, documents on website www.ieee.org.

- The plethora of information and options available for a mobile wireless operator to integrate 802.11 into the wireless data and overall service offerings.

2.3 IEEE 802.11 STANDARDS

- When Local Area Networks (LANs) first began to emerge as potential business tools in the late 1970s, the IEEE realized that there was a need to define certain LAN standards. To accomplish this task, the IEEE launched what became known as Project 802, named for it began of February 1980.

- Although the published IEEE 802 standards actually predated the ISO standards, both were in development at roughly the same time, and both shared information that resulted in the creation of two compatible models.

- Project 802 defined network standards for the physical components of a network (the interface card and the cabling) that are accounted for in the physical and data link layers of the OSI reference model.
- The 802 specifications set standards for:
  (i)   Network interface cards (NICs).
  (ii) Wide area network (WAN) components.
  (iii) Components used to create twisted–pair and coaxial cable networks.
- The 802 specifications define the ways NICs access and transfer data over physical media. These include connecting, maintaining, and disconnecting network devices.
- The LAN standards defined by the 802 committees are classified into 16 categories that can be identified by their 802 number as shown in Table 2.1.

Table 2.1 : 802 Specification Categories

Specification	Description
802.1	Sets Internetworking standards related to network management.
802.2	Defines the general standard for the data link layer. The IEEE divides this layer into two sublayers: the LLC and MAC layers. The MAC layer varies with different network types and is defined by standard IEEE 802.3.
802.3	Defines the MAC layer for bus networks that use Carrier–Sense Multiple Access with Collision Detection (CSMA/CD). It is the Ethernet Standard.
802.4	Defines the MAC layer for bus networks that use a token–passing mechanism (Token Bus LAN).
802.5	Defines the MAC layer for token ring networks (Token Ring LAN).
802.6	Sets standards for Metropolitan Area Networks (MANs), which are data networks designed for towns or cities. In terms of geographic breadth, MANs are larger than LANs, but smaller than WANs. MANs are usually characterized by very–high–speed connections using fiber–optic cables or other digital media.
802.7	Used by the Broadband Technical Advisory Group.
802.8	Used by the Fiber Optic Technical Advisory Group.
802.9	Defines integrated voice/data networks.
802.10	Defines network security.
802.11	Defines Wireless Network Standards.
802.12	Defines Demand Priority Access LAN, 100BaseVG Any LAN.
802.13	Unused.
802.14	Defines cable modem standards.
802.15	Defines Wireless Personal Area Networks (WPAN).
802.16	Defines broadband wireless standards.

- The 802.11 standard describes the functions and services required by an IEEE 802.11 compliant device including the requirements for privacy, security, and authentication.
- Even 802.11 has a variety of standards, each with a letter suffix.
- These cover everything from the wireless standards themselves, to standards for security aspects, quality of service and the like:

Specification	Description
802.11a	Wireless network bearer operating in the 5 GHz ISM band with data rate up to 54 Mbps.
802.11b	Wireless network bearer operating in the 2.4 GHz ISM band with data rates up to 11 Mbps.
802.11e	Quality of service and prioritisation
802.11f	Handover
802.11g	Wireless network bearer operating in 2.4 GHz ISM band with data rates up to 54 Mbps.
802.11h	Power control
802.11i	Authentication and encryption.
802.11j	Interworking.
802.11k	Measurement reporting.
802.11n	Wireless network bearer operating in the 2.4 and 5 GHz ISM bands with data rates up to 600 Mbps.
802.11s	Mesh networking.
802.11ac	Wireless network bearer operating below 6 GHz to provide data rates of at least 1Gbps per second for multi–station operation and 500 Mbps on a single link.
802.11ad	Wireless network bearer providing very high throughput at frequencies up to 60GHz.
802.11af	Wi-Fi in TV spectrum white spaces (often called White–Fi).
802.11ah	Wi-Fi using unlicensed spectrum below 1 GHz to provide long range communications and support for the Internet of Everything.

2.4 Wi-Fi PROTOCOLS

- IEEE 802.11 is a main Wi-Fi/WLAN protocol. As seen in previous section there are several other Wi-Fi protocols. Sometimes IEEE 802.15 (Bluetooth) is also referred to as a WLAN protocol. The IEEE 802.11 standards i.e. most widely known as the network bearer standards, 802.11a, 802.11b, 802.11g and now 802.11n.
- There are two unlicensed bands viz. 5 GHz Unlicensed National Information Infrastructure (UNII) band and 2.4 GHz Industrial, Scientific, and Medical (ISM) band. Wi-Fi protocols operate in these unlicensed bands.

- Following table 2.2 gives the details of these protocols.

Table 2.2 : Wi-Fi Protocols

WLAN	801.11a	802.11b	802.11g	802.11n	Bluetooth
Primary application	Wireless LAN	Wireless LAN	Wireless LAN	Wireless LAN	Wireless PAN
Frequency band	5 GHz UNII	2.4 GHz ISM	2.4 GHz ISM	5 GHz UNII 2.4 GHz ISM	2.4 GHz ISM
Access Protocol	CSMA/CA	CSMA/CA	CSMA/CA	CSMA/CA	PPP
FEC	Convolutional code	None	Convolutional code	Convolutional code	None
Mobility	In development	In development	In development	In development	NA
Max data rate	54 Mbit/s	11 Mbit/s	54 Mbit/s	540 Mbit/s	1 Mbit/s (v1.2) 3 Mbit/s (v2.0) 24 Mbps (v3.0)
Number of none verlapping channels	11	3	3	3/11	79
Range	50 m	50 m	50 m	50 m	1–10 m
Modulation /coding	OFDM	CCK, HR/DSS HR/DSS/ short HR / DSSS / PBCC	DSSS/CCK or OFDM	OFDM	FHSS
Power	0.05/0.25/1W	+20 dBm	0.05/0.25/1W	0.05/0. 25/1W UNII +20 dBm ISM	0 dBm

Following things can be Observed from the Table 2.2.

- 802.11a and 802.11n operatein 5 GHz UNII band but 802.11n is high speed and also operates in ISM band. The higher speed is due to increased bandwidth and better modulation schemes.
- 802.11g is meant to increase the data rate to 54 Mbps while providing backward–compatibility for 802.11b (Wi-Fi) equipment.
- Bluetooth operates in ISM band causing interference with 802.11b,g and n.

- 802.11a operates in the UNII band and can operate at a much greater Effective Radiated Power (ERP). The data rate in the chart for 802.11a and 802.11b shows a range in speeds that are, dependent on the modulation format used, power, and the interference experienced.
- 802.11Provides direct mobile data interoperability between the wired LAN and the wireless operator's system.
- Hiperlan is a European (ETSI) standardization initiative for a high performance wireless Local Area Network. The maximum data rate for the user depends on the distance of the communicating stations. HiperLAN/2 has similar physical layer properties as 802.11a as below
- It uses Orthogonal Frequency Division Multiplexing (OFDM).
- It is deployed in the 5 GHz band.
- However, the Media Access Control (MAC) layers are different, hence the different technology specification, in that HiperLAN uses a Time Division Multiple Access (TDMA) format as compared with 802.11a, which uses OFDM.

2.4.1 802.11b

- This is the most widespread variant of the standards.
- In 1999 the 802.11b standard was published and has been adapted widely by manufacturers of infrastructure, such as APs, routers, and bridges.
- 802.11b operates in the ISM band at 2.4 GHz and specifies data rates of up to 11 Mbps.
- It is the one typically found in "hot spots," with 802.11g quickly becoming more dominant.
- It is also adapted widely by vendors of interface devices for laptops, desktops, and PDAs.
- The standard specifies Direct Sequence Spread Spectrum (DSSS) and several modulation schemes, including Complimentary Code Keying (CCK) and Packet Binary Convolution Coding (PBCC).

2.4.2 802.11g

- 802.11g is backward compatible with 802.11b. This means any 802.11g device must be able to coexist with 802.11b devices.
- Wi-Fi specification 802.11g provides higher data rates (up to 54 Mbps) than 802.11b.
- The 802.11g standard employs DSSS/*Frequency Hopping Spread Spectrum* (FSSS) and OFDM.
- An 802.11g equipped laptop must work in an 802.11b Access Point (AP) coverage area.
- If an 802.11b laptop comes into an 802.11g AP coverage area, then 802.11g AP must be able to serve the device.
- A drawback to this is the fact that when an 802.11b device is detected in the 802.11g serving area, additional overhead is introduced. This overhead diminishes actual throughput by as much as 25 %.

2.4.3 802.11a

- It is important to note that while 802.11a and 802.11b/802.11g are not compatible, it is not unusual to use them both in an enterprise network.

- Wi-Fi systems using the 802.11a specification operate in UNII band, which enables systems using this particular network to operate not only at higher speeds but also at high power, enabling more reach.

- 802.11a operates in the UNII band at 5 GHz and uses OFDM as its modulation scheme.

- 802.11a is designed to provide data rates of up to 54 Mbps.

- Most users may be employing 802.11b/802.11g, whereas power users may be assigned 802.11a.

- These networks would be overlapping and not interoperating.

- Although not required by any standard, APs are available that offer both 802.11b/802.11g and 802.11a.

2.4.4 802.11n

- The 802.11n protocol is designed to effectively replace 802.11a, b, and g for local area networking.

- 802.11n enables speeds of 540 Mbps through improved modulation schemes and increased channel bandwidth.

- The increased channel bandwidth is achieved by combining two channels therefore increasing the bandwidth from 20 MHz to 40 MHz.

- In addition, 802.11n uses Multiple Input Multiple Output (MIMO) i.e. multiple antennas to both send and receive information.

- The use of MIMO not only increases the range of the 802.11n network, but also the throughput as well.

- 802.11n systems are also meant to be backward compatible, therefore incorporating legacy devices like 802.11a, b, and g networks.

- The vision for 802.11n systems is to render the wired networks in the home unnecessary, allowing for high–definition streaming video and other broadband–intensive applications to be leveraged in the home and office environment.

2.4.5 802.11ac

- 802.11ac is a logical extension, or rather evolution, of the 802.11n standard that is widely deployed.

- 802.11ac is compatible with 802.11n with the exception that it only operates in the 5 GHz band, which is typically less congested than the 2.4 GHz band. What 802.11ac brings to the table are several key attributes that enable it to deliver higher data rates than those available with 802.11n.

- The higher data rates are possible with 802.11ac through the use of higher modulation schemes where 256 QAM is achieved.

- Additionally, the radio channel size was increased to 80 MHz and 160 MHz. Also, 802.11ac is able to provide multiple spatial streams at the same time, up to 8 as compared to 802.11n which can only do 1.

- The spatial stream for a single user or device is referenced as SU–MIMO while the multiple user spatial stream is referenced as MU–MIMO.

2.5 FREQUENCY ALLOCATION

- IEEE 802.11g/b wireless nodes communicate with each other using radio frequency signals in the ISM (Industrial, Scientific, and Medical) band between 2.4 GHz and 2.5 GHz. Neighboring channels are 5 MHz apart.

- However, due to the spread spectrum effect of the signals, a node sending signals using a particular channel will utilize frequency spectrum 12.5 MHz above and below the center channel frequency.

- As a result, two separate wireless networks using neighboring channels (for example, channel 1 and channel 2) in the same general vicinity will interfere with each other.

- Applying two channels that allow the maximum channel separation will decrease the amount of channel cross–talk and provide a noticeable performance increase over networks with minimal channel separation.

2.5.1 802.11b and 802.11g

- Channel allocation within the ISM band for 802.11b,g services for a number of regions around the world.

- It is important to note that the spectrum or channel allocations are not uniform throughout the world.

- The radio frequency channels used are listed in Table 2.3:

- The preferred channel separation between the channels in neighboring wireless networks is 25 MHz (five channels).

- This means that you can apply up to three different channels within your wireless network. In the United States, only 11 usable wireless channels are available, so we recommended that you start using channel 1, grow to use channel 6, and add channel 11 when necessary, because these three channels do not overlap.

- The channel identifiers, channel center frequencies, and regulatory domains of each IEEE 802.11a 20–MHz–wide channel are shown in Table 2.3.

Table 2.3 : Cahnnels for IEEE 802.11 a

Channel	Center Frequency	Regulatory Domains				
		North America	EMEA	Japan	China	Australia
Identifier	(MHz)	(–A)	(–E)	(–P)	(–C)	(–N)
34	5170	–	–	–	–	–
36	5180	X	X	X	–	X
38	5190	–	–	–	–	–
40	5200	X	X	X	–	X
42	5210	–	–	–	–	–
44	5220	X	X	X	–	X
46	5230	–	–	–	–	–
48	5240	X	X	X	–	X
52	5260	X	X	X	–	X
56	5280	X	X	X	–	X
60	5300	X	X	X	–	X
64	5320	X	X	X	–	X
100	5500	–	X	–	–	–
104	5520	–	X	–	–	–
108	5540	–	X	–	–	–
112	5560	–	X	–	–	–
116	5580	–	X	–	–	–
120	5600	–	X	–	–	–
124	5620	–	X	–	–	–
128	5640	–	X	–	–	–
132	5660	–	X	–	–	–
136	5680	–	X	–	–	–
140	5700	–	X	–	–	–
149	5745	X	–	–	X	X
153	5765	X	–	–	X	X
157	5785	X	–	–	X	X
161	5805	X	–	–	X	X

- The channel identifiers, channel center frequencies, and regulatory domains of each IEEE 802.11b 22 MHz–wide channel are shown in Table 2.4.

Table 2.4 : Channels for IEEE 802.11b

| Channel Identifier | Center Frequency (MHz) | Regulatory Domains | | | China | Australia |
| | | America | | | | |
		(–A)	EMEA (–E)	Japan (–P)	(–C)	(–N)
1	2412					
2	2417	X	X	X	X	X
3	2422	X	X	X	X	X
4	2427	X	X	X	X	X
5	2432	X	X	X	X	X
6	2437	X	X	X	X	X
7	2442	X	X	X	X	X
8	2447	X	X	X	X	X
9	2452	X	X	X	X	X
10	2457	X	X	X	X	X
11	2462	X	X	X	X	X
12	2467	X	X	X	X	X
13	2472	–	X	X	X	X
14	2484	–	X	X	X	–

- The channel identifiers, channel center frequencies, and regulatory domains of each IEEE 802.11g 22 MHz–wide channel are shown in Table 2.5.

Table 2.5: Channels for IEEE 802.11g

| Channel Identifier | Center Frequency (MHz) | Regulatory Domains | | | China | Australia |
| | | America | EMEA | Japan | | |
		(–A)	(–E)	(–P)	(–C)	(–N)
1	2412	X	X	X	X	X
2	2417	X	X	X	X	X
3	2422	X	X	X	X	X
4	2427	X	X	X	X	X

...Conti.

5	2432	X	X	X	X	X
6	2437	X	X	X	X	X
7	2442	X	X	X	X	X
8	2447	X	X	X	X	X
9	2452	X	X	X	X	X
10	2457	X	X	X	X	X
11	2462	X	X	X	X	X
12	2467	–	X	X	X	X
13	2472	–	X	X	X	X
14	2484	–	–	X		–

- The channel identifiers, channel center frequencies, and regulatory domains of each IEEE 802.11n 22 MHz–wide channel are shown in Table 2.6.

Table 2.6 : Channels for IEEE 802.11n 2.4 GHz Radio Band

Channel	Center Frequency	Regulatory Domains		
		Americas	EMEA	Japan
Identifier	(MHz)	(–A)	(–E)	(–P)
1	2412	X	X	X
2	2417	X	X	X
3	2422	X	X	X
4	2427	X	X	X
5	2432	X	X	X
6	2437	X	X	X
7	2442	X	X	X
8	2447	X	X	X
9	2452	X	X	X
10	2457	X	X	X
11	2462	X	X	X
12	2467	–	X	X
13	2472	–	X	X
14	2484	–	–	–

- The channel identifiers, channel center frequencies, and regulatory domains of each IEEE 802.11n 20 MHz–wide channel are shown in Table 2.7.

Table 2.7 : 5 GHz Radio Band

Channel Identifier	Center Frequency (MHz)	Regulatory Domains				
		North America (–A)	EMEA (–E)	Japan (–P)	China (–C)	Isreal (–I)
36	5180	X	X	X	–	X
40	5200	X	X	X	–	X
44	5220	X	X	X	–	X
48	5240	X	X	X	–	X
52	5260	X	X	X	–	X
60	5300	X	X	X	–	X
64	5320	X	X	X	–	X
100	5500	–	X	–	–	–
104	5520	–	X	–	–	–
108	5540	–	X	–	–	–
112	5560	–	X	–	–	–
116	5580	–	X	–	–	–
120	5600	–	X	–	–	–
124	5620	–	X	–	–	–
128	5640	–	X	–	–	–
132	5660	–	X	–	–	–
136	5680	–	X	–	–	–
140	5700	–	X	–	–	–
149	5745	X	–	–	X	–
153	5765	X	–	–	X	–
157	5785	X	–	–	X	–
161	5805	X	–	–	X	–
165	5809	X	–	–	X	–

2.6 MODULATION AND CODING SCHEMES

There are several coding schemes used by the Wi-Fi variants of 802.10. While Wi-Fi is a CDMA technology, the modulation and coding schemes are significantly different than those of 2.5/3G and 4G technologies used by mobile wireless systems.

2.6.1 802.11b

In order to develop higher data rates for 802.11b, several modulation schemes were added to the standard.

Complementary Code Keying (CCK)

- The addition of this modulation scheme enables the higher data rates of 5.5 Mbps and 11 Mbps.

- The higher data rate capability is known as High Rate Direct Sequence Spread Spectrum (HR/DSSS).

- The same preamble and header are used as the earlier basic rate DSSS method. This allows the HR/DSSS and basic DSSS to coexist in the same Basic Services Set (BSS).

- The standard also offers optional features that can be used to increase data throughput. These features allow Wi-Fi vendors to differentiate their product offerings.

- They include HR/DSSS/short essentially HR/DSSS with a short preamble and HR/DSSS/PBCC. This optional implementation can coexist under limited conditions. For example, this can be implemented on different channels.

2.6.2 802.11g, 802.11a, and 802.11n

- These standards both incorporate the modulation scheme of OFDM.

- This technique breaks down a wide carrier into several smaller subcarriers. Data is transmitted on each of the subcarriers and then combined into one code division channel.

2.7 NETWORK ARCHITECTURE

- The network architecture of Wi-Fi is dependent on different configurations we can have. Following is a list of these configurations.

1. Wi-Fi with Single AP

2. Wi-Fi with multiple Aps

3. Wi-Fi with connectivity to wired LAN/internet/any other network as shown in Fig. 2.4.

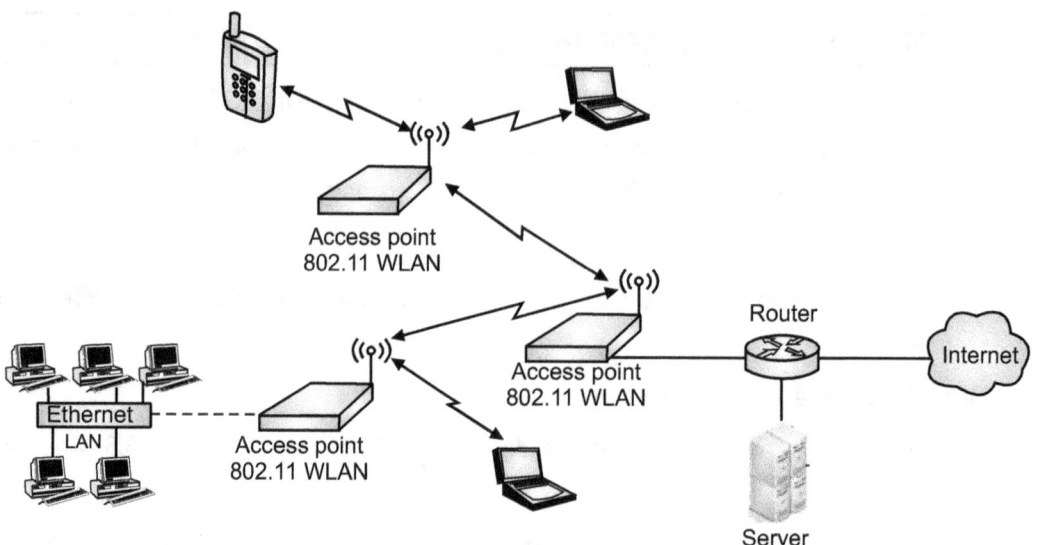

Fig. 2.4 : Wireless local area network

- To meet the above configuration requirements, the network architecture of Wi-Fi consists of following entities :

  1. Basic Services Set (BSS): This is a simple Wi-Fi network where it is simply the association of two stations in an ad hoc network.

  2. Distribution System (DS): is another network architecture that involves Communication etween a Station (CPE) and an Access Point (AP). A DS can and does handle the interworking with multiple BSSs.

  3. Third general type of architecture is the Extended Services Set (ESS) that allows for communication between two or more DSs.

- Each computer, mobile, portable or fixed, is refered to as a station in 802.11. The difference between a portable and mobile station is that a portable station moves from point to point but is only used at a fixed point.

- Mobile stations access the LAN during movement. When two or more stations come together to communicate with each other they form a Basic Service Set (BSS). The minimum BSS consists of two stations. 802.11 LANs use the BSS as the standard building block.

- A BSS which stands alone and is not connected to a base is called an Independent Basic Service Set (IBSS) or is refered to as an Ad–Hoc Network. An ad–hoc network is a network where stations communicate only peer to peer.

- There is no base and no one gives permission to talk. Mostly these networks are spontaneous and can be set up rapidly. Ad–Hoc or IBSS networks are characteristically limited both temporally and spatially.

- When BSS's are interconnected the network becomes one with infrastructure. 802.11 infrastructure has several elements.

- Two or more BSS's are interconnected using a Distribution System or DS. This concept of DS increases network coverage. Each BSS becomes a component of an extended, larger network.

- Entry to the DS is accomplished with the use of Access Points (AP).

- An access point is a station, thus addressable. So data moves between the BSS and the DS with the help of these access points.

- Creating large and complex networks using BSS's and DS's leads us to the next level of hierarchy, the Extended Service Set or ESS.

- The beauty of the ESS is the entire network looks like an independent basic service set to the Logical Link Control layer (LLC). This means that stations within the ESS can communicate or even move between BSS's transparently to the LLC.

- One of the requirements of IEEE 802.11 is that it can be used with existing wired networks. 802.11 solved this challenge with the use of a Portal. A portal is the logical integration between wired LANs and 802.11.

- It also can serve as the access point to the DS. All data going to an 802.11 LAN from an 802.X LAN must pass through a portal. It thus functions as brigde between wired and wireless.

- The implementation of the DS is not specified by 802.11. So a distribution system may be created from existing or new technologies. A point to point bridge connecting LANs in two seperate buildings could become a DS.

- While the implementation for the DS is not specified, 802.11 does specify the services which the DS must support. Services are divided into two sections, Station Servies (SS) and Distribution System Services (DSS).

- There are five services provided by the DSS. Association, Reassociation, Disassociation, Distribution, and Integration. The first three services deal with station mobility. If a station is moving within its own BSS or is not moving, the stations mobility is termed No–transition.

- If a station moves between BSS's within the same ESS, its mobility is termed BSS–transition. If the station moves between BSS's of differing ESS's it is ESS transition.

- A station must affilliate itself with the BSS infrastructure if it wants to use the LAN. This is done by Associating itself with an access point. Associations are dynamic in nature because stations move, turn on or turn off. A station can only be associated with one AP. This ensures that the DS always knows where the station is asociation supports no–transition mobility but is not enough to support BSS–transition. Enter Reassociation.

- This service allows the station to switch its association from one AP to another. Both association and reassociation are initiated by the station.

- Disassociation is when the association between the station and the AP is terminated. This can be initiated by either party. A disassociated station cannot send or receive data.

Notice that I have not mentioned ESS–transition. That is because it is not supported. A station can move to a new ESS but will have to reinitiate connections.

- Distribution and Integration are the remaining DSS's. Distribution is simply getting the data from the sender to the intended receiver.

- The message is sent to the local AP (input AP), then dstributed through the DS to the AP (output AP) that the receipiant is associated with. If the sender and receiver are in the same BSS, the input and out AP's are the same. So the distribution service is logically invoked whether the data is going through the DS or not. Integration is when the output AP is a portal. Thus 802.x LANs are integrated into the 802.11 DS.

- Station services are Authentication, Deauthentication, Privacy, and MAC Service Data Unit (MSDU) Delivery. With a wireless system, the medium is not exactly bounded as with a wired system.

- In order to control access to the network, stations must first establish their identity. This is much like trying to enter a radio net in the military.

- Before you are acknowledged and allowed to converse, you must forst pass a series of tests to ensure that you are who you say you are. That is really all authentication is.

- Once a station has been authenticated, it may then associate itself. The authentication relationship may be between two stations inside an IBSS or to the AP of the BSS.

- Authentication outside of the BSS does not take place. There are two types of authentication services offered by 802.11. The first is Open System Authentication. This means that anyone who attempts to authenticate will receive authentication. The second type is Shared Key Authentication.

- In order to become authenticated the users must be in possesion of a shared secret. The shared secret is implemented with the use of the Wired Equivalent Privacy (WEP) privacy algorithm.

- The shared secret is delivered to all stations ahead of time in some secure method (such as someone walking around and loading the secret onto each station).

- Deauthentication is either the station or AP wishes to terminate a stations authenication. When this happens the station is automatically disassociated.

- Privacy is an encryption algorithm which is used so that other 802.11 users cannot eavesdrop on your LAN traffic. IEEE 802.11 specifies Wired Equivalent Privacy (WEP) as an optional algorithm to satisfy privacy.

- If WEP is not used then stations are "in the clear" or "in the red", meaning that their traffic is not encrypted. Data transmitted in the clear are called plaintext. Data transmissions which are encrypted are called ciphertext.

- All stations start "in the red" until they are authenticated. MSDU delivery ensures that the information in the MAC service data unit is delivered between the medium access control service access points.

- The bottom line is this, authentication is basically a network wide password. Privacy is whether or not encryption is used.
- Wired Equivalent Privacy is used to protect authorized stations from eavesdroppers. WEP is reasonably strong.
- The algorithm can be broken in time. The relationship between breaking the algorithm is directly related to the length of time that a key is in use. So WEP allows for changing of the key to prevent brute force attack of the algorithm.
- WEP can be implemented in hardware or in software. One reason that WEP is optional is because encryption may not be exported from the United States.
- This allows 802.11 to be a standard outside the U.S. albeit without the encryption.

2.7.1 Network Components

- There are two basic components to an 802.11 WLAN: AP and the station.
- The AP allows for communications among stations as well as access (in some cases) to a wired LAN.

The access point contains all the functions of a station (station services) as well as DSS.

Functions available in an AP:

- Authentication,
- Association,
- Deauthentication,
- Disassociation,
- Distribution,
- Integration,
- Privacy,
- MAC Services Data Units (MSDU) delivery
- Reassociation.

Functions available in a station device (CPE):

- Authentication,
- Deauthentication,
- Privacy,
- MSDU delivery.

2.7.2 Ad Hoc Network

When two stations communicate directly with each other the network is called Adhoc network as shown in Fig. 2.5.

- There is no need of Access point.
- The two stations establish point–to–point connectivity like Bluetooth.
- Useful when only two users want to share data.

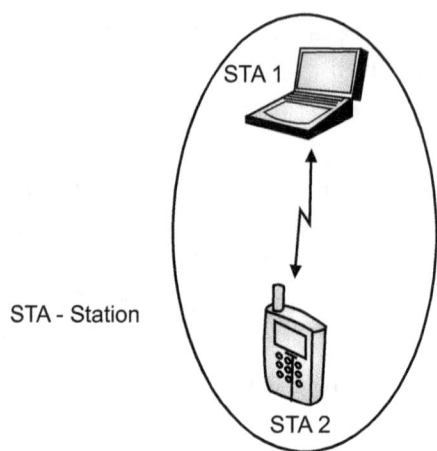

STA - Station

Fig. 2.5 : Ad hoc network

- Ad hoc mode networks works fine in small environment, like building, homes etc.
- No extra hardware (Access point) is required to use ad hoc mode, therefore it reduces the cost.
- If devices have wireless network adapters in them already then that will do the job as far as building ad hoc networks is concern.
- Ad hoc can be useful as back up option for time being if network based on infrastructure mode and access points are malfunctioning.

2.7.3 Infrastructure Network

- Infrastructure mode is one of the two methods for connecting to wireless networks with Wi-Fi enabled devices such as laptops, PDAs, I–phone etc.
- These devices are connected to wireless network with the help of Access Point (AP) as shown in Fig. 2.6.
- Wireless Access Points are usually routers or switches which are connected to internet by Ethernet port.
- Wireless Access points are always required for infrastructure mode of wireless networking. It is necessary to use SSID while configuring AP, this SSID should be known to clients for their computers to connect WLAN. SSID is basically security key which help prevent UN authorized access to WLAN.
- The Access point is then connected to wire network (Internet) to provide wireless internet connectivity to clients.
- Multiple access points can be added in the WLAN, this increases the reach of infrastructure for supporting many number of wireless clients.
- If we are to compare ad hoc with infrastructure mode then infrastructure mode provide much more stability, scalability, ease of management and improved security.

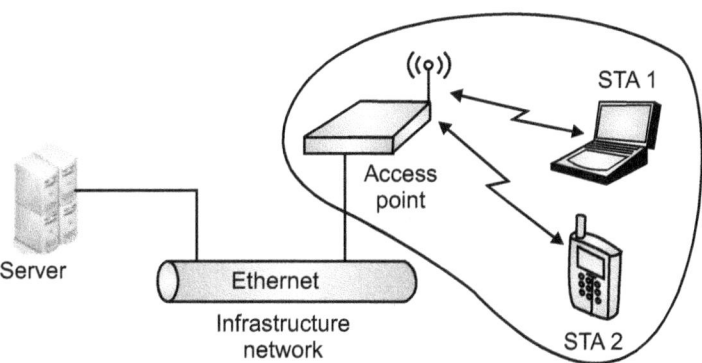

Fig. 2.6 : Infrastructure mode

- Ad hoc on the other hand does not provide security to that level and managing can be difficult incase of network growth.
- Performance suffers as we increase devices as well.
- The only disadvantage associated with infrastructure mode is extra cost to for Access points (routers and switches).
- Compared to the alternative, adhoc wireless networks, infrastructure mode networks offer the advantage of scalability, centralized security management and improved reach.
- The disadvantage of infrastructure wireless networks is simply the additional cost to purchase AP hardware.
- In addition, an infrastructure BSS can consist of more than one interconnected APs that establishes an Extended Service Set (ESS) network as shown in Fig. 2.7.

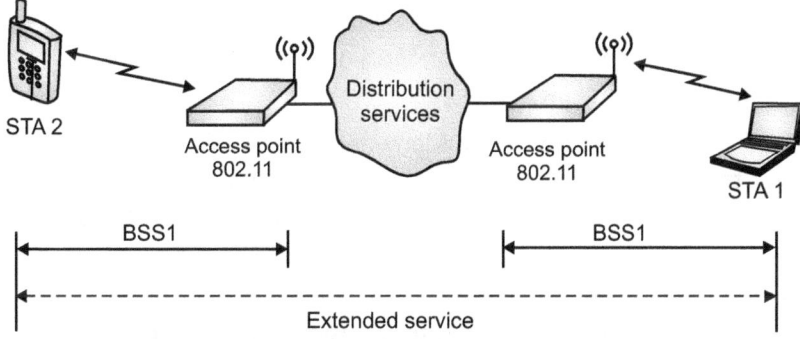

Fig. 2.7 : Extended Service Set (ESS)

- This configuration not only handles portable stations but also mobile stations.
- That is to say, a station can move from the coverage area of one AP to another.
- This method allows the expansion of coverage within or around a building. It also provides additional capacity.
- Each AP within the BSS network provides 802.11 authentication and authorization services for access to the BSS network, as well as privacy services for the encryption of data sent through the BSS network.
- In addition, each AP can act as a bridge between the wireless and wired LANs, allowing stations on either LAN to communicate with each other as shown in Fig. 2.8.

- This allows the combination of the users wired LAN and his Wi-Fi LAN.

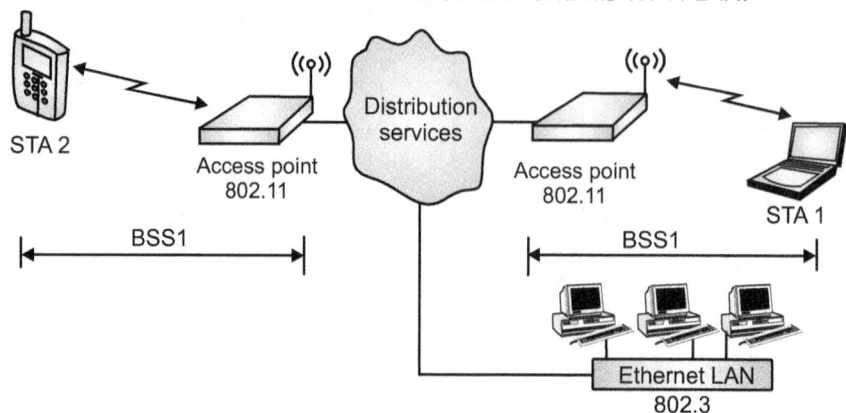

Fig. 2.8 : Portal

2.8 TYPICAL Wi-Fi CONFIGURATIONS

- There are three basic Wi-Fi configurations from the point of view of application and integration of Wi-Fi with other networks.
  - Small Office Home Office (SOHO) Wi-Fi Network
  - Enterprise application,
  - Campus deployment.

2.8.1 SOHO Wi-Fi Network

- A Small Office Home Office (SOHO) application is shown in Fig. 2.9.
- As the name suggests, this network is used in s a home or small office.
- SOHO Wi-Fi makes sense when:
- **Maximum of Five Real World Users:** Many data sheets will state a higher number than this, however this only takes into consideration the number of connected devices, rather than their data utilisation. Remember a wireless AP's bandwidth is divided amongst everybody.
- **Simple Deployments; Limited Scale:** As these devices are designed for home use or small sized offices, they are provided with a basic configuration wizard for ease of use. However if you have many users or plan to grow your wireless network, then scalability is a major limitation with these devices, as they are not designed to work beyond the SOHO environment. Administrators face increased management overhead and users can face a bad experience such as poor roaming or decreased speed if SOHO grade equipment is deployed

Characteristics of a SOHO Wi-Fi Solution:

- Stand alone Access Point (Autonomous) set up one by one These devices will be configured individually, causing increased IT resources and potential inconsistent network settings.

- **Low Cost; Easy Set Up:** These devices are aimed at very small deployments and generally provide few features required by larger organisations such as increased security, management and mobility needs on a larger scale.

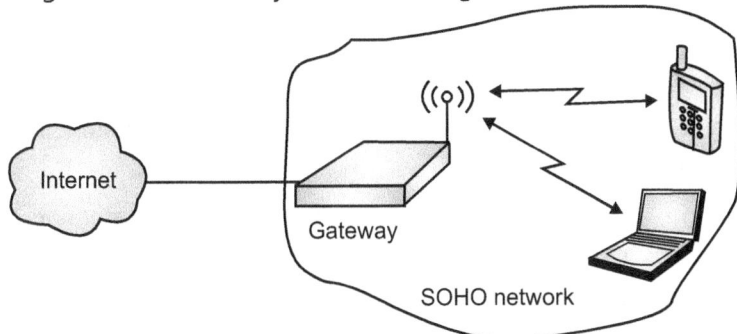

Fig. 2.9 : SOHO configuration

2.8.1.1 Design Issues

1. Technology: As we have seen earlier, there are multiple Wi-Fi standards and they are incompatible with each other. Hence selection of one of the standards IEEE 802.11 is a major design decision. Depending on the devices that you have in hand, the technology can be decided.

Since 802.11n protocol supports backward compatibility, it can be an obvious choice. But one needs to cater for differentiating services between 802.11b/g and 802.11a if desired.

Due to the backwards compatibility of 802.11g, it shares the previous advantage of hot spot access.

Because 802.11a operates in 5GHz band, it offers higher data rates. The spectrum also has less interference because for using this spectrum there are more rules for control and very few technologies are using it at present. But 802.11a is not compatible with other devices and the network cannot be portable.

2. Coverage and Capacity : As mentioned earlier, these two issues are not significant in SOHO. The coverage can however be extended by use of AP.

3. Security: Since network is small, simple security measures will be required. *Wired Equivalency Privacy* (WEP) keys can be distributed to the users. Simple privacy and securitymeasures can be employed to avoid the intruders such as use of MAC address, customizing SSID etc.

2.8.2 Enterprise Application

- Wi-Fi network for a business or commercial application will be more complex than the SOHO application.
- Enterprise Wi-Fi makes sense when:

5+ Users: High density features including even client distribution amongst AP's, guaranteed service levels, and quality of service, ensure that an AP's bandwidth is optimised for increased numbers of users, devices and services.

Bigger Deployments; Ability to Scale: Centralised management (local or cloud) and coordinated AP's provide stable wireless environments, consistent security policies and a seamless mobile workplace.

Characteristics of an Enterprise Wi-Fi solution:

True Mobility : Increased speeds and seamless roaming for users moving between AP's.

Much more reliable Wi-Fi connectivity and quality Increased redundancy provided by coverage hole detection and enhanced failover mechanisms such as mesh.

Security, Monitoring, and Reporting: BYOD management, MDM integration (JAMF), strong authentication methods and protection from outside threats.

Higher Quality Hardware: Assist with battery saving whilst increasing performance.

All of this Managed from One Place: VM and Cloud web–based centralised management.

A typical enterprise application of Wi-Fiis shown in Fig. 2.10.

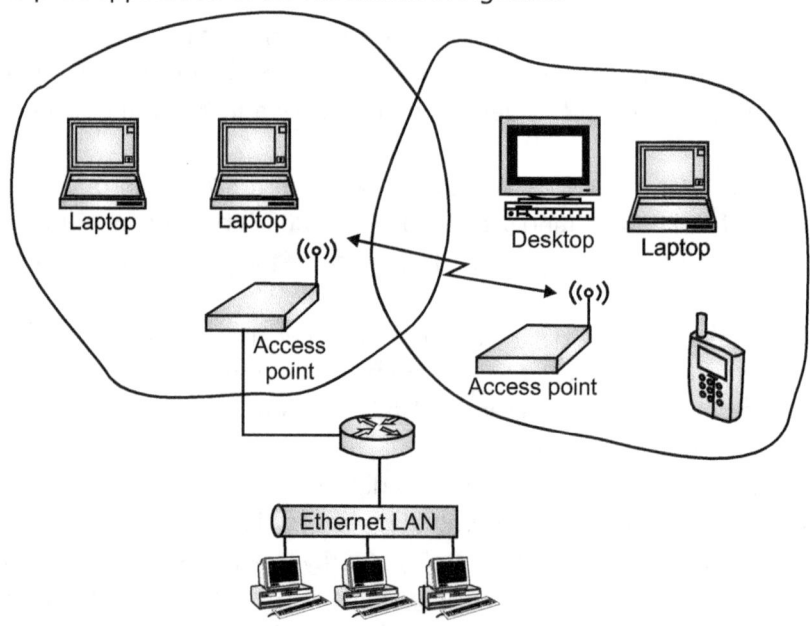

Fig. 2.10 : Enterprise Wi-Fi

Several issues will impact design of a Wi-Fi for enterprise application as discussed below.

2.8.3 Design Issues

1. Technology: Which of the Wi-Fi standard 802.11a, b, or g beadopted will be decided on user's requirements such as capacity, application, mobility, telecommuting etc. The other issues such as availability of resources and devices, current capacity utilization will also impact this decision. A combination of the technologies may be required depending on the user requirements.

2. Coverage and Capacity: The coverage and capacity will be dependent on number and types of AP's used. To extend the coverage addition of an AP may be sufficient. For capacity improvement in some area multiple channels can be employed with proper frequency planning. Frequency planning becomes necessary when channel reuse is required. For example, in the United States there are 11 channels available to 802.11b/g. These channels overlap so that in reality only three of them can be used without interference caused by overlap. These are channels 1, 6, and 10. In the case where capacity demands multiple APs, these APs need to be set to one of these three unique channels. If more than three APs are required for capacity reuse, these channels need to Maximize Radio Frequency (RF) separation to minimize interference.

In addition to coverage, survey may be required. In the simplest case, the installation of an access point in conjunction with software and a laptop may be sufficient. Once the AP is up and running, signal strength measurements can be recorded throughout the service area.

Site survey issues that factor into the design process include:

- Likely point for installing APs,
- Available power,
- Floor plans, electrical diagrams, and blueprints if available,
- Obstructions to coverage such as metal walls,
- Test transmitter locations and AP testing plan (RF coverage).

3. Security: The security and privacy measures mentioned for SOHO can be implemented in Enterprise network also. But enterprise having more users it will not be complicated and unmanageable to use WEP and MAC address techniques. In the case of an enterprise, Wi-Fi network additional security methods are to be used. In addition, there should be a mechanism to detect and locate all wireless Aps and ensure their security and authenticity.

2.8.4 Campus Deployment

Campus deployment of Wi-Fi will have following requirements.

- Indoor/outdoor or both area Coverage.
- Access required at number of different locations/buildings.

2.8.4.1 Design Issues

- The design issues for the campus deployment are somewhat similar to enterprise except that the campus deployment will have a larger area to be covered.
- The requirement for interconnecting the various locations or buildings in the campus is the major issue. 802.11 provide number of compliant solutions to address this issue. They include wired facilities such as DSL, cable modems, T1 circuits, unlicensed microwave solutions, or even optical solutions.
- Fig. 2.11 shows a typical campus deployment network.

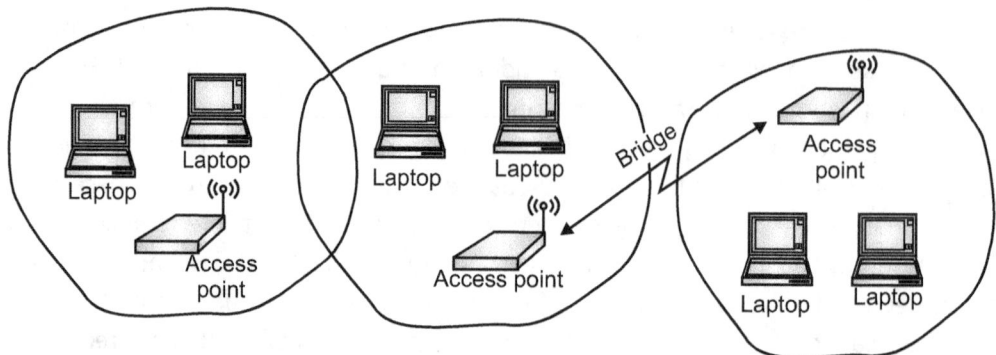

Fig. 2.11 : Campus deployment of Wi-Fi network

2.9 SECURITY

- The security issue should address authentication and privacy sufficient to bring wireless LANs at par with their wired LAN.

- 802.11 Again WEP plays most important role in security. But a variety of security protocols are specified by 802.11 such as WPA–PSK, WPA2, IEEE 802.1x/RADIUS, WDS, WEP, TKIP, and CCMP (AES) encryption.

- When WEP is enabled, No user can participate in the communication unless he has the key. Additional security can be implemented by using other forms of security and authentication protocols.

- In the case of mobile users Virtual Private Network (VPN) can be used for providing security between the mobile user and the campus network.

2.9.1 WEP

- WEP security involves two parts, Authentication and Encryption. Authentication in WEP involves authenticating a device when it first joins the LAN.

- The authentication process in the wireless networks using WEP is to prevent devices/stations joining the network unless they know the WEP key.

- There are two types of authentication in 802.11: Open authentication and shared key authentication.

1. Open Systems Authentication: Open System Authentication is the default authentication protocol for the 802.11 standard. It consists of a simple authentication request containing the station ID and an authentication response containing success or failure data. Upon successful authentication, both stations are considered mutually authenticated. It can be used with WEP (Wired Equivalent Privacy) protocol to provide better communication security, however it is important to note that the authentication management frames are still sent in clear text during authentication process. WEP is used only for encrypting data once the client is authenticated and associated. Any client can send its station ID in an attempt to associate with the AP. In effect, no authentication is actually done.

2. Shared Key Authentication: Shared Key Authentication is a standard challenge and response mechanism that makes use of WEP and a shared secret key to provide authentication. Upon encrypting the challenge text with WEP using the shared secret key, the authenticating client will return the encrypted challenge text to the access point for verification. Authentication succeeds if the access point decrypts the same challenge text.

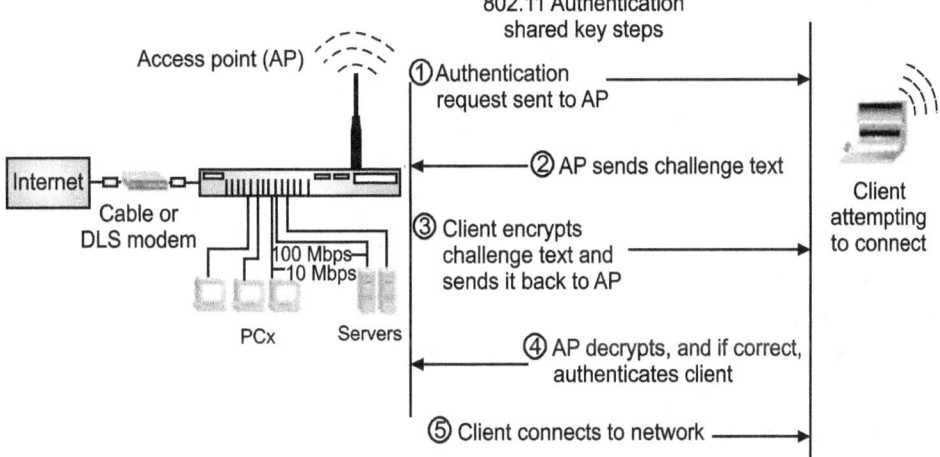

Fig. 2.12

The following steps occur when two devices use Shared Key Authentication:

- The station sends an authentication request to the access point.
- The access point sends challenge text to the station.
- The station uses its configured 64-bit or 128-bit default key to encrypt the challenge text, and it sends the encrypted text to the access point.
- The access point decrypts the encrypted text using its configured WEP key that corresponds to the station's default key. The access point compares the decrypted text with the original challenge text. If the decrypted text matches the original challenge text, then the access point and the station share the same WEP key, and the access point authenticates the station.
- The station connects to the network.

If the decrypted text does not match the original challenge text (that is, the access point and station do not share the same WEP key), then the access point will refuse to authenticate the station, and the station will be unable to communicate with either the 802.11 network or Ethernet network.

2.9.2 Encryption with WEP

- The IEEE 802.11 standard supports two types of WEP encryption: 40-bit and 128-bit. The 64-bit WEP data encryption method allows for a five-character (40-bit) input. Additionally, 24 factory-set bits are added to the forty-bit input to generate a 64-bit encryption key. (The 24 factoryset bits are not user-configurable).

- This encryption key will be used to encrypt/decrypt all data transmitted via the wireless interface. Some vendors refer to the 64-bit WEP data encryption as 40- bit WEP data encryption because the user-configurable portion of the encryption key is 40 bits wide. The 128-bit WEP data encryption method consists of 104 user-configurable bits. Similar to the 40- bit WEP data encryption method, the remaining 24 bits are factory-set and not user-configurable.

- The 128-bit encryption is stronger than 40-bit encryption, but 128-bit encryption may not be available outside the United States due to U.S. export regulations. When configured for 40-bit encryption, 802.11 products typically support up to four WEP keys.

- Each 40-bit WEP key is expressed as five sets of two hexadecimal digits (0 to 9 and A to F). For example, "12 34 56 78 90" is a 40-bit WEP key. When configured for 128-bit encryption, 802.11g products typically support four WEP keys, but some manufacturers support only one 128-bit key.

- The 128-bit WEP Key is expressed as 13 sets of two hexadecimal digits (0 to 9 and A to F). For example, "12 34 56 78 90 AB CD EF 12 34 56 78 90" is a 128-bit WEP key.

- Typically, 802.11 access points can store up to four 128-bit WEP keys, but some 802.11 client adapters can only store one. Therefore, make sure that your 802.11 access and client adapters' configurations match.

- Whatever keys you enter for an access point, you must also enter the same keys for the client adapter in the same order. In other words, WEP key 1 on the AP must match WEP key 1 on the client adapter, WEP key 2 on the AP must match WEP key 2 on the client adapter, etc.

- WEP was designed to prevent casual eavesdropping. The objective was to provide equivalent privacy to that of a wired LAN. In other words, if you were not on the LAN you would not see messages.

- The WEP algorithm is far from unbreakable. Depending on the length of the key used; the frequency of changing the key; and the ability to key the secret key, secret WEP provides a protection from brute force attacks.

- WEP is self-synchronizing which makes it less susceptible to message delivery problems inherent in the wireless environment.

- It can be implemented in hardware as well as software allowing it to be very efficient. It is illegal to export many encryption algorithms from the United States. Every effort was made by the standards body to make WEP exportable. Use of WEP is optional within the standard.

2.9.3 Alternatives to WEP

- WEP is not completely secure protocol. It can be easily breached. One has to implement other additional forms of security like AES for more sensitive information.

2.9.4 SSID

- An SSID is a 32-character (maximum) alphanumeric key identifying the name of the wireless local area network. Some vendors refer to the SSID as the network name. For the wireless devices in a network to communicate with each other, all devices must be configured with the same SSID. Using this SSID user has to connect to the suitable AP.
- Thus unauthorized users are prevented from accessing the network. The SSID can be learned by the hackers.

2.9.5 MAC Address

- The network will allow traffic only to the user whose MAC address is valid. This also can be breached as the hacker simply observes network traffic and assumes the MAC address and IP address of a genuine user.
- The administrator has to maintain the list of MAC addresses.

2.9.6 Extensible Authentication Protocol (EAP)

- EAP is a general protocol for authentication that also supports multiple authentication methods, such as token cards, Kerberos, one–time passwords, certificates, public key authentication and smart cards. IEEE 802.1x specifies how EAP should be encapsulated in LAN frames.
- WEP is a data encryption method and is not intended as a user authentication mechanism.
- Wi-Fi Protected Access (WPA) user authentication is implemented using 802.1x and the Extensible Authentication Protocol (EAP).
- Support for 802.1x authentication is required in WPA.
- In the 802.11 standard, 802.1x authentication was optional. With EAP a client is unable to gain access to the LAN without first going through a log–in procedure the process follows:
- EAP was originally developed for PPP. It is also a general purposed protocol. EAP support multiple authentication methods, for example, one–time password, certificate, public key authentication, smart key, Kerberos (IETF RFC 1510).
- There may be different authentication mechanism in authentication layer. It is based on EAP and also new mechanism can be easily added.
- In general EAP is a protocol that defines how your authentication in network is carried out. But actually it is an EAP method such as, EAP–TLS, EAP–PEAP, and EAP–LEAP and so on that actually determines your valid existence in network.
- We can summarize the EAP authentication process as:
    - The client first sends a user name and password to a RADIUS server.
    - The server sends a challenge message to the client.
    - The client then uses his password to supply a response to the RADIUS server's challenge.

- The server then authenticates the client.
- The process is then repeated in reverse.
- The client and server then create a WEP key.
- This key is delivered to the AP over the wired LAN.
- The AP then sends the WEP key to the client and this key is used for the session.

Note : In this process the use of the WEP key is reduced to only this one session.

2.10 802.11 SERVICES

- The 802.11 standard defines services that provide the functions that the LLC layer requires for sending MAC Service Data Units (MSDUs) between two entities on the network. These services, which the MAC layer implements, fall into two categories:

1. **Station Services:** These include Authentication, Deauthentication, Privacy, and MSDU delivery.

2. **Distribution System Services:** These include Association, Disassociation, Distribution, Integration, and Reassociation.

1. **Station Services :** The 802.11 standard defines services for providing functions among stations. A station may be within any wireless element on the network, such as a handheld PC or handheld scanner. In addition, all access points implement station services. To provide necessary functionality, these stations need to send and receive MSDUs and implement adequate levels of security.

- The 802.11 standard defines services for providing functions among stations. A station may be within any wireless element on the network, such as a handheld PC or handheld scanner. In addition, all access points implement station services. To provide necessary functionality, these stations need to send and receive MSDUs and implement adequate levels of security.

- **Authentication**

The wireless LANs have limited physical security to prevent unauthorized access, 802.11 defines authentication services to control LAN access to a level equal to a wired link. Every 802.11 station, whether part of an independent BSS or an ESS network, must use the authentication service prior to establishing a connection (referred to as an association in 802.11 terms) with another station with which it will communicate. Stations performing authentication send a unicast management authentication frame to the corresponding station.

The IEEE 802.11 standard defines the following two authentication services:

Open system authentication. This is the 802.11 default authentication method. It is a very simple two–step process.

(i) First the station wanting to authenticate with another station sends an authentication management frame containing the sending station's identity. The receiving station then sends back a frame indicating whether it recognizes the identity of the authenticating station.

(ii) Shared key authentication This type of authentication assumes that each station has received a secret shared key through a secure channel independent from the 802.11 network. Stations authenticate through shared knowledge of the secret key. Use of shared key authentication requires implementation of the Wired Equivalent Privacy algorithm (WEP).

- **Deauthentication**

When a station wants to disassociate from another station, it invokes the deauthentication service. Deauthentication is a notification and cannot be refused. A station performs deauthentication by sending an authentication management frame (or group of frames to multiple stations) to advise of the termination of authentication.

- **Privacy**

With a wireless network, all stations and other devices can hear data traffic taking place within range on the network, seriously affecting the security level of a wireless link. IEEE 802.11 counters this problem by offering a privacy service option that raises the security level of the 802.11 network to that of a wired network.

2. Distribution System Services

Distribution system services, as defined by 802.11, provide functionality across a distribution system. Access points provide distribution system services. The following sections provide an overview of the services that distribution systems need to provide proper transfer of MSDUs.

- **Association**

Each station must initially invoke the association service with an access point before it can send information through a distribution system. The association maps a station to the distribution system via an access point. Each station can associate with only a single access point, but each access point can associate with multiple stations. Association is also a first step to providing the capability for a station to be mobile between BSSs.

- **Disassociation**

A station or access point may invoke the disassociation service to terminate an existing association. This service is a notification; therefore, neither party may refuse termination. Stations should disassociate when leaving the network. An access point, for example, may disassociate all its stations if being removed for maintenance.

- **Distribution**

A station uses the distribution service every time it sends MAC frames across a distribution system. The 802.11 standard does not specify how the distribution system delivers the data. The distribution service provides the distribution system with only enough information to determine the proper destination BSS.

- **Integration**

The integration service enables the delivery of MAC frames through a portal between a distribution system and a non–802.11 LAN. The integration function performs all required media or address space translations. The details of an integration function depend on the distribution system implementation and are beyond the scope of the 802.11 standard.

- **Reassociation**

The reassociation service enables a station to change its current state of association. Reassociation provides additional functionality to support BSS–transition mobility for associated stations. The reassociation service enables a station to change its association from one access point to another. This keeps the distribution system informed of the current mapping between access point and station as the station moves from one BSS to another within an ESS. Reassociation also enables changing association attributes of an established association while the station remains associated with the same access point. The mobile station always initiates the reassociation service.

2.11 HOT SPOTS

- A hotspot is any location where Wi-Fi Internet access (sometimes for free) is made publicly available. You can often find hotspots in some public areas, coffee shops, and restaurants. Most of these hot spots are 802.11b systems.
- Apart from internet access, the hotspots will make some sophisticated services available to the users such as establish VPN with their inherent security between the mobile user and his corporate Network.
- Wi-Fi technology is essentially for off loading data traffic from cellular networks in high density areas. Hence Wi-Fi hot spots have become increasingly important to wireless carriers to off–load their existing licensed spectrum traffic to a hot spot which is typically off–net. However roaming agreements have been extended to the wireless mobile carriers enabling combined "cellular" and Wi-Fi capable devices to hook up to the hot spot while in its coverage area. Under a roaming agreement it is possible for a "handing off" to the cellular network when leaving the hot spot.

2.11.1 Security at Hot Spots

The security at hotspots is a major issue. We can say that the security at hot spots is nonexistent. The unknown users are frequently entering and leaving the premises. WEP keys will be there with everyone. Simple login procedures can be used to minimize access.

2.12 VIRTUAL PRIVATE NETWORKS (VPNS)

- A VPN or Virtual Private Network is a method used to add security and privacy to private and public networks, like Wi-Fi Hotspots and the Internet.
- VPNs are most often used by corporations to protect sensitive data.
- However, using a personal VPN is increasingly becoming more popular as more interactions that were previously face–to–face transition to the Internet.
- Privacy is increased with a VPN because the user's initial IP address is replaced with one from the VPN provider.

- This method allows subscribers to attain an IP address from any gateway city the VPN service provides. For instance, you may live in Pune, but with a VPN, you can appear to live in Mumbai, Delhi, or any number of gateway cities.
- A VPN is a shared network where private data is segmented from other traffic so that only the intended recipient has access.
- The term VPN was originally used to describe a secure connection over the Internet. Today, however, VPN is also used to describe private networks, such as Frame Relay, Asynchronous Transfer Mode (ATM), and Multiprotocol Label Switching (MPLS).
- Privacy and security are added to each IP packet, which is encapsulated inside another IP packet. This is known as tunneling. In the case of a VPN, the actual data is contained inside the IP packet visible to the Internet.
- A key aspect of data security is that the data flowing across the network is protected by encryption technologies. Private networks lack data security, which can allow data attackers to tap directly into the network and read the data.
- IPSec–based VPNs use encryption to provide data security, which increases the network's resistance to data tampering or theft.
- IPSec is one of the most complete, secure, and commercially available, standards–based protocols developed for transporting data. IPSec is an Internet Engineering Task Force (IETF) standard suite of protocols that provides data authentication, integrity, and confidentiality as data is transferred between communication points across IP networks.
- IPSec provides data security at the IP packet level. A packet is a data bundle that is organized for transmission across a network, and it includes a header and payload (the data in the packet).
- IPSec emerged as a viable network security standard because enterprises wanted to ensure that data could be securely transmitted over the Internet.
- IPSec protects against possible security exposures by protecting data while in transit. While IPSec does not provide authentication it does provide confidentiality. With IPSec each user must have an IPSec client on his PC.

2.13 MOBILE VPN

- A mobile VPN is a network configuration in which mobile devices such as notebook computers or Personal Digital Assistants (PDAs) access a Virtual Private Network (VPN) or an intranet while moving from one physical location to another.
- The concept of virtual private networks predates data networking. The term is used by traditional phone companies to refer to services offered to various entities. In some cases, it is as simple as a leased line facility. In others it is a complete outsourced network that is carved out of the "public network" for entities' exclusive use.
- VPN combines two concepts: virtual networking and private networking. In a virtual network, geographically distributed and remote nodes can interact with each other the way they do in a network where the nodes are collocated.

- The topology of the virtual network is independent of the physical topology of the facilities used to support it. A casual user of the virtual network, not aware of the physical network setup, would only be able to detect the topology of the virtual network. A virtual network is also managed as a single administrative entity.
- Private networks are usually defined as nonshared networking facilities combining hosts and clients that belong to the same administrative entity. A good example of a private network is a corporate intranet, which can only be used by a certain number of authorized individuals belonging to that particular corporation.
- Virtual private networking, thus, is the emulation of private secure data networks over public shared insecure telecommunications facilities
- VPN properties include mechanisms for data protection and establishing trust among hosts in virtual networks and incorporation of various methods to enforce and maintain Service Level Agreements (SLAs) and Quality of Service (QoS) for all entities that make up a Virtual Private Network. VPN can be defined from many perspectives.

2.13.1 Advantages to Using VPNs

- There are a number of compelling reasons to use VPN. In particular, for telecommuters. The rapid increase in telecommuters is forcing IT departments to provide remote access to more and more users.
- Traditionally this access was provided through dial–up procedures; however, with ever–increasing costs and the relatively low speeds users are moving to high–speed access.

VPN has tons of advantages and benefits, that includes but not limited to:

Add–on Security : By connecting to the internet through VPN tunnel, the network data are all well encrypted and secured by the VPN standard, all information are very safe from attack's eyes;

Network Anonymity : Through VPN people can surf the websites in complete anonymity. Comparing to the web proxy method or special IP hiding software, VPN allows users to access internet in 100% anonymous way from any software or application installed in the computer system.

Unblock Web Sites and Bypass Web Filters : In this days one of the major usage of VPN is to access blocked websites to bypass network filters from local ISP or internet authorities, especially in some countries that the Internet censorship is applied to web browsers;

Change the Internet IP Address : VPN service from different country can give the VPN users the IP address from that country as well, this is very convenient sometimes of the websites require you to access from domestic location, for example some online banking or stock investment websites for safety reason;

Improved Network QoS and Performance: Depends on how the VPN network infrastructure is setup, sometimes the internet download speed and quality of service like Jitter and packet delay can dramatically get improved by using VPN connections.

Reduce Costs: Business teams like to use VPN to setup multiple remote locations as a virtual local network to save the cost to rent dedicated internet connections. The maintenance of establishing LAN connection through internet VPN is very low comparing to some traditional dedicated line solutions.

Remote Work: Enterprise like to provide VPN connections to employees who work from home or from outside during the business travels just like they are virtually sit in the cube of office buildings, VPN increases productivity in business environment and becomes the most popular method for remote work requirements in corporation network;

Sharing Information: VPN is often used to connect multiple offices in different locations or countries to share the same documents or files around the world in a secure and cost down way.

2.14 VPN TYPES

- There are two approaches to the classification of VPN technology:
- (i) Architecture taxonomy deals with how VPN is architected and deployed.
- (ii) Tunneling taxonomy deals with how underlying tunneling techniques are implemented.
- Historically, architecture taxonomy is more often used in sources dealing with wireline data VPNs, while tunneling–based taxonomy is usually applied in sources addressing cellular systems.
- The examples of VPN classifications include compulsory versus voluntary, which is based on tunneling taxonomy, and site–to–site versus remote access, which is based on architecture taxonomy.
- All IP VPNs can be implemented using basic tunneling methods:
  - (a) End–to–end, or voluntary.
  - (b) Network–based, or compulsory.
  - (c) Chained or mediated tunnels, which fall somewhere in the middle
- Based on the tunneling method being used, the VPN itself can be classified as voluntary, compulsory, or combined. We will now take a closer look at all three methods.

2.14.1 Voluntary VPNs

- Voluntary IP VPN provides remote users with the ability to create a tunnel from their terminals, such as mobile phones or PDAs, to certain tunnel termination point, such as a VPN gateway that resides within the private network.
- Private networks are usually protected by firewalls and require firewall traversal and security mechanisms for instance, user authentication and data integrity and confidentiality protection applied to the remote access traffic.
- Consequently, remote user equipment must support proper protocols to satisfy these requirements.
- For example, a remote user equipped with a device such as a PDA could establish an IPSec ESP tunnel to a corporate network using PKI–based key distribution (also known as

an asymmetric keys approach) or predistributed shared secret key (also known as a symmetric keys approach).

- All data between such mobile stations and the private network would then be encapsulated in the secure end–to–end IPSec tunnel.

- The end–to–end tunneling in this example exists only for the duration of the session and is torn down when the remote users do not require private network access, or when the user must be preemptively disconnected based on a set of predefined events, such as session duration or limits in access rights.

- This type of VPN service is depicted in Fig. 2.13, which uses mobile dial–up access over a GSM network as an example.

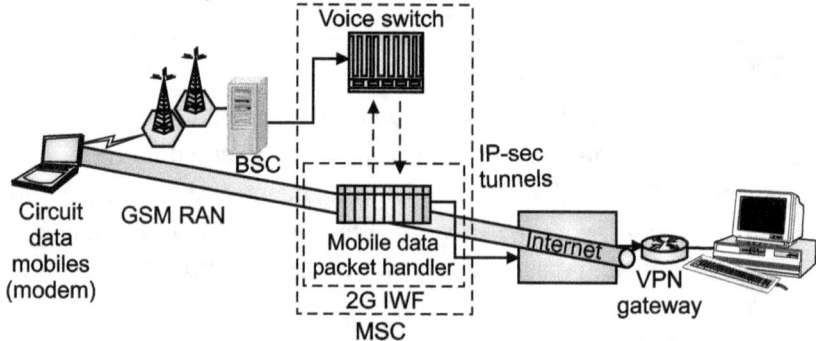

Fig. 2.13 : Voluntary VPN

- In this scenario, the remote user establishes a VPN connection to a private network after a wireless carrier grants him or her Internet access.

- Note that both wireless and wireline–based access to the Internet allow roaming users to establish this type of VPN at will, by "voluntarily" opening a communication channel to the private network when they need it hence the name of the approach.

- Voluntary VPN carries a number of significant advantages. For private network IT administrators and often for remote users, this is the simplest way to establish a remote access VPN.

- Remote users simply need access to the Internet or any other public IP network, and a VPN client in their mobile or fixed devices. All that the private network IT department needs to do is to provision a VPN gateway connected to the Internet and capable of terminating a particular type of tunneling, and establish a proper set of policies and security procedures.

- The service provider offering Internet access service cannot access the end–to–end encrypted private data being transmitted between remote user and private network, and hence it will not have to be entrusted with it.

- Voluntary VPN also does not require any preestablished relationship between corporations and service providers.

- Therefore, there are no multiple SLAs and legal agreements about data confidentiality.

- However, the user and the corporation should be ready to accept a network access service that may be less predictable and often qualitatively inferior to the service provided to parties that instead enter in a SLA, unless the service provider offers predefined levels of service such as a "business class" Internet access option.

- Voluntary VPNs require that public, topologically correct IP addresses be assigned to remote users' equipment.

- This requirement along with other properties of an end–to–end tunneling creates a number of potential drawbacks to voluntary VPN service. Because of the limited number of IPv4 addresses available to service providers especially for mobile operators that would like to offer "always on" connectivity to the Internet to their subscribers reliance on private addressing schemes to conserve valuable IP address space, combined with various subnetting and address translation techniques such as NAT, is very common.

- Until recently, this made end–to–end tunneling, where public IP addresses were required, impossible.

- For example, IPSec AH mode is not compatible with NAT, which would not even allow for the tunnel to be established. Luckily, a few mechanisms allowing for NAT traversal have been recently introduced by the IETF and are being widely implemented by the industry.

- Also, the emergence of an IPv6–based network and the expected gradual conversion to an all–IPv6 Internet should resolve problems with insufficient addresses.

- Another disadvantage of voluntary VPN arises from the nature of secure end–to–end tunneling, in which the contents of the tunneled packets are encapsulated and thus not available for inspection by any nodes on the tunneled packet's path except the tunnel endpoints. This makes QoS, Classe of Service (CoS), and the majority of traffic–shaping mechanisms requiring multifield packet inspection a difficult to impossible task. Monitoring equipment and certain firewalling functions will fail to work properly as well.

- When Mobile VPNs are implemented in a cellular wireless environment, voluntary tunneling will lead to an extra layer of encapsulation over the last–hop wireless link.

- This will consume more of already scarce and expensive radio resources. Also, complex encryption and security algorithms may not be suitable for implementation in small wireless devices, which typically have limited processing and battery power.

- Additionally, widely mutable radio conditions and lossy wireless environment are not friendly to the establishment and preservation of IPSec tunnels.

- This may translate in a long tunnel setup time, or in extreme cases, to complete failure and perhaps the need to move to a region with better coverage. Note that this is not only affecting cellular systems but also Wireless LAN–based access networks.

- For these reasons, while voluntary tunneling provides a clean and secure end–to–end solution for access to private networks, often greater VPN efficiency and unique services can be achieved with a participation of service providers prompting an introduction of another VPN type.

2.14.2 Compulsory VPN

- A service provider may offer compulsory VPN service by concatenating or chaining multiple tunnels or provisioning a single tunnel for a part of a data path between two participating endpoints.

- For example, a compulsory VPN can be based on a tunnel created between a private network and a service provider and not extended to reach all the way to a remote user that is using the network access service.

- As a result, with compulsory VPN service the remote user does not need to have any involvement into VPN establishment process and is "forced" to use the available preprovisioned service whenever the access to the private network is required, hence the name.

- This VPN type assumes that the operator's network infrastructure features the intelligence and functionality necessary to support VPN services based on the tunnels or sets of tunnels provisioned between the private network and service provider's networks rather than all the way to the end–user device.

- In both cases, the enterprise must preestablish a detailed SLA with the service provider responsible for VPN service and must trust it to handle its valuable data with the necessary care and confidentiality.

- The service provider often participates in the network's access control, and the corporation must trust the service provider to deny access to nonauthorized users according to the network access policy defined by the corporate network administrator.

- One possible compulsory VPN scenario implemented in the CDMA2000 infrastructure based on Mobile IP is depicted in Fig. 2.14.

- In Fig. 2.14 the user data is encapsulated into Mobile IP tunnel only between the PDSN in carrier's network and the HA owned by corporation.

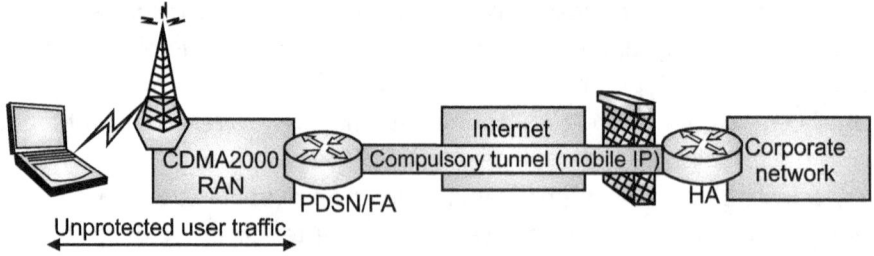

Fig. 2.14 : Compulsory VPN

- The need to keep a part of the private data path unprotected, to trust the service provider, and to establish multiple SLAs and complex data confidentiality agreements are some of the drawbacks of compulsory VPN.

- In mobile environment, security problems become even more serious, since the user traffic is being sent over potentially insecure radio channels.

- During packet data roaming, the unprotected traffic to and from the mobile station must also traverse the visited carrier network (which may or may not have established SLA with the corporation served by a home wireless carrier) before being tunneled to original carrier's network.

- If there are insecure links in this network, especially unencrypted links in the backhaul section, this could present serious security problems.

- These problems are hard to address unless the provider puts careful service provisioning in place.

- For instance, gateway–to–gateway IPSec tunnels in critical points of the network could address this problem.

- On the positive side, the compulsory approach better utilizes the air interface by avoiding over–the–air encapsulation overhead, which is especially advantageous for cellular wireless systems, and by simplifying the user equipment.

- When compulsory VPN is used, the end–user equipment does not have to support any VPN clients or tunneling or security capability at times they could be CPU–hungry and battery–life–consuming.

- Also, the user is not involved in VPN creation and only needs to request the service when accessing the service provider's network.

- Compulsory VPN presents a number of other significant advantages to service providers. Offering and marketing compulsory VPN as a feature can potentially enable new business models and carrier service offerings.

- With the voluntary approach, service providers do not get involved in provisioning and often are not even aware of the existence of encrypted and encapsulated traffic unless they offer special access points to the Internet associated to publicly routable IP addresses or NAT traversal–compliant devices.

- In contrast, compulsory VPN access offerings can be marketed in different forms by carriers to a variety of private enterprises and ISPs interested in outsourcing their remote access function.

- This will bring new revenue streams, along with greater differentiation from the competition service offerings.

- Another benefit of compulsory VPN for service providers lies in greater control over the user. In a compulsory model, the service provider is usually involved in user authentication and IP address assignment (though the latter might be a mixed blessing in some situations), which allows it to control user provisioning to a greater extent.

- IP addresses can be assigned to remote users from the customers' networks private address space, thus saving the usage of publicly routable IP addresses from the provider side.

2.14.3 Chained VPN

- The third type of VPN is not easily classified as either voluntary or compulsory.
- Chained tunnel VPN consists of a set of concatenated tunnels that extend all the way to the end–user equipment. Chained tunnel VPN can come in many different forms, as shown in Fig. 2.15, which depicts a few tunnel chaining options in the GPRS network.

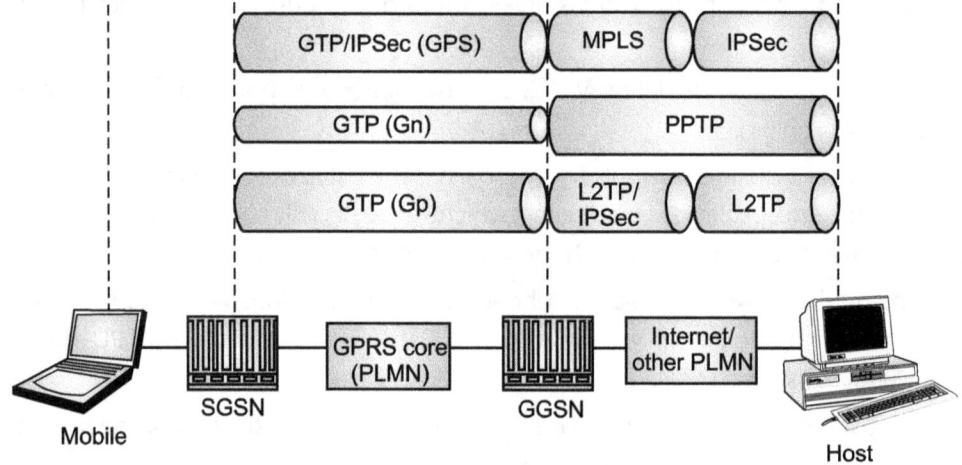

Fig. 2.15 : Chained VPN

- Similar to the voluntary VPN approach, chained tunnel VPN provides end–to–end user data protection, and the user participates in tunnel initiation.
- Like compulsory VPN, the service provider is involved in chained tunnel VPN provisioning and construction and can easily apply QoS and traffic shaping at the tunnel concatenation points.
- This participation does necessitate SLA and data handling agreements, though.
- In our opinion, all of these VPN types have their positives and negatives and will coexist in future networks. The service providers can offer them interchangeably, depending on the available technology, suitability to task, and business environment.

2.15 Wi-Fi INTEGRATION WITH 3G/4G

- Though the cellular and Wi-Fi radio technologies originated and evolved from two fundamentally different objectives, each has trended towards the other, with wireless data a central use of cellular technology today while over–the–top services provide voice over data networks.

- This confluence seems headed towards an integrated cellular and Wi-Fi landscape, but the evolutionary nature of the trend has resulted in a broad variety of approaches and solutions.

- There has been a great deal of interest of late in using Wi-Fi to offload traffic from heavily congested mobile networks. Early deployments consisted of building a parallel Wi-Fi offload network that takes traffic directly to the Internet. The mobile network operator would implement some kind of proprietary client that would manage the offload function.

- Many subscribers have implemented their own offload strategy by selecting Wi-Fi when its available

- Now, the industry is shifting its focus toward integrating Wi-Fi RANs into the mobile packet core.

- In this approach, Wi-Fi would take its place alongside 3G/LTE as a cornerstone technology in the mobile world. The mobile device selects the best radio access technology based on the conditions (typically signal strength, application type, default to Wi-Fi, etc.) and the subscriber is automatically authenticated and connected. All RAN traffic is brought back into the mobile packet core as defined in the 3GPP evolved packet core standards.

  The following points justify the need for Wi-Fi offload and also build up a business case for the cellular operators to adopt the same:

  - It will cater to the growing mobile data demand and the smart devices usage patterns that have the characteristics of short sessions, high throughput and low latency.

  - It will enhance the end user experience by improving service capacity and capability. Also the end user devices are so designed that they perform with better data speeds in Wi-Fi networks and so Wi-Fi has an edge over cellular network in this case as well.

  - Using a solution which is more economically viable for providing indoor services will reduce the operating expenditure of the service providers as cellular broadband is more expensive than Wi-Fi.

  - Address the issue of spectrum crunch whereby the cellular operators can provide high bandwidth consuming services through Wi-Fi.

There are two general classifications of mobile data users, casual and business. It is important to note that data requirements are individual specific.

- The linking of 3G/4G with Wi-Fi is dependent on network and user devices. Linking 3G/4G networks with Wi-Fi networks involves both business and technical considerations.

- The type of services and its management and the rates are the business considerations. This is in addition to the determination of what services specifically will be used or available.
- The technical considerations involve design, deployment, provisioning, and ongoing support. Technical issues generally involve billing and authentication and increase in complexity when the networks are owned by different companies.
- Therefore the demarcation and how the networks will interact with each other in the delivery of services is another area of technical interaction. But the ongoing support is of course a critical decision that involves problem identification, resolution, and enhancements.

2.15.1 Loose and Tight Coupling

- An integrated data offload approach provides the operator with full control over subscribers as well as the ability to deliver any subscribed content while the users are on theWi-Fi network.
- This is achieved by the integration of cellular and Wi-Fi networks so that abridge can be formed between the two networks through which data flow can be established. There are two architectures for coupling cellular and Wi-Fi networks; loose coupling and tight coupling.
- In loose coupling architecture, the networks are independent requiring no major cooperation between them as shown in Fig. 2.16. The Wi-Fi network is connected indirectly to the cellular core network through an external IP network such as the Internet.

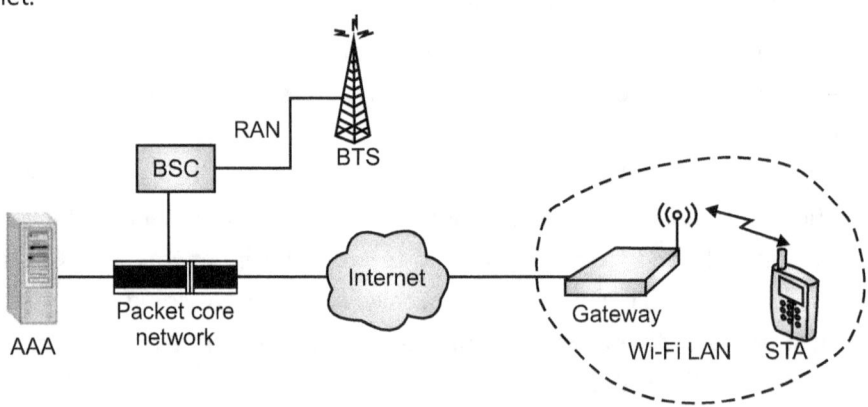

Fig. 2.16 : Loose integration

- Service connectivity is provided by roaming between the two networks
- The tightly coupled integration has the Wi-Fi LAN directly connected to the mobile operator's core packet network as shown in Fig. 2.17.
- In a tightly coupled system, the networks share a common core and majority of network functions such as vertical handover, resource management, and billing are controlled and managed centrally.

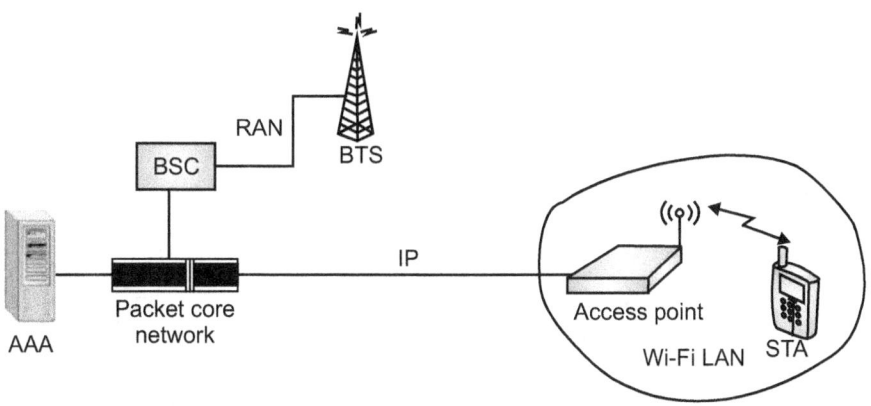

Fig. 2.17 : Tight integration

2.15.2 GSM and Wi-Fi

Fig. 2.18 shows how Wi-Fi and GSM network are integrated that utilizes GPRS and/or EDGE. The Wi-Fi systems can be integrated directly into the operator's network or through a roaming agreement providing access to the GSM subscriber.

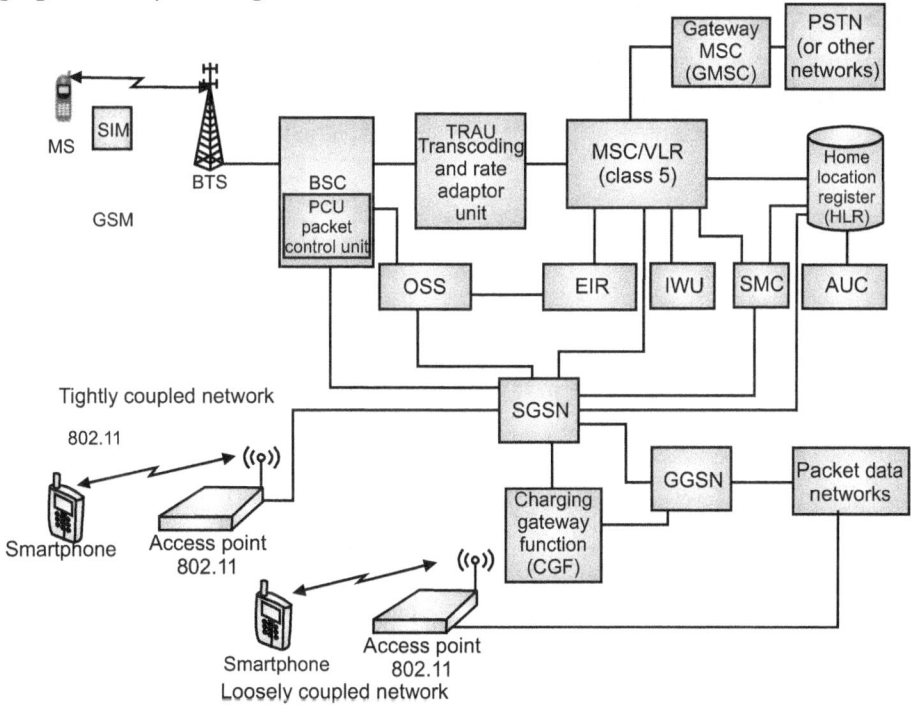

Fig. 2.18 : GSM and Wi-Fi convergence

2.15.3 CDMA/EVDO and Wi-Fi

Fig. 2.19 shows a high–level configuration where an EVDO network is connected to both loose and tight–coupled Wi-Fi networks. This configuration is similar in concept to that of Fig. 2.19 with the exception that the underlying RAN is CDMA2000/EVDO.

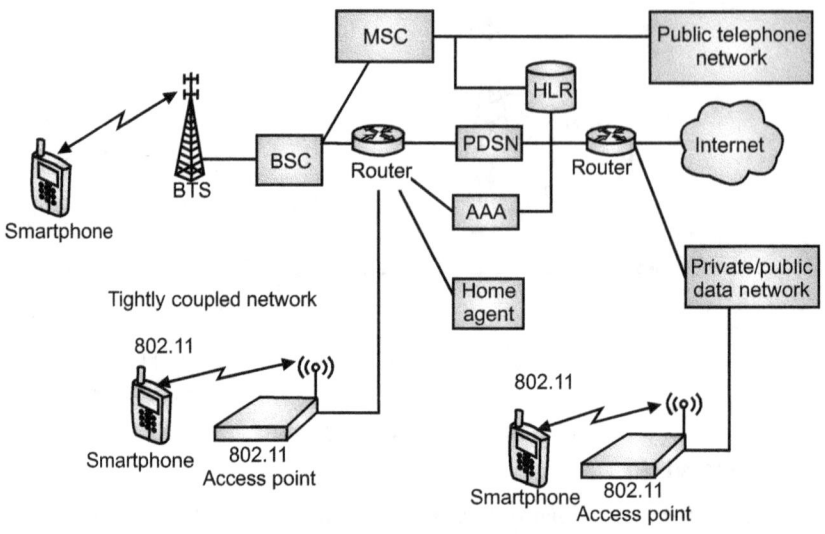

Fig. 2.19 : CDMA2000/EVDO and Wi-Fi convergence

2.15.4 GSM/HSPA and Wi-Fi

- Fig. 2.20 shows how a wireless operator that migrates from GSM to UMTS/HSPA integrates with an Wi-Fi system. UMTS/HSPA connectivity and integration with 802.11 systems is relatively the same as that for GSM due to the commonality of the core packet network.

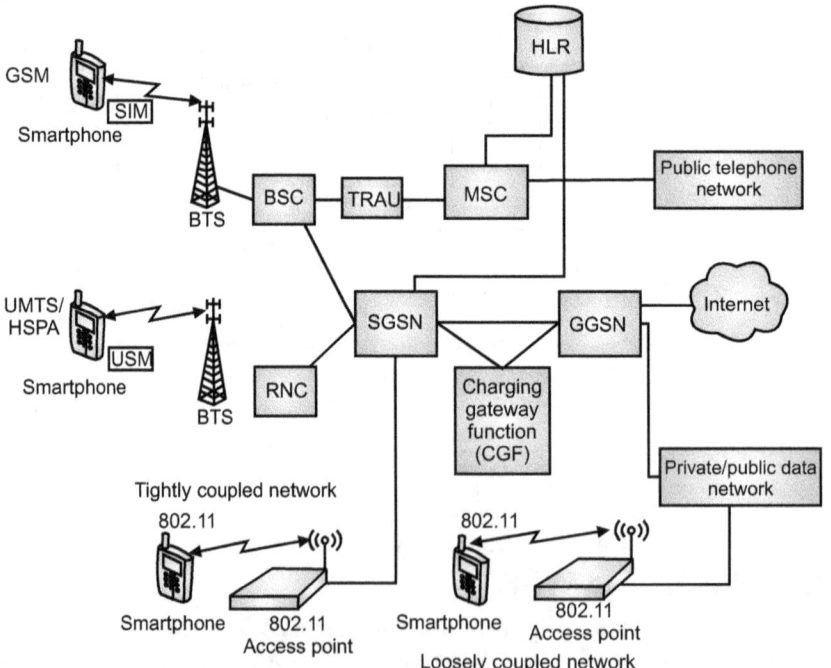

Fig. 2.20 : UMTS/HSPA and Wi-Fi

2.15.5 LTE and Wi-Fi

Fig. 2.21 shows how a wireless operator having LTE as the RAN integrates with an Wi-Fi system.

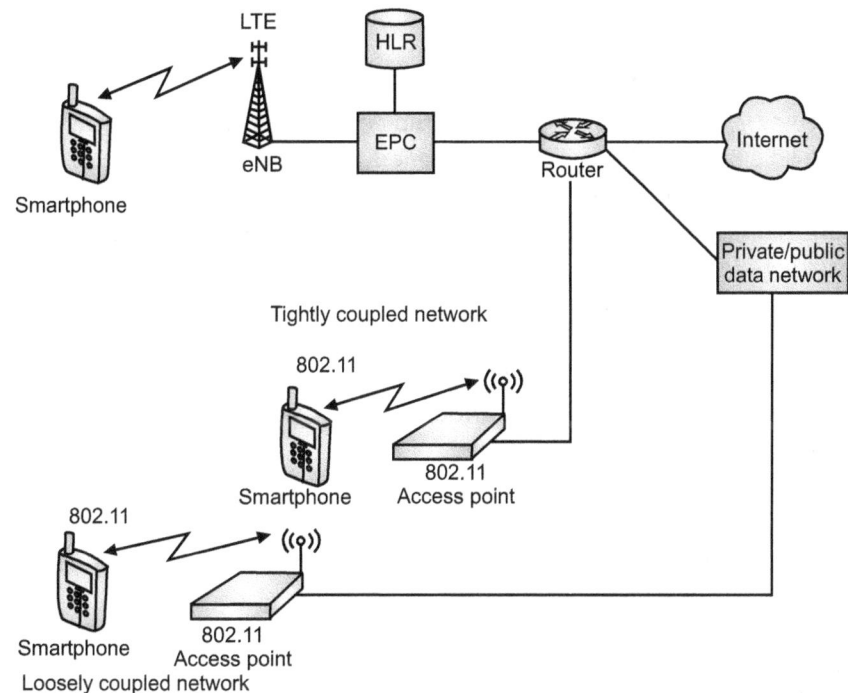

Fig. 2.21 : LTE and Wi-Fi

2.16 BENEFITS OF CONVERGENCE OF Wi-Fi AND WIRELESS MOBILE

- Wi-Fi competes with high speed data access capabilities of 3G/4G. Wi-Fi is provides high data rates but no mobility whereas 3G/4G technologies provide mobility but data rates are lower. When both technologies are combined, it will be beneficial to the user.

- For example a group of users belonging to an organization can be provided with IP–based Wi-Fi enabled handsets. The handsets can also be provided with mobile service. These users can access Wi-Fiservice while in the building and mobility and 3G/4G data services outside the premises.

- Thus Wi-Fi and 4G/3G technologies can complement each other. Thus if these services are provided by same operator there will increase in revenue for the operator and spectrum will also be saved.

- The convergence of Wi-Fi and Wireless mobile is beneficial if one can evaluate some aspects such as objective behind such convergence, deployment plan, optimality of technology etc.

QUESTIONS

1. Explain different components in Wi-Fi architecture.
2. What are characteristics of access point ?
3. What are characteristics of wireless adapter ?
4. What are advantages and disadvantages of Wi-Fi.
5. What are key issues to be addressed for implement of Wi-Fi.
6. What are IEEE 802 standards ? Explain in brief.
7. Write the various IEEE 802.11 standards.
8. What are various Wi-Fi protocols ? Explain features of any one of them.
9. Compare various Wi-Fi protocols.
10. What is Adhoc Wi-Fi network ? Explain.
11. Explain following terms w.r.t. Wi-Fi.
    (i)   Access point   (ii) Basic service set
    (iii) Extended service set   (iv) Distributed system
12. What is infrastructure Wi-Fi Network ? Explain.
13. What does portal mean in Wi-Fi?
14. Explain SOHO Wi-Fi configuration.
15. Explain enterprise Wi-Fi configuration.
16. What is WEP ? Explain.
17. What is open system authentication?
18. What is shared key authentication ?
19. What are alternatives for WEP ?
20. What are drawbacks of WEP ?
21. What is SSID ?
22. What is MAC address security ?
23. Explain EAP for Wi-Fi.
24. What are the two types of services defined by 802.11 standard ?
25. Explain following series defined by 802.11 standard.
    (i)   Association   (ii) Disassociation
    (iii) Reassociation   (iv) Integration
    (v)   Authentication
26. What is Wi-Fi Hot spot ? What is its use ?
27. What are virtual Private Networks ?
28. What are advantages using VPN?
29. What are the types of VPN ? Explain any are of them.
30. Write a short note on Wi-Fi integration with 34/44.
31. What are advantages / benefits of convergence of Wi-Fi and wireless mobile.

Unit - III

THIRD GENERATION (3G) OVERVIEW

3.1 INTRODUCTION

- It is in the mid-1980s that the concept for IMT-2000, "International Mobile Telecommunications", was born at the ITU as the third generation system for mobile communications. After over ten years of hard work under the leadership of the ITU, a historic decision was taken in the year 2000 : unanimous approval of the technical specifications for third generation systems under the brand IMT-2000.

- The spectrum between 400 MHz and 3 GHz is technically suitable for the third generation. The entire telecommunication industry, including both industry and national and regional standards-setting bodies gave a concerted effort to avoiding the fragmentation that had thus far characterized the mobile market. This approval meant that for the first time, full interoperability and interworking of mobile systems could be achieved.

- IMT-2000 is the result of collaboration of many entities, inside the ITU (ITU-R and ITU-T), and outside the ITU (3GPP, 3GPP2, UWCC and so on)

- IMT-2000 offers the capability of providing value-added services and applications on the basis of a single standard. The system envisages a platform for distributing converged fixed, mobile, voice, data, Internet and multimedia services.

- One of its key visions is to provide seamless global roaming, enabling users to move across borders while using the same number and handset. IMT-2000 also aims to provide seamless delivery of services, over a number of media (satellite, fixed, etc...).

- It is expected that IMT-2000 will provide higher transmission rates: a minimum speed of 2Mbit/s for stationary or walking users, and 348 kbit/s in a moving vehicle. Second-generation systems only provide speeds ranging from 9.6 kbit/s to 28.8 kbit/s. IMT-2000 has following characteristics.

1. Flexibility

- With the large number of mergers and consolidations occurring in the mobile industry, and the move into foreign markets, operators wanted to avoid having to support a wide range of different interfaces and technologies. This would surely have hindered the growth of 3G worldwide.

- The IMT-2000 standard addresses this problem, by providing a highly flexible system, capable of supporting a wide range of services and applications.

- The IMT-2000 standard accommodates five possible radio interfaces based on three different access technologies (FDMA, TDMA and CDMA):

2. Affordability

There was agreement among industry that 3G systems had to be affordable, in order to encourage their adoption by consumers and operators.

3. Compatibility with Existing Systems

IMT-2000 services have to be compatible with existing systems. 2G systems, such as the GSM standard (prevalent in Europe and parts of Asia and Africa) will continue to exist for some time and compatibility with these systems must be assured through effective and seamless migration paths.

4. Modular Design

The vision for IMT-2000 systems is that they must be easily expandable in order to allow for growth in users, coverage areas, and new services, with minimum initial investment.

In addition, IMT-2000 has the following key characteristics:

- Global standard,
- High quality,
- Worldwide common frequency band,
- Small terminals for worldwide use,
- Worldwide roaming capability,
- Multimedia application services and terminals,
- Improved spectrum efficiency,
- High-speed packet-data rates,

Fig. 3.1 shows the linkage between the various platforms that make up the IMT-2000 specification group.

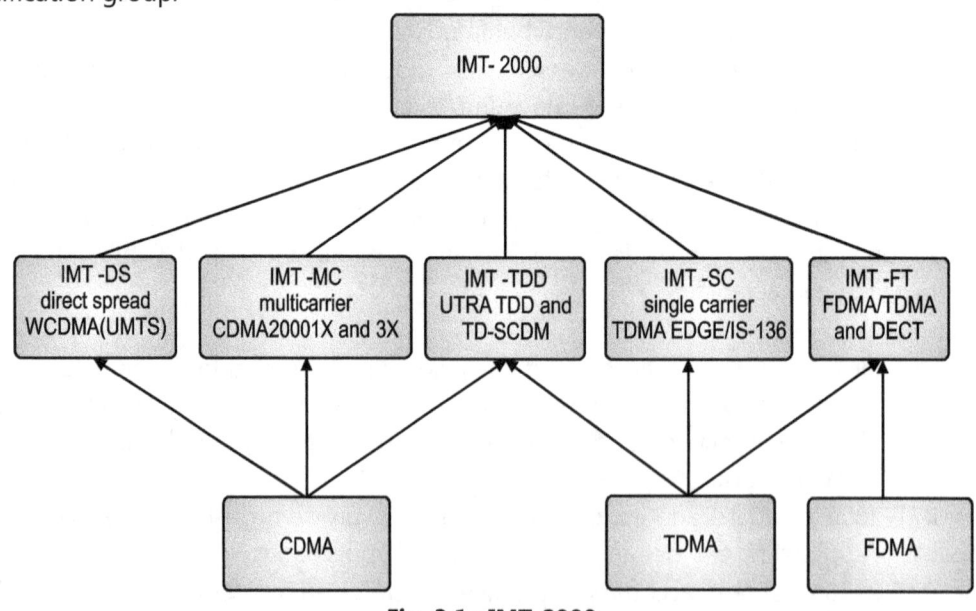

Fig. 3.1 : IMT-2000

- The radio access platforms that make up the IMT-2000 specification are all different, and it should be no wonder that it is difficult to obtain a simple answer when asked to describe what a 3G system will look like.

  (a) IMT-2000/3G can be described as being used to reference a multitude of technologies covering many frequency bands, channel bandwidths, and of course, modulation formats.

  (b) No single 3G infrastructure platform, technology, or application exists.

  (c) 3G is applied to mobile and stationary wireless applications involving high-speed data. IMT-2000 mandates data speeds of 144 kbps at driving speeds, 384 kbps for outside stationary use or walking speeds, and 2 Mbps for indoors.

- Along with the different platforms that make up the IMT-2000 standard is the fact that existing First-Generation/Second-Generation (1G/2G) platforms need to transition into the 3G arena.

- The transition method that an operator must select and spend money on is, of course, a difficult decision and will determine how successful the wireless operator will be in the future.

- The interim platform that bridges the 2G systems into a 3G environment is referred to as 2.5G. Table 3.1 attempts to group some of the major technology platforms by wireless generation.

Table 3.1

Property	First Generation (1G)	Second Generation (2G)	Second-(2.5) Generation (2.5 G)	Third Generation (3G)
Started	1970-1984	1980-1991	1985-1999	1990-2002
Technology used	Analog signalling	Digital signalling	Digital signalling	Broad bandwidth
Standard	AMPS, TACS, NMT	GSM, TDMA, CDMA	GPRS, MODE, HSCSD, EDGE	WCDMA, CDMA-2000
Bandwidth (bps)	1.9 kbps	14.4 kbps	14.4 kbps	2 mbps
Multi-address Technique	FDMA	TDMA, CDMA	TDMA, CDMA	CDMA

...Conti.

Corenetwork	PSTN	PSTN	PSTN and packet network	Packet network
Switching	circuit	Circuit	Circuit for access network and air interface, packet for core and network data	Packet except circuit for air interface
Service type	Voice mono-service person to person	Voice sms mono-media person to person	Higher capacity, packetized data	Integrated with high quality audio, video and data
Comments	Traditional analog cellular depolyment scheme	Digital modulation scheme implemented Deployment in 800-900, 1800-1900 MHz bands Spectrum clearing required for 1900 MHz in United States Spectrum refarming equired for existing 1G perators to implement 2G ystems	Overlay approach used except in new spectrum Packet-data enhancements to existing 2G operators	Defined by IMT-2000 Europe (UMTS WCDMA / ULTRA TDD) America (UMTS/CDMA2000/ULTRA TDD and WiMAX) Asia (UMTS / CDMA2000 / TD-SCDMA/ULTRA TDD and WiMAX) Overlay approach for existing operators of 2/2.5G networks

- What follows is a brief visualization of the interaction between the major 1G, 2G, 2.5G, and 3G platforms.

- Obviously, if an operator chooses to implement more than one technology platform for marketing and strategic reasons, then the lines of transition become more complicated than those shown in Fig. 3.2.

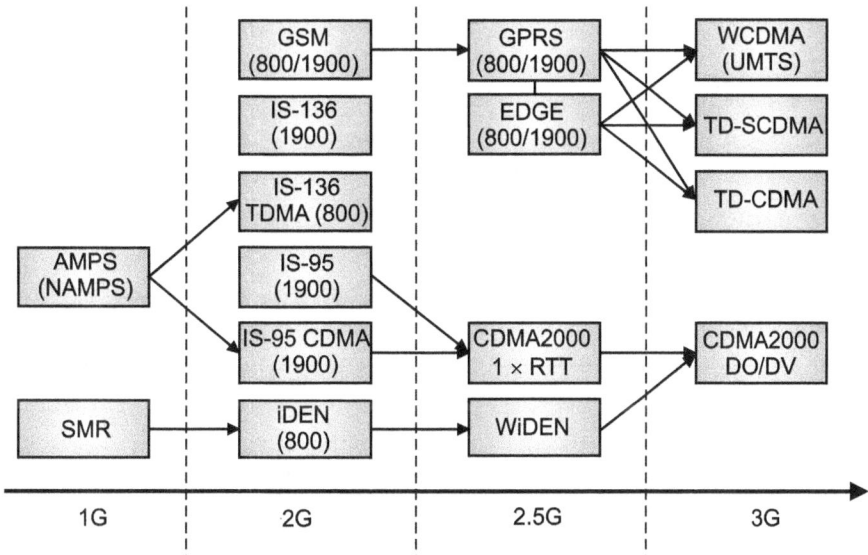

Fig. 3.2 : Migration path

- Both WCDMA and CDMA2000 depicted in Fig. 3.2 include various enhancements that are discussed in later units of specific interest for the enhancements includes HSDPA and HSUPA for WCDMA and Rev 0, A and B for EVDO.

- 3G is a mobile radio and network access scheme that enables high-speed data to be used, allowing for true multimedia capabilities in a mobile wireless system. Presently, voice has been the primary wireless application, with the use of the Short Message Service (SMS) being the largest packet-data service.

- Today's wireless cellular and Personal Communications Services (PCS) systems have the same radio bandwidth allocated for both voice and data. Some of the 2.5G transition or migration plans call for the use of a dedicated spectrum just for data applications. IMT-2000 specifies that data speeds of 144 kbps for vehicular, 384 kbps for pedestrian, and 2 Mbps for indoor applications are the desired goals and have been built into the specifications.

- Table 3.2 is a brief grouping of the various major technology platforms and the data speeds that are associated with each.

Table 3.2 : 2G, 2.5G, and 3G Comparison

2G Technology	Data Capability	Spectrum Required	Comment
Note: TD-SCDMA and TD-CDMA are TDD and are unpaired.			
GSM	9.6 or 14.4 kbps	200 kHz	Circuit-switched data
IS-136	9.6 kbps	30 kHz	Circuit-switched data
iDEN	9.6 kbps	25 kHz	Circuit-switched data
CDMA (IS-95A/J-STD-008)	9.6 bps/14.4 kbps, 64 bps (IS-95B)	1.25 MHz	Circuit-switched data
2.5G Technology	**Data Capability**	**Spectrum Required**	**Comment**
HSCSD	28.8/56 kbps	200 kHz	Circuit/packet data
GPRS	128 kbps	200 kHz	Circuit/packet data
Edge	384 kbps	200 kHz	Circuit/packet data
CDMA2000-1XRTT	153 kbps	1.25 MHz	Circuit/packet data
3G Technology	**Data Capability**	**Spectrum Required**	**Comment**
WCDMA	144 kbps vehicular 384 kbps outdoors 2 Mbps indoors	5 MHz	Packet data
CDMA2000-DO/EV	144 kbps vehicular 384 kbps outdoors 2 Mbps indoors	1.25 MHz	Packet data
TD-CDMA (Ultra TDD)	144 kbps vehicular 384 kbps outdoors 2 Mbps indoors	5 MHz	Packet data
TD-SCDMA	144 kbps vehicular 384 kbps outdoors 2 Mbps indoors	1.6 MHz	Packet data

- In examining Table 3.2, it is apparent that not all of the IMT-2000 platform standards are included, and that is on purpose. The platforms that are listed in both are Wideband Code Division Multiple Access(WCDMA), CDMA2000, TD-CDMA, and TD-SCDMA;

- WCDMA and CDMA2000 will receive more attention and the reason for the two-platform focus lies in the primary issue that a vast majority of wireless operators use one of these two standards, which are part of the IMT-2000 specification.

- CDMA2000 and WCDMA have received more acceptance right now than TD-CDMA and TD-SCDMA. TD-CDMA has experienced some level of rollout but not the same level that CDMA2000 and WCDMA have. In addition, TD-SCDMA implementation and adoption have localized to China.

- In referencing Table 3.2 the data rates listed for 3G are those for compliance with IMT-2000. In practice each of the platforms listed have several enhancements that enable the technology to exceed the IMT-2000 requirements.

3.2 UNIVERSAL MOBILE TELECOMMUNICATIONS SERVICE (UMTS)

- The International Mobile Telecommunications-2000, IMT-2000 standard is actually a family of standards for Third Generation (3G) wireless communications. It defines the broad outlines and requirements for standards that can be called 3G standards. It was set in place by the International Telecommunications Union (Radio Communications section), ITU-R.

- In the 1980s work started on looking at, what was termed in the ITU-R the "Future Public Land Mobile Telecommunications System". However with the deployment on GSM and other 2G technologies the impetus for the development of the next generation system was not present.

- It was not until the early 1990s that progress was seen. A working group was set up and also the 1992 World Administrative Radio Conference (WARC'92) allocated 230 MHz of spectrum between 1885 and 2025 and 2110 and 2200 MHz.

- A number of organizations recognized the need for a global standard for the next generation of mobile telecommunications services. ETSI in Europe moving towards what they termed their Universal Mobile Telecommunications System, UMTS and in Japan the forerunner of the Association of Radio Industries and Businesses, ARIB undertaking a study. To enable a single standard to be adopted the ITU-R requested each regional Standards Development Organisation (SDO) to submit proposals for a Radio Transmission Technology.

- As a result, between 1996 and 1998 companies and regional SDOs worked towards their proposal submissions.

- A total of 17 different proposals were submitted. Of these eleven were for terrestrial systems and the remain six were for satellite systems. The evaluation of the proposals was completed during 1998 but during early 1999 it was necessary to gain some form of consensus. Once this was complete, by the end of 1999 the specification for the radio Transmission Technology was released by the end of 1999.

- Although many proposals were submitted there were several that were considerably more important than others. These included:
- UMTS / WCDMA: The Universal Mobile Telecommunications System using wideband CDMA was the successor to the highly successful GSM system that was initially deployed around Europe, but was spreading rapidly worldwide.
- CDMA2000:   This scheme was the successor to the cdmaOne system defined under Interim Standard IS-95 which was the first system to be deployed using CDMA technology.
- TDS-CDMA: This was a scheme developed in China that adopted many elements of the GSM / UMTS technology but was optimised for Time Division Duplex.
- Of the main IMT-2000 systems, history has shown that UMTS has became the most widely deployed of the 3G systems. It offered global roaming as well as being designed to enable more applications than many of its competitors. Also as it followed on from GSM, it had a very wide base on which to build 3.2.1 Migration Path to UMTS and the Third Generation Partnership

3.2.1 Project (3GPP)

- In 1998 the various SDOs interested in UMTS banded together to form the 3rd Generation Partnership Programme, 3GPP by signing the 3rd Generation Partnership Project Agreement. Historically, the scope of 3GPP was to produce technical specifications and reports for a 3G system based on evolved GSM core networks, and the resulting radio access technology, i.e. both FDD and TDD versions of UMTS.
- The work on the UMTS standard progressed rapidly and the first release, known as Release 99 took place in 1999. Further releases have appeared periodically since then to incorporate additional changes and additions to the standards including High Speed Packet Downlink Access - HSDPA, High Speed Packet Uplink Access - HSUPA and Long Term Evolution - LTE.
- The success of 3GPP subsequently lead to the organisation taking on the maintenance and development the GSM, GPRS and EDGE technical specifications and reports. Ore recently it has undertaken the development of the 3G LTE and LTE Advanced technical specifications and reports.
- A similar organisation, known as the 3rd Generation Partnership Programme 2, 3GPP2, was set up to develop and manage the standards and reports for the CDMA2000 cellular telecommunications system.
- The radio access for UMTS is known as Universal Terrestrial Radio Access (UTRA). This is a WCDMA-based radio solution that includes both FDD and TDD modes.
- The Radio Access Network (RAN) is known as UTRAN. It takes more than an air-interface or an access network to make a complete system, however.

- The core network also must be considered, because of the widespread deployment and success of Global System for Mobile Communications (GSM) it is appropriate to base the UMTS core network on an evolution of the GSM core network.

- The initial release of UMTS (3GPP Release 1999) makes use of the same core network architecture as defined for GSM/GPRS, albeit with some enhancements.

- Moreover, the core network is required to support both UMTS and GSM radio access networks (i.e., both UTRAN and the GSM BSS).

- Evolution of the GSM Base-Station Subsystem (BSS) has not stopped, however, enhancements such as the Enhanced Data Rates for Global Evolution (EDGE) have been made. With this requirements for the continued evolution of GSM and for the GSM to meet UMTS requirements, it makes sense for the continued maintenance and evolution of GSM specifications to be undertaken by 3GPP. Consequently, 3GPP, rather than ETSI, is now responsible for GSM specifications as well as UMTS-specific specifications.

- Sine, last several years various enhancements to GSM have been developed according to yearly releases. Thus, for a given GSM specification, versions have been related to Release 1996, Release 1997, and Release 1998. Initially, the 3GPP determined to continue with this approach.

- Therefore, the first release of specifications from the 3GPP is known as 3GPP Release 1999.

- The release includes not only new specifications for the support of a UTRAN access but also enhanced versions of existing GSM specifications (such as for the support of EDGE).

- The 3GPP Release 1999 specifications were completed in March, 2000. It subject to some revisions and corrections as errors and inconsistencies are discovered during test and deployment.

- The next release of 3GPP specifications was originally termed *3GPP Release 2000*. This included major changes to the core network. The changes were so significant, however, that they could not all be handled in a single step.

- Thus Release 2000 was divided into two releases: Release 4 and Release 5. Going forward, the concept of yearly releases will no longer apply, and releases will be structured and timed according to defined functionality.

- For the most part (although not exclusively), 3GPP Release 1999 focuses mainly on the access network (including a totally new air interface) and the changes needed to the core network to support that access network. Release 4 focuses more on changes to the architecture of the core network. Release 5 introduces a new call model, which means changes to user terminals, to the core network, and to the access network (although the fundamentals of the air interface remain the same).

- The air interface is new in Release 1999 and that it does not change drastically in later releases, it is the best to begin our description of UMTS technology with the WCDMA air interface.
- The FDD mode of operation, with less emphasis on TDD. First, however, we need a few words about the types of services that UMTS can offer.

3.3 UMTS SERVICES

- There are four different QoS classes:
  - (i)   Conversational class.
  - (ii) Streaming class.
  - (iii) Interactive class.
  - (iv) Background class.

Traffic Class	Conversational Class	Streaming Class	Interactive Class	Background Class
	Real Time	Real Time	Best Effort	Best Effort
Fundamental characteristics	- Preserve time relation (variation) between information entities of the stream - Conversational pattern (stringent and low delay)	- Preserve time relation (variation) between information entities of the stream	- Request response pattern -Preserve payload content	-Destination is not expecting the data within a certain time -Preserve payload content
Example of the application	voice	streaming video	web browsing	telemetry, emails

- **Conversational:** The best-known application of this class is speech service over circuit-switched bearers. With Internet and multimedia, a number of new applications will require this type, for example voice over IP and video telephony. Real-time conversation is always performed between peers (or groups) of live (human) end-users. This is the only type of the four where the required characteristics are strictly imposed by human perception. Real-time conversation is characterised by the fact that the end-to-end delay is low and the traffic is symmetric or nearly symmetric. The maximum end-to-end delay is given by the human perception of video and audio conversation: subjective evaluations have shown that the end-to-end delay has to be less than 400 ms. Therefore the limit for acceptable delay is strict, as failure to provide sufficiently low delay will result in unacceptable quality

- **Interactive:** When the end-user, either a machine or a human, is on line requesting data from remote equipment (e.g. a server), this scheme applies. Examples of human interaction with the remote equipment are Web browsing, database retrieval, and server access. Examples of machine interaction with remote equipment are polling for measurement records and automatic database enquiries (tele-machines). Interactive traffic is the other classical data communication scheme that is broadly characterised by the request response pattern of the end-user. At the message destination there is an entity expecting the message (response) within a certain time. Round-trip delay time is therefore one of the key attributes. Another characteristic is that the content of the packets must be transparently transferred (with low bit error rate).
- **Streaming:** Multimedia streaming is a technique for transferring data such that it can be processed as a steady and continuous stream. Streaming technologies are becoming increasingly important with the growth of the Internet because most users do not have fast enough access to download large multimedia files quickly. With streaming, the client browser or plug-in can start displaying the data before the entire file has been transmitted. For streaming to work, the client side receiving the data must be able to collect the data and send it as a steady stream to the application that is processing the data and converting it to sound or pictures. Streaming applications are very asymmetric and therefore typically withstand more delay than more symmetric conversational services. This also means that they tolerate more jitter in transmission. Jitter can be easily smoothed out by buffering.
- **Background:** Data traffic of applications such as e-mail delivery, SMS, downloading of databases and reception of measurement records can be delivered background since such applications do not require immediate action. The delay may be seconds, tens of seconds or even minutes. Background traffic is one of the classical data communication schemes that is broadly characterised by the fact that the destination is not expecting the data within a certain time. It is thus more or less insensitive to delivery time. Another characteristic is that the content of the packets does not need to be transparently transferred. Data to be transmitted has to be received error free. Examples include server-to-server e-mail delivery (as opposed to user retrieval of e-mail), SMS, and performance/measurement reporting. Background applications require error-free delivery.

3.3.1 UMTS Speech Service

- The speech codec in UMTS will employ the Adaptive Multi-rate (AMR) technique. The multi-rate speech coder is a single integrated speech codec with eight source rates: 12.2 (GSM EFR), 10.2, 7.95, 7.40 (IS-641), 6.70 (PDC-EFR), 5.90, 5.15 and 4.75 kbps. The AMR bit rates can be controlled by the radio access network. To facilitate interoperability with existing cellular networks, some of the modes are the same as in existing cellular networks. The 12.2 kbps AMR speech codec is equal to the GSM EFR codec, 7.4 kbps is equal to the US-TDMA speech codec, and 6.7 kbps is equal to the Japanese PDC codec.

The AMR speech coder is capable of switching its bit rate every 20 ms speech frame upon command. For AMR mode switching in-band signalling is used.

- The AMR coder operates on speech frames of 20 ms corresponding to 160 samples at the sampling frequency of 8000 samples per second. The coding scheme for the multi-rate coding modes is the so-called Algebraic Code Excited Linear Prediction Coder (ACELP). The multi-rate ACELP coder is referred to as MR-ACELP. Every 160 speech samples,the speech signal is analysed to extract the parameters of the CELP model (LP filter coefficients, adaptive and fixed codebooks' indices and gains). The speech parameter bits delivered by the speech encoder are rearranged according to their subjective importance before they are sent to the network. The rearranged bits are further sorted based on their sensitivity to errors and are divided into three classes of importance: A, B and C. Class A is the most sensitive, and the strongest channel coding is used for class A bits in the air interface.

- During a normal telephone conversation, the participants alternate so that, on the average, each direction of transmission is occupied about 50% of the time. The AMR has three basic functions to utilise effectively discontinuous activity:
  - Voice Activity Detector (VAD) on the TX side.
  - Evaluation of the background acoustic noise on the TX side, in order to transmit characteristic parameters to the RX side.
  - The transmission of comfort noise information to the RX side is achieved by means of a Silence Descriptor (SID) frame, which is sent at regular intervals.
  - Generation of comfort noise on the RX side during periods when no normal speech frames are received.

- DTX has some obvious positive implications: in the user terminal battery life will be prolonged or a smaller battery could be used for a given operational duration. From the network point of view, the average required bit rate is reduced, leading to a lower interference level and hence increased capacity.

3.3.2 UMTS Data Service

- Packet data are a key attribute, WCDMA is designed to offer great flexibility in transmission of user data across the air interface. For example, data rates can change on a frame-by-frame basis (every 10 ms). Moreover, it is possible to support a mix and match of different types of services. For example, a subscriber may be sending and receiving packet data while also involved in a voice call.

- When sending information over the air interface, physical control channels are used in combination with physical data channels. While the physical data channels carry the user information, the physical control channels carry information to support the correct interpretation of the data carried on the corresponding Dedicated Physical Data Channel (DPDCH) frame plus power control commands and feedback indicators.

- Packet-data services in the 3GPP Release 1999 architecture use largely the same mechanisms as used for GPRS/EDGE data, the big difference being the user data rates that can be supported. Packet-data services are established in UMTS through the activation of a PDP context with an Access Point Name (APN), Quality-of-Service (QoS) criteria, etc.

- From the air-interface perspective, UMTS provides greater flexibility than GPRS/EDGE in terms of how resources are allocated for packet-data traffic. Not only does UMTS offer a greater range of speeds, the WCDMA air interface has a selection of different channel types that can be used for packet data.

3.4 THE UMTS AIR INTERFACE

- The UMTS air interface is a Direct-Sequence CDMA (DS-CDMA) system, given that this is a radical departure from the TDMA techniques of GSM, GPRS, and EDGE, it is worth briefly describing the concepts involved.
- All 3G platforms WCDMA, CDMA2000, TD-CDMA, and TD-SCDMA use variants of CDMA.

3.4.1 WCDMA Basics

- DS-CDMA is a technique in which data are spread over a wider bandwidth through multiplication by a sequence of pseudo-random(PN) bits called chips.
- Fig. 3.3 provides a conceptual depiction of this spreading. The user can see the data, at a relatively low rate compared with the rate of the spreading code, are spread over a signal that has a higher bit rate.
- The signal transmitted i.e. spread signal will also be pseudo-random in nature.
- Thus the spread signal looks like noise.

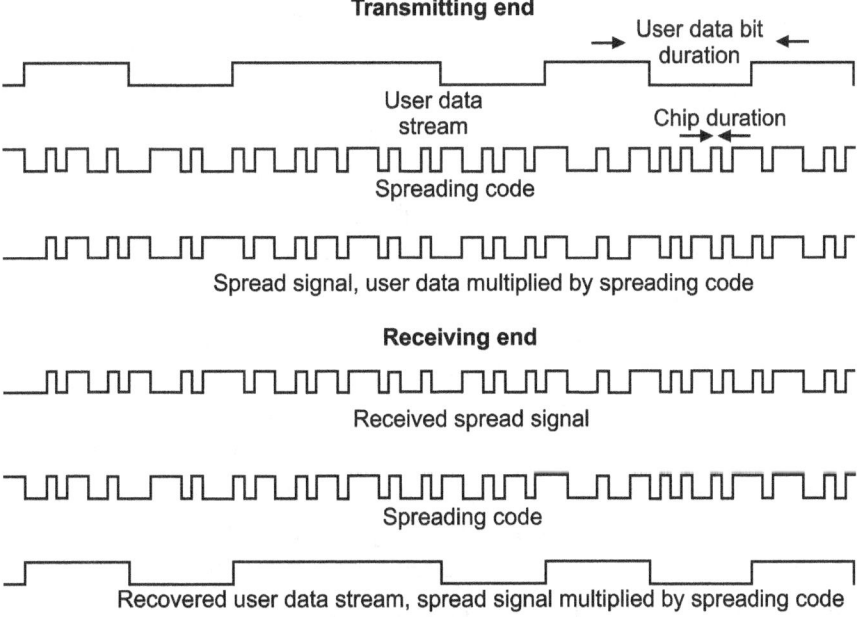

Fig. 3.3 : CDMA basic concept

- When multiple users transmit simultaneously on the same frequency, then the stream of data from each user needs is spread using different pseudo-random sequence.
- At the receiving end the same PN code is used , to recover the set of received signals. What is being despread the complete set of signals received from all users that are transmitting.
- For example, two users (U1 and U2) are transmitting on the same frequency but with two different spreading codes. If, at the receiving end, the received signal is despread with the spreading code applicable to user U1, then the original data stream from user U1 is recovered.
- The data stream i.e. recovered to some noise created by the received signal also contains user data from user U2. The noise, however, is small.
- Similarly, if the received signal is despread according the spreading code used by user U2, then the original data stream from user U2 is recovered, with a little noise generated by the presence of user U1's data within the spread signal. Provided that the rate of the spreading signal (the chip rate) is far larger than the user data rate, then the noise (i.e., the interference) generated by the presence of other users will be sufficiently small not to inhibit recovery of the data stream from a given user. As the number of simultaneous users increases, the interference occurs and it eventually becomes impossible to recover a specific user's data with any confidence.
- In other way, for a given bit of recovered user data, the signal-to-noise ratio must be sufficiently high.
- In CDMA, we used to E_b/N_o, where E_b is the energy per bit of recovered user data, and N_o is the noise power spectral density. Provided that E_b/N_o is sufficiently large, then the user data can be recovered.
- The ratio of the chip rate to the user data symbol rate is known as the spreading factor.
- The ability to recover the user's signal is directly influenced by the spreading factor. The higher spreading factor, the greater is the ability to recover the user's signal.
- In terms of transmission and reception, a higher spreading factor has an equivalent effect as transmitting at a higher power.
- Thus, the magnitude of the spreading factor can be considered a type of gain and is known as the processing gain. In decibels, the processing gain is given by 10×10 log10 (spreading rate/user rate). In some cases, this can be quite a large number and it can help to overcome the effect of interference generated by the presence of other users.
- For example, the processing gain for a given CDMA service were 20 dB, and if an E_b/N_o value of 5 dB were needed, then for a given user, the signal-to-interference ratio can be as low as −15 dB, and the user's signal still can be recovered.
- This is the despreading benefits from the processing gain of 20 dB. Note that for a given chip rate, the processing gain for low-bit-rate user applications is greater than the high-

bit-rate applications, which often means that lower-bit-rate applications can tolerate more interference than high-bit-rate applications.

- The first Multiple Access Third Generation Partnership Project (3GPP) Wideband Code Division networks (WCDMA) were launched in 2002. At the end of 2005, there were 100 WCDMA networks open and a total of more than 150 operators with licenses for frequencies WCDMA operation. Currently, WCDMA networks are deployed in UMTS band of around 2 GHz in Europe and Asia, including Japan and America Korea. WCDMA is deployed in the 850 and 1900 of the existing frequency allocations and the new 3G band 1700/2100 should be available in the near future. 3GPP has defined WCDMA operation for several additional bands, which are expected to be commissioned in the coming years.

- As WCDMA mobile penetration increases, it allows WCDMA networks to carry a greater share of voice and data traffic. WCDMA technology provides some advantages for the operator in that it allows the data, but also improves the voice of base. Voice capacity offered is very high due to interference control mechanisms, including frequency reuse of 1, fast power control, and soft handover.

- WCDMA can offer a lot more voice minutes to customers. Meanwhile WCDMA can also improve broadband voice service with AMR codec, which clearly provides better voice quality than fixed telephone landline. In short, WCDMA can offer more voice minutes with better quality.

- In addition to the high spectral efficiency, third-generation (3G) WCDMA provides even more dramatic change in capacity of the base station and the efficiency of the equipment. The high level of integration in the WCDMA is achieved due to the broadband carrier: a large number of users supported by the carrier, and less Radio Frequency (RF) carriers are required to provide the same capacity.

- With less RF parts and more digital baseband processing, WCDMA can take advantage of the rapid evolution of digital signal processing capability. The level of integration of the high base station enables efficient building high capacity sites since the complexity of RF combiners, additional antennas or power cables can be avoided. WCDMA operators are able to provide useful data services, including navigation, person to person video calls, sports and video and new mobile TV clips.

- WCDMA enables simultaneous voice and data which allows, for example, browsing or email when voice conferencing or video sharing in real time during voice calls.

- The operators also offer mobile connectivity to the Internet and corporate intranet with maximum bit rate of 384 kbps downlink and both uplink. The first terminals and networks have been limited to 64 to 128 kbps uplink while the latter products provide 384 kbps uplink.

- The WCDMA air interface of UMTS (hereafter simply WCDMA) has a nominal bandwidth of 5 MHz. While 5 MHz is the nominal carrier spacing, it is possible to have a carrier spacing of 4.4 to 5 MHz in steps of 200 kHz. This enables spacing that might be needed to avoid interference, particularly if the next 5 MHz block is allocated to another carrier.

- The chip rate in WCDMA is 3.84×10^6 chips per second (3.84 Mcps). In theory, for a speech service at 12.2 kbps (and, for now, assuming that no extra bandwidth for error correction), the spreading factor would be $3.84 \times 10^6/12.2 \times 10^3 = 314.75$.
- This would equate to a processing gain of 25 dB. In reality, however, WCDMA does include extra coding for error correction. Consequently, a spreading factor as high as 314.75 is not supported, at least not in the uplink.
- The supported uplink spreading factors are 4, 8, 16, 32, 64, 128, and 256. The highest spreading factor (256) is used mostly by the various control channels that require low data throughput. Some control channels also can use lower spreading factors, whereas user services generally use lower spreading factors, the lower spreading rate allows for higher data throughput.
- Table 3.3 provides a summary of the spreading factors and the corresponding data rates on the uplink.

Table 3.3 : Uplink Spreading Factors and Data Rates

Spreading Factor	Gross Data Rate (kbps)	User Data Rate (kbps) (Assuming Half-Rate Coding for Error Correction)
256	15	7.5
128	30	15
64	60	30
32	120	60
16	240	120
8	480	240
4	960	480

- At first glance, it appears that the lowest spreading factor (4) provides a gross rate of only 960 kbps and a usable rate of only 480 kbps. This does not meet the requirements of IMT-2000, which states that a user should be able to achieve speeds of 2 Mbps.
- In order to meet that requirement, UMTS supports the capability for a given user to transmit up to six simultaneous data channels.
- Thus, if a user wants to transmit user data at a user rate greater than 480 kbps, then multiple channels are used, each with a spreading factor of 4.
- With six parallel channels, each with a spreading factor of 4, a single user can obtain speeds of over 2 Mbps. This requires 6×5 MHz (30 MHz $\times$ 30 MHz) of FDD spectrum.
- In the downlink, the same spreading factors are available, with a spreading factor of 512 also possible. One difference between the uplink and downlink, however, is the number of bits per symbol. The uplink effectively uses 1 bit per user symbol, whereas the downlink effectively uses 2 bits per user symbol. Consequently, for a given spreading factor, the user bit rate in the downlink is greater than the corresponding bit rate in the uplink.

- The user rate in the downlink is not quite twice that in the uplink, however, owing to differences in the way that control channels and traffic channels are multiplexed on the air interface.
- Table 3.4 provides a summary of the spreading factors and the corresponding data rates on the downlink.

Table 3.4 : Downlink Spreading Factors and Data Rates

Spreading Factor	Gross Air-Interface Bit Rate (kbps)	User Data Rate (kbps) (Including Coding for Error Correction)	Approximate Net User Data Rate (kbps) (Assuming Half-Rate Coding)
512	15	3 - 6	1 - 3
256	30	12 - 24	6 - 12
128	60	42 - 512	21 - 25
64	120	90	45
32	240	210	105
16	480	432	216
8	960	912	456
4	1920	1872	936

- The uplink, WCDMA supports multiple simultaneous user data channels in the downlink so that a single user can achieve rates of over 2 Mbps.
- It should be noted, however, that Table 3.4 does not tell the whole story of possible data rates on the downlink. WCDMA supports a concept known as compressed mode, whereby gaps exist in downlink transmission so that the terminal can take measurements on other frequencies.
- When compressed mode is used, a reduction will take place in the data rate compared with as shown in above Table 3.4.
- An important capability of WCDMA is that user data rates do not need to be fixed. In WCDMA, channels are transmitted with a 10 ms frame structure. It is possible to change the spreading factor on a frame-by-frame basis. Thus, within one frame, the user data rate is fixed, but the user data rate can change from frame to frame.
- This capability means that WCDMA can offer bandwidth on demand. Note that rate changes every 10 ms do not apply to AMR speech because each speech packet is 20 ms in duration, so the speech rate can change every 20 ms if needed, but not every 10 ms.

3.4.2 Spectrum Allocation

- Here is the summary of UMTS frequencies:
- Paired Uplink and downlink outside North America are 1920-1980 and 2110-2170 MHz Frequency Division Duplex (FDD, W-CDMA), channel spacing is 5 MHz and raster is 200 kHz. An Operator needs 3 - 4 channels (2×15 MHz or 2×20 MHz) to be able to build a high-speed, high-capacity network. In the United States, the separation is 80 MHz and with the Uplink 1850 to 1915 MHz; Downlink 1930 to 1995 MHz. Although 5 MHz is the

nominal carrier spacing, it is possible to have a carrier spacing of 4.4 to 5 MHz in steps of 200 kHz.

- 1900-1920 and 2010-2025 MHz Time Division Duplex (TDD, TD/CDMA) Unpaired, channel spacing is 5 MHz and raster is 200 kHz. Tx and Rx are not separated in frequency. 1980-2010 and 2170-2200 MHz Satellite uplink and downlink.

- UMTS is an overlay for an existing wireless operator using a 2G/2.5G RAN. The implementation of UMTS requires new spectrum or spectrum segmentation. In some instances, PCS operators may not have sufficient spectrum to offer WCDMA because they have only a single 5 × 5 MHz license that has existing GSM customers on it.

3.5 OVERVIEW OF THE 3GPP RELEASE 1999 NETWORK ARCHITECTURE

- Fig. 3.4 shows the UMTS architecture as specified in 3GPP Release 99. The system architecture is based on the enhanced GSM Phase 2+ core network with GPRS and a new radio network called UMTS Terrestrial Radio Access Network (UTRAN). UTRAN is connected with the core network by the Iu interface.

- UTRAN consists of several Radio Network Subsystems (RNSs). An RNS is supported by the core network. Each RNS consists of base stations, termed as Node B in UMTS, and a radio network controller (RNC). The RNC is a BSC equivalent and controls several Node Bs. As shown in Fig. 3.4, the 3G terminals (UE) interface with UTRAN using the Uu interface, which is a WCDMA-based radio link.

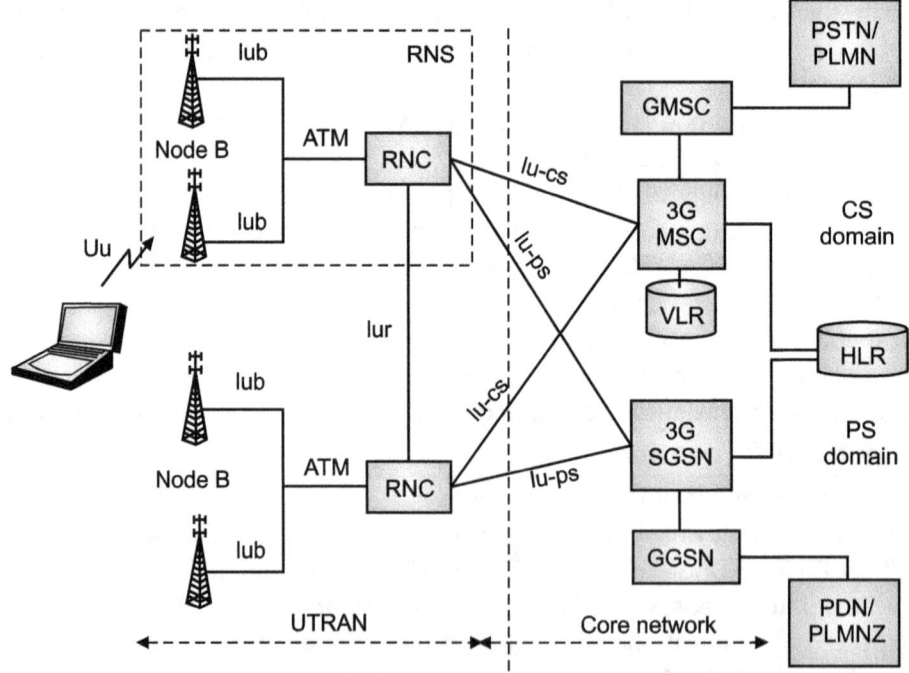

Fig. 3.4 : 3GPP Release 1999 network architecture.

- The Node Bs are connected to the RNC by Iub interfaces. Unlike the Abis interface, the Iub interface is well defined. This ensures interoperability in a multivendor environment where Node Bs and RNCs are supplied by different vendors. Another point to note here is that, unlike GSM BSCs, Node Bs are connected to each other by the Iur interface. This is required for inter-RNC handover.

- A UE may attach to the several RNCs. The RNC that controls Node B is known as Controlling RNC (CRNC). It is responsible for managing radio resources for all the Node Bs under its control. The RNC that controls the connection between a UE and the core network is known as a Serving RNC (SRNC). In many cases, the CRNC and the SRNC are same. UTRAN supports soft handover. The soft handover occurs between Node Bs supported by different RNCs. During soft handover, the UE starts communicating with the new RNC, i.e., a Drift RNC (DRNC), before it takes over the role of SRNC.

- As shown in Fig. 3.4, the core network consists of network elements to support subscriber control and circuit and packet switching. The core network also supports interfaces to the external network. The RNCs are connected to a 3G MSC by the Iu-CS interface, which supports circuit-switched services. Iu-CS is equivalent to the A interface in GSM. The RNCs are also connected to a 3G SGSN by the Iu-PS interface, which supports packet-switched data services. Iu-PS is equivalent to the Gb interface in GPRS. All the new interfaces, i.e., Iub, Iur, Iu-CS, and Iu-PS, are based on ATM.

- In UMTS, the User Equipment (UE) or Mobile Station (MS) comprises Mobile Equipment (ME) and a UMTS Subscriber Identity Module (USIM).

- It can be seen from Fig. 3.4 that all the interfaces in the UTRAN of 3GPP Release 1999 are based on Asynchronous Transfer Mode (ATM). ATM was chosen because of its ability to support a range of different service types (such as a variable bit rate for packet-based services and a constant bit rate for circuit-switched services).

- From Fig. 3.4 that the core network uses the same basic architecture as GSM/GPRS. This was done purposely so that the new radio access technology could be supported by an established, robust core network technology. It should be possible for an existing core network to be upgraded to support UTRAN so that a given MSC, for example, could connect to both a UTRAN RNC and a GSM BSC.

- In fact, UMTS specifications include support for a hard handover from UMTS to GSM and vice versa. This is an important requirement because the widespread rollout of UMTS coverage will take time to complete, and if holes exist in UMTS coverage, it is desirable that a UMTS subscriber should receive service from the more ubiquitous GSM coverage.

If UTRAN and the GSM BSS are supported by different MSCs, then an intersystem handover could be achieved through an inter-MSC handover. Given that many of the functions of the MSC/VLR are similar for UMTS and GSM, however, it makes sense for a given MSC to be able to support both types of access simultaneously. Similar logic suggests that a given SGSN should be able to support an Iu-PS connection to an RNC and a Gb interface to a GPRS BSC simultaneously.

- In most vendor implementations, many of the network elements are being upgraded to support GSM/GPRS/EDGE and UMTS simultaneously. Such network elements include the MSC/VLR, the Home Location Register (HLR), the SGSN, and the GGSN. For some vendors, the base stations deployed for GSM/GPRS/EDGE have been designed so that they can be upgraded to support both GSM and UMTS simultaneously.

- This is a major consideration for network operators who want to deploy a UMTS network in parallel with an existing GSM network. For some vendors, the BSC is being upgraded to act as both a GSM BSC and a UMTS RNC.

- This configuration is rare, however. The different interfaces and functions (such as a soft handover) required of a UMTS RNC mean that its technology is quite different from that of a GSM BSC. Consequently, it is normal to find separate UMTS RNCs and GSM BSCs.

3.6   OVERVIEW OF THE 3GPP RELEASE 4 NETWORK ARCHITECTURE

- Fig. 3.5 illustrates the Release 4 architecture. As can be noticed, the core network is evolved further and introduces changes in the CS domain. The 3G MSC functions are divided into two parts, i.e., MSC server and media gateways. The MSC server contains call control and mobility management logic. The MSC server also contains a VLR to hold mobile subscriber service data. The media gateway contains the switching function and is controlled by the MSC server. MGW terminates the bearer channels from the circuit-switched network. The same applies to the GMSC server, which is split into GMSC server and media gateway.

- Separating the call control and physical interfaces has distinct advantages. It offers scalability and lower cost. Moreover, the information transfer between MS server, media gateways and other components are IP based. Therefore, many components in the core network, including SGSN, GGSN, and MSC server, can be hooked up on the intra PLMN IP backbone, taking advantage of shared and cheaper IP transport.

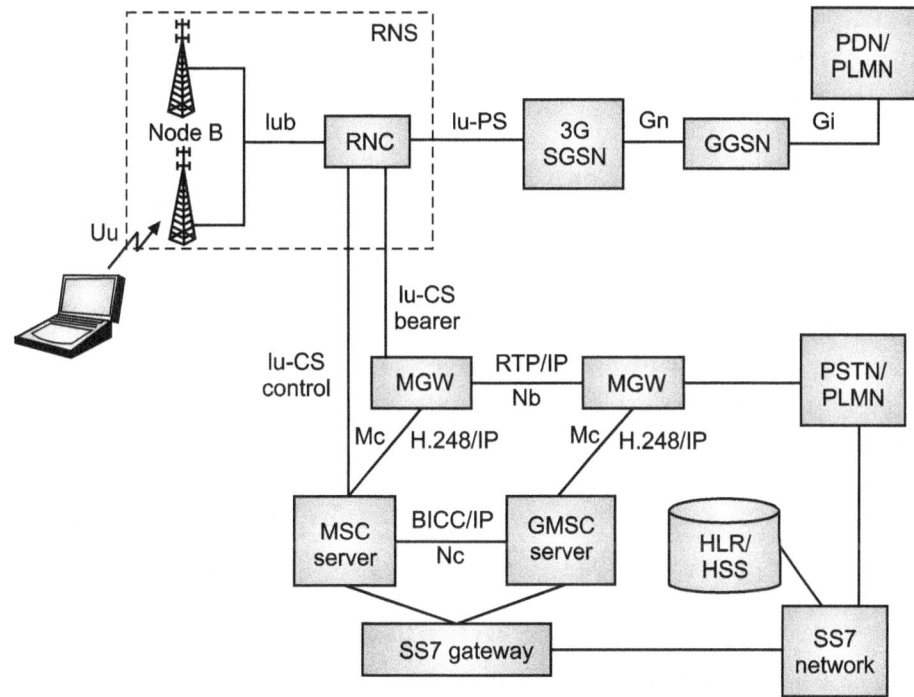

Fig. 3.5 : 3GPP Release 4 distributed network architecture.

- The MSC server uses ITU-T H.248 to control the media gateway. The ITU-T BICC (bearer-independent call control) protocol is used between the MSC and the GMSC server The core network supports coexistence of both UTRAN and GSM/GPRS Radio Access Network (GRAN).

- Basically, the MSC is divided into an MSC server and a Media Gateway (MGW). The MSC server contains all the mobility management and call-control logic that would be contained in a standard MSC. It does not, however, contain a switching matrix.

- The switching matrix is contained within the MGW, which is controlled by the MSC server and can be placed remotely from the MSC.

- Control signaling for circuit-switched calls is between the RNC and the MSC server. The media path for circuit-switched calls is between the RNC and the MG. Typically, an MG will take calls from the RNC and routes those calls toward their destinations over a packet backbone. In many cases, that packet backbone will use the Real-Time Transport Protocol (RTP) over the Internet Protocol (IP).

- As can be seen from Fig. 3.5, packet-data traffic from the RNC is passed to the SGSN and from the SGSN to the GGSN over an IP backbone. Given that data and voice both can use IP transport within the core network, a single backbone can be constructed to support both types of service.

- This can mean significant savings of capital and operating expenses compared with construction and operation of separate packet- and circuit-switched backbone networks.

- At the remote end, where a call needs to be handed off to another network, such as the Public Switched Telephone Network (PSTN), another MGW is controlled by a Gateway MSC server (GMSC server).

- This MGW will convert the packetized voice to standard Pulse Code Modulation (PCM) for delivery to the PSTN. It is only at this point that transcoding needs to take place. Assuming, for example, that speech over the air interface is carried at 12.2 kbps, then the voice does not need to be converted up to 64 kbps until it reaches the MGW that interfaces with the PSTN.

- This packetized transport can mean significant bandwidth savings on the backbone network, particularly if the two MGWs are some significant distance apart.

- The control protocol between the MSC server or GMSC server and the MGW is the ITU H.248 protocol. This protocol was developed jointly by the ITU and the Internet Engineering Task Force (IETF).

- It also goes by the name Media Gateway Control (MEGACO). The call-control protocol between the MSC server and the GMSC server can be any suitable call-control protocol. The 3GPP standards suggest but do not mandate the Bearer Independent Call Control (BICC) protocol, which is based on ITU-T recommendation Q.1902.

- In many cases, an MSC server also will support the functions of a GMSC server. Moreover, one MGW may have the ability to interface both with the RAN and with the PSTN. In this case, calls to or from the PSTN can be handed off locally. This can represent another major savings.

- Consider, for example, a scenario where an RNC is located in one city (city A) and is controlled by an MSC in another city (city B). Let's assume that a subscriber in city A makes a local phone call.

- Without a distributed architecture, the call needs to travel from city A to city B (where the MSC is), only to be connected back to a local PSTN number in city A. With a distributed architecture, the call can be controlled by an MSC server in city B, but the actual media path can remain within city A, thereby reducing transmission requirements and network operations costs.

- One also will notice in Fig. 3.5 that the HLR also may be known as a Home Subscriber Server (HSS). The HSS and HLR are functionally equivalent, with the exception that interfaces to an HSS will use packet-based transports such as IP, whereas an HLR is likely to use standard Signaling System 7 (SS7)–based interfaces. Although not shown, a logical interface exists between the SGSN and HLR/HSS and between the GSN and HLR/HSS.

- Many of the protocols used within the core network are packet-based, using either IP or ATM. However, the network must interface with traditional networks through the use of media gateways. Moreover, the network also must interface with standard SS7 or CC7 networks.

- This interface is achieved through the use of an SS7 Gateway (SS7 GW).

- This is a gateway that on one side supports the transport of an SS7 message over a standard SS7 transport. On the other side, it transports SS7 application messages over a packet network such as IP.
- Entities such as the MSC server, the GMSC server, and the HSS communicate with the SS7 gateway using a set of transport protocols specially designed for carrying SS7 messages on an IP network. This suite of protocols is known as SIGTRAN.
- Many of the protocols mentioned in this brief discussion (e.g., RTP, H.248, and SIGTRAN).

3.7 OVERVIEW OF THE 3GPP RELEASE 5 ALL-IP NETWORK ARCHITECTURE

- Fig. 3.6 shows the Release 5 architecture. The salient point for this architecture is that it is all IP based. The voice is over IP, and hence there is no need of circuit switching within PLMN. At the gateway, appropriate conversion is required to interconnect to legacy systems. The SGSN and the GGSN are enhanced to support circuit-switched services such as voice.
- The new Roaming Signaling Gateway (R-SGW) and Transport Signaling Gateway (T-SGW) are needed to provide interworking with the external system over legacy SS7 and SS7-over-IP. The call State Control Function (CSCF) provides call control functions for multimedia sessions. The Media Gateway Control Function (MGCF) controls media gateways, which are IP multimedia subsystems. The Media Resource Function (MRF) supports features such as multiparty conferencing and "meet me."

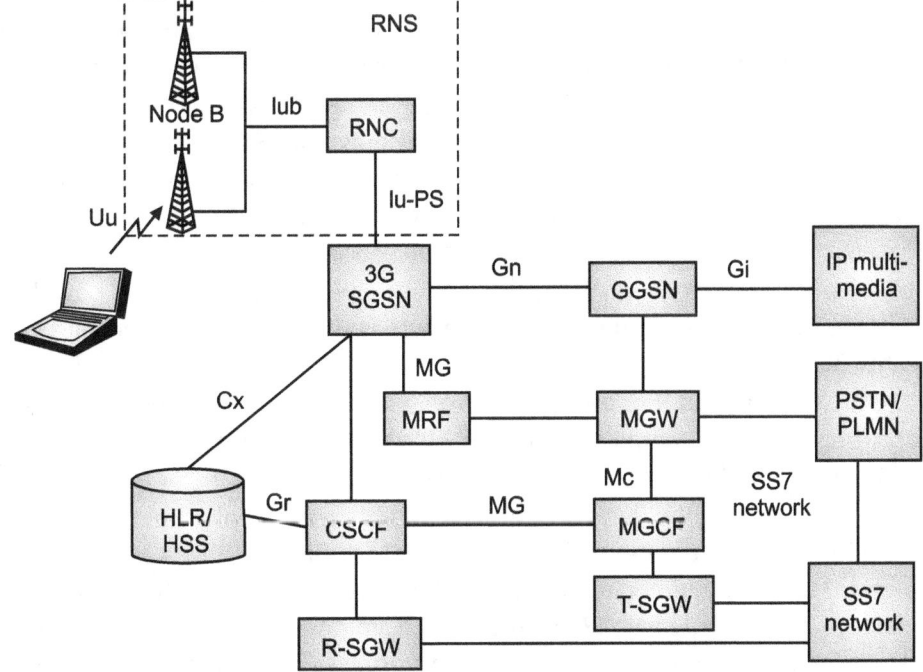

Fig. 3.6 : 3GPP IP multimedia network architecture

- In Release 5, not only is the core enhanced, but the uplink data rate also is improved through the introduction of High-Speed Uplink Packet Access (HSUPA).

- As we can see from Fig. 3.6, voice and data no longer need separate interfaces; just a single Iu interface can carry all the media. Within the core network, that interface terminates at the SGSN there is no separate media gateway.

- We also find a number of new network elements, notably the Call State Control Function (CSCF), the Multimedia Resource Function (MRF), the Media Gateway Control Function (MGCF), the Transport Signaling Gateway (T-SGW), and the Roaming Signaling Gateway (R-SGW).

- An important aspect of the all-IP architecture is the fact that the user equipment is greatly enhanced. Significant logic is placed within the UE. In fact, the UE supports the Session Initiation Protocol (SIP). The UE effectively becomes an SIP user agent. As such, the UE has far greater control of services than previously.

- The CSCF manages the establishment, maintenance, and release of multimedia sessions to and from user devices. This includes functions such as translation and routing. The CSCF acts like a proxy server/registrar, as defined in the SIP architecture.

- The SGSN and GGSN are enhanced versions of the same nodes used in GPRS and UMTS Releases 1999 and 4. The difference is that these nodes, in addition to data services, now support services that traditionally have been circuit-switched such as voice. Consequently, appropriate QoS capabilities need to be supported either within the SGSN and the GGSN or, at a minimum, in the routers immediately connected to them.

- The Multimedia Resource Function (MRF) is a conference bridging function used to support features such as multiparty calling and meet-me conference service.

- The Transport Signaling Gateway (T-SGW) is an SS7 gateway that provides SS7 interworking with standard external networks such as the PSTN. The T-SGW will support SIGTRAN protocols. The Roaming Signaling Gateway (R-SGW) is a node that provides signaling interworking with legacy mobile networks that use standard SS7. In many cases, the T-SGW and R-SGW will exist within the same platform.

- The MGW performs interworking with external networks at the media path level. The MGW in the 3GPP Release 5 network architecture is the same as the equivalent function within the 3GPP Release 4 architecture.

- The MGW is controlled by a Media Gateway Control Function (MGCF). The control protocol between these entities is ITU-T H.248. The MGCF also communicates with the CSCF. The protocol of choice for this interface is SIP.

- It should be noted that the Release 5 all-IP architecture is an enhancement to an existing Release 1999 or Release 4 network. It is effectively the addition of a new domain in the core network the IP-Multimedia(IM) domain. This new domain, which enables both voice and data to be carried over IP all the way from the handset, uses the services of the Packet Switched (PS) domain for transport purposes i.e. it uses the SGSN, GGSN, Gn, Gi, etc., nodes and interfaces that belong to the PS domain.

3.8 OVERVIEW CDMA2000

- CDMA2000 is the evolution of the original IS-95 cdmaOne system. CDMA2000 has a number of evolutions of which the first was CDMA2000 1x, sometimes also called CDMA2000 1xRTT.
- CDMA2000 1x which is also standardised as IS-2000 supports circuit-switched voice, and has the capability to provide up and sometimes beyond 35 simultaneous call per sector and as such it doubles the capacity of the original IS-95 networks. It also enables the transmission and reception of data at rates up to 153 kbps in both directions. It was recognized by the International Telecommunications Union (ITU) as an IMT-2000 standard in November 1999.
- The aim of the CDMA2000 is to provide a migration path from the original cdmaOne / IS-95 system through the CDMA2000 1x format to further high speed formats. These different standards have all been standardised under the IS-format and as shown in Fig. 3.7 of the migration path is given below:.

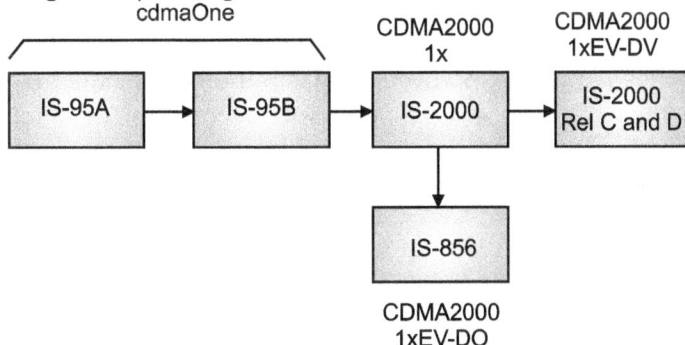

Fig. 3.7 : CDMA2000 evolution process

- The CDMA2000 1x format is the basic 3G standard, but in what is termed CDMA2000 1xEv, there are further developments. There are basically two routes for the evolution that were initially proposed, only one of which was deployed:
- CDMA2000 1x EV-DO: The first of these known as CDMA2000 1xEV-DO (EVolution Data Only or as is becoming more widely known Evolution Data Optimised) is something of a sideline from the main evolutionary development of the standard. It is defined under IS-856 rather than IS-2000, and as the name indicates it only carries data, but at speeds up to 3.1 Mbps in the forward direction and 1.8 Mbps in the reverse direction, the speed in the reverse link being upgraded as part of Release A of the standard. The first commercial CDMA2000 1xEV-DO network was deployed by SK Telecom (Korea) in January 2002.
- CDMA2000 1s EV-DV: The second is CDMA2000 1s EV-DV (Evolution Data and Voice). The idea was that this system would carry both data and voice services. It was never deployed as the EV-DO system was deployed in preference and there was no requirement for a data and voice service as voice could be carried on DO as either VoIP or by falling back to the CDMA2000 1X format.

- The CDMA2000 1xRTT and 3xRTT terms refer to what are termed "Radio Transmission Technologies". The original IS-95 and deployments of CDMA2000 utilised the 1.25 MHz channel spacing. This provided what is effectively the first phase of the 3G development and roll out. However to enhance the performance beyond that possible using the technologies such as 1xEV-DO and 1xEV-DV, the channel bandwidth of 1.25 MHz was deemed insufficient for even higher data rates. Accordingly by increasing the bandwidth, higher data rates were possible. The further evolution of the CDMA2000 system involves utilising channel bandwidths of 3 times the standard 1.25 MHz bandwidth under what was termed 3XRTT. Further bandwidth increases to 5X, 7X and so forth could in theory be contemplated.

- For CDMA2000 1xRTT technology, a Spreading Rate 1 (SR1) was used where the signal was spread to occupy a bandwidth of 1.25 MHz. Here the spread rate was the same as that used for IS-95, i.e. 1.2288 Mcps. For 3xRTT technology, Spreading Rate 3 (SR3) was used. Here the spreading rate was 3.6864 Mcps. It was found that if the spreading rate remained the same but the data rate increased, as happens with video downloads and other 3G applications, the processing gain decreased. Accordingly the coverage and signal strength needed to be improved to match the new conditions. By increasing the spreading rate, the performance could be boosted without the need for improvements in coverage.

3.8.1 Migration Path

- The migration path that a wireless operator must take to realize CDMA2000 as envisioned for 3G is usually thought of as a staged approach for implementation. The concept behind the phased approach is to enable wireless operators using IS-95 platforms to migrate toward 3G without having to either forklift their existing platforms or acquire a new spectrum.

- However, upgrading to 1xRTT and/or EVDO will require hardware and software changes. An important concept is that CDMA2000 is backward-compatible with existing 2G CDMA systems, thereby speeding time to market.

- From an operator's point of view, the migration from 2G to 3G and the realization of 3G must include the following:
    - It needs to be cost-effective based on the capital infrastructure already in place.
    - It needs increased capacity and throughput in both voice and data services that use existing spectrum allocations.
    - It needs standard systems that enable both backward and forward compatibility with other network and data platforms.
    - It needs the flexibility to meet ever-changing market conditions.

- CDMA2000 phase 1 is an interim step between IS-95B and full realization of the IMT-2000 specification. The multicarrier approach for CDMA2000 has been abandoned at this time in favor of a more robust single-carrier solution. However, EVDO Rev B is planned to utilize multiple carriers but this specification has not been finalized at this writing. CDMA2000 can be and has been deployed in an existing IS-95 channel or system and will exhibit the numerous enhancements, some of which are included here:

- 1.25-MHz channel support,
- 144-kbps packet-data rates,
- 2× increase in voice capacity,
- 2× increase in standby time,
- Improved handoff.

- IS-95 and CDMA2000 1xRTT, EVDO, and EVDV can and will coexist in the same market and possibly at the same cell site. Obviously, one can take numerous approaches in the course of implementing any technology platform, and CDMA2000 is by no means unique to this situation. However, several common migration paths are being pursued for implementing CDMA2000. The migration path, depends on whether the operator is currently using IS-95A/B, J-STD-008, or CDMA2000 (1xRTT) and upgrading to CDMA2000 EVDO/EVDV or is in the process of either installing a new system or segmenting existing spectrum to facilitate introduction of CDMA2000 EVDO/EVDV into the network (Table 3.5). Please keep in mind that there are several releases for CDMA2000 and EVDO that are driving toward harmonization in the future.

Table 3.5 : CDMA Path

Standard	Salient Issues
IS-95A	9600 bps or 14.4 kbps.
IS-95B	Primarily voice, data on forward link, improved handoff, and data speeds of 64/56 kbps.
CDMA2000	SR1 (1.2288 Mcps), voice and data (packet data via separate channel). 128 Walsh codes (256 future). 2 × voice capacity over IS-95. 144 kbps using 1xRTT with SR1.
IS-856 (EVDO)	SR1 (1.2288 Mcps), Packet data only, Higher data rate, 3 Mbps DL, 2 Mbps UL.

The following are three possible migration paths an operator may pursue:

1. CDMAOne (IS-95A) → CDMA2000 (1 x RTT) → CDMA2000 (EVDO)
2. CDMAOne (IS-95A) → CDMAOne (IS-95B) → CDMA2000 (1 x RTT) → CDMA2000 (EVDV)
3. CDMA2000 (1xRTT) → EVDV and EVDO

- To complicate matters a little more for migration issues, several interim steps within the CDMA2000 implementation process bear mentioning relative to the single-carrier (1×) aspects. The expected migration path or, rather, the options for possible deployment of a CDMA2000-1X system are shown in Fig. 3.7.

- For instance there are several migration steps for EVDO starting with EVDO Rev 0 and then progressing to Rev A and then to Rev B. Many enhancements and also hardware and software changes are required to realize this migration.

3.8.2 System Architecture

- The system architecture that will make up a CDMA2000 network is a logical extension of an existing CDMAOne network, with the fundamental difference being the introduction of packet-data services.

- The implementation of a CDMA2000 system is meant to involve upgrades to the BTS and BSC for the purpose of handling the packet-data services. Additionally, the use of packet-data services also necessitates the introduction of a packet server complex that may exist already to support services such as Cellular Data Packet Data (CDPD).

- However, it is recommended that the existing packet-data network should not by default be considered for inclusion into the CDMA2000 network architecture. The system architecture for a CDMA2000 network, owing to packet-data services, can be either centralized or distributed. The decision whether the system uses a distributed or centralized system depends on the design requirements as well as operational issues.

- Fig. 3.8 is an example of a stand-alone CDMA2000 system that has the inclusion of a Packet Data Serving Node (PDSN) for handling packet-data services.

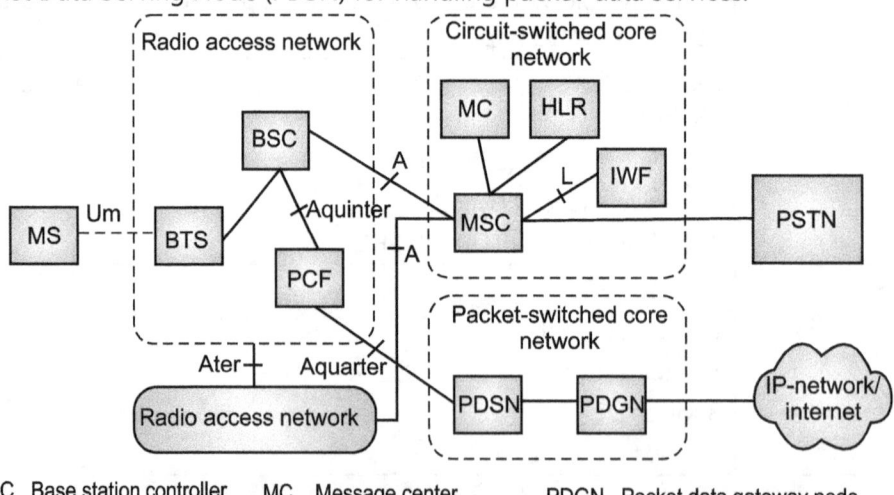

BSC	Base station controller	MC	Message center
BTS	Base transceiver station	MS	Mobile station
HLR	Home location register	MSC	Mobile switching center
IWF	Inter working function	PCF	Packet control function

PDGN	Packet data gateway node
PDSN	Packet data support node
PSTN	Packet switched telephone network

Fig. 3.8 : Generic CDMA2000 system architecture

3.8.3 Spectrum

- The spectrum requirements for a CDMA2000 system have their roots in IS-95, but some differences exist.

- A comparison for spectrum requirements between IS-95, CDMA2000-1×RTT, and EVDO carriers is shown in Fig. 3.9.

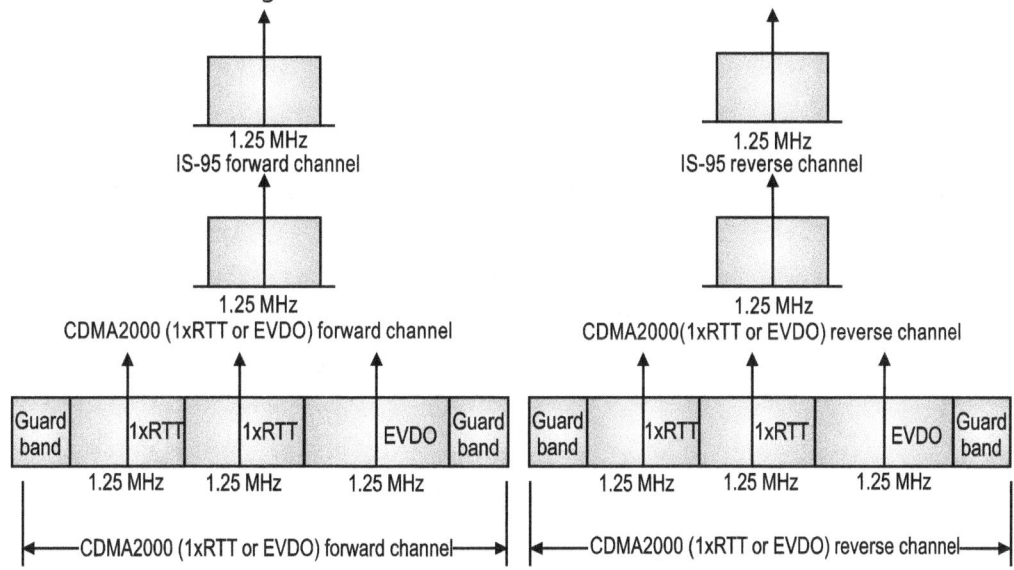

Fig. 3.9 : 1 × RTT and EVDO

Table 3.6

Wireless Data Tech.	Channel BW	Duplex	Infrastructure Change	Requires New Spectrum	Requires New Handsets
IS-95B	1.25 MHz	FDD	Require new software in BSC	No	Yes, new handsets will work on IS-95B at 64 kbps and IS-95A at 14.4 Kbps. Cdma one phones can work in IS-95B at 14.4 Kbps
Cdma2000 1xRTT	1.25 MHz	FDD	Requires new s\w in backbone and new channel cards at base stations. Also need to build a new packet service node.	No	Yes, new handsets will work on 1xRTT at 144 Kbps, IS-95B at 64 Kbps, IS-95A at 14.4 Kbps. Older handsets can work in 1xRTT but at lower speeds.

... Contd

| Cdma2000 1xEV (DO & DV) | 1.25 MHz | FDD | Requires s\w and digital card upgrade on 1xRTT networks | No | Yes, new handsets can work on 1xEV at 2.4 Mbps, 1xRTT at 144 Kbps, IS-95B at 64 Kbps, IS-95A at 14.4 Kbps. Older handsets can work in 1xEV but at lower speeds. |
| Cdma2000 3xRTT | 3.75 MHz | FDD | Requires backbone modifications and new channel cards at base stations. | Maybe | Yes, new handsets will work on 95A at 14.4 Kbps, 95B at 64 Kbps, 1xRTT at 144 Kbps, 3xRTT at 2 Mbps. Older handsets can work in 3x but at lower speeds. |

- The channel depicted in the Fig. 3.9 indicates that for whatever version of CDMA2000-1× the operator decides to deploy, it can be overlaid onto the existing IS-95 channel through a 1:1 or N:1 upgrade. Concurrently, an EVDO system can be overlaid onto an existing 1xRTT network in a 1 : 1 or N : 1 method as well. CDMA2000-1x introduces several enhancements, including a reverse pilot channel.

- When the decision is made to migrate to an EVDO system, the operator allocates its own specific spectrum for EVDO and thus operates on its own channel, which is effectively an overlay system. Depending on the plan, the CDMA2000 channel locations will need to be though in advance.

3.9 TD-CDMA

- Time Division- Code Division Multiple Access is part of the UMTS standard for the 3rd Generation of mobile communications (3G). TD-CDMA is also referred to as UMTS UTRA TDD High Chip Rate. TD-CDMA uses unpaired spectrum. The uplink and the downlink are both accommodated on the same frequency. This makes a flexible allocation of resources to the uplink and downlink possible to accommodate asymmetric services.

- TD-CDMA is best suited to accommodate users with a demand for high data rates and low mobility (stationary/pedestrian) in hot spot areas.

- TD-CDMA, also referred to as HCR TDD and UMTS TDD, is an IMT-2000–compliant air-interface specification using packet data. The TD-CDMA system interfaces with a GSM/UMTS core network, which allows it to be overlaid on top of the existing network or built as a new system.

- UMTS TDD uses many of the same basic parameters as UMTS FDD. The same 5 MHz channel bandwidths are used. UMTS TDD also uses direct sequence spread spectrum and different users and what can be termed "logical channels" are separated using different spreading codes. Only when the receiver uses the same code in the correlation process, is the data recovered. In W-CDMA all other logical channels using different spreading codes appear as noise on the channel and ultimately limit the capacity of the system. In UMTS TDD, a scheme known as multi user detection (MUD) is employed in the receiver and improves the removal of the interfering codes, allowing higher data rates and capacity.

- In addition to the separation of users by using different logical channels as a result of the different spreading codes, further separation between users may be provided by allocating different time slots. There are 15 time slots in UMTS TDD. Of these, three are used for overhead such as signalling, etc and this leaves twelve time slots for user traffic. In each timeslot there can be 16 codes. Capacity is allocated to users on demand, using a two dimensional matrix of timeslots and codes.

- In order for UMTS TDD to achieve the best overall performance, the transport format, i.e. the modulation and forward error correction can be altered for each user. The schemes are chosen by the network, and will depend on the signal characteristics in both directions. Higher order forms of modulation enable higher data speeds to be accommodated, but they are less resilient to noise and interference, and this means that the higher data rate modulation schemes are only used when signal strengths are high. Additionally the levels of forward error correction can be changed. When errors are likely, i.e. when signal strengths are low or interference levels are high, Similarly higher levels of forward error correction are needed under low require additional data to be sent and this slows the payload transfer rate. Thus it is possible to achieve much higher data transfer rates when signals are strong and interference levels are low.

3.9.1 Generic TD-CDMA Architecture

- A TD-CDMA network architecture is very similar to other IMT-2000 networks. In fact, the RAN interface is the primary difference, where the core network uses Releases 99, 4, and 5.

- Fig. 3.10 shows a sample TD-CDMA network that interfaces with an SGSN, enabling it to be used as a data-solution offering for a GSM/GPRS/EDGE, WCDMA, or even TD-SCDMA systems.

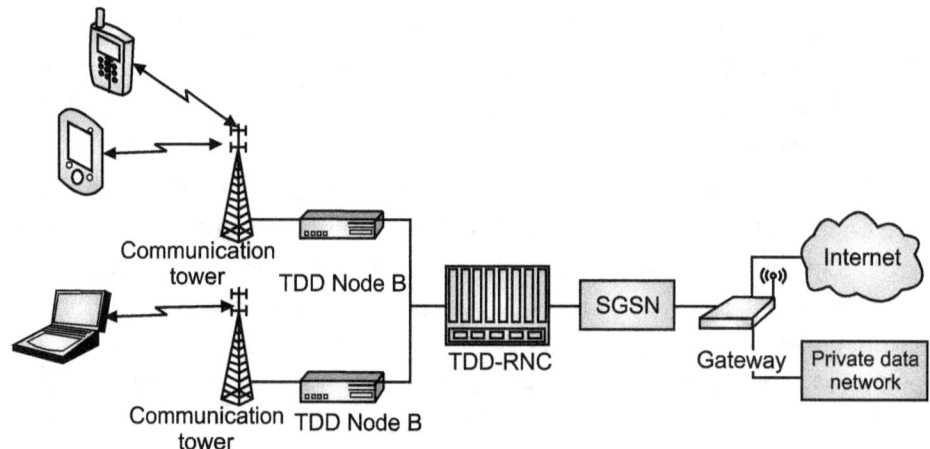

Fig. 3.10 : TD-CDMA system architecture

3.9.2 Radio Network

- TD-CDMA supports both circuit and packet services and is designed primarily to support the asymmetric characteristics of IP data, enabling broadband to the edge of the network.

- TD-CDMA uses TDD, and therefore, uplink and downlink traffic share the same physical radio channel. However, each radio channel has 15 time slots.

- Additionally, in each time slot, up to 16 separate codes, which are orthogonal to each other, can be transmitted, where each user can be allocated individual codes or groups of codes for higher data throughput.

- Uplink and downlink channel allocation can be done by the system or the operator. A minimum of one uplink and one downlink always needs to be allocated per TD-CDMA carrier.

- In order to support both packet and circuit services, TD-CDMA uses both shared channels and dedicated channels. This is in comparison with an FDD system such as WCDMA, which supports only dedicated channels on the uplink. TD-CDMA, however, supports shared channels in both directions, enabling it to be more efficient with bursty traffic such as IP traffic.

3.9.3 RAN

- TD-CDMA requires 5 MHz of radio bandwidth to operate a single channel. The 5 MHz of bandwidth as well as the 3.84 Mcps is meant to facilitate coexistence with WCDMA networks, enabling operators to deploy both technologies in the same market. TD-CDMA can operate on all the IMT-2000 frequency bands.

- The channel structure for the TD-CDMA radio access uses TDMA, FDMA, and CDMA. In addition, TD-CDMA uses the same chip rate, modulation, and bandwidth (non-duplex) that are used by WCDMA.

- The heart of the TD-CDMA radio access is the TDD access method. Each radio carrier is divided into 15 time slots, each containing 16 separate and unique codes; this is depicted in Fig. 3.11.

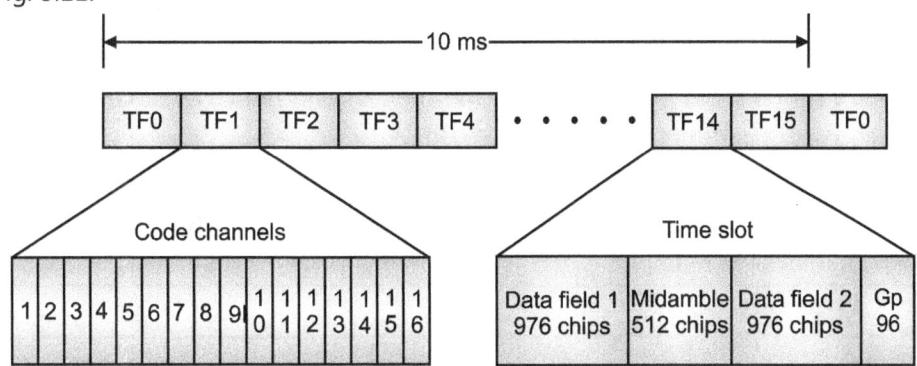

Fig. 3.11 : TD-CDMA channel structure

- The specific uplink and downlink transmissions alternate on the same radio-frequency (RF) channel by allocating time slots to either the uplink or downlink, with the ratio determining the relative uplink and downlink bandwidth.

- An important aspect is that TD-CDMA supports both packet data (IP) and circuit-switched voice, and when it is supporting circuit-switched traffic, it allocates a symmetric uplink and downlink channel.

- Several coding schemes are used with TD-CDMA. In TD-CDMA spreading, scrambling, and channelization codes are used. Spreading codes are an essential element in a TD-CDMA network. There are a total of 16 spreading codes, and all are orthogonal to each other and, like all CDMA codes, are part of a tree. In TDD, the power control in TD-CDMA is done via a closed loop for the downlink, and for the uplink, an open loop method is used.

3.9.4 Handover

For a TD-CDMA system, the parameters needed in the cell-selection monitoring set may include :

- SIR
- Path loss
- Interference power
- Received power level on BCH, etc.

The handover process is implemented in the mobile unit and the RNS. Measurement of serving radio connection downlink performance and candidate cell received signal strengths and quality is made in the UE. The RNS measures the uplink performance, as well as the position information for the UE being served, and uses these measurements in conjunction with defined thresholds and handover strategy to make a handover decision.

3.9.5 Implementation

- Multiple scenarios are possible for implementing a TD-CDMA system. However, all these implementation methods fall into one of two categories: new spectrum or overlay.

- The specific methodology for implementing a TD-CDMA system largely depends on two elements: your business plan relating to the services and the coverage area you want to service and the spectrum that you have to use.

- There are, of course, other considerations, but without spectrum and a valid business plan defining what you want to provide, it is difficult to establish a proper implementation plan.

3.10 TD-SCDMA

- TD-SCDMA is designed for TDD/TDMA operation with synchronous CDMA technology. Its TDD mode supports a flexible uplink/downlink system with flexible switching points to achieve very high use of the allocated spectrum. TD-SCDMA has distinctive features to support the services required in 3G-based systems. The duplexing mode is TDD, combined with CDMA technology. Time slots and spreading codes separate the users in a cell. Each time slot can contain up to 16 users uniquely separated by their own individual spreading code. A key feature of TD-SCDMA is that the uplink is received synchronously in the base station, allowing better channel separation and the use of truly orthogonal codes

- In addition to TDMA and CDMA, TD-SCDMA includes support for innovative use of key technologies such as smart antennas, joint detection, and dynamic channel allocation to achieve near optimal performance, as follows:
  - Eliminate Multiple Access Interference (MAI).
  - Minimize intra-cell and inter-cell interference.
  - Support high data rates (up to 2 Mb/s).
  - Support dynamic traffic and applications with a flexible uplink and downlink design.
  - Provide large cell coverage (up to 40 Km in radius).
  - Support high mobility users (up to 120 Km/h).
  - Achieve high spectrum efficiency.

3.10.1 System Architecture

- The fundamental architecture for a TD-SCDMA wireless system has a similar set of network components as all 3G networks. TD-SCDMA uses a 3GPP core network while at the RAN and therefore can be connected to an existing GSM, WCDMA, or TD-CDMA network.

- However, the primary implication is to interface with an existing GSM network, providing a migration path to 3G. The RAN portion of the TD-SCDMA, node B, network employs a combination of FDMA, TDMA, and CDMA protocols.

- Fig. 3.12 is a general depiction of a TD-SCDMA network that interfaces with a 3GPP core network. Only one TD-SCDMA cell is shown; other radio access systems are not shown, but they could be included easily, provided that they interface at the MSC/SGSN.

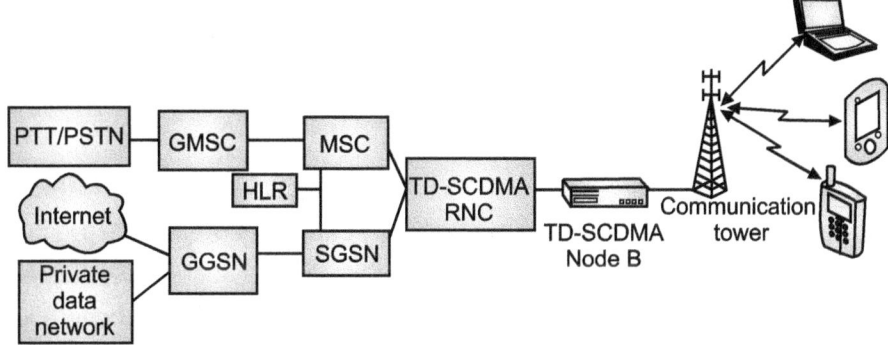

Fig. 3.12 : TD-SCDMA system architecture

- TD-SCDMA has an IP-based network following Release 4 and Release 5 for UMTS. The use of an IP-based core network facilitates many services and addresses the issue of interfacing with numerous appliances and services in the future.

- TD-SCDMA uses TDD as the access method, allowing for both asynchronous and synchronous operation.

- Because of the TD-SCDMA is a TDD network, it needs to reduce interference through a combination of interference-mitigation techniques that include the use of "smart" antennas and joint detection (mobile rake receiver) and the previously mentioned uplink synchronization. All these techniques help to reduce interference, thereby increasing pole capacity.

- The RAN interface only requires the use of 1.6 MHz of spectrum, enabling it to have multiple carriers in the same bandwidth as a WCDMA, CDMA2000, or TD-CDMA carrier. There are two variations to TD-SCDMA: TSM and LCR. LCR is low chip rate and requires that Release 4 be implemented in the core network. A TSM TD-SCDMA system for mobile communication involves leveraging a GSM core platform.

- TD-SCDMA is designed currently to operate in the 2010- to 2025-MHz frequency band, but since it is IMT-2000-compliant, it is possible, via the specification, to operate in all IMT-2000 bands.

- An important aspect of the all-IP architecture is the fact that the user equipment is greatly enhanced. Significant logic is placed within the UE. In fact, the UE supports the Session Initiation Protocol (SIP). The UE effectively becomes an SIP user agent. As such, the UE has far greater control of services than previously.

- TD-SCDMA supports circuit-switched services in addition to packet (IP) services. Circuit-switched rates are defined as 12.2, 64, 144.4, 384, and 2048 kbps. Packet-data rates are defined as 9.6, 64, 144.4, 384, and 2048 kbps.

- The radio spectrum required for a TD-SCDMA network can begin with as simple as 1.6 MHz of contiguous spectrum for an individual channel, with a possible use of a guard band of 100 to 200 kHz.

- The guard-band requirements will need to be specified when differing technologies are spectrally adjacent to each other. In many countries around the world, TDD spectrum has been allocated for potential use for mobility. In China, where TD-SCDMA is being sponsored heavily, a total of 155 MHz of frequency bandwidth has been allocated for TDD.

- Simple math indicates that with a 1.6-MHz carrier, a total of 96 unique TD-SCDMA carriers are possible.

3.10.2 Channel Structure

- For time division synchronous code division multiple access (TD-SCDMA) system, as is illustrated in figure below, radio frame has a period of 10 ms, which can be divided into two subframes, with 5 ms's duration for each. Furthermore, each subframe is comprised of seven normal and three special time slots. Due to its time division duplex (TDD) nature, it can support asymmetry service, such as download. In the figure, time slots for downlink and uplink are colored with blue and green, respectively. The yellow colored time slots indicate that they can be flexibly used as downlink or uplink. In addition, all the gaps are grey colored.

- Each normal time slot, such as TS0, TS1, ..., TS6, has two data fields, including 352 chips for each, spaced by a 144 chips long midamble, and appended by a 16 chips long gap at the end. The number of symbol carried by each data field depends on the spreading factor, which can be 1, 2, 4, 8, 16 for uplink and 1, 16 for downlink. Correspondingly, the symbol number can be 352, 176, 88, 44, 22 for uplink and 352, 22 for downlink. The midamble is just a alias of training sequence in TD-SCDMA system, which is used for channel estimation for both downlink and uplink. Hence, it is not spreaded nor scrambled before transmission.

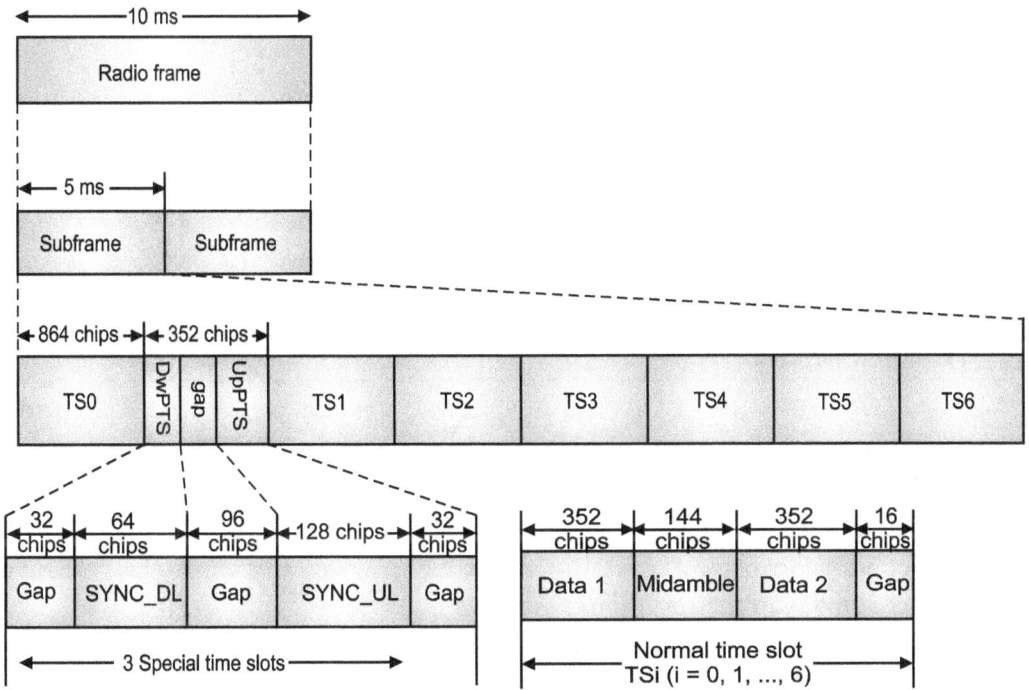

Fig. 3.13 : TD-SCDMA channel structure

- A total of 16 spreading codes are used with TD-SCDMA. The codes are all orthogonal to each other and, like all CDMA codes, are part of a tree. The tree for the code sequence dictates the potential data throughput that can occur.

3.10.3 Interference-Mitigation Techniques

- TD-SCDMA, because it uses a TDD method for access, has unique self-interference problems that need to be addressed in order to take advantage of system capabilities. To help mitigate interference, TD-SCDMA uses a combination of interference-mitigation techniques that include the use of "smart" antennas and joint detection, terminal (uplink) synchronization, and dynamic channel allocation. All these techniques help to reduce interference, thereby increasing pole capacity:
  - (a) Smart antennas
  - (b) Joint detection
  - (c) Terminal synchronization

3.10.4 Handover

For a TD-SCDMA system, the parameters needed in the cell-selection monitoring set may include:
- SIR
- Path loss

- Interference power
- Received power level on BCH, etc.

The handover process is implemented in the mobile unit and the RNS. Measurements of serving radio connection downlink performance and candidate cell received signal strengths and quality are made in the UE. The RNS measures the uplink performance as well as the position information for the UE being served and uses these measurements in conjunction with defined thresholds and handover strategy to make a hand-over decision.

3.11 COMMONALITY AMONG WCDMA, CDMA2000, TD-CDMA, AND TD-SCDMA

- WCDMA, CDMA2000, TD-CDMA, and TD-SCDMA are part of the IMT-2000 platform specification and have many similarities. All four platforms use CDMA technology and require, in their final versions, a total of either 1.25, 1.6, or 5 MHz of spectrum.
- All four systems will be able to interoperate with one another, and it is possible for a wireless operator to deploy several or all of the 3G platforms in the same network, provided that the requisite spectrum is available.
- CDMA2000 and TD-SCDMA can be deployed jointly. The starting point for WCDMA, TD-CDMA, and TD-SCDMA is GSM 2G network, as does CDMA2000 with IS-95.
- All systems have a migration path from existing 2G platforms to 3G.
- All four platforms are designed to operate in multiple frequency bands and can operate in the same frequency bands, provided that the spectrum is available.
- Therefore, the commonalities can be summed up in the following brief points that were introduced at the beginning of this unit :
    - Compatibility of service within IMT-2000 and other fixed networks.
    - High quality.
    - Worldwide common frequency band.
    - Small terminals for worldwide use.
    - Multimedia application services and terminals.
    - Improved spectrum efficiency.
    - Flexibility for evolution to the next generation of wireless systems.
    - Worldwide roaming capability.
    - High-speed packet-data rates.
    - 2 Mbps for fixed environment.
    - 384 kbps for pedestrian.
    - 144 kbps for vehicular traffic.
    - Global standard.

- Following Table 5.7 gives the detailed comparison

Table 5.7

Specifications	TD-SCDMA	WCDMA	CDMA2000
Full Form	Time Division-Synchronous Code Division Multiple Access, Utilizes concept of TDMA,FDMA,CDMA and SDMA	Wideband Code Division Multiple Access	Also known as IMT-2000, as the specifications introduced in service in the years 2000-2002. Supports 1x EV-DO (Evolution Data Only) and 1x EV-DV (Evolution Data and Voice)
RF Carrier Frequency	It is utilized in China, uses frequencies between 1785-2220 MHz	For 2100 MHz Band: 1920-1980 Uplink, 2110-2170 downlink, For 1900 MHz band: 1850-1910 Uplink, 1930-1990 Downlink,	806-960 MHz, 1710-2025 MHz, 2110-2200 MHz 2500-2690 MHz
Channel Bandwidth	Uplink and downlink share 1.6 MHz band(for 1.28 Mcps) with 7 timeslots per frame, 16 codes per timeslot. 5MHz band is also specified for 3.84Mcps TDD case.	5 MHz	1.25 MHz
Frame Structure	Super frame=720ms, radio frame=10 ms, sub frame=5ms	10 ms	20 ms
Duplex technique	TDD	FDD	FDD
Spectrum Allocation	Need unpaired spectrum for both Downlink(DL) and Uplink(UL)	Need paired spectrum one for UL and the other for DL	>Need paired spectrum one for UL and the other for DL

...Conti.

Spectrum Efficiency	For asymmetric traffic,the slots are allocated according to uasage and hence single spectrum is efficiently used for both DL and UL(TDD case).	For asymmetric traffic, as the bands are allocated dedicately for DL and UL, the spectrum gets wasted when there is no data to be send/receive.	For asymmetric traffic, as the bands are allocated dedicately for DL and UL, the spectrum gets wasted when there is no data to be send/receive.
Chip rate per carrier	1.28 Mchips/sec	3.84 Mchips/sec	1.2288 Mchips/sec
Modulation supported	QPSK,8PSK,16QAM	QPSK, 16QAM	QPSK,8PSK,16QAM
Spreading Factor	1/2/4/8/16	4 to 256	-
Forum website link	www.tdscdma-forum.org/en/	www.umts-forum.org/	www.umts-forum.org/

QUESTIONS

1. Differentiate between 2G and 3G.
2. Explain the IMT 2000.
3. Write a short note on : (i) UMTS (ii) 2G (iii) 3G (iv) UMTS services
4. Explain the project (3GPP) of UMTS.
5. Write a short note on the UMTS air Interface.
6. Draw and Explain the 3GPP release 1999 network architecture.
7. Draw and Explain the 3GPP release 4 network architecture.
8. Explain the 3GPP release 5 architecture and draw the 3GPP IP multimedia network architecture.
9. Write a short note on CDMA 2000.
10. Draw and explain the system architecture of CDMA 2000.
11. Explain the TD-CDMA of the UMTS standard for the 3G of mobile communication.
12. Draw the generic architecture of TD-CDMA.
13. Write a short note on : (i) Radio network (ii) RAN (iii) Handover
14. Write a short note on TD-SCDMA and draw the system architecture of TD-SCDMA.
15. Draw and explain the TD-SCDMA channel structure.
16. Differentiate between the TD-SCDMA, WCDMA and CDMA 2000.

LONG TERM EVOLUTION

4.1 INTRODUCTION

- LTE, Long Term Evolution, the successor to UMTS and HSPA is now being deployed and is the way forwards for high speed cellular services. In its first forms it was a 3G or as some would call it a 3.99G technology, but with further additions the technology fulfilled the requirements for a 4G standard. In this form it was referred to as LTE Advanced.

- Long–Term Evolution (LTE) is an exciting new wireless mobility technology that has thrust itself upon the industry. This unit will cover many of the important areas of LTE it self.

- The main goal of LTE is to provide a high data rate, low latency and packet optimized radio access technology supporting flexible bandwidth deployments. Same time its network architecture has been designed with the goal to support packet–switched traffic with seamless mobility and great quality of service.

LTE has several advantages as listed below:

- **High Throughput:** High data rates can be achieved in both downlink as well as uplink. This causes high throughput.

- **Low Latency:** Time required to connect to the network is in range of a few hundred milliseconds and power saving states can now be entered and exited very quickly.

- **FDD and TDD in the Same Platform:** Frequency Division Duplex (FDD) and Time Division Duplex (FDD), both schemes can be used on same platform.

- **Superior End–User Experience:** Optimized signaling for connection establishment and other air interface and mobility management procedures have further improved the user experience. Reduced latency (to 10 ms) for better user experience.

- Seamless Connection: LTE will also support seamless connection to existing networks such as GSM, CDMA and WCDMA.

- **Plug and Play:** The user does not have to manually install drivers for the device. Instead system automatically recognizes the device, loads new drivers for the hardware if needed, and begins to work with the newly connected device.

- **Simple Architecture:** Because of Simple architecture low operating expenditure (OPEX).

- LTE is also capable of interworking with legacy wireless systems as well.

There are some more facts about LTE summarized below.

- LTE is the successor technology not only of UMTS but also of CDMA 2000.

- LTE is important because it will bring up to 50 times performance improvement and much better spectral efficiency to cellular networks.

- LTE introduced to get higher data rates, 300Mbps peak downlink and 75 Mbps peak uplink. In a 20MHz carrier, data rates beyond 300Mbps can be achieved under very good signal conditions.

- LTE is an ideal technology to support high date rates for the services such as voice over IP (VOIP), streaming multimedia, videoconferencing or even a high–speed cellular modem.

- LTE uses both Time Division Duplex (TDD) and Frequency Division Duplex (FDD) mode. In FDD uplink and downlink transmission used different frequency, while in TDD both uplink and downlink use the same carrier and are separated in Time.

- LTE supports flexible carrier bandwidths, from 1.4 MHz up to 20 MHz as well as both FDD and TDD. LTE designed with a scalable carrier bandwidth from 1.4 MHz up to 20 MHz which bandwidth is used depends on the frequency band and the amount of spectrum available with a network operator.

- All LTE devices have to support (MIMO) Multiple Input Multiple Output transmissions, which allow the base station to transmit several data streams over the same carrier simultaneously.

- All interfaces between network nodes in LTE are now IP based, including the backhaul connection to the radio base stations. This is great simplification compared to earlier technologies that were initially based on E1/T1, ATM and frame relay links, with most of them being narrowband and expensive.

- Quality of Service (QoS) mechanism have been standardized on all interfaces to ensure that the requirement of voice calls for a constant delay and bandwidth, can still be met when capacity limits are reached.

- Works with GSM/EDGE/UMTS systems utilizing existing 2G and 3G spectrum and new spectrum. Supports hand–over and roaming to existing mobile networks.

4.2 LTE ECOSYSTEM

- LTE has many components that can make up the network; however, there are five main elements.

- Fig. 4.1 shows an LTE network reference model, consisting of LTE entities (UE and eNB) and EPC entities (S–GW, P–GW, MME, HSS, PCRF, SPR, OCS and OFCS). A PDN is an internal or external IP domain of the operator that a UE wants to communicate with, and provides the UE with services such as the Internet or IP Multimedia Subsystem (IMS)

- The high–level network architecture of LTE is comprised of following three main components:

- The User Equipment (UE).

- The Evolved UMTS Terrestrial Radio Access Network (E–UTRAN).

- The Evolved Packet Core (EPC).

- The evolved packet core communicates with packet data networks in the outside world such as the internet, private corporate networks or the IP multimedia subsystem. The interfaces between the different parts of the system are denoted Uu, S1 and SGi as shown in Fig. 4.1

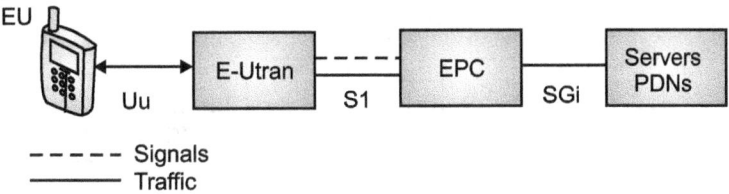

Fig. 4.1(a) : Basic LTE network

- **The User Equipment (UE):** The internal architecture of the user equipment for LTE is identical to the one used by UMTS and GSM which is actually a Mobile Equipment (ME).

The E–Utran (The Access Network):

- The architecture of evolved UMTS Terrestrial Radio Access Network (E–UTRAN) is shown in Fig. 4.1(b)

- The E–Utran handles the radio communications between the mobile and the evolved packet core and just has one component, the evolved base stations, called eNodeB or eNB. Each eNB is a base station that controls the mobiles in one or more cells. The base station that is communicating with a mobile is known as its serving eNB.

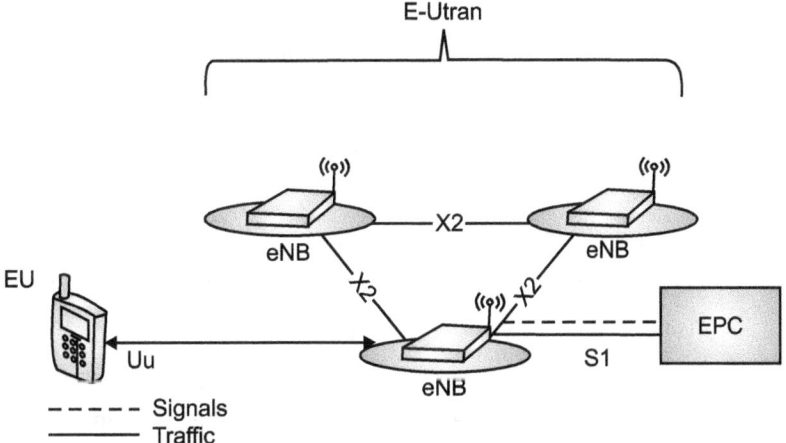

Fig. 4.1(b) : E–Utran

The architecture of Evolved Packet Core (EPC) has been shown in Fig. 4.1(c)

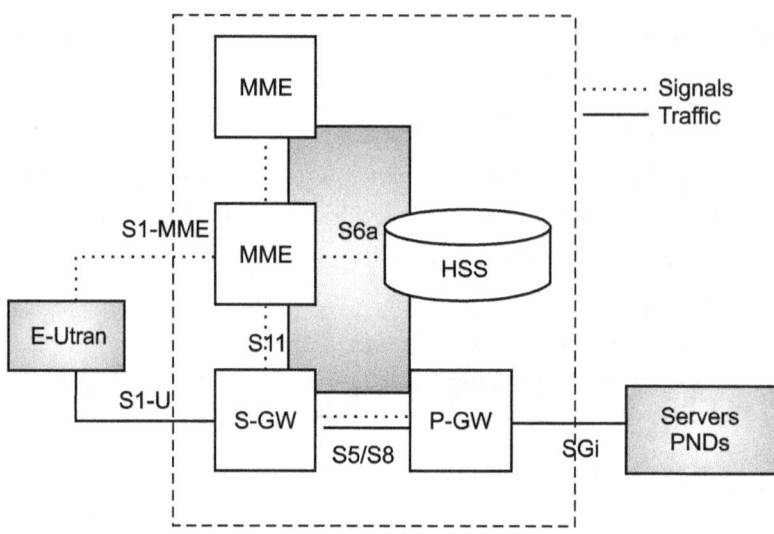

Fig. 4.1(c) : Evolved Packet Core (EPC)

- The Home Subscriber Server (HSS) component has been carried forward from UMTS and GSM and is a central database that contains information about all the network operator's subscribers.

- The Packet Data Network (PDN) Gateway (P–GW) communicates with the outside world ie. Packet Data Networks (PDN), using SGi interface. Each packet data network is identified by an Access Point Name (APN). The PDN gateway has the same role as the GPRS support node (GGSN) and the serving GPRS Support Node (SGSN) with UMTS and GSM.

- The Serving Gateway (S-GW) acts as a router, and forwards data between the base station and the PDN gateway.

- The Mobility Management Entity (MME) controls the high–level operation of the mobile by means of signalling messages and Home Subscriber Server (HSS).

- The Policy Control and Charging Rules Function (PCRF) is a component which is not shown in the above diagram but it is responsible for policy control decision–making, as well as for controlling the flow–based charging functionalities in the Policy Control Enforcement Function (PCEF), which resides in the P-GW.

- At a high level, Table 4.1 tries to identify some of the major changes as compared to some of the other wireless access technologies. Because LTE is a flat architecture utilizing an all IP signaling scheme it is able to facilitate faster data rates as well as significantly reduced latency enabling it to be very suitable for video applications.

Table 4.1 : Wireless Access Technology Comparison

	WCDMA	HSPA	HSPA+	LTE	LTE Advanced
Max downlink speed	384 k	14 M	28 M	100 M	1 G
Max uplink speed	128 k	5.7 M	11 M	50 M	500 M
Spectrum (FDD)	5 MHz	5 MHz	5 MHz	10 MHz	100 MHz
Latency round trip	150 ms	100 ms	50 ms (max)	~10 ms	~10 ms
3GPP release	Rel 99/4	Rel 5/6	Rel 7	Rel 8/9	Rel 10
Access method	CDMA	CDMA	CDMA	OFDMA/SC–FDMA	OFDMA/SC–FDMA

- In the LTE ecosystem, once the UE has acquired the network it is basically an always–on connection. In the always–on mode even if the UE is in idle mode, it still has its IP address; and the connection between the Serving Gateway (SGW) and Packet Data Network Gateway (PGW) remains. However, the connection between the SGW and the eNodeB may be torn in the idle mode. The always–on connection even in idle mode enables fast session setup and is ideal for applications requiring a fast response time.

- When looking at Fig. 4.1 several new elements are defined. However, one key change is that the functionality that was associated with the RNC in CDMA and the NodeB in WCDMA/HSPA has now moved to the eNodeB in LTE. This puts a lot of the decisions for processing data sessions at the edge of the network in LTE.

- LTE can operate either as a TDD or FDD system. LTE at this time is typically deployed as an FDD network. However the TDD configuration is also possible and enables LTE to be deployed in unpaired spectrum configurations like that associated with WiMAX.

- The amount of spectrum, or rather bandwidth, the LTE can occupy is flexible. Specifically LTE is so structured that it can operate with a variety of Common Carriers (CC).

- The typical deployment for LTE involves a 10 MHz channel that is deployed in an FDD configuration as a 10×10 channel.

- However, LTE can have different common carriers. There are a total of 6 CC bandwidths associated with LTE and they are 1.4, 3, 5, 10, 15, and 20–MHz–wide CCs. The designation of the bandwidth is for a single CC whether it is an FDD or TDD deployment.

- Therefore, a 5 MHz LTE CC for an FDD system is made up of two 5 MHz paired channels while a TDD system only has a single 5 MHz channel used jointly for transmit and receive.

- Within LTE there is a more robust adaptation for different Quality of Service (QoS) is possible, where there are nine Quality Class Identifiers (QCI) defined as per standard.

4.3 LTE STANDARDS

- LTE is a standards–based wireless access system. The standards for LTE are driven by the 3GPP organization.

- As with all standards, there are several major releases, with release 9 being the primary release at this time and release 10 in the near future.

- Additional releases will follow release 10; however, for the moment we will only briefly discuss release 9 and release 10, LTE Advanced.

- Each LTE release has its unique attributes and benefits which are highlighted in Table 4.2.

Table 4.2 : LTE Releases Major Features

Release 8	Release 8 introduced LTE for the first time, with a completely new radio interface and core network, enabling substantially improved data performance compared with previous systems. Highlights included: • Up to 300Mbit/s downlink and 75Mbit/s uplink. • Latency down to 10ms. • Implementation in bandwidths of 1.4, 3 ,5 , 10, 15 or 20MHz, to allow for different deployment scenarios. • Orthogonal Frequency Domain Multiple Access (OFDMA) downlink. • Single–Carrier Frequency Domain Multiple Access (SC–FDMA) uplink. • Multiple Input Multiple Output (MIMO) antennas. • Flat radio network architecture, with no equivalent to the GSM BSC or UMTS RNC, and functionality distributed among the base stations (eNodeBs). • All IP core network, the System Architecture Evolution (SAE).
Release 9	Release 9 brought a number of refinements to features introduced in Release 8, along with new developments to the network architecture and new service features. These included: • Introduction of LTE femtocells in the form of the Home eNodeB (HeNB) • Self Organising Network (SON) features, such as optimisation of the random access channel • Evolved Multimedia Broadcast and Multicast Service (eMBMS) for the efficient delivery of the same multimedia content to multiple destinations • Location Services (LCS) to pinpoint the location of a mobile device.

...Conti.

Release 10	Release 10 provided a substantial uplift to the capacity and throughput of the LTE system and also took steps to improve the system performance for mobile devices located at some distance from a base station. Notable features included:
	• Up to 3Gbit/s downlink and 1.5Gbit/s uplink
	• Carrier Aggregation (CA), allowing the combination of up to five separate carriers to enable bandwidths up to 100MHz
	• Higher order MIMO antenna configurations up to 8×8 downlink and 4×4 uplink
	• Relay nodes to support Heterogeneous Networks ("HetNets") containing a wide variety of cell sizes
	• Enhanced Inter–Cell Interference Coordination (eICIC) to improve performance towards the edge of cells.

4.4 RADIO SPECTRUM

- There is a growing number of LTE frequency bands that are being designated as possibilities for use with LTE.

- FDD spectrum requires pair bands, one of the uplink and one for the downlink, and TDD requires a single band as uplink and downlink are on the same frequency but time separated. As a result, there are different LTE band allocations for TDD and FDD. In some cases these bands may overlap, and it is therefore feasible, although unlikely that both TDD and FDD transmissions could be present on a particular LTE frequency band.

- The greater likelihood is that a single UE or mobile will need to detect whether a TDD or FDD transmission should be made on a given band. UEs that roam may encounter both types on the same band. They will therefore need to detect what type of transmission is being made on that particular LTE band in its current location.

- The different LTE frequency allocations or LTE frequency bands are allocated numbers. Currently the LTE bands between 1 and 22 are for paired spectrum, i.e. FDD, and LTE bands between 33 and 41 are for unpaired spectrum, i.e. TDD.

- There is a large number of allocations or radio spectrum that has been reserved for FDD, frequency division duplex, LTE use.

- The FDD LTE frequency bands are paired to allow simultaneous transmission on two frequencies. The bands also have a sufficient separation to enable the transmitted signals not to unduly impair the receiver performance. If the signals are too close then the receiver may be "blocked" and the sensitivity impaired. The separation must be sufficient to enable the roll–off of the antenna filtering to give sufficient attenuation of the transmitted signal within the receive band.

- Table 4.3 gives LTE bands for FDD configuration. More bands can be and will be added.

Table 4.3 : LTE FDD Bands

LTE Band Number	Uplink (MHz)	Downlink (MHz)	Width of Band (MHz)	Duplex Spacing(MHz)	Band Gap (MHz)
1	1920–1980	2110–2170	60	190	130
2	1850–1910	1930–1990	60	80	20
3	1710–1785	1805–1880	75	95	20
4	1710–1755	2110–2155	45	400	355
5	824–849	869–894	25	45	20
6	830–840	875–885	10	35	25
7	2500–2570	2620–2690	70	120	50
8	880–915	925–960	35	45	10
9	1749.9–1784.9	1844.9–1879.9	35	95	60
10	1710–1770	2110–2170	60	400	340
11	1427.9–1452.9	1475.9–1500.9	20	48	28
12	698–716	728–746	18	30	12
13	777–787	746–756	10	−31	41
14	788–798	758–768	10	−30	40
15	1900–1920	2600–2620	20	700	680
16	2010–2025	2585–2600	15	575	560
17	704–716	734–746	12	30	18
18	815–830	860–875	15	45	30
19	830–845	875–890	15	45	30
20	832–862	791–821	30	−41	71
21	1447.9–1462.9	1495.5–1510.9	15	48	33
22	3410–3500	3510–3600	90	100	10
23	2000–2020	2180–2200	20	180	160
24	1625.5–1660.5	1525–1559	34	−101.5	135.5
25	1850–1915	1930–1995	65	80	15
26	814–849	859–894	30 / 40		10
27	807–824	852–869	17	45	28
28	703–748	758–803	45	55	10
29	n/a	717–728	11		
30	2305–2315	2350–2360	10	45	35
31	452.5–457.5	462.5–467.5	5	10	5

With the interest in TDD LTE, there are several unpaired frequency allocations that are being prepared for LTR TDD use. The TDD LTE bands are unpaired because the uplink and downlink share the same frequency, being time multiplexed. Table 4.4 gives LTE bands for TDD configuration.

Table 4.4 : LTE TDD Bands

LTE Band Number	Allocation (MHz)	Width of Band (MHz)
33	1900–1920	20
34	2010–2025	15
35	1850–1910	60
36	1930–1990	60
37	1910–1930	20
38	2570–2620	50
39	1880–1920	40
40	2300–2400	100
41	2496–2690	194
42	3400–3600	200
43	3600–3800	200
4	703–803	100

- What is always important to consider when determining the band to operate in the wireless access is the selection of the User Equipment (UE). Most UEs are band–specific, even though the chip sets that reside in the devices can operate in any of the designed LTE bands. However, it is the Radio Frequency (RF) component of the UE which needs to match the frequency bands of operation. In reviewing the bands in Table 4.3 and 4.4, the possible bandwidths are different.

- Additionally in Table 4.3 the duplex spacing is unique for each band number; and this is important to note since some of the band numbers have transmit and receive reversed, bands 13 and 14, as compared to other bands.

4.5 LTE ARCHITECTURE

- The LTE architecture is a flat IP network and consists of many elements. The simplified version is shown in Fig. 4.2(a) whereas Fig. 4.2(b) is a more detailed illustration of an LTE network.

- The various major elements comprising an LTE network will be defined. However, the key concept is that the eNodeB now has many of the functions that were associated with a Node B/BSC and the BTS/RNC. All non–LTE network components are referred to as non–3GPP.

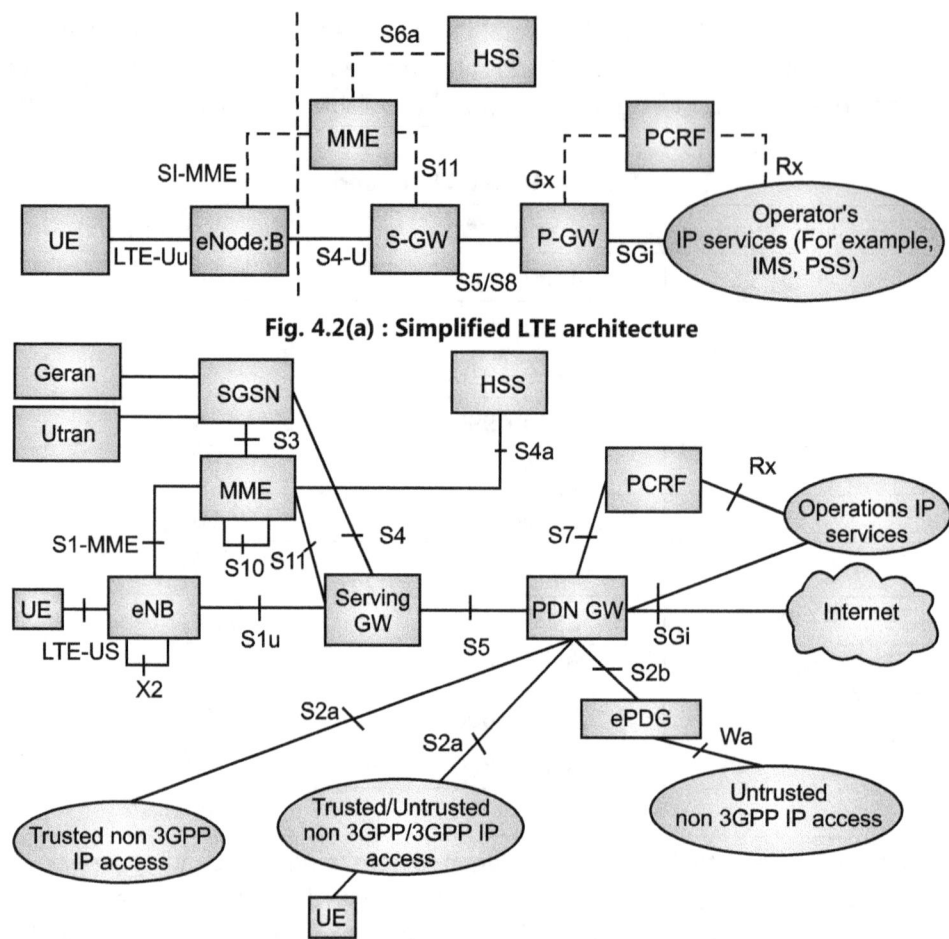

Fig. 4.2(a) : Simplified LTE architecture

Fig. 4.2(b) : Detailed LTE architecture

- At a high level, the network is comprised of the Core Network (EPC) and the access network E–utran. While the CN consists of many logical nodes, the access network is made up of essentially just one node, the evolved NodeB (eNodeB), which connects to the UEs. Each of these network elements is interconnected by means of interfaces that are standardized in order to allow multi–vendor interoperability.

- In an LTE network an eNodeB can be connected to other eNodeBs via an X2 link which facilitates communication between the eNodeBs for handovers and other traffic management functions.

- Several eNodeBs are typically connected to an MME and SGW. The SGW handles the bearer traffic and communicates with a PGW, if required, for service delivery. However, the MME is only involved in the control plane portion and does not handle bearer traffic.

- As mentioned, several eNodeBs will be connected to an MME and SGW. There will be numerous MME and SGWs in an LTE network depending on the amount of eNodeBs and the network configuration.

- Additionally, there can be several PGWs depending on a particular service type or class associated with each PGW.

- You can ultimately break down the LTE network into either the subscriber (UE), radio access network (eNodeBs) or the core network (EPC).

4.6 USER EQUIPMENT (UE)

- The UE is the device that the subscriber to the LTE wireless network interfaces with the most. Typically the UE can be thought of as either a handset, Smartphone, or aircard.

- However, many LTE UE devices are being integrated into appliances, vehicles, and clothing to mention a few alternative UE device locations and types.

- The mobile equipment comprised of the following important modules:

  Mobile Termination (MT): This handles all the communication functions.

  Terminal Equipment (TE): This terminates the data streams.

  Universal Integrated Circuit Card (UICC): This is also known as the SIM card for LTE equipment. It runs an application known as the Universal Subscriber Identity Module (USIM).

- There are five different LTE UE categories that are defined. As can be seen in the table below, the different LTE categories have a wide range in the supported parameters and performance.

Table 4.5 : LTE UE Categories

Parameter	LTE CAT 1	LTE CAT 2	LTE CAT 3	LTE CAT 4	LTE CAT 5
Bandwidth	1.4, 3, 5, 10, 15 and 20				
MIMO	2×2	2×2 4×4	2×2 4×4	2×2 4×4	2×2 4×4
Modulation Uplink	QPSK 16QAM	QPSK 16QAM 64QAM	QPSK 16QAM 64QAM	QPSK 16QAM 64QAM	QPSK 16QAM 64QAM
Modulation Downlink	QPSK, 16QAM, 64QAM				
Data Rate Uplink (Mbps)	5	25	51	75	75
Data Rate Downlink (Mbps)	10	51	10	30	30
Duplexing	FDD H–FDD TDD	FDD H–FDD TDD	FDD H–FDD TDD	FDD H–FDD TDD	FDD H–FDD TDD

- All the LTE UEs can support different bandwidths in addition to TDD and FDD channel configurations. However, the UEs will not support every frequency band listed in the LTE bands.
- The limitation is not due to the LTE components for the UE, but due to the RF components that enable the UE to operate in a specific portion of the radio spectrum band.

4.7 ENHANCED NODE B (eNODEB)

- The eNodeB can be defined as three major components involving the antennas system, radio elements, and digital processing components. The eNodeB therefore provides the physical radio connection between the LTE network and the UE. However, the eNodeB does much more than simply providing a physical connection.
- LTE Mobile communicates with just one base station and one cell at a time and there are following two main functions supported by eNodeB:
- The eNodeB sends and receives radio transmissions to all the mobiles using the analogue and digital signal processing functions of the LTE air interface.
- The eNode B controls the low–level operation of all its mobiles, by sending them signalling messages such as handover commands.
- Each eNodeB connects with the EPC by means of the S1 interface and it can also be connected to nearby base stations by the X2 interface, which is mainly used for signalling and packet forwarding during handover.
- The eNodeB performs all radio resource management functions, such as radio bearer control, radio admission control, radio mobility control, scheduling, and dynamic allocation of resources to UEs in both uplink and downlink. More specifically the eNodeB runs the scheduler, which is one of the most important components in resource allocations with an LTE Network.
- Additionally the eNodeB is connected to both the MME and an SGW through S1 signaling links. The eNodeB routes all user plane data to the appropriate SGW and ensures that all data sent over the radio interface are encrypted.
- Fig. 4.3 shows how a typical eNodeB is connected to an MME, SGW, and another eNodeB via an X2 interface.
- The S1 interface is divided into S1–U and S1–MME. The S1–U is where the traffic data is routed and the S1–MME is where the control information, or, control plane protocol, transverses over. The X2 link, however, is shared directly between eNodeBs and is used to coordinate handovers and data transfers.
- Two modulation formats are used by eNodeB: Orthogonal Frequency Division Multiple Access (OFDMA) for downlink and Single Carrier Frequency Division Multiple Access (SC–FDMA) for uplink.

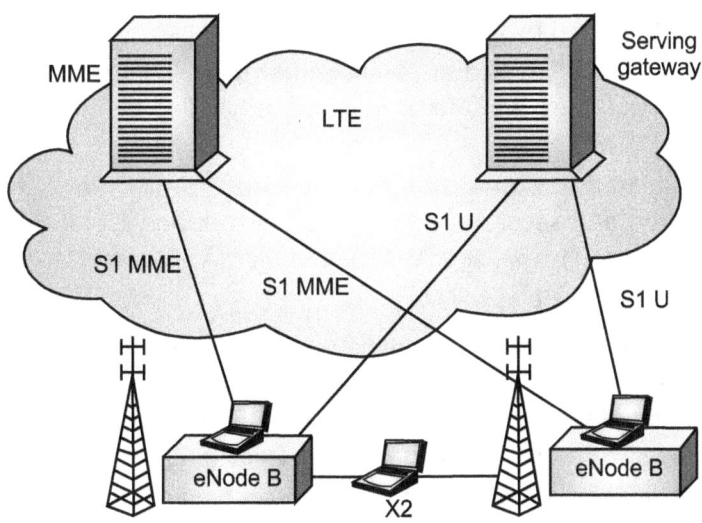

Fig. 4.3 : S1 interface

4.8 CORE NETWORK (EPC)

- The core network (EPC) for LTE consists Mobility Management Entity (MME), SGW, PGW and Home Subscriber Server (HSS) as shown in Fig. 4.3

4.8.1 Mobility Management Element (MME)

- The Mobility Management Entity (MME) is the control node that processes the signaling between the UE and the EPC. The protocols running between the UE and the CN are known as the Non Access Stratum (NAS) protocols.

- The MME keeps track of the UE that is associated with the eNodeBs that are connected to the MME. The UE can be in one of three states that the MME keeps track off:

1. **Connected**
   - UE has registered with the network.
   - UE has established a Radio Resource Connection (RRC).
   - Handovers are network controlled.
   - Measurement reports sent from UE to eNodeB.

2. **Idle**
   - UE has been inactive for an extended period of time.
   - Cell selection and reselection are under complete UE control.
   - UE is not connected to the network and is just monitoring the network for messages.

3. **Dormant**
   - UE is not connected or monitoring the network.
   - UE could be out of service area or powered off.

The main functions supported by the MME can be classified as:

- **Functions Related to Bearer Management:** This includes the establishment, maintenance and release of the bearers and is handled by the session management layer in the NAS protocol.
- **Functions Related to Connection Management:** This includes the establishment of the connection and security between the network and UE and is handled by the connection or mobility management layer in the NAS protocol layer.

The main functions of MME are as below:

- **Network Access Control:** MME manages authentication and authorization for the UE. It also facilitates UE access to the network to gain IP connectivity.
- **Radio Resource Management:** MME works with the HSS and the RAN to decide the appropriate radio Resource Management strategy (RRM) that can be UE–specific.
- **Mobility Management:** One of the most complex functions MME performs. Providing seamless inter–working has multiple use cases such as Inter–eNB and Inter–RAT, among others. The use cases become more complex depending on a change in MME, S–GW, P–GW or inter–working across other wireless networks.
- **Roaming Management:** MME supports outbound and inbound roaming subscribers from other LTE/EPC systems and legacy networks.
- **UE Reach–ability:** MME manages communication with the UE and HSS to provide UE reach–ability and activity–related information.
- **Tracking Area Management:** Allocates and reallocates a tracking area identity list to the UE.
- **Lawful Intercept:** Since MME manages the control plane of the network, MME can provide the whereabouts of a UE to a law enforcement monitoring facility.
- **Load Balancing Between S–GWs:** Directs UEs entering an S–GW pool area to an appropriate S–GW. This achieves load balancing between S–GWs.

4.8.2 Serving Gateway (SGW)

- All user IP packets are transferred through the Serving Gateway, which serves as the local mobility anchor for the data bearers when the UE moves between eNodeBs.
- It also retains the information about the bearers when the UE is in the idle state (known as "EPS Connection Management IDLE" [ECM–IDLE]) and temporarily buffers downlink data while the MME initiates paging of the UE to reestablish the bearers.
- In addition, the S–GW performs some administrative functions in the visited network such as collecting information for charging (for example, the volume of data sent to or received from the user) and lawful interception.
- It also serves as the mobility anchor for interworking with other 3GPP technologies such as general packet radio service (GPRS) and UMTS.
- The SGW also serves as the mobility anchor for interworking with other 3GPP technologies like UMTS.

4.8.3 Packet Data Network Gateway (PGW)

- The PDN Gateway is responsible for IP address allocation for the UE, as well as QoS enforcement and flow–based charging according to rules from the PCRF.
- It is responsible for the filtering of downlink user IP packets into the different QoS–based bearers. This is performed based on Traffic Flow Templates (TFTs).
- The P-GW performs QoS enforcement for Guaranteed Bit Rate (GBR) bearers.
- It also serves as the mobility anchor for interworking with non–3GPP technologies such as CDMA2000 and WiMAX network

4.8.4 Home Subscriber Server (HSS)

- The Home Subscriber Server contains users' SAE subscription data such as the EPS-subscribed QoS profile and any access restrictions for roaming. Thus HSS is similar in function to a Home Location Register (HLR) except that it is IP–based.
- It also holds information about the PDNs to which the user can connect. This could be in the form of an Access Point Name (APN) (which is a label according to DNS naming conventions describing the access point to the PDN) or a PDN address (indicating subscribed IP addresses).
- In addition the HSS holds dynamic information such as the identity of the MME to which the user is currently attached or registered. The HSS may also integrate the Authentication Center (AUC), which generates the vectors for authentication and security keys.

4.8.5 Policy Control and Charging Rules Function (PCRF)

- The Policy Control and Charging Rules Function is responsible for policy control decision–making, as well as for controlling the flow–based charging functionalities in the Policy Control Enforcement Function (PCEF), which resides in the P-GW.
- The PCRF provides the QoS authorization (QoS Class Identifier [QCI] and bit rates) that decides how a certain data flow will be treated in the PCEF and ensures that this is in accordance with the user's subscription profile.
- The PCRF while not technically part of the LTE core network plays an important role in delivering services for the subscriber.

4.9 RADIO CHANNEL COMPONENTS

- In order that data can be transported across the LTE radio interface, various "channels" are used. These are used to segregate the different types of data and allow them to be transported across the radio access network in an orderly fashion.
- Effectively the different channels provide interfaces to the higher layers within the LTE protocol structure and enable an orderly and defined segregation of the data.
- There are three categories into which the various data channels may be grouped.
  - **Physical Channels:** These are transmission channels that carry user data and control messages.

- **Transport Channels:** The physical layer transport channels offer information transfer to Medium Access Control (MAC) and higher layers.
- **Logical Channels:** Provide services for the Medium Access Control (MAC) layer within the LTE protocol structure.

- The radio access medium is the Uu, air interface layer, that is shown in Fig. 4.4. The Uu is the air interface between UE and eNodeB and transports all signaling messages and data between the UE and the eNodeB.

- The radio access medium involves both layer 1 and layer 2 components. The layer 1 is the actual radio communication or Physical Layer (PHY) that is responsible for functions like Modulation, Error Correction, interleaving, and HARQ.

- The layer 2 components consist of three functional areas. The first is the Packet Data Convergence Protocol (PDCP), which provides header compression and encryption for the information sent between the UE and the eNodeB.

- Then there is the Radio Link Control (RLC), which is responsible for the successful segmentation and concatenation of the data that is sent between the UE and eNodeB. The third part of the layer 2 components is the Medium Access Control (MAC) and this is used for scheduling the uplink and downlink resources.

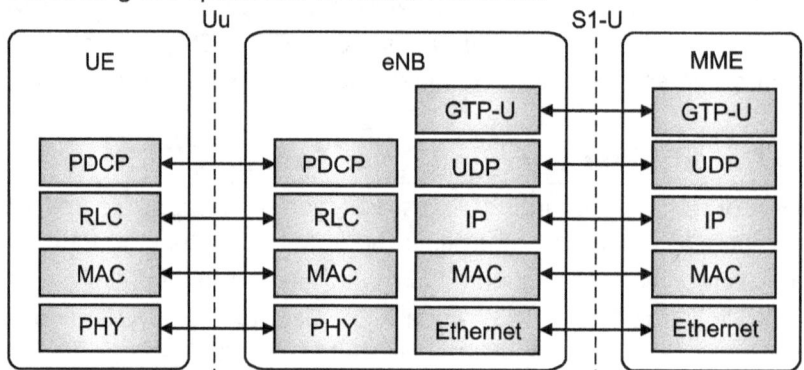

Fig. 4.4 : Layers 1 and 2

4.9.1 LTE Channel Types

In LTE over the Uu interface, there are uplink and downlink channels which have many channels within them. These channels reside in the layer 2 portion discussed in the previous section. However, whether the channel is an uplink or downlink it can be categorized as either of the following three types of channels.

1. **Logical Channels**
   - Distinguish type of information to be carried.
   - Can carry more than one data stream (multiple users)

2. **Transport Channels**
   - Indicates how information is formatted and coded.
   - Carries one or more logical channels.

3. **Physical Channels**
    - Defines the source and destination of the information.
    - Can carry one or more transport channels.

4.9.1.1 Downlink Channels

- Fig. 4.5 is a logical layout of the downlink channels for LTE. The interaction between each of the channels indicates that a particular channel can have several types of messages which it can convey regarding the transport or physical channel.
- It is important to note that the physical channel described is not at the layer 1 but at layer 2.

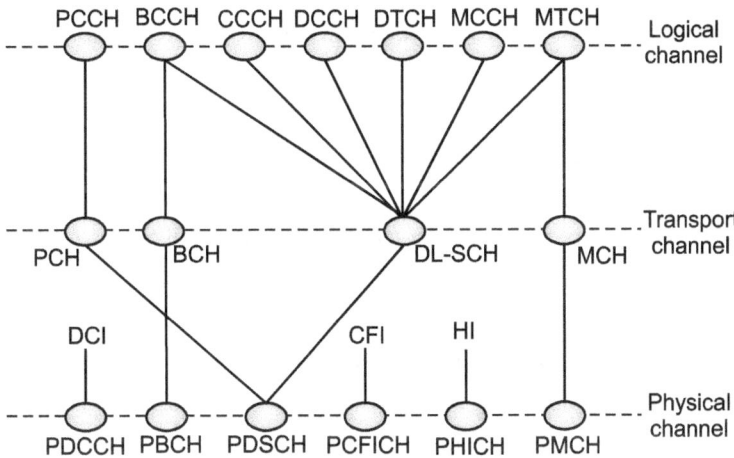

Fig. 4.5 : Downlink channel relationships

Logical Channels

- **PCCH (Physical Downlink Control Channel):** This instructs mobile about the type of data and its scheduling including defining the resource blocks to use on the uplink. This control channel is used for paging information when searching a unit on a network.
- **BCCH (Broadcast Control Channel):** This control channel provides system information to all mobile terminals connected to the eNodeB.
- **DTCH (Dedicated Traffic Channel):** Each UE is assigned a dedicated traffic channel which is shared with other UEs. This traffic channel is used for the transmission of user data.
- **Common Control Channel (CCCH):** This channel is used for random access information, e.g. for actions including setting up a connection.
- **Multicast Control Channel (MCCH):** This control channel is used for Information needed for multicast reception.
- **DCCH (Dedicated Control Channel):** This is used to send information for the management of the DTCH. This control channel is used for carrying user–specific control information, e.g. for controlling actions including power control, handover, etc.

- **Multicast Traffic Channel (MTCH):** This channel is used for the transmission of multicast data.

Transport Channels

- **PCH (Paging Channel):** This is used for sending pages. To convey the PCCH

- **BCH (Broadcast Channel):** This carries cell–specific content and is used by all UEs on the site. The LTE transport channel maps to Broadcast Control Channel (BCCH).

- **DL–SCH (Downlink Shared Channel):** This multiplexes both the DTCH and DCCH as well as the BCCH on to the PDSCH. This transport channel is the main channel for downlink data transfer. It is used by many logical channels.

- **Multicast Channel (MCH):** This transport channel is used to transmit MCCH information to set up multicast transmissions

Physical Channels

- **PBCH (Physical Broadcast Channel):** This physical channel carries system information for UEs requiring to access the network. It only carries what is termed Master Information Block, MIB, messages. The modulation scheme is always QPSK and the information bits are coded and rate matched – the bits are then scrambled using a scrambling sequence specific to the cell to prevent confusion with data from other cells.

- **PDSCH (Physical Downlink Shared Channel):** This is the main data–bearing channel providing user data such as control signaling, broadcast information including System Information Blocks (SIB) and paging information.

- **PCFICH (Physical Control Format Indication Channel):** This is used by eNodeB to inform UEs about the number of OFDMA symbols used for the PDCCH. As the name implies the PCFICH informs the UE about the format of the signal being received. It indicates the number of OFDM symbols used for the PDCCHs, whether 1, 2, or 3. The information within the PCFICH is essential because the UE does not have prior information about the size of the control region.

- **PDCCH (Physical Downlink Control Channel):** This carries control information from the eNodeB to the UE, scheduling grants and UL and DL resource allocations, and UL power control.

- **PHICH (Physical Hybrid Automatic Repeat Request (ARQ) Indicator Channel):** This is a physical channel that carries Hybrid ARQ Indicator (HI). The HI contains the ACK/NACK feedback to the UE pertaining to the uplink blocks.

- **PMCH (Physical Mulicast Channel):** This carries the multicast/broadcast channel information for Multimedia Broadcast and Multicast Services (MBMS).

Within the downlink signaling there are some key signals which help in the UE in establishing and maintaining communication with the eNodeB. The key signals in the downlink involve both synchronization and reference signals.

Synchronizaton Signals

- **Primary Synchronization:** This is used by UE to obtain subframe synchronization. In the cell search process the UE determines the timing and center frequency of the downlink carrier.
- **Secondary Synchronization:** This is used by UE to obtain frame–level synchronization and allows the UE to obtain the cell–identity group of the eNodeB.

Reference Signals

- Reference signals enable UE to mitigate amplitude, phase, and timing errors by providing a known reference signal so the UE can make corrections.
- Three types of downlink reference signals are:
  (a) Cell–specific reference signals.
  (b) MBSFN reference signals.
  (c) UE–specific reference signals.

4.9.1.2 Uplink Logical Channel Structure

Fig. 4.6 is a logical layout of the uplink channels for LTE between the UE and the eNodeB. The interaction between each of the channels indicates that a particular channel can have several types of messages which it can convey regarding the transport or physical channel.

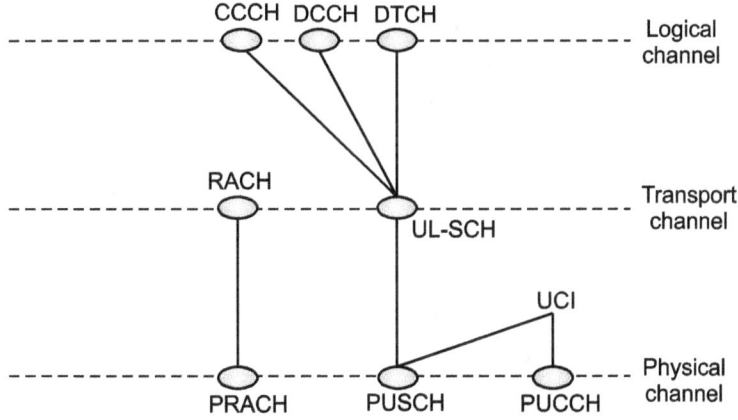

Fig. 4.6 : Uplink channel relationships

Logical Channels

- **CCCH (Common Control Channel):** This controls information sent to UE when UE has no RRC connection with the network. This channel is used for random access information, e.g. for actions including setting up a connection.
- **DCCH (Dedicated Control Channel):** This is a point–to–point bidirectional channel that transmits dedicated control information to and from the UE. This control channel is used for carrying user–specific control information, e.g. for controlling actions including power control, handover, etc..
- **DTCH (Dedicated Traffic Channel):** Point–to–point dedicated channel to UE for the data traffic. This traffic channel is used for the transmission of user data.

Transport Channels

- **UL–SCH (Uplink Shared Channel):** This transport channel is the main channel for uplink data transfer. It is used by many logical channels. Channel Quality Indicator (CQI), Precoding Matrix Indicator (PMI), Rank Indication (RI), and Redundancy Version (RV).

- **RACH (Random Access Channel):** This is used for random access requirements.

Physical Channels

- **PUSCH (Physical Uplink Shared Channel):** This physical channel found on the LTE uplink is the Uplink counterpart of PDSCH This carries data traffic, as well as the Uplink Shared Channel (UL–SCH) and the Uplink Control Information (UCI).

- **PRACH (Physical Random Access Channel):** This uplink physical channel is used for random access functions. This is the only non–synchronised transmission that the UE can make within LTE. The downlink and uplink propagation delays are unknown when PRACH is used and therefore it cannot be synchronised.

- **PUCCH (Physical Uplink Control Channel):** It provides the various control signalling requirements. There are a number of different PUCCH formats defined to enable the channel to carry the required information in the most efficient format for the particular scenario encountered. It includes the ability to carry SRs, Scheduling Requests.

Just like the downlink, the uplink has some key signals which help in the UE in establishing and maintaining communication with the eNodeB.

- **DMRS (Demodulation Reference Signal):** This is used for synchronization and uplink channel estimation. There are two DMRSs: one for PUSCH and the other for the PUCCH.

- **SRS (Sounding Reference Signal):** This is used by the eNodeB to estimate uplink channel condition when PUCCH and PUSCH are not being used.

4.9.1.3 Hybrid Automatic Repeat Request (HARQ)

- One of the purpose of LTE to come in is to bring in high data rates. To achieve this UE must embrace some techniques where it can transmit data quickly and reliably.

- What happens when there are error packets received on UE or eNB. Of–course, there would be some sort of mechanism applied on the devices to rectify the errors. Therefore, in LTE two mechanisms are followed to detect and correct the errors. A mechanism HARQ is implemented to correct the error packets in the PHY layer. Furthermore, there might be a chance that some packets are still left with errors and might be acceptable to some applications. Hence, these are passed to upper layers. The second mechanism (ARQ) is implemented in RLC layer which takes care of these residual errors. It either fixes those errors or discards the packets.

- HARQ is used in LTE to facilitate good communication and ensure data is sent and received properly. This is essentially a Stop and Wait protocol which is sent in a subframe of a message and offset in time. HARQ works by sending a packet to the destination receiver and ACK/NACK is received before the next process is allowed to begin.

- In HARQ, if the received data has an error then the Receiver buffers the data and requests a re–transmission from the sender. When the receiver receives the re–transmitted data, it then combines it with buffered data prior to channel decoding and error detection. This helps the performance of the re–transmissions.

- In general, HARQ schemes can be categorized as adaptive–synchronous, non–adaptive–synchronous, adaptive–asynchronous and non–adaptive–asynchronous. In a synchronous HARQ schemes, the retransmission time relative to the first transmission is specified and so there is no need for an information signal, for example a HARQ process number.

- However, in an asynchronous HARQ scheme, the retransmissions can happen at any time after the first transmission, which causes asynchronous HARQ to need extra signalling to transmit the HARQ process number to the receiver. As a result, synchronous HARQ schemes have the advantage of decreasing the signalling load and the disadvantage of less flexibility in scheduling compared to asynchronous HARQ schemes.

- Fig. 4.7 and 4.8 illustrate the various signaling sequences associated with resource assignments.

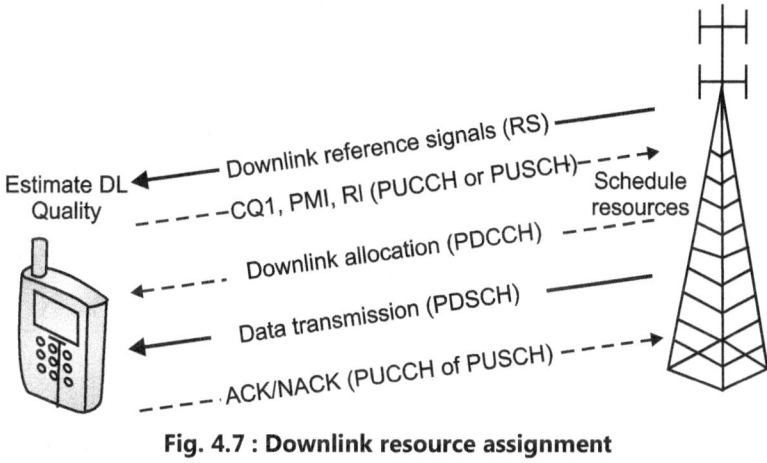

Fig. 4.7 : Downlink resource assignment

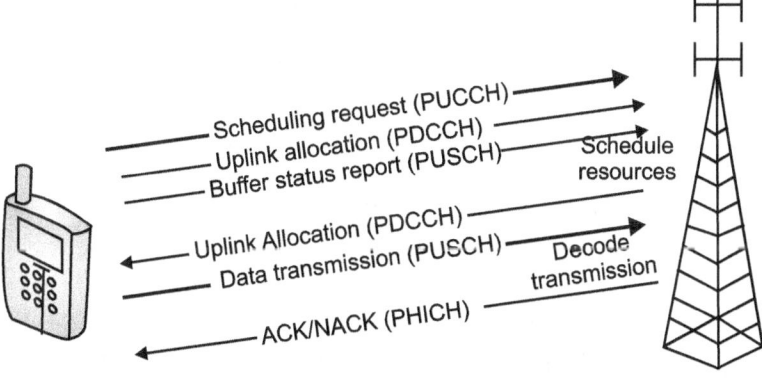

Fig. 4.8 : Uplink resource request and assignment

4.9.1.4 QCI (QoS Class Identifier)

- There are premium subscribers who always want to have better user experience on their 4G LTE device. These users are willing to pay more for high bandwidth and better network access on their devices. Not only the subscribers but some services itself need better priority handling in the network (e.g. VoIP call). To be able to full fill this, QOS plays the key role. QOS defines priorities for certain customers / services during the time of high congestion in the network

- QoS Class Identifier (QCI) and Allocation and Retention Priority (ARP) are two key parameters in LTE, which define the particular service treatment for a UE on a bearer level.

- There are several QCI settings which are shown in Table 4.6. The QCI setting describes the errors and delay that are expected with a particular service treatment including whether the service is a Guaranteed Bit Rate (GBR) or is a Nonguaranteed Bit Rate (Non–GBR).

Table 4.6 : QCI

QCI	Bearer Type	Priority	Packet Delay	Packet Loss	Example
1	GBR	2	100 ms	10^{-2}	VoIP call
2		4	150 ms	10^{-3}	Video call
3		3	50 ms		Online Gaming (Real Time)
4		5	300 ms		Video streaming
5	Non-GBR	1	100 ms	10^{-6}	IMS signaling
6		6	300 ms		IMS signling
7		7	100 ms	10^{-3}	Video, TCP based serices e.g. email, chat, ftp etc.
8		8	300 ms	10^{-6}	Video, video, interactive gaming
9		9	300 ms		Video, TCP based services e.g. email, chat, ftp etc

- If a bearer is a GBR, then the GBR provisioned is an average bit rate that the user can expect. Coupled with the GBR is a Maximum Bit Rate (MBR) and this is the maximum burst rate that can be provided for that service.

- If the QCI assigned is a Non-GBR, then there are two primary parameters which help regulate or define its throughput. The first parameter is the per APN Aggregate Maximum Bit Rate (APN-AMBR) and is used to limit the total bit rate of non-GBR bearers for a UE on a particular eNodeB or access point. Coupled with the APN-AMBR is the UE–

AMBE or per UE aggregate bit rate limits the total bit rate of all non–GBR bearers for a particular UE.

- The purpose of the QCI values is to provide uniformity of service delivered inside the network, on–net, or when using another network which adheres to the same QCI values. It is important to note that every bearer has a QCI; however, these QoS parameters are not mandatory and are in fact just guidelines for network operators.

- The other partner to QCI is the Allocation and Retention Priority (ARP) parameter. These are used to either keep a bearer up or have it torn down based on congestion levels.

- There are 15 ARP values and each is associated with a particular UE or service profile. ARP 1 has the highest priority and ARP 15 has the lowest.

- However, a key point is that the ARP values are set by the network operator.

4.9.2 System Information Messages (SIB)

The system information is very essential and the same is broadcasted by LTE eNB over logical channel BCCH. This logical channel information is further carried over transport channel BCH or carried by DL–SCH.

There are two parts in SI static part and dynamic part. Static part is called as Master Information Block (MIB) and is transmitted using BCH and carried by PBCH once every 40ms. MIB carries useful information which includes channel bandwidth, PHICH configuration details; transmit power, no. of antennas and SIB scheduling information transmitted along with other information on the DL–SCH.

Dynamic part is called as SIB and is mapped on RRC SI messages(SI–1,2,3,4,5,6,7,8,9,10,11) over DL–SCH and transmitted using PDSCH at periodic intervals. SI–1 transmitted every 80ms, SI–2 every 160ms and SI–3 every 320 ms.

LTE System Information Blocks	Description
MIB	Carries physical layer information of LTE cell which in turn help receive further SIs, i.e. system bandwidth
SIB1	Contains information regarding whether or not UE is allowed to access the LTE cell. It also defines the scheduling of the other SIBs. carries cell ID, MCC, MNC, TAC, SIB mapping.
SIB2	Carries common channel as well as shared channel information. It also carries RRC, uplink power control, preamble power ramping, uplink Cyclic Prefix Length, sub–frame hopping, uplink EARFCN
SIB3	Carries cell re–selection information as well as Intra frequency cell re–selection information

...Conti.

SIB4	Carries Intra Frequency Neighbors(on same frequency); carries serving cell and neighbor cell frequencies required for cell reselection as well handover between same RAT base stations(GSM BTS1 to GSM BTS2) and different RAT base stations(GSM to WCDMA or GSM to LTE or between WCDMA to LTE etc.), Covers E–UTRA and other RATs as mentioned
SIB5	Carries Inter Frequency Neighbors(on different frequency); carries E–UTRA LTE frequencies, other neighbor cell frequencies from other RATs. The purpose is cell reselection and handover.
SIB6	Carries WCDMA neighbors information i.e. carries serving UTRA and neighbor cell frequencies useful for cell re–selection
SIB7	Carries GSM neighbours information i.e. Carries GERAN frequencies as well as GERAN neighbor cell frequencies. It is used for cell re–selection as well as handover purpose.
SIB8	carries CDMA–2000 EVDO frequencies, CDMA–2000 neighbor cell frequencies.
SIB9	Carries HNBID (Home eNodeB Identifier)
SIB10	Carries ETWS prim. notification
SIB11	Carries ETWS sec. notification

4.9.3 LTE DL RF Channel

- The downlink RF channel used for LTE has many unique properties that enable it to provide high data rates in a very spectral efficient fashion.

- LTE employs OFDM for downlink data transmission and SC–FDMA for uplink transmission LTE utilizes a modulation technique called Orthogonal Frequency–Division Multiple Access (OFDMA). OFDMA is similar to OFDM; however, there are some key differences that need to be highlighted.

- Fig. 4.9 shows both OFDM and OFDMA showing subscribers and symbols. In **OFDM** systems, only a single user can transmit on all of the sub–carriers at any given time. In order to support multiple users time and/or frequency division access techniques are used in OFDM. The major setback to this static multiple access scheme is the fact that the different users see the wireless channel differently is not being utilized. OFDMA, on the other hand, allows multiple users to transmit simultaneously on the different sub–carriers per OFDM symbol.

- The dynamic approach to assigning subcarriers leads to better trunking efficiency which equates to usable bandwidth that can be delivered to the subscriber.

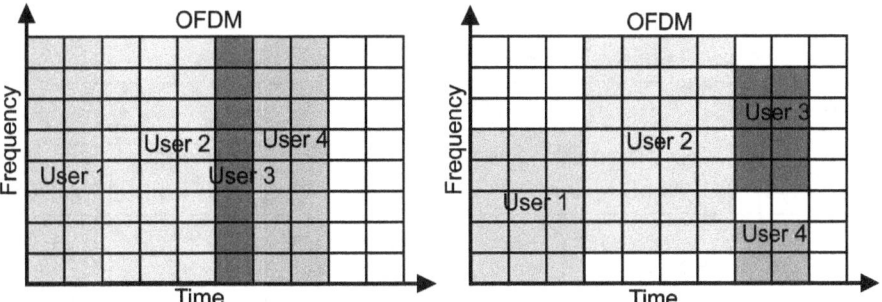

Fig. 4.9 : OFDM and OFDMA

- OFDMA was chosen for the downlink modulation format for LTE because it has high spectral efficiency. Additionally OFDMA is also resilient to multipath propagation problems and it has the added benefit of reduced receiver complexity. The receiver complexity simplification is important for the UE aspect to keep the overall cost and battery consumption at a minimum.

- OFDMA also enables MIMO capability in the downlink. However, as indicated in Fig. 4.9, with OFDMA resources can be both in the time domain (symbols) and the frequency domain (subcarriers) in addition to supporting parallel data streams to the UE. Fig. 4.10 shows the time and frequency relationship for the OFDMA signal.

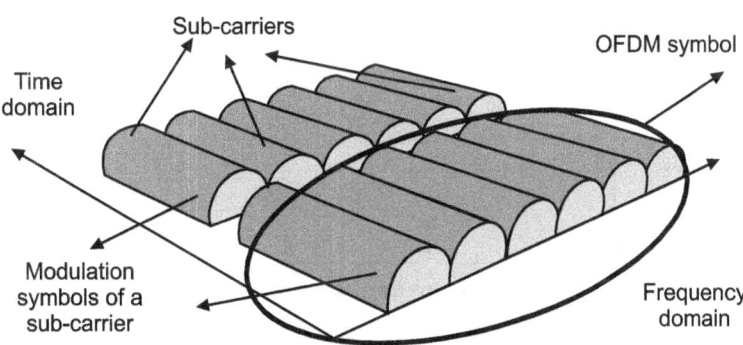

Fig. 4.10 : Downlink

- The OFDM signal used in LTE comprises a maximum of 2048 different sub–carriers having a spacing of 15 kHz. Although it is mandatory for the mobiles to have capability to be able to receive all 2048 sub–carriers, not all need to be transmitted by the base station which only needs to be able to support the transmission of 72 sub–carriers. In this way all mobiles will be able to talk to any base station.

- Within the OFDM signal it is possible to choose between three types of modulation for the LTE signal:
  - **QPSK (= 4QAM):** 2 bits per symbol.
  - **16QAM:** 4 bits per symbol.
  - **64QAM:** 6 bits per symbol.

Following table 4.7 gives comparison of OFDM and OFDMA.

Table 4.7 : Compare OFDM and OFDMA

Features	OFDM	OFDMA
Full Form	Orthogonal Frequency Division Multiplexing	Orthogonal Frequency Division Multiple Access
Capacity Allocation	One user is assigned full OFDM symbol with all the data subcarriers as well as pilot subcarriers, Data subcarriers are used for data transmission and pilot subcarriers are used to carry known symbols. The pilot subcarriers help in channel estimation and equalization. For example, in fixed wimax 1 OFDM symbol consists of total 256 subcarriers. This 256 subcarriers are divided into 192 data, 8 pilots, 1 DC, 28 left guard and 27 right guard subcarriers. Here resource allocation to user is TDMA based.	Here one user is assigned unique one or more subchannels. The subchannel is composed of distributed or contiguous subcarriers based on OFDMA type. These subcarriers are spread across multiple OFDM symbols. Here resource allocation to user is both TDMA and FDMA based.
Robustness against fading/interference	Less robust to fading as well as interference.	More robust to fading as well as interference compare to OFDM.

4.9.4 LTE UL RF Channel

- For the LTE uplink, a different concept is used for the access technique. Although still using a form of OFDMA technology, the implementation is called Single Carrier Frequency Division Multiple Access (SC–FDMA).

- One of the key parameters that affects all mobiles is that of battery life. Even though battery performance is improving all the time, it is still necessary to ensure that the mobiles use as little battery power as possible.

- With the RF power amplifier that transmits the radio frequency signal via the antenna to the base station being the highest power item within the mobile, it is necessary that it operates in as efficient mode as possible. This can be significantly affected by the form of radio frequency modulation and signal format. Signals that have a high peak to average ratio (PAPR) and require linear amplification do not lend themselves to the use of efficient RF power amplifiers.

- As a result it is necessary to employ a mode of transmission that has as near a constant power level when operating. Unfortunately OFDM has a high peak to average ratio. While this is not a problem for the base station where power is not a particular problem, it is unacceptable for the mobile.

- As a result, LTE uses a modulation scheme known as SC–FDMA – Single Carrier Frequency Division Multiplex which is a hybrid format. This combines the low Peak to Average Ratio offered by single–carrier systems with the multipath interference resilience and flexible subcarrier frequency allocation that OFDM provides.

- Fig. 4.11 shows the uplink SC–FDMA format. In comparing the OFDMA scheme in Fig. 4.10 with the one in Fig. 4.11, similarities and differences stand out. By having a single carrier instead of multiple carriers, battery and UE cost savings come at some reduction in trunking efficiency.

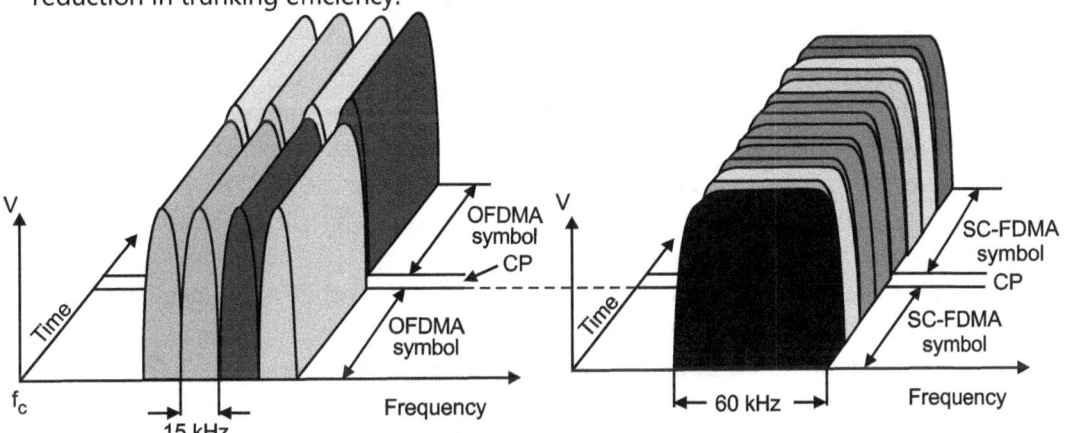

Fig. 4.11 : SC–FDMA compared with OFDMA

Transmission Scheme	OFDMA		SC-FDMA	
Analysis bandwidth	15 kHz	Signal BW (M × 15 kHz)	15 kHz	Signal BW (M × kHz)
Peak to Average Power Ration (PAR)	Same as data symbol	High PAR (Gaussian)	<data symbol (not meaningful)	Same as data symbol
Observable IQ constellation	Same as data symbol at	Not meaningful (Gaussian)	< data symbol (not meaning)	Same as data symbol at M × 66.7 μs rate

4.9.5 Resource Blocks (RBs)

- In the downlink, the subcarriers are split into resource blocks. This enables the system to be able to compartmentalize the data across standard numbers of subcarriers.

- Resource blocks comprise 12 subcarriers, regardless of the overall LTE signal bandwidth. They also cover one slot in the time frame.

- This means that different LTE signal bandwidths will have different numbers of resource blocks.
- Table 4.8 shows the relationship between resource blocks available and the LTE RF channel bandwidth.

Table 4.8 : Resource Blocks

Bandwidth (MHz)	1.4	3	5	10	15	20
Resource Blocks	6	15	25	50	75	100

- **Resource Element:** A resource Element is the smallest unit. It is one OFDM subcarrier for the duration of one OFDM symbol as shown in Fig. 4.13.
- **OFDM Subcarrier Spacing:** The Orthogonal Frequency Division Multiplexing spacing between the individual sub–carriers in LTE is 15 kHz. There is no frequency guard band between these Sub–carrier frequencies, rather a guard Period called a Cyclic Prefix (CP) is used in the time domain to help prevent Multipath Inter–Symbol Interference (ISI) between Sub–carriers.
- **Cyclic Prefix:** The Cyclic Prefix (CP) is a guard period transmitted before each OFDM symbol in each subcarrier to prevent ISI due to multipath etc. The last FFT samples of the symbol are pre–transmitted at the front of the symbol as the CP. The entire symbol (all FFT samples including the last ones) is then transmitted. This creates a nice mathematical way to process the FFTs at the receiver to get the original symbol. The Cyclic Prefix for LTE comes in two flavors Normal CP =5 usec and Extended CP= 17 usec. The extended one is intended for use for very large rural cells.
- **LTE Slot:** 0.5 msec period of an LTE downlink frame corresponding to 7 OFDM symbols (and 7 CPs) when Normal CP = 5 usec is used (the standard case). AN LTE slot is only 6 OFDM symbols (and 6 CPs) when the Extended CP = 17 usec is used.
- Combining the above information we can now define a Resource Block.
- **Resource Block:** A Resource Block is 12 OFDM subcarriers transmitting for the duration of one LTE Slot (0.5 msec). 12 subcarriers x 7 symbols = 84 symbols (or resource elements) comprise a normal Resource Block. There are 72 symbols in a Resource Block with the extended CP. Since 12 OFDM subcarriers are used in a RB, the bandwidth of a Resource Block is 180 KHz.
- So 1 Resource Block maps to the following:

  180 kHz, 84 Symbols and 0.5 ms in duration.

  LTE Subframe : two slots or 1 msec in time.

  LTE Frame : 10 msec or 10 subframes or 20 slots.
- LTE flexible Bandwidth 1.08 MHz to 19.8 MHz. The Downlink LTE Bandwidth can be configured with anywhere between 6 Resource Blocks to 110 Resource Blocks. The system is designed so all the initial signaling channels are contained in the first 6 blocks. Additional Resource Blocks add bandwidth. When there are 6 RBs the LTE Downlink bandwidth is 6x180 kHz = 1.08 MHz. When there are the maximum 110 RBs, the LTE Downlink Bandwidth is $110 \times 180 = 19.8$ MHz.

- Visualization of a 6 to 110 Resource block System is given in Fig. 4.13. Each row represents 180 KHZ of bandwidth across a 10 ms radio frame :

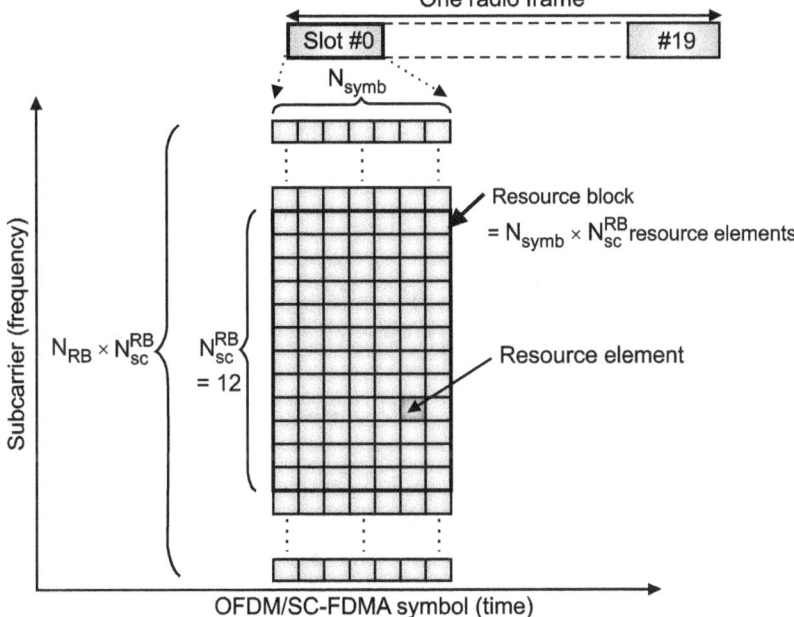

Fig. 4.12: LTE FDD frame to resource element relationship

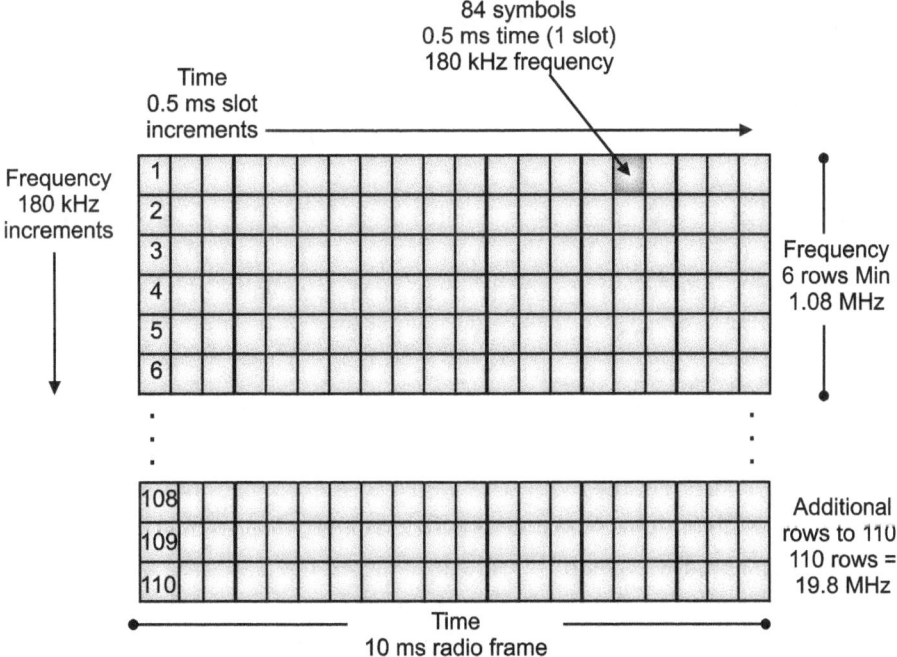

Fig. 4.13 : Visualization of a 6 to 110 Resource block System

4.10 TD-LTE

- TDD and FDD are two topologies by which critical resources time and frequency are shared among mobile subscribers or terminals. LTE uses both of these flavors to provide facility for the mobile subscribers or UEs to utilize the scares resource efficiently based on the need.

- While both LTE TDD (TD-LTE) and LTE FDD will be widely used, it is anticipated that LTE FDD will be the more widespread, although LTE TDD has a number of significant advantages, especially in terms of higher spectrum efficiency that can be used by many operators.

- TD-LTE does not require a paired spectrum since transmission and reception occurs in the same channel. In FD-LTE, it requires a paired spectrum with different frequencies with a guard band.

- TD-LTE is cheaper than FD-LTE since in TD-LTE there is no need for a diplexer to isolate transmission and receptions.

- In TD-LTE, it's possible to change the uplink and downlink capacity ratio dynamically according to the needs. In FD-LTE, capacity is determined by frequency allocation by regulatory authorities, making it difficult to make a dynamic change.

- In TD-LTE, a larger guard period is necessary to maintain the uplink and downlink separation that will affect the capacity. In FD-LTE, the same concept is referred to as a guard band for isolation of uplink and downlink, which will not affect capacity.

- In LTE a TDD configuration is referred to as a Type 2 LTE network and with the TDD classification there are possibly seven different configurations possible.

- Operating LTE in a TDD configuration enables several possible options. One key option is that LTE TDD can be deployed into existing TDD wireless access spectrum, which is currently using another technology as one possibility.

- LTE TDD is in theory more spectral–efficient than an LTE FDD system due to the fact the same channel is used for uplink and downlink communication where an FDD system has dedicated channels, bandwidth, for both uplink and downlink.

- The spectral efficiency comes about due to the issue that data is not symmetric.

- As suspected LTE TDD does not have the same air interface as LTE FDD due to the issue that the frame structure is different.

- However, unlike an FDD system the channel propagation characteristics are the same for both directions which enables transmit and receive to use one set of propagation parameters due to the duplex spacing for FDD channels.

- In an LTE TDD system, the UL and DL capacity ratio can be changed dynamically to match demand allowing for better handling of data traffic.

- However, in LTE TDD systems the base stations need to be synchronized with respect to the uplink and downlink transmission times. If neighboring base stations use different uplink and downlink assignments and share the same channel, then some level of mutual interference may occur between cells.

- Fig. 4.14 shows LTE TDD frame. The 10 ms frame comprises two half frames, each 5 ms long. The LTE half–frames are further split into five subframes, each 1ms long.

- The subframes may be divided into standard subframes of special subframes. The special subframes consist of three fields;

- **DwPTS:** Downlink Pilot Time Slot

- **GP:** Guard Period

- **UpPTS:** Uplink Pilot Time Stot.

- These three fields are also used within TD–SCDMA and they have been carried over into LTE TDD (TD–LTE) and thereby help the upgrade path. The fields are individually configurable in terms of length, although the total length of all three together must be 1ms.

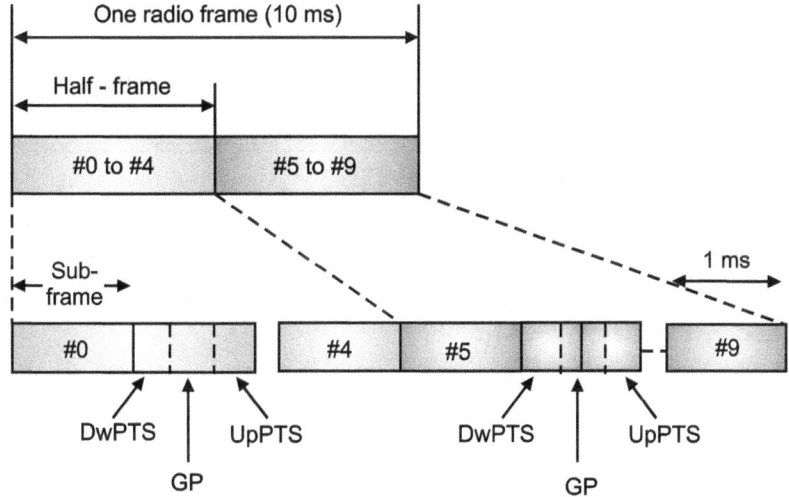

Fig. 4.14 : LTE TDD frame structure.

4.10.1 LTE TDD Configuration

- One of the advantages of using LTE TDD is that it is possible to dynamically change the up and downlink balance and characteristics to meet the load conditions. In order that this can be achieved in an ordered fashion, a number of standard configurations have been set within the LTE standards.

- A total of seven up / downlink configurations have been set, and these use either 5 ms or 10 ms switch periodicities. In the case of the 5ms switch point periodicity, a special subframe exists in both half frames. In the case of the 10 ms periodicity, the special subframe exists in the first half frame only. It can be seen from the table below that the subframes 0 and 5 as well as DwPTS are always reserved for the downlink. It can also be seen that UpPTS and the subframe immediately following the special subframe are always reserved for the uplink transmission. LTE TDD has several different configurations possible. Each of the seven configurations is listed in Table 4.9.

- In the table,
  D is a subframe for downlink transmission
  S is a "special" subframe used for a guard time
  U is a subframe for uplink transmission

Table 4.9 : LTE TDD Configurations

Uplink–Downlink Configuration	Downlink/Uplink Periodicity	Subframe Number									
		0	1	2	3	4	5	6	7	8	9
0	5ms	D	S	U	U	U	D	S	U	U	U
1	5ms	D	S	U	U	D	D	S	U	U	D
2	5ms	D	S	U	D	D	D	S	U	D	D
3	10ms	D	S	U	U	U	D	D	D	D	D
4	10ms	D	S	U	U	D	D	D	D	D	D
5	10ms	D	S	U	D	D	D	D	D	D	D
6	5ms	D	S	U	U	U	D	S	U	U	D

4.11 MULTIPLE INPUT MULTIPLE OUTPUT

- MIMO, Multiple Input Multiple Output is another of the LTE major technology innovations used to improve the performance of the system. This technology provides LTE with the ability to further improve its data throughput and spectral efficiency above that obtained by the use of OFDM.
- Although MIMO adds complexity to the system in terms of processing and the number of antennas required, it enables far high data rates to be achieved along with much improved spectral efficiency. As a result, MIMO has been included as an integral part of LTE.
- MIMO is used either in spatial diversity, spatial multiplexing or beamforming mode mode. Since the different streams transmitted from different antenna can undergo different fading, the possibility of receiving better signal atleast from one antenna increases compared to single antenna system(SISO).
- When spatial diversity is employed, LTE MIMO scheme utilises the transmission of the same information stream from multiple antennas. LTE supports two or four for this technique.. The information is coded differently using Space Frequency Block Codes. This mode provides an improvement in signal quality at reception and does not improve the data rate. Accordingly this form of LTE MIMO is used on the Common Channels as well as the Control and Broadcast channels.
- MIMO increases the overall bit rate through the transmission of two or more different data streams on two or more different antennas; however, the data streams use the same

frequency and the same reference signal to differentiate them. This is called spatial multiplexing mode.

- The typical MIMO configurations used in LTE for MIMO are:

  (i) 1Tx, 2Rx or

  (ii) 2Tx, 2Rx.

- It is possible to have LTE operate with 8Tx and 4Rx per eNodeB leading to increased throughput at the expense of antenna real estate. However the more common configuration for an eNodeB is a 2Tx, 2Rx configuration, or 2 × 2.

- UE devices are MIMO capable; however, their form factor limits the amount of available options and presently the mandatory configuration for UEs is a 1Tx and 2Rx configuration.

- Fig. 4.15 shows one possible MIMO configuration for both the eNodeB as well as the UE. In Fig. 4.15, the eNodeB is set up as 4 × 4 configuration; however, the UE can only support a 1 × 2 configuration. In this situation each of the UEs receives data streams from both receive antennas and transmit antennas of the eNodeB.

- However, the UE has one transmit antenna to send information on the uplink channel which is received by two of the eNodeB receive antennas; in reality all four eNodeB receive antennas can be utilized.

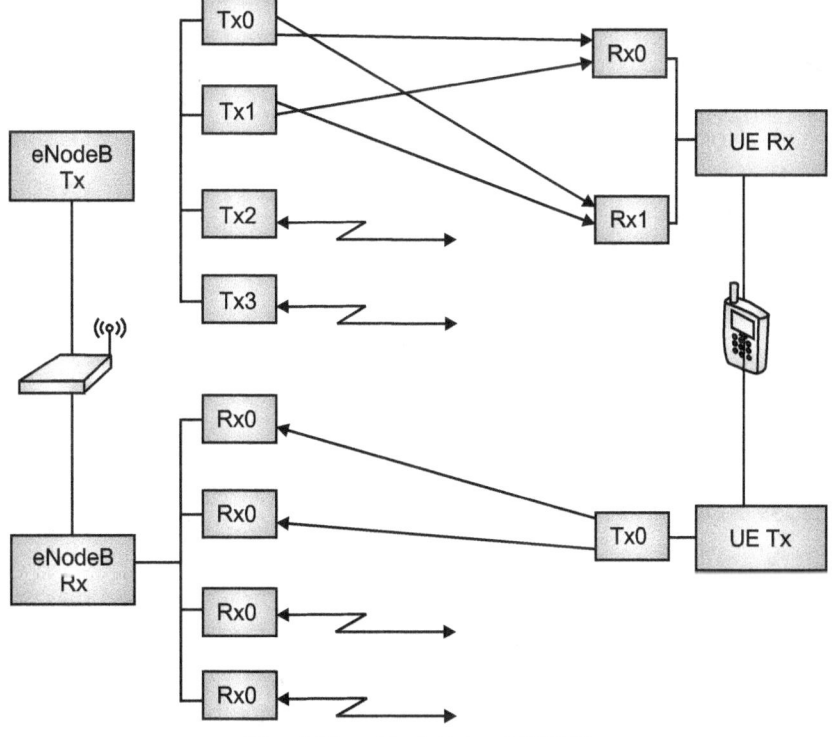

Fig. 4.15 : eNodeB 4 × 4 MIMO

- To help with MIMO communication several reference signals are sent from the eNodeB to help in the establishment of the communication link between the eNodeB and the UE. Specifically, the reference signals are related to the Resource Block (RB), which subcarriers are sent via different antennas.

4.12 LTE SCHEDULER

- Scheduling is the process through which eNB decides which UEs should be given resources to send or receive data . In LTE, scheduling is done per subframe level

- The scheduler for the LTE system is a critical component and directly influences the performance of the LTE network itself. Specifically, the scheduler located in the eNodeB is responsible for scheduling all LTE resources between the eNodeB and the UE. Scheduling is a network–controlled function at the eNodeB, and the UE can only make resource requests.

- The eNodeB scheduler dynamically controls which resources in time and frequency are allocated to a certain user at a given time.

- The downlink control signaling informs the UE(s) what resources and respective transmission formats have been allocated. Additionally the eNodeB MAC sublayer is responsible for scheduling transmissions over the LTE air interface in both the downlink and uplink directions.

- Sitting just above the Physical layer, the MAC Scheduler assigns bandwidth resources to user equipment and is responsible for deciding on how uplink and downlink channels are used by the eNodeB and the UEs of a cell. It also enforces the necessary Quality of Service for UE connections. QoS is a set of rules that come from the Policy and Charging Rules Function (PCRF) in the core network. These rules define priority, bit rate and latency requirements for different connections to the UE. They is usually based on the types of applications using the UE connection

  - In order to take its resource allocation decisions, the MAC Scheduler receives information such as:

  - QoS data from the PCRF: minimum guaranteed bandwidth, maximum allowed bandwidth, packet loss rates, relative priority of users, etc.

  - Messages from the UEs regarding the radio channel quality, the strength or weakness of the signal, etc.

  - Measurements from the radio receiver regarding radio channel quality, noise and interference, etc.

  - Buffer status from the upper layers about how much data is queued up waiting for transmission

- Data is transferred between the MAC sublayers in the UE and eNodeB using transport blocks which are sent via the downlink and uplink shared transport channels (DL–SCH and UL–SCH). In LTE the scheduling decisions utilize multiple inputs including link adaptation and HARQ.

- When allocating resources and managing the QoS the scheduler makes numerous decisions based on its unique algorithm that it is coded with. Some of the variables that go into the scheduler decision involve:

  - System bandwidth,
  - Min and max data rate,
  - Channel Quality Indicator (CQI) reports from the UEs,
  - UE capabilities,
  - Pending retransmissions,
  - Quality–of–service parameters and measurements,
  - Available power allocation,
  - BER target requirements according to the service,
  - Latency requirement, depending on the service,
  - Payloads buffered in the eNodeB ready for scheduling
  - UE sleep cycles and measurement gaps/periods

- The scheduler optimizes the eNodeB throughput for the current loading condition using a scheduling policy. There are two scheduling policies that can be utilized.

- Fair allocation scheme in which each UE (in DL or UL) is allocated the same amount of available Proportional Resource Blocks (PRBs). The number of allocated PRBs per UE changes only when the number of UE in the cell changes, that is, either increases or decreases.

- Proportional allocation scheme in which the user bandwidth is adapted to the changing channel conditions.

- The MME provides the inputs (variables) to the eNodeB scheduler.

4.13 CARRIER AGGREGATION

- To achieve these very high data rates it is necessary to increase the transmission bandwidths over those that can be supported by a single carrier or channel. The method being proposed is termed carrier aggregation, CA, or sometimes channel aggregation. Using LTE Advanced carrier aggregation, it is possible to utilise more than one carrier and in this way increase the overall transmission bandwidth.

- These channels or carriers may be in contiguous elements of the spectrum, or they may be in different bands.

- Spectrum availability is a key issue for 4G LTE. In many areas only small bands are available, often as small as 10 MHz. As a result carrier aggregation over more than one band is contained within the specification, although it does present some technical challenges.

- Carrier aggregation is supported by both formats of LTE, namely the FDD and TDD variants. This ensures that both FDD LTE and TDD LTE are able to meet the high data throughput requirements placed upon them.

- With Releases 8 and 9, carrier aggregation is not possible and the maximum channel bandwidth is 20 MHz. However, with carrier aggregation it is possible to obtain a 100–MHz–wide RF channel in both the uplink and downlink through aggregating five individual 20 MHz channels for a total of 100 MHz.

- When carrier aggregation is used for 5×20 MHz for a 100–MHz–wide LTE FDD system the following data rates are possible.

  (a) Downlink : 1 Gps (using 8 Tx antennas),

  (b) Uplink : 500 Mbps (using 4 Rx antennas).

- There are a number of ways in which LTE carriers can be aggregated:

- **Intra–Band:**   This form of carrier aggregation uses a single band. There are two main formats for this type of carrier aggregation:

- **Contiguous:** The Intra–band contiguous carrier aggregation is the easiest form of LTE carrier aggregation to implement. Here the carriers are adjacent to each other. The aggregated channel can be considered by the terminal as a single enlarged channel from the RF viewpoint. In this instance, only one transceiver is required within the terminal or UE, whereas more are required where the channels are not adjacent. However as the RF bandwidth increases it is necessary to ensure that the UE in particular is able to operate over such a wide bandwidth without a reduction in performance. Although the performance requirements are the same for the base station, the space, power consumption, and cost requirements are considerably less stringent, allowing greater flexibility in the design. Additionally for the base station, multi–carrier operation, even if non–aggregated, is already a requirement in many instances, requiring little or no change to the RF elements of the design. Software upgrades would naturally be required to cater for the additional capability.

- **Non–contiguous:** Non–contiguous intra–band carrier aggregation is somewhat more complicated than the instance where adjacent carriers are used. No longer can the multi–carrier signal be treated as a single signal and therefore two transceivers are required. This adds significant complexity, particularly to the UE where space, power and cost are prime considerations.

- **Inter–band non–contiguous:** This form of carrier aggregation uses different bands. It will be of particular use because of the fragmentation of bands – some of which are only 10 MHz wide. For the UE it requires the use of multiple transceivers within the single item, with the usual impact on cost, performance and power. In addition to this there are also additional complexities resulting from the requirements to reduce intermodulation and cross modulation from the two transceivers

- Each aggregated carrier is referred to as a Component Carrier, CC. The component carrier can have a bandwidth of 1.4, 3, 5, 10, 15 or 20 MHz and a maximum of five component carriers can be aggregated, hence the maximum aggregated bandwidth is 100 MHz. In FDD the number of aggregated carriers can be different in DL and UL, see figure 1. However, the number of UL component carriers is always equal to or lower than the number of DL component carriers. The individual component carriers can also be of different bandwidths. For TDD the number of CCs as well as the bandwidths of each CC will normally be the same for DL and UL.

- The easiest way to arrange aggregation would be to use contiguous component carriers within the same operating frequency band (as defined for LTE), so called intra–band contiguous. This might not always be possible, due to operator frequency allocation scenarios. For non–contiguous allocation it could either be intra–band, i.e. the component carriers belong to the same operating frequency band, but have a gap, or gaps, in between, or it could be inter–band, in which case the component carriers belong to different operating frequency bands, see Fig. 4.16.

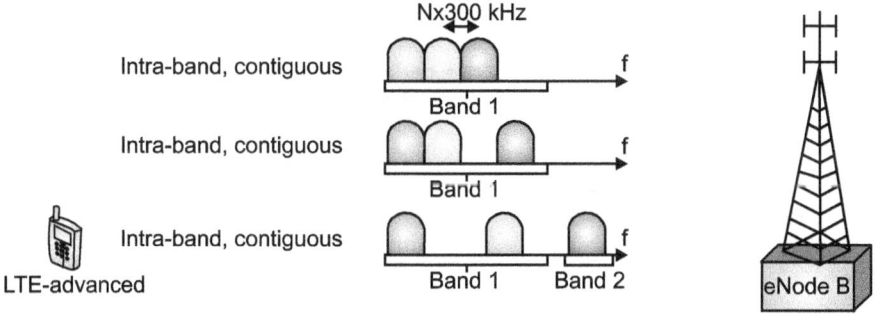

Fig. 4.16 : Carrier aggregation

- A very important attribute with carrier aggregation is that aggregating carriers can be mixed and matched so that you have different UL and DL carriers used for aggregation. Additionally, the carriers aggregated do not have to have the same bandwidth.

- Also when using non–continuous carriers, whether intraband or interband, the carriers will have different coverage areas and this needs to be factored into the design where the high–frequency carrier is the limiting case. Of course, this assumes that the power and other key attributes are the same.

- Another point to factor in the design process is that the RRC messaging is handled by one of the CCs and this is typically referred to as the LTE, Primary CC (PCC). Other CCs are called Secondary CCs (SCC); however, each CC effectively forms a unique cell with different coverage areas.

4.14 CELL SEARCH

- A cell search procedure is used by the UE to acquire time and frequency synchronization with a LTE cell and UE detects the Physical Layer Cell ID (PCI) of that cell.

- Although there can be many algorithms defined for this procedure the basic sequence is as follows and shown in Fig. 4.17.

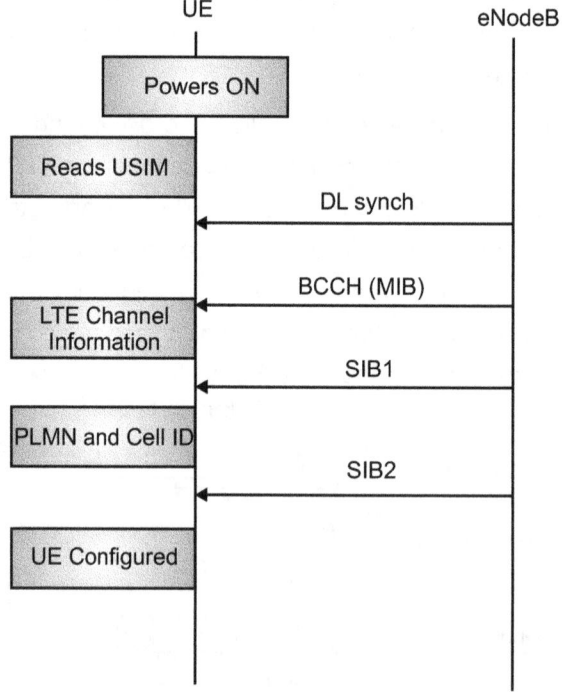

Fig. 4.17 : Cell search

- After being powered on, UE tunes the RF and attempts to measure the wideband Received Power (RSSI) for specific frequencies (channels as commanded by higher layer) over a set of supported frequency bands one after another and ranks those cells based on signal strength.

- From the list of all channels with RSSI a threshold value is determined..

- UE decodes sync/reference signals and find Physical Cell Id of each candidate from step 2.

- Of all the cells of step 3. UE decode MIB and SIB. Now, UE has a list if frequency, PCI and PLMN of the filtered cells.

- From all of the above information, UE makes a descision of on which of these cells it would select.

4.15 CELL RESELECTION

Cell reselection is a process where the UE is always scanning nearby cells in order to find the best cell to camp on. Once the UE camps on a cell (cell selection), it will continue to look for a better cell which is called cell reselection.

During the scanning for a possible cell reselection, the UE will consider a new cell if it is better than the current cell it is camped on provided that:

- The current cell is not suitable.

- The downlink signal strength is insufficient.

- The new cell must also meet the normal PLMN, TAI, and status requirements.

4.16 ATTACH AND DEFAULT BEARER ACTIVATION

Once the UE has selected a cell site to camp on, it will attempt to attach to the cell and if successful a default bearer will be assigned to the UE.

The overall process can be briefly summarized as

- Upon power up, UE scans channels for a suitable network.

- The UE synchronizes with the best cell to get system configuration information.

- UE then can request a Radio Resource Connection (RRC) to exchange signaling information with network.

- RRC is used to register the UE (attach).

- Network establishes the default bearer path.

- UE is assigned IP address.

Fig. 4.18 shows attach and default bearer assignment process.

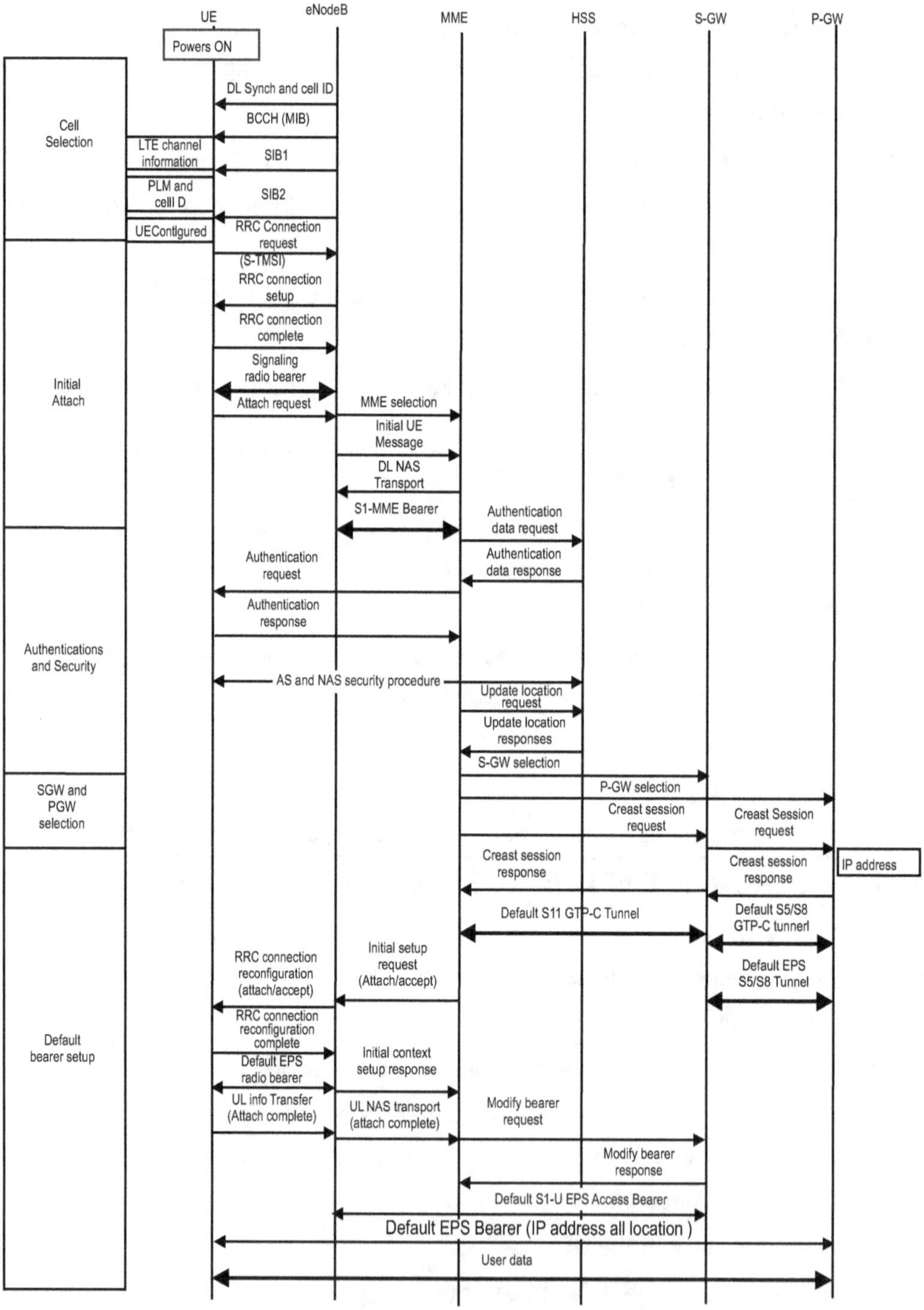

Fig. 4.18 : Attach and bearer assignment

An important point to note is that when the UE no longer needs a data session, the default access bearer remains, that is, PGW to SGW. The SGW to eNodeB connection is torn down; however, the IP address associated with the UE is still maintained.

4.17 HANDOVER (X2, S1, INTER–MME)

- Handover procedure is intended to reduce the interruption time, less than the circuit–switched handover in 2G networks, and it is an important function for LTE eNB.
- In LTE there are three different types of handover can be possible
    - **Intra–LTE Handover:** In this case source and target cells are part of the same LTE network.
    - **Inter–LTE Handover:** Handover happens towards other LTE nodes. (Inter–MME and Inter–SGW)
    - **Inter–RAT Handover:** Handover between different radio technologies. For example handover from LTE to WCDMA.

Intra–LTE handover is of two types:

- Intra–LTE (Intra–MME/SGW) handover using the X2 interface
- Intra–LTE Handover Using the S1 Interface

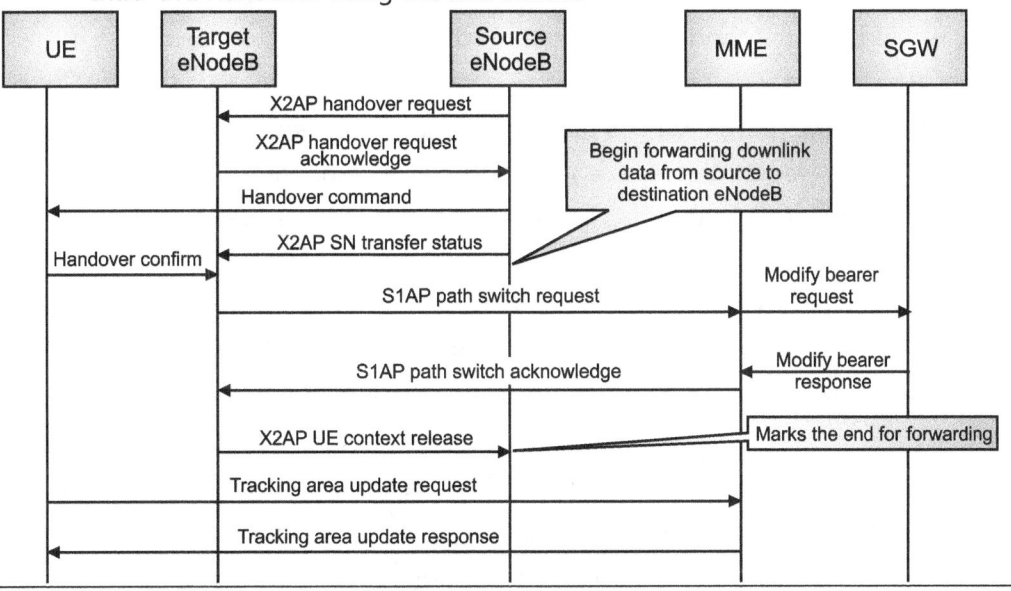

Fig. 4.19 : X2 handover

4.17.1 X2 Handover

- Intra–LTE (Intra–MME/SGW) handover using the X2 interface is used to handover a UE from a source eNodeB (S–eNB) to a target eNodeB (T–eNB) using the X2 interface when the Mobility Management Entity (MME) and Serving Gateway (SGW) are unchanged.
- This scenario is possible only when there is a direct connection exists between source eNodeB and target eNodeB with the X2 interface.

- In case of intra–LTE handover using X2 interface the UE is source eNodeB and is in connected stated and the goal is to move the UE to target eNodeB. The X2 handover procedure is performed without Evolved Packet Core (EPC) involvement, i.e. preparation messages are directly exchanged between the S–eNB and T–eNB. The release of the resources at the source side during the handover completion phase is triggered by the T–eNB.

  Fig. 4.19 shows call flows for an X2 handover and described as below:

- UE is in connected state and a data call is up. Data packets are transferred to/from the UE to/from the network in both directions (DL as well as UL).

- The network sends the measurement control REQ message to the UE to set the parameters to measure and set thresholds for those parameters. Its purpose is to instruct the UE to send a measurement report to the network as soon as it detects the thresholds.

- The UE sends the measurement report to the S–eNB after it meets the measurement report criteria communicated previously. The S–eNB makes the decision to hand off the UE to a T–eNB using the handover algorithm; each network operator could have its own handover algorithm.

- The S–eNB issues the resource status request message to determine the load on T–eNB (this is optional). Based on the received resource status response, the S–eNB can make the decision to proceed further in continuing the handover procedure using the X2 interface.

- The S–eNB issues a handover request message to the T–eNB passing necessary information to prepare the handover at the target side (e.g., UE Context which includes the Security Context and RB Context (including E–RAB to RB Mapping) and the Target cell info).

- The T–eNB checks for resource availability and, if available, reserves the resources and sends back the handover request acknowledge message including a transparent container to be sent to the UE as an RRC message to perform the handover. The container includes a new C–RNTI, T–eNB security algorithm identifiers for the selected security algorithms, and may include a dedicated RACH preamble and possibly some other parameters (i.e., access parameters, SIBs, etc.).

- The S–eNB generates the RRC message to perform the handover, i.e, RRC connection reconfiguration message including the mobility Control Information. The S–eNB performs the necessary integrity protection and ciphering of the message and sends it to the UE.

- The S–eNB sends the eNB status transfer message to the T–eNB to convey the PDCP and HFN status of the E–RABs.

- The S–eNB starts forwarding the downlink data packets to the T–eNB for all the data bearers (which are being established in the T–eNB during the handover REQ message processing).

- In the meantime, the UE tries to access the T–eNB cell using the non–contention–based Random Access Procedure. If it succeeds in accessing the target cell, it sends the RRC connection reconfiguration complete to the T–eNB.

- The T–eNB sends a path switch request message to the MME to inform it that the UE has changed cells, including the TAI+ECGI of the target. The MME determines that the SGW can continue to serve the UE.

- The MME sends a modify bearer request (eNodeB address and TEIDs for downlink user plane for the accepted EPS bearers) message to the SGW. If the PDN GW requested the UE's location info, the MME also includes the User Location Information IE in this message.

- The SGW sends the downlink packets to the target eNB using the newly received addresses and TEIDs (path switched in the downlink data path to T–eNB) and the modify bearer response to the MME.

- The SGW sends one or more "end marker" packets on the old path to the S–eNB and then can release any user plane / TNL resources toward the S–eNB.

- The MME responds to the T–eNB with a path switch REQ ACK message to notify the completion of the handover.

- The T–eNB now requests the S–eNB to release the resources using the X2 UE context release message. With this, the handover procedure is complete.

4.17.2 S1 Handover

- The S1–based handover procedure is used when the X2–based handover cannot be used. These are some examples when S1–based handover can be used.

- There is no X2 connectivity to the target eNodeB;

- by an error indication from the T–eNB after an unsuccessful X2–based handover;

- or by dynamic information learnt by the S–eNB using the status transfer procedure.

- The S–eNB initiates the handover by sending a Handover required message over the S1–MME reference point. The EPC does not change the decisions taken by the S–eNB.

- The availability of a direct forwarding path is determined in the S–eNB (based on the X2 connectivity with the T–eNB) and indicated to the source MME. If a direct forwarding path is not available, indirect forwarding will be used. The source MME uses the indication from the S–eNB to determine whether to apply indirect forwarding or not.

- S1 handovers are the most prevalent handovers in LTE if the network topology is laid out correctly. Fig. 4.20 shows a simple signaling flow for an S1 handover.

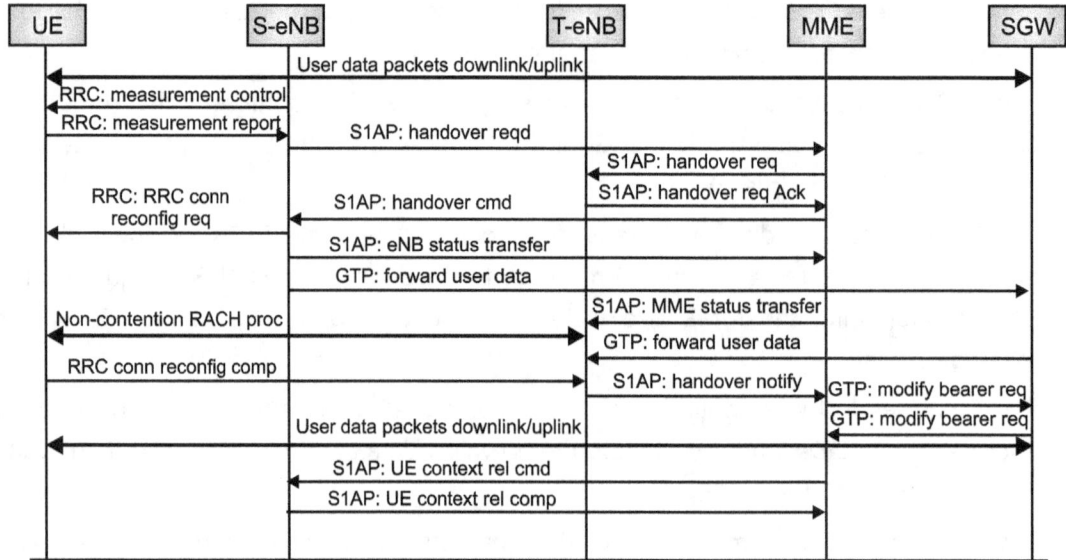

Fig. 4.20 : S1 handover

- Based on the measurement report from the UE, the S–eNB decides to Handover the UE to another eNodeB (T–eNB).

- The handover procedure for Intra–LTE handover using the S1 interface is very similar to that of Intra–LTE Handover Using the X2 Interface, except the involvement of the MME in relaying the handover signaling between the S–eNB and T–eNB.

- There are two main differences here:

  (a) No need for the path switch Procedure between the T–eNB and MME, as MME is aware of the Handover.

  (b) The SGW is involved in the DL data forwarding if there is no direct forwarding path available between the S–eNB and T–eNB.

- Once the Handover is complete, the MME clears the logical S1 connection with the S–eNB by initiating the UE context release procedure.

4.17.3 Inter–MME Handover

- In LTE, inter–MME handovers is used where the target eNodeB resides on a different MME and this signaling flow is shown in Fig. 4.21.

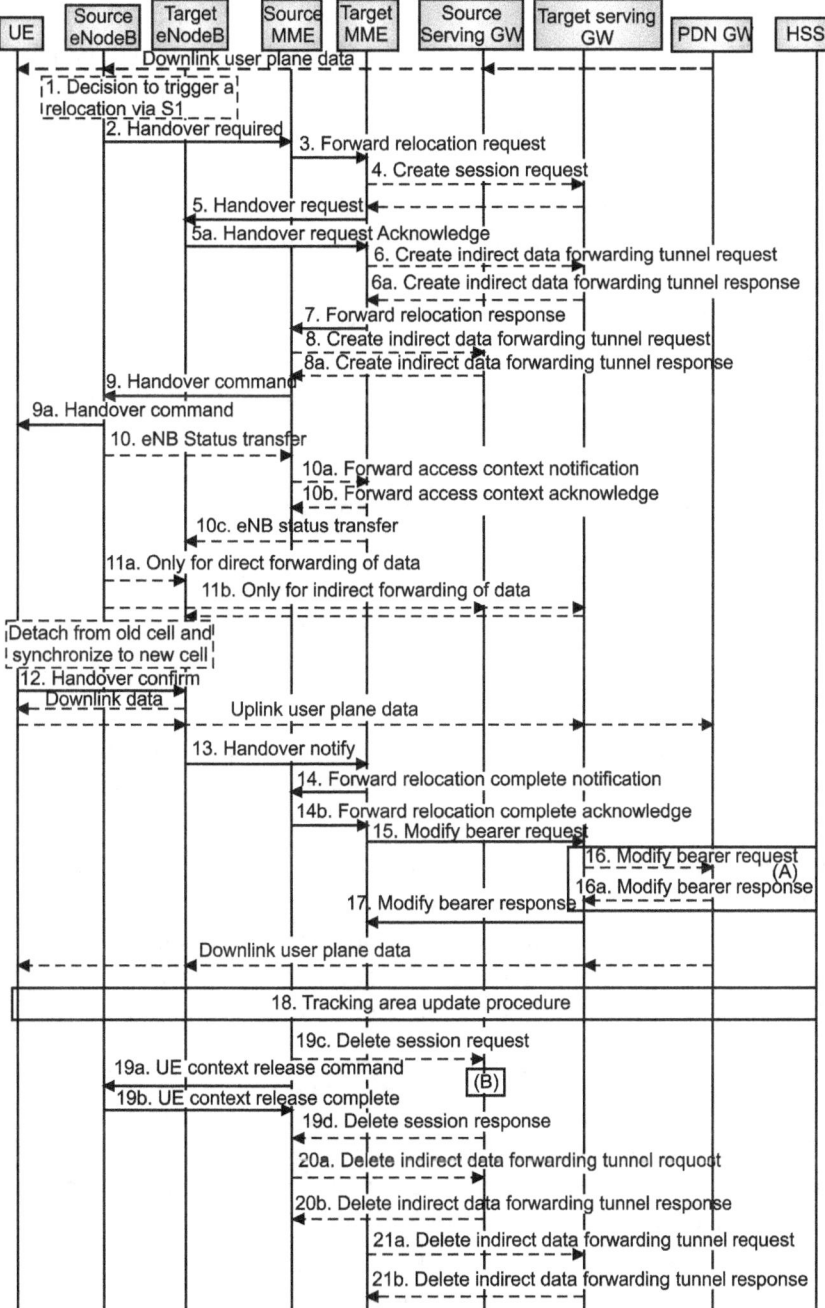

Fig. 4.21 : Inter–MME handover

4.18 SELF–ORGANIZING NETWORKS (SONS)

- The rate at which cellular or mobile communications is growing is increasing. With increasing data usage, more dense and complicated networks, radio network planning and maintenance is more complicated than in the early days of mobile communications.

- Much of this has been brought about by the introduction of LTE where micro and femto cells as well as relay nodes are being relied upon to ensure that the required overall capacity can be met. This brings many challenges in terms of network planning and management.

- LTE supports the functions of SONs. It enables the SONs to automate network configuration and optimization processes for the introduction of a new node, as well as for the removal of the one on a permanent or temporary basis. A temporary removal of a node could be simply due to maintenance–related events.

- The Third Generation Partnership Project, 3GPP has introduced the concept of self–organising networks, SON into Release 8 of their standards, and in addition to this the Next Generation Mobile Networks, NGMN alliance introduced the concept of SON with the aims of:

  - Reducing the operating cost by reducing the level of human intervention in network design, build and operation

  - Reducing capital expenditure by optimising the use of available resources

  - Protecting revenue by reducing the number of human errors

- The main functionality of SON includes: self–configuration, self–optimization and self–healing.

- Self–configuration process is defined as the process where newly deployed nodes (eNBs) are configured by automatic installation procedures to get the necessary basic configuration for system operation.

- Self–optimization process is defined as the process where UE and eNB measurements and performance measurements are used to autotune the network.

- Self–healing function aims at automatic detection and localization of most of the failures and applies self–healing mechanisms to solve several failure classes, such as reducing the output power in case of temperature failure or automatic fallback to previous software version.

4.19 RELAY CELLS

- One of the main drivers for the use of LTE is the high data rates that can be achieved. However all technologies suffer from reduced data rates at the cell edge where signal levels are lower and interference levels are typically higher.

- The use of technologies such as MIMO, OFDM and advanced error correction techniques improve throughput under many conditions, but do not fully mitigate the problems experienced at the cell edge.

- As cell edge performance is becoming more critical, with some of the technologies being pushed towards their limits, it is necessary to look at solutions that will enhance performance at the cell edge for a comparatively low cost. One solution that is being investigated and proposed is that of the use of LTE relays.

- Fig. 4.24 shows one possible configuration for a relay cell. In the Fig. 4.24, the Relay Node (RN) is connected to a Donner eNodeB (DeNB). The fact that the RN is connected to a DeNB differentiates it from a typical small cell, which is an independent cell site, that is, small/pico/femto. A DeNB can have multiple RNs associated with it

- LTE relaying is different to the use of a repeater which re–broadcasts the signal. A relay will actually receive, demodulates and decodes the data, apply any error correction, etc to it and then re–transmitting a new signal. In this way, the signal quality is enhanced with an LTE relay, rather than suffering degradation from a reduced signal to noise ratio when using a repeater.

- For an LTE relay, the UEs communicate with the relay node, which in turn communicates with a donor eNB.

- Relay nodes can optionally support higher layer functionality, for example decode user data from the donor eNB and re–encode the data before transmission to the UE.

- The LTE relay is a fixed relay – infrastructure without a wired backhaul connection, that relays messages between the Base Station (BS) and Mobile Stations (MSs) through multihop communication.

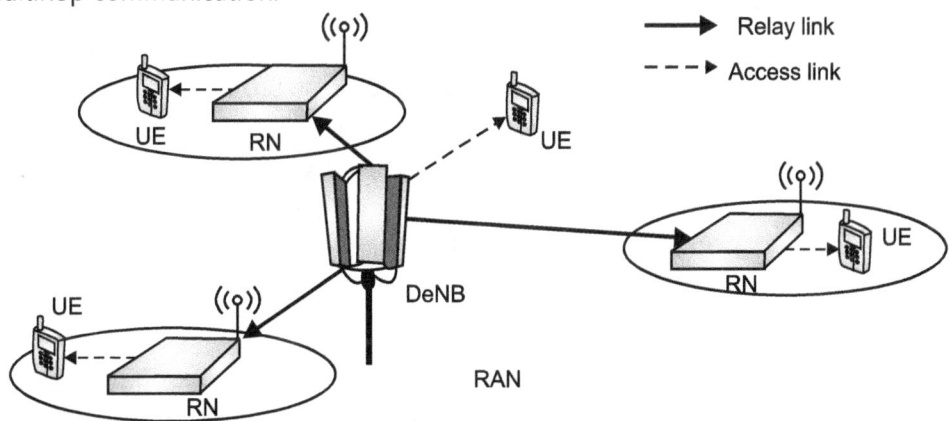

Fig. 4.22 : Relay Cell

4.20 HETEROGENEOUS NETWORK (HETNET)

- To achieve this LTE and LTE Advanced operators need to adopt a variety of approaches to meet the needs of a host of scenarios that will occur within the network.

- Different types of user will need use the network in different places and for different applications. Coupled to this operators introducing LTE and LTE Advanced networks will have many legacy systems available. In any LTE heterogeneous network it will be necessary to accommodate other radio access technologies including HSPA, UMTS and even EDGE and GPRS. In addition to this other technologies including Wi–Fi also need to be accommodated.

- These solutions for LTE heterogeneous networks need to incorporate not only the radio access network solutions, but also the core network as well. In this way a truly heterogeneous network can become functional.

- To ensure the best use is made of the available capabilities, all the various elements need to be operated in a manner that is truly seamless to the user. The user should be given the best experience using the best available technology at any given time. The performance and hence the user experience should also be very much the same whatever the location and whatever the application.

4.20.1 Small Cell

- The term small cell has gained a lot of attention and will have a major impact on how LTE and other wireless access technology platforms are deployed.

- Specifically, a small cell is what some can classify as a pico or femto cell. However, small cells are meant to address the issues like spot capacity and coverage problems, at the same time requiring a small physical footprint for the infrastructure.

- Small cells when included in a HetNet design can augment macro cell sites and in fact could possibly replace future macro cell deployments.

- Presently, small cells are implemented in an underlay approach for a macro network. However, there is nothing that would preclude a large deployment of small cells from replacing the current macro cell deployment schemes in an urban environment.

- Therefore, there are two views of what defines a small cell. One view is that physical footprint the small cell occupies from an infrastructure aspect.

- The other, and probably the best, definition is the coverage area that the small cell provides. By defining small cells based on their coverage area, the use of Remote Radio Heads (RRH) and femtocells plus other delivery platforms would easily be classified as a small cell.

4.20.2 HeNB

- A femto cell is a radio access network element that supports one or more of the GSM/WCDMA family of radio interfaces, operates in a limited geographic area in licensed spectrum, may operate over the public internet, and supports a limited number of simultaneous users in a home environment.

- Its principal functions are for coverage extension and for offloading users from the cellular network.

- Femto cell offers advantage to both subscribers and opertaors. It will reduce network infrastructure cost and reduce traffic on traditional radio network. And subscribers will get better indoor coverage.

- 3GPP Release 8 describes the femto architecture. 3G femto access point is called Home NodeB(HNB). LTE femto access point is called HeNB.

- Key components to the advancement of a heterogeneous network architecture are femtocell or in LTE world the Home eNodeB (HeNB).

- The HeNB uses licensed spectrum; however, a HeNB is not a relay node primarily since it gets its backhaul from existing DSL/cable connections. A HeNB is mainly used for indoor coverage.

- The HeNB includes the functions of an eNodeB as well as some additional HeNB–specific configuration/security functions. The HeNB accesses the core network and can support a large number of S1 interfaces with the use of a HeNB–Gateway (HeNB GW).

- Three different access modes are defined for HeNBs. These are closed, hybrid, and open and are associated with the Closed Subscriber Group (CSG).

    (a) **Closed Access:** Mode provides services only to its associated CSG members.

    (b) **Hybrid Access:** Mode provides services to its associated CSG members and to nonmembers. In a hybrid mode, the CSG members are prioritized over nonmembers.

    (c) **Open Access :** Mode has the HeNB appear as a normal eNodeB.

The HeNB cells operate as either a closed or hybrid cell for access. The HeNB broadcasts its access configuration to help the UE in identifying the characteristics of the HeNB. The parameters that support the UE in the identification of closed/hybrid cell are:

    (i)   CSG indicator

    (ii) CSG identity (CSG ID)

    (iii) HeNB name

4.21 REMOTE RADIO HEADS (RRH)

- One important deployment method for LTE is the use of RRH. An RRH is typically meant for outdoor deployments; however, it can also be used for building systems in place of or augmenting DAS.

- The main funtions of development of RRH(Remote Radio Head) are as follows:

    1. Offload IF and RF processing from base station.

    2. Increase in distance between RF antenna and Base Station Hardware.

    3. Use of cheap optical fibre to carry data between RRH and Base Station Controller.

- The RRH is a radio head in an LTE transmitter which can be mounted close to the antenna and connected to an RRH controller through an Ethernet or fiber connection.

- Fig. 4.23 shows a high–level depiction of some possible locations where an RRH can be utilized.

- In essence, an RRH enables a very small physical footprint for the LTE base station or sector making it possible to be installed in locations that were previously prohibited due to space or other issues.

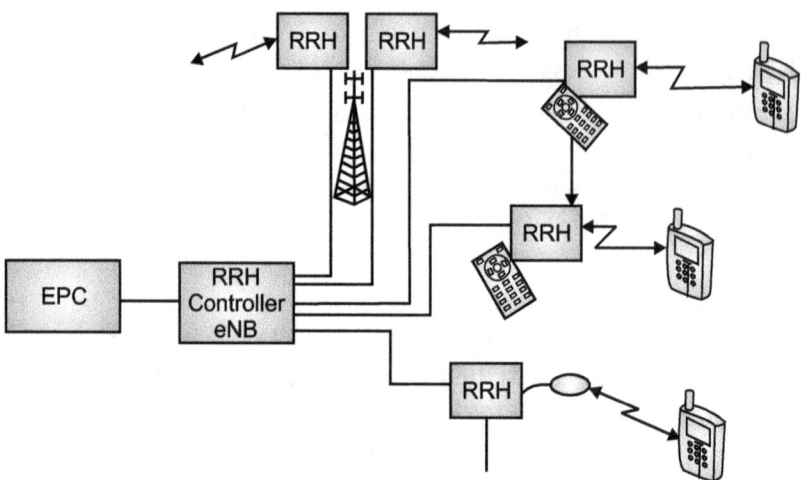

Fig. 4.23 : Remote Radio Head

4.21.1 Common Packet Radio Interface (CPRI)

- Common Packet Radio Interface (CPRI) is a fiber–optic communication standard that enables the use of RRH. CPRI defines the interface between an LTE eNodeB controller and a remote radio head for LTE.
- CPRI is essentially a layer 1 and layer 2 protocol that is IP–based utilizing an Ethernet connection.
- With CPRI the IP payload is referred to as an antenna carrier meant for a particular RRH.
- With multiple transmitters and receivers for LTE, each has its own CPRI antenna carrier payload.

4.22 VoLTE

- The Voice over LTE, VoLTE scheme was devised as a result of operators seeking a standardised system for transferring traffic for voice over LTE.
- Originally LTE was seen as a completely IP cellular system just for carrying data, and operators would be able to carry voice either by reverting to 2G / 3G systems or by using VoIP in one form or another.
- VoLTE is a logical evolution or migration of voice services onto one platform. How LTE handles VoIP or VoLTE is important, since LTE is a packet–based system and voice services are effectively a circuit–based service. VoIP, is understood. However, the EPC for an LTE network does not have a VoIP gateway to interface to a TDM network.
- Therefore, VoLTE uses an IP Multimedia Service (IMS) approach for VoIP treatment. The IMS platform is not part of the EPC, but as expected, referencing the EPC diagrams interfaces to the EPC via a PGW.
- The two methods used involved Circuit Switched Fall Back (CSFB) and Simultaneous Voice LTE (SV–LTE). With CSFB when a voice call needed to be placed or received from a TDM network, the UE would fall back to a 2G or 3G network. SV–LTE is slightly different than CSFB in that packet traffic is still handled by the LTE bearer and voice services use a CSFB.

- However, these techniques require two different radio access networks to serve the subscriber.

4.23 LTE ADVANCED

- 3GPP release 11 and beyond is referred to as LTE Advanced and is the next level or improvement for LTE. With work starting on LTE Advanced, a number of key requirements and key features are coming to light. Although not fixed yet in the specifications, there are many high level aims for the new LTE Advanced specification.
- These will need to be verified and much work remains to be undertaken in the specifications before these are all fixed.
- Currently some of the main headline aims for LTE Advanced can be seen below:
  - **Peak Data Rates:** Downlink – 1 Gbps; uplink – 500 Mbps.
  - **Spectrum Efficiency:** 3 times greater than LTE.
  - **Peak Spectrum Efficiency:** Downlink – 30 bps/Hz; uplink – 15 bps/Hz.
  - **Spectrum Use:** The ability to support scalable bandwidth use and spectrum aggregation where non–contiguous spectrum needs to be used.
  - **Latency:** from Idle to Connected in less than 50 ms and then shorter than 5 ms one way for individual packet transmission.
- Cell edge user throughput to be twice that of LTE.
- Average user throughput to be 3 times that of LTE.
  - **Mobility:** Same as that in LTE
  - **Compatibility:** LTE Advanced shall be capable of interworking with LTE and 3GPP legacy systems.
  - There are a number of key technologies that will enable LTE Advanced to achieve the high data throughput rates that are required. MIMO and OFDM are two of the base technologies that will be enablers. Along with these there are a number of other techniques and technologies that will be employed.
  - Orthogonal Frequency Division Multiplex, OFDM OFDM forms the basis of the radio bearer. Along with it there is OFDMA (Orthogonal Frequency Division Multiple Access) along with SC–FDMA (Single Channel Orthogonal Frequency Division Multiple Access). These will be used in a hybrid format. However the basis for all of these access schemes is OFDM.
  - **Carrier Aggregation, CA:** As many operators do not have sufficient contiguous spectrum to provide the required bandwidths for the very high data rates, a scheme known as carrier aggregation has been developed. Using this technology operators are able to utilise multiple channels either in the same bands or different areas of the spectrum to provide the required bandwidth.
  - **LTE Relaying:** LTE relaying is a scheme that enables signals to be forwarded by remote stations from a main base station to improve coverage.

- **Device to Device, D2D:** LTE D2D is a facility that has been requested by a number of users, in particular the emergency services. It enables fast swift access via direct communication – a facility that is essential for the emergency services when they may be on the scene of an incident.
- **Coordinated Multipoint :** One of the key issues with many cellular systems is that of poor performance at the cell edges. Interference from adjacent cells along with poor signal quality lead to a reduction in data rates. For LTE–Advanced a scheme known as coordinated multipoint has been introduced. In short, CoMP enables multiple downlink and uplink transmissions for a mobile device, thereby not only improving throughput but also potentially improving the battery life of the end user device.

QUESTIONS

1. Write a short note on LTE.
2. Describe the LTE Ecosystem.
3. Explain the LTE standards.
4. Explain the uplink and downlink of LTE bands for FDD configuration.
5. Explain the uplink and downlink of LTE bands for TDD configuration.
6. Draw and Explain the LTE architecture.
7. Write a short note on:
   (i) User Equipment (UE) (ii) (eNode B) (iii) Core network (EPC)
   (iv) Mobility Management Element (MME) (v) Serving Gateway (500w)
   (v) Packet data Network Gateway (PGW)
8. Explain the radio channel components.
9. What are the LTE channel types ? Explain each of them.
10. Draw and Explain the uplink logical channel structure.
11. Explain the Hybrid Automatic Repeat Request (HARD).
12. Write a short note on QCI.
13. Explain the System Information messages (SIB).
14. Draw and Explain the LTE RF channel.
15. Draw and Explain the LTE UL channel.
16. Describe the TD-LTE and Explain the LTE TDD configuration.
17. Draw and Explain the eNodeB 4×4 MIMO
18. Explain the LTE scheduler.
19. Write a short note on : (i) Carrier Aggregation (ii) Cell search (iii) Cell reselection.
20. Draw and Explain the X2 handover.
21. Draw and Explain the S1 Handover.
22. Explain following terms : (i) Relay Cells (ii) HETNET (iii) RRH (iv) VoLTE (v) SON
23. Write features of LTE advanced.

Unit - V

WiMAX

5.1 INTRODUCTION

- The Worldwide Interoperability for Microwave Access (WiMAX) is used for providing broadband internet using wireless medium mainly at 2.5GHz, 3.5GHz and 5.8GHz radio frequencies. It is also known as 4G technology. It delivers about 4 times fast internet compared to its 3G counterpart. OFDM is behind this increase in speed as it carry multiple carriers, each carrying more than one data bits based on modulation techniques (QPSK, 16QAM). This carriers are concisely packed together to save bandwidth. Intel is behind the development and proliferation of WIMax throughout the world.

- WiMAX is a broadband wireless access method that is based on the Data over Cable Service Interface Specification (DOCSIS) protocol and uses OFDMA as the modulation scheme. WiMAX is not a 3GPP standard, but it is an IEEE standard.

- WiMAX is based on the IEEE 802.16 set of standards for an IP packet-based system and can be deployed as an FDD or TDD configuration. WiMAX is also a complimentary broadband service to Wi-Fi (IEEE 802.11).

- The WiMAX IEEE 802.16 standards cover the following scenarios:

  (i)   WiMAX for backhaul solutions (point to point),

  (ii) Fixed wireless access WiMAX (point to multipoint),

  (iii) Mobile WiMAX (mobility).

- Mobile WiMAX is also classified as a 3G (IMT-2000) and 4G (IMT-2000 advanced) wireless radio access technology. WiMAX using 802.16e comes under the 3G classification while WiMAX using 802.16m is classified as a 4G technology.

- WiMAX, which originally began as a fixed wireless point-to-multipoint wireless network, was previously referred to as Local Multipoint Distribution Systems (LMDS). However LMDS systems were designed and deployed before the IEEE standard series of 802.16 x was established.

- Additionally LMDS was designed for fixed locations providing last mile broadband access using a variety of protocols.

- However with the advent of IEEE 802.16, the adaptation of WiMAX has greatly enhanced since it is no longer vendor-driven proprietary protocols but a standards-based solution.

- The WiMAX IEEE 802.16, or 802.16, is an evolving IEEE standards that are applicable to a vast array of applications and defined spectrum bands currently ranging from 400 MHz to 66 GHz, which include both licensed and unlicensed (license exempt) bands.
- WiMAX is used presently in many deployment configurations around the world ranging from last mile broadband access for both fixed and mobile as well as point-to-point links for backhaul.
- Fig. 5.1 briefly depicts the various areas within wireless access that WiMAX plays a role.

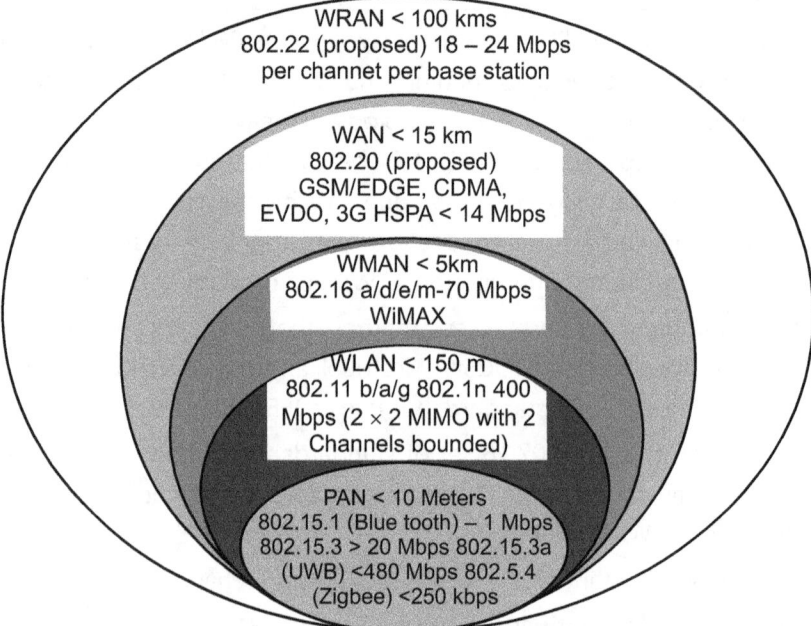

Fig. 5.1 : WiMAX wireless access relationship

- In reviewing Fig. 5.1, it is apparent that WiMAX meets a variety of wireless access requirements.
- Some of the uses for fixed WiMAX include :
  - (a) Last mile wireless broadband connections as an alternative for DSL and cable modems.
  - (b) Broadband access in developing countries as an alternative to installing fixed infrastructure like copper.
  - (c) Hotspots and high-speed connectivity for business customers.
  - (d) Backhaul connectivity as a point-to-point microwave link using licensed, lightly licensed, and unlicensed spectrum.
- WiMAX also supports wireless mobility enabling:
  - (a) Broadband mobility (3G and 4G).
  - (b) Nomadic connectivity, that is, hot spots and or hot zones.

- WiMAX enables the convergence of both mobility and fixed wireless access through a common radio access protocol.

- An important attribute of WiMAX is the reliance on specific profiles for the Access Node (AN) and the Subscriber Station (SS).

- The profiles define the specific Radio Frequency (RF) characteristics, as well as the services that are supported.

- Profiles consist of both system and certification profiles. The system profiles define mandatory and options physical and MAC layer features, whereas the certification profiles define the operating frequency, RF channel bandwidth, and duplexing mode (TDD, FDD) and are tied to the system profile selected.

- When WiMAX equipment is certified it is certified based on interoperability using a given certification profile.

- For a more detailed read on the specifications related to 802.16, there are several excellent sources for obtaining information and existing vendor interoperability, for example, www.wimaxforum.org and www.ieee802.org/16.

5.2 STANDARDS

- The standards board of the IEEE (Institute of Electrical and Electronics Engineers) based in the USA set up a working group to address Broadband Wireless Access Standards under the 802.16 banner. Its aim was to prepare formal standards that would be used for the deployment of broadband metropolitan area networks around the world.

- Although the standards for the physical and MAC layers are defined under 802.16, the technology has been named WiMAX (Worldwide interoperability of Microwave Access) and issues, including interoperability, certification and promotion of the system are handled by the WiMAX Forum.

- Fig. 5.2 attempts to show some of the relationships between some of the more prevalent IEEE 802 standards and WiMAX.

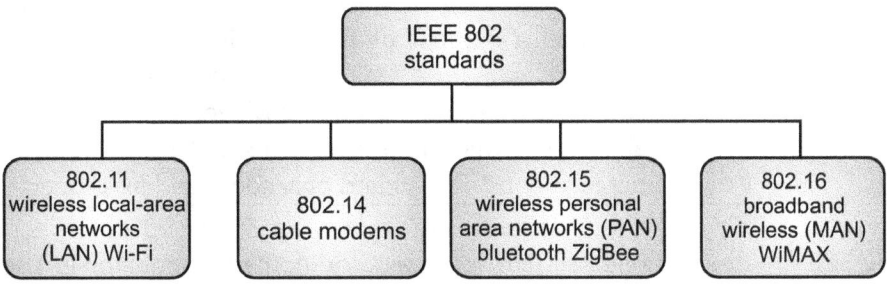

Fig. 5.2 : IEEE 802

- Like all other standards within the 802 series like Wi-Fi and Bluetooth/Zigbee, the 802.16 series, referred to as WiMAX has many sections which make up this standard. However, WiMAX can be grouped into two basic standard types, fixed and mobile. The WiMAX standards like all standards are continuously evolving and diligence is needed to keep up-to-date on the various advances that are being made with it unique series or protocols.

- The unique aspect with WiMAX is that while the term is general its application can be widely different. For instance WiMAX can be used for point-to-point communication for backhaul or it can be used for mobility or fixed broadband. Because of the plethora of WiMAX configurations possible, a brief overview of the relevant 806.16 standards is shown in Table 5.1. There are other 806.16 specifications as part of the series that provide additional enhancements and functionality; however, they will not be covered here.

Table 5.1 : 806.16 Variants

Standard/Amendment	Description
802.16	Now withdrawn. This is the basic 802.16 standard that was released in 2001. It provided for basic high data links at frequencies between 11 and 60 GHz.
802.16a	Now withdrawn. This amendment addressed certain spectrum issues and enabled the standard to be used at frequencies below the 11 GHz minimum of the original standard.
802.16b	Now withdrawn. It increased the spectrum that was specified to include frequencies between 5 and 6 GHz while also providing for Quality of Service aspects.
802.16c	Now withdrawn. This amendment to 802.16 provided a system profile for operating between 10 and 66 GHz and provided more details for operations within this range. The aim was to enable greater levels of interoperability.
802.16d (802.16-2004)	This amendment was also known as 802.16-2004 in view of the fact that it was released in 2004. It was a major revision of the 802.16 standard and upon its release, all previous documents were withdrawn. The standard / amendment provided a number of fixes and improvements to 802.16a including the use of 256 carrier OFDM. Profiles for compliance testing are also provided, and the standard was aligned with the ETSI HiperMAN standard to allow for global deployment. The standard only addressed fixed operation.
802.16e (802.16-2005)	This standard, also known as 802.16-2005 in view of its release date, provided for nomadic and mobile use. With lower data rates of 15 Mbps against to 70 Mbps of 802.16d, it enabled full nomadic and mobile use including handover.
802.16f	Management information base
802.16g	Management plane procedures and services

...Conti.

802.16h	Improved coexistence mechanisms for license-exempt operation
802.16j	Multi-hop relay specification
802.16k	802.16 bridging
802.16m	Advanced air interface. This amendment is looking toth e future and it is anticipated it will provide data rates of 100 Mbps for mobile applications and 1 Gbps for fixed applications. It will allow cellular, macro and micro cell coverage, with currently there are no restrictions on the RF bandwidth although it is expected to be 20 MHz or more.

- Further expanding upon Table 5.1 is Table 5.2 which briefly highlights some of the technical parameters associated with the mobility aspects for WiMAX.

Table 5.2 : WiMAX Mobilty

	802.16e	802.16m
Operating bandwidth	5 to 20 MHz single carrier	5 to 20 MHz per carrier Multiple carrier aggregation (100 MHz)
Duplex	TDD, FDD, H-FDD (MS)	TDD, FDD, H-FDD (MS)
MIMO	**DL** 1×1 (baseline), 2×2, 2×4, 4×4, 4×8, 8×8 **UL** 1×1 (baseline), 1×2, 1×4, 2×4, 4×4	**DL** 2×2 (baseline), 2×4, 4×4, 4×8, 8×8 **UL** 1×2(baseline), 1×4, 2×4, 4×4
Frame length	Variable; 2 to 20 ms	5 ms, (superframe = 20 ms)

- The WiMAX Forum like the IEEE plays an important role in the development and refinement of the WiMAX standards through promoting the standardization of WiMAX and obviously the compatibility and interoperability of devices that make up the WiMAX ecosystem.

- Difference between various 802.16 standards and many offered up.

- 802.16 is a point-to-multipoint protocol with a centralized base station and is a Wireless Metropolitan Area Network (WMAN) technology that provides both backhaul and an alternative for last mile broadband access as well as connecting 802.11 hot spots to the Internet. 802.16 standard specifies two convergent service layers that form the basis of protocol, and those two convergent service layers are ATM and Packet (IP).

- 802.16a focuses on spectrum that is below 10 GHz. In the United States the key spectrum for 802.16 is in the MMDS bands, mostly from 2.5 to 2.7 GHz. Worldwide, 3.5 GHz and 10.5 GHz. Because Non-Line-of-Sight (NLOS) operation and lower component costs, these bands have seen good use as fixed wireless for both residential and small-business services. 802.16a has the same access method as HiperMAN.

- The 802.16e standard added mobility and offers an alternative access method other than 3G mobility access methods.

- The 802.16m standard is an enhancement to the 802.16e standard focusing on higher throughput capabilities and defined in 4G technology. 802.16m is also meant to support Voice over IP (VoIP):

  (a) **DL:** 300 Mbps/20 MHz (4 × 4)

  (b) **UL:** 135 Mbps/20 MHz (2 × 4)

- Specifically, 802.16m has these additional attributes:

  (a) Multicarrier operation (100-MHz bandwidth).

  (b) Extended MIMO.

  (c) Fixed frame length to reduce round trip times (5 ms).

  (d) Superframe structure.

5.3 GENERIC WiMAX ARCHITECTURE

- The WiMAX architecture developed by the WiMAX form supports is a unified network architecture to support fixed, nomadic and mobile operation. The WiMAX network architecture is based upon an all-IP model.

- The WiMAX network architecture comprises three major elements or areas.

- **Remote or Mobile Stations:** These are the user equipments that may be mobile or fixed and may be located in the premises of the user.

- **Access Service Network, ASN:** This is the area of the WiMAX network that forms the radio access network at the edge and it comprises one or more base stations and one or more ASN gateways.

- **Connectivity Service Network, CSN:** This part of the WiMAX network provides the IP connectivity and all the IP core network functions. It is what may be termed the core network in cellular parlance.

- As shown in the Fig. 5.3 Subscriber Station (SS) or MS seeking to enter wimax network will connect first with Base Station(BS). BS already has been interfaced with ASN gateway/CSN router to provide internet service. For complete frame exchange between BS and SS read our article on MAC protocol inside.

- CSN router is connected with Application service provider which consists of AAA (Authentication, authorization and accounting) server, DHCP server, HA (Home Agent), DNS server, PSTN and other networks (such as 3GPP). ASN stands for Access Service Network and CSN stands for connectivity service network. For more on gateway and router pl. refer our pages as mentioned in useful links as shown in Fig. 5.3 below.

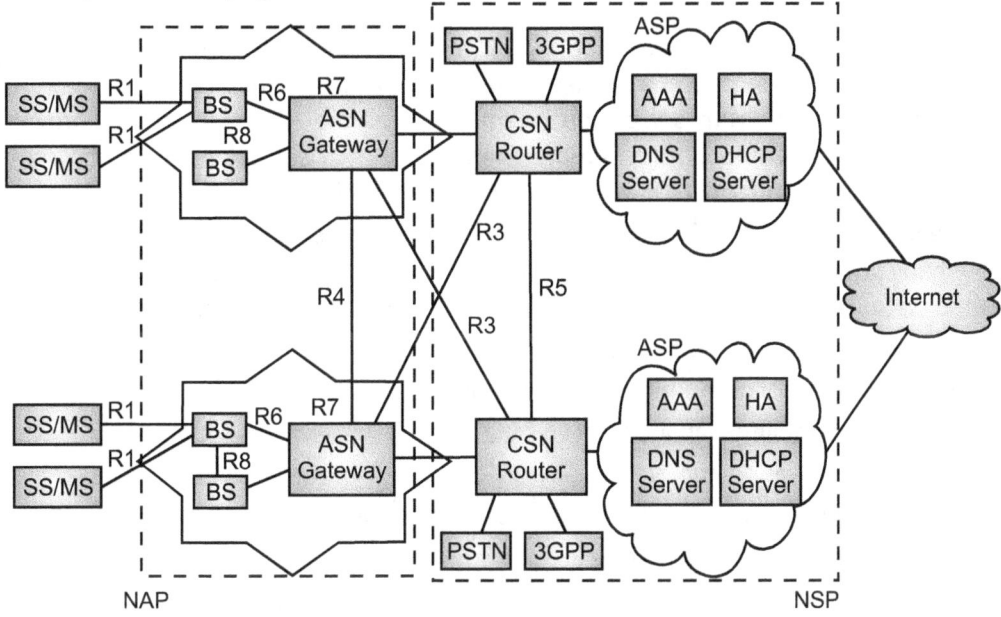

Fig. 5.3 : WiMAX Network Reference Model

- The overall WiMAX network comprises a number of different entities that make up the different major areas described above. These include the following entities

- **Subscriber Station, SS / Mobile Station, MS:** The Subscriber station, SS may often be referred to as the Customer Premises Equipment, CPE. These take a variety of forms and these may be termed "indoor CPE" or "outdoor CPE" the terminology is self-explanatory. The outdoor CPE has the advantage that it provides better performance as a result of the better position of the antenna, whereas the indoor CPE can be installed by the user. Mobile Stations may also be used. These are often in the form of a dongle for a laptop, etc.

- **Base Station, BS:** The base-station forms an essential element of the WiMAX network. It is responsible for providing the air interface to the subscriber and mobile stations. It provides additional functionality in terms of micro-mobility management functions, such as handoff triggering and tunnel establishment, radio resource management, QoS policy enforcement, traffic classification, DHCP (Dynamic Host Control Protocol) proxy, key management, session management, and multicast group management.

- **ASN Gateway, ASN-GW:** The ASN gateway within the WiMAX network architecture typically acts as a layer 2 traffic aggregation point within the overall ASN.

- The ASN-GW may also provide additional functions that include: intra-ASN location management and paging, radio resource management and admission control, caching of subscriber profiles and encryption keys. The ASN-GW may also include the AAA client functionality(see below), establishment and management of mobility tunnel with base stations, QoS and policy enforcement, foreign agent functionality for mobile IP, and routing to the selected CSN.

- **Home Agent, HA:** The Home Agent within the WiMAX network is located within the CSN. With Mobile-IP forming a key element within WiMAX technology, the Home Agent works in conjunction with a "Foreign Agent", such as the ASN Gateway, to provide an efficient end-to-end Mobile IP solution. The Home Agent serves as an anchor point for subscribers, providing secure roaming with QoS capabilities.

- **Authentication, Authorisation and Accounting Server, AAA:** As with any communications or wireless system requiring subscription services, an Authentication, Authorisation and Accounting server is used. This is included within the CSN.

Defining a few of the nodes a little more:

The ASN provides the following high-level functions:

- L2 session/mobility management.
- Network entry and handover.
- Radio resource management and admission control.
- QoS and policy enforcement.
- Foreign agent.
- Forwarding all data and messaging to and from the selected CSN.
- Paging and location management

The ASN-GW, which is part of the ASN, performs the following high-level functions:

- Layer 2 traffic aggregation.
- Management, network optimization.
- Forwarding of all subscriber traffic to and from the MS and CSN.
- Routing to the desired CSN, if more than one.
- AAA client functionality.
- Idle mode control.

The CSN provides a host of functions of which some are:

- IP and traffic management.
- QoS and policy.
- Authentications for all SS devices.
- Roaming support.
- Billing.
- O and M functions.

The various interfaces for a WiMAX system are R1-R5 and R8 and they are described briefly.

- R1 is the interface between the MS and the ASN and is the air interface specification for (PHY and MAC).

- R2 is the interface between the MS and the CSN. The R2 interface enables authentication, service authorization, IP host configuration management, and mobility management. The R2 interface is a logical interface and is not a physical protocol interface between the SS and CSN.

- R3 is the interface between the ASN and CSN and is meant to support AAA, policy enforcement, and mobility management. The R3 interface provides the bearer plane tunneling for IP data between the ASN and the CSN.

- R4 interface is the control and bearer plane protocols within the ASN to coordinate MS mobility between ASNs.

- R5 is a set of control plane and bearer plane protocols providing interworking between CSNs.

- R6 is the communication interface between the BS and the ASN-GW for the control and bearer plane.

- R8 is control plane messages for the bearer plane data flows between the BS for handovers.

5.3.1 Fixed

- WiMAX can and is used as a point-to-point communication system for backhaul. The frequency band that is used for point-to-point communication can be any band. However there are some preferred bands that a point-to-point WiMAX link should utilize. Fig. 5.4 is a high-level diagram of a simple point-to-point communication like using WiMAX.

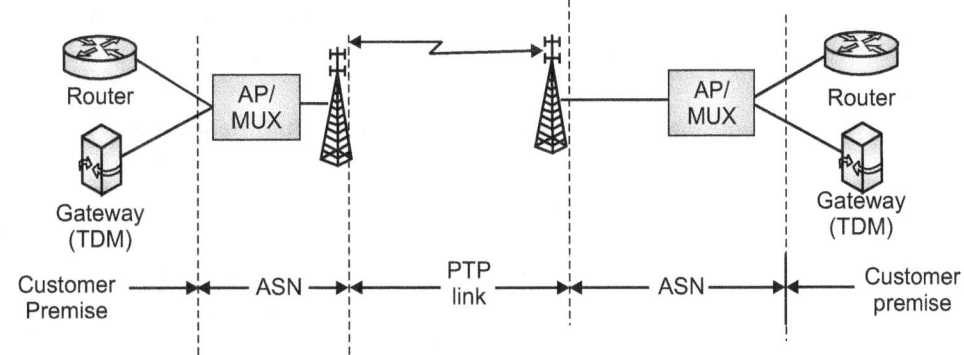

Fig. 5.4 : Point-to-point communication

- Adherence to Fresnel zones is essential for good link quality.

5.3.2 Point to Multipoint (PMP)

- 802.16 is the enabling technology or standard that is intended to provide WMAN access to locations, usually buildings, by use of exterior illumination typically from a centralized base station as shown in Fig. 5.5.
- The simplified system shown in the Fig. 5.5 could also have multiple subscribers that would be referred to as Subscriber Stations (SSs).

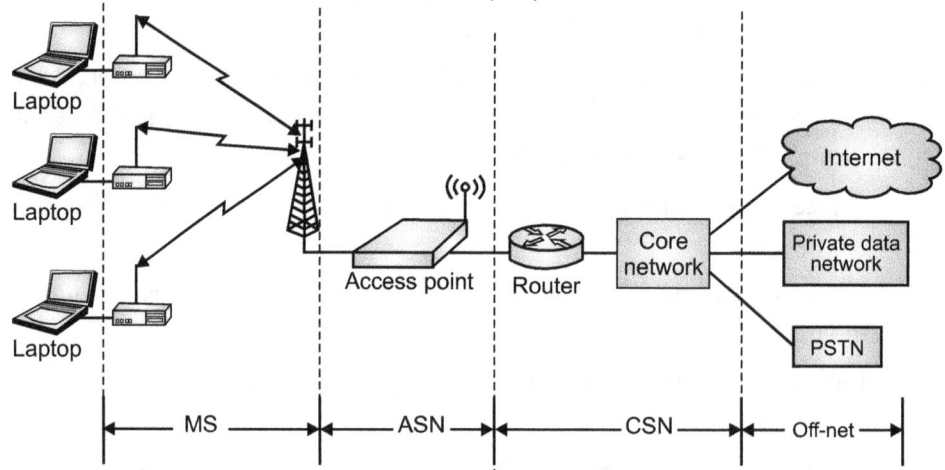

Fig. 5.5 : 802.16 general configuration

- Local Multipoint Distribution Systems (LMDSs), Fixed Wireless Point-to-Multipoint (FWPMP), and Multichannel Multiple-Point Distribution Systems (MMDSs) have been in existence for quite some time now. However, each of the LMDS, FWPMP, and MMDS, while being superb in delivering a vast array of broadband services, has suffered from the proprietary systems which have not seen the reduction in total cost of deployment or ownership being reduced to a level that competes with the existing wired broadband services.
- Wireless Internet Service Providers (WISPs) have also been active in delivering broadband services. WISPs have used both licensed and licensed exempt bands for service delivery. WISPs have been using point-to-multipoint or mesh systems along with 802.11 to serve their customers.
- However, with the advent of the 802.16, standard equipment manufacturers and operators now had a standard for access profiles as well as known interoperability levels allowing for multivendor environments.
- The PMP is a concept where multiple subscribers can access the same radio platform utilizing both a multiplexing method as well as queuing. 802.16 systems operate in the microwave frequency band and utilize similar radio technology as a point-to-point microwave system.
- The point-to-multipoint protocol used is a connection-oriented system that can take on a star or mesh configuration using both FDD and TDD.

- In addition, 802.16 is in itself protocol-independent in that it can transport both ATM and IP depending on the content desired to be ported. In addition, 802.16 utilizes both contention and contention less access supporting services that are ATM Adaption Layer 1(AAL1) to AAL5.

- The system configuration used for an 802.16 system is designed to operate efficiently within the spectrum that is allocated. To achieve this, 802.16 is a wireless system that employs cellular-like design and reuse with the exception that there is no handoff.

- However, 802.16 is different from 802.11 and wireless mobility systems like GSM, CDMA, and UMTS. 802.16 is a unique wireless access system whose purpose is to provide broadband access to multiple subscribers or locations within the same geographic area. It utilizes microwave radio as the fundamental transport media and is not fundamentally a new technology but rather an adaptation and standardization of existing technology for broadband service implementation.

- For a wireless service provider 802.16 is one of the many tools that can be used to help improve the network and drive operating and capital costs downward.

802.16 systems can be effectively deployed where:

  - Users are dissatisfied with the current packet and or network interface.
  - Network operators need to reach customers cost-effectively without deploying fiber/copper.

5.3.3 Mesh

- Fig. 5.6 depicts a generalized mesh network for WiMAX. A mesh environment is very efficient for low network traffic levels since each node needs to transport its own traffic plus the associated node it is meant to relay, which can be multiple layers deep.

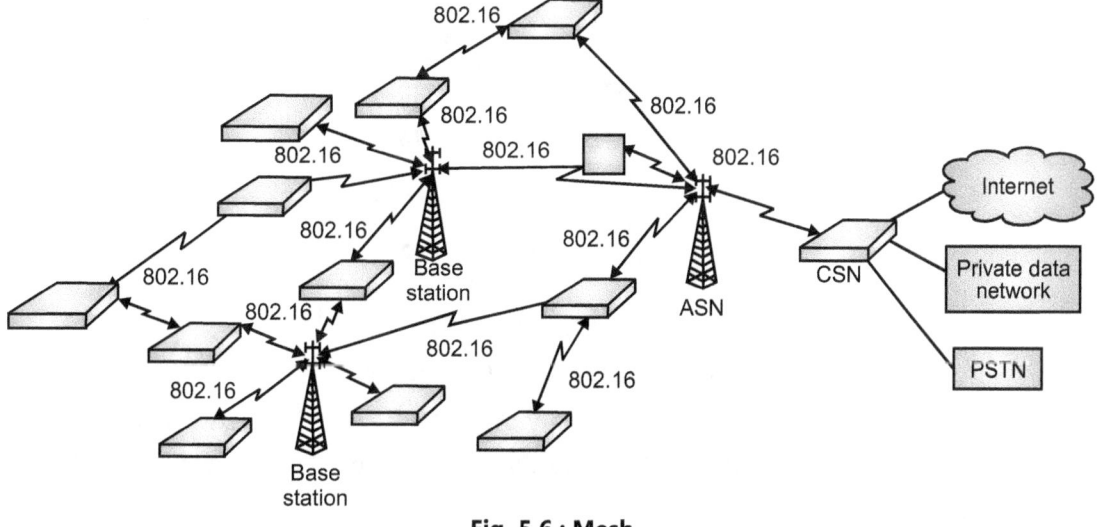

Fig. 5.6 : Mesh

- However, the key advantage with a mesh environment is the flexibility it affords, as well as reducing some of the fixed infrastructure requirements when the customer base and true concentrations are not known from the beginning.

5.3.4 Mobility

- A key criterion for WiMAX to be both a 3G and 4G wireless access media is the ability to provide mobility. Fig. 5.7 is a very simplified depiction of a WiMAX mobility network.

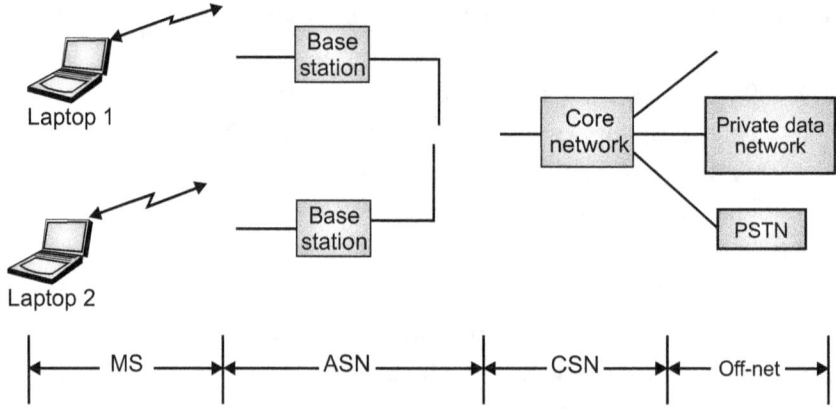

Fig. 5.7 : WiMAX mobile system

5.4 CORE NETWORK

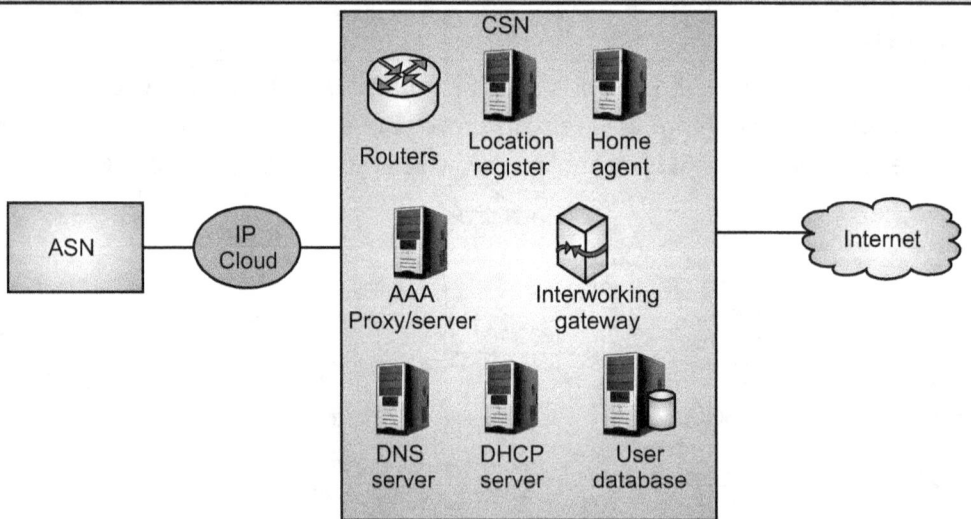

Fig. 5.8 : Structure of WiMAX network

- WiMAX network structure mainly includes WiMAX Access Service Network and WiMAX Connectivity Service Network. CSN is the core network of WiMAX. It provides the IP connection service for the users.

- As you can see in CSN, it includes the router, location register, home agent and AAA-server. Router connects CSN with the other modules. Location register record the user's login and location information. In order to support the mobility, CSN provides mobile IP function.

- Home agent is responsible for maintaining MS position imformation and sending the packets to the network of MS. AAA proxy/server provide authentication, authorization and accounting services. As to connect Internet or any other IP network, CSN may also include user database and interworking gateway devices, DHCP server and DNS server.

- The main components for a CSN are:
  - Core packet switch (IMS).
  - Authentication, Authorization, and Accounting (AAA) server.
  - Dynamic Host Control Protocol (DHCP) server.
  - Domain Name Service (DNS) server.
  - Network Time Protocol (NTP) server.
  - Home agent.
  - OSS/BSS.
  - Service Edge Router/Gateway.

- CSN is defined as the combination of network function. It includes these performances:
  - MS IP address and endpoint parameter allocation for user sessions
  - Internet access
  - AAA services
  - Policy and Admission Control based on user subscription profiles
  - ASN-CSN tunneling support
  - WiMAX subscriber billing and inter-operator settlement
  - Inter-CSN tunneling for roaming
  - Inter-ASN mobility
  - Connectivity to WiMAX services such as IP multimedia services (IMS), location based services, peer-to-peer services and provisioning.

5.5 RADIO NETWORK

The WiMAX radio network is referred to as the Access Network System (ASN) shown in Fig. 5.9 and includes the following main components:

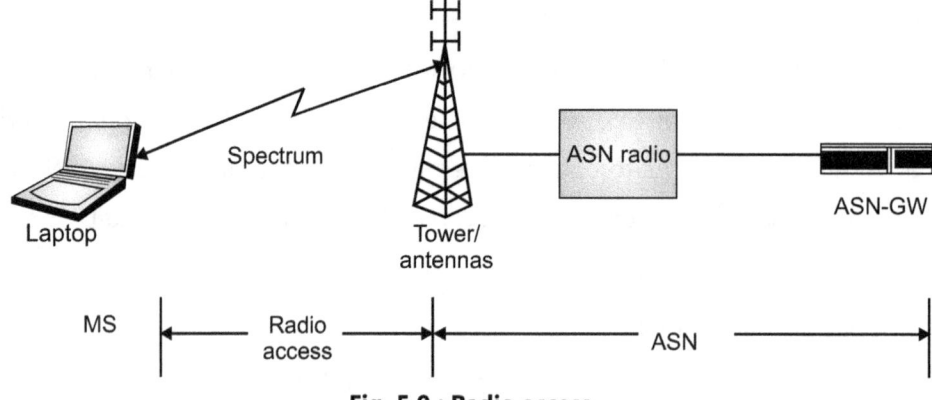

Fig. 5.9 : Radio access

- Spectrum
- Base station
- ASN radio equipment
- ASN-GW

Within the functionality of the ASN is the scheduler. WiMAX draws upon the DOCSIS protocol for defining its service-scheduling techniques.

5.6 WiMAX SPECTRUM

- The IEEE 802.16 WiMAX standard allows data transmission using multiple broadband frequency ranges. The original 802.16a standard specified transmissions in the range 10 - 66 GHz, but 802.16d allowed lower frequencies in the range 2 to 11 GHz. The lower frequencies used in the later specifications means that the signals suffer less from attenuation and therefore they provide improved range and better coverage within buildings. This brings many benefits to those using these data links within buildings and means that external antennas are not required.

- Different bands are available for WiMAX applications in different parts of the world. The frequencies commonly used are 3.5 and 5.8 GHz for 802.16d and 2.3, 2.5 and 3.5 GHz for 802.16e but the use depends upon the countries:

- Presently, WiMAX has several frequency bands below 10 GHz that are associated with the mobility and edge devices. The frequency bands below 10 GHz currently meant for WiMAX are:

    - **450 MHz:** 470 MHz (IMT-2000),
    - **698 MHz:** 960 MHz,

- **1710 MHz:** 2025 MHz (IMT-2000),
- **2110 MHz:** 2200 MHz (IMT-2000),
- **2300 MHz:** 2400 MHz,
- **2500 MHz:** 2690 MHz,
- **3400 MHz:** 3600 MHz.

- Additionally through the use of the IMT frequency bands WiMAX user terminals can have access all around the world. Specifically, 802.16-compliant equipment is meant to operate in multiple spectrum plans around the world.

- The two major spectrum channel plans are defined by the Federal Communications Commission (FCC) and European Telecommunications Standards Institute (ETSI). The channel plans, in addition to spectrum locations, are different for both the FCC and ETSI allocations.

- The typical FCC allocation for broadband systems is 20 or 25 MHz, while for Europe the spectrum allotted is 28 MHz with both allocation methods favoring duplexed operation.

- The standard also supports Frequency Division Duplexing (FDD) and Time-Division Duplexing (TDD). The inclusion of TDD is aimed at regulatory environments where structured channel pairs do not exist.

- In the United States, the FCC channel allocation plan is done in increments of 5 MHz ranging from 5, 10, 15, 20, and 25 MHz channels that can be either FDD or TDD in nature. The FCC channel plan and spectrum also need to adhere to CFR 47 part 101 as well as parts 1, 15, and 17. While the ETSI channel plan for 802.16 has different channel bandwidths or channel plans than that used in the United States.

- 802.16 operating in the 10-GHz or higher frequency bands is meant for fixed applications. The channel plans are based on increments of 3.5 MHz ranging from 3.5, 7, 14, 28, 56, and 112 MHz depending on the country and spectrum that the system is to operate within.

- However with respect to the bands below 10 GHz, WiMAX is deployed in both licensed and unlicensed bands. As previously mentioned, some of the typical bands for global WiMAX deployment are 2.3 GHz, 2.5 GHz, 3.5 GHz, and 5.7 GHz.

- In the United States, the 2.5-GHz band is licensed spectrum and goes from 2.5 GHz to 2.7 GHz (2.690 GHz). It also allocated in such countries like canda, Brazil, South east Asia etc.

- In the United States, this band is referred to as the Broadband Radio Service (BRS) band, and since 1998 it is allowed to operate not only as a TDD but also as an FDD configuration for both fixed and mobile operation. In the United States the BRS is broken into eight licenses of 22.5 MHz each.

- The 2.3-GHz band is a licensed band and has been allocated in the United States, Australia, New Zealand, and South Korea (WiBro). The 2.3-GHz band in the United States is called the Wireless Communications Services (WCSs) band and is allocated in 30-MHz blocks. However, a unique aspect with this band in the United States is its proximity to the DARSs (Digital Audio Radio Services) band, which is adjacent to the WCSs band that places significant restrictions on out-of-band emissions to protect DARSs.

- The 3.5-GHz band is a licensed band also and has been allocated for fixed wireless broadband services in many countries (except the United States).

- The UNII (Unlicensed National Information Infrastructure) or licensed license-exempt 5 GHz (sometimes referred to as 5.7 GHz or 5.8-GHz band) is allocated for unlicensed operation in many countries. In the United States, the UNII band includes about 200 MHz of total spectrum.

- However, Table 5.3 tabularizes the above information.

Table 5.3 : Lower 10 GHz WiMAX Spectrum

	Frequency	Channel Bandwidth (MHz)
MMDS	2150–2162 and 2500–2690	1.5, 3, 6, 12, 24
MMDS	2150–2162 and 2500–2690	1.5, 3, 6, 12, 24
WCS	2305–2320 and 2345–2360	2.5, 5, 10, 15
ETSI	3410–4200, 10000–10680	1.75, 3.5, 7, 14, 28
UNII	5250–5360 and 5725–5825	Unspecified

5.7 MODULATION

- Number of modulation schemes such as QAM 4 (PSK), QAM-16, QAM-64, and QAM-256 are used in WiMAX.

- These modulation schemes are used with OFDM, OFDMA, and SOFDM. OFDMA is similar to OFDM; however, there are some key differences that need to be highlighted. What is unique is that in OFDM the subcarrier allocation is fixed per user; however, with OFDMA the subcarrier allocation is dynamic.

- The dynamic approach to assigning subcarriers leads to better trunking efficiency which equates to usable bandwidth that can be delivered to the subscriber.

- OFDMA was chosen for use in WiMAX because it has high spectral efficiency. Additionally OFDMA is also resilient to multipath propagation problems and it has the added benefit of reduced receiver complexity.

- The receiver complexity simplification is important to keep the overall cost and battery consumption at a minimum.

- Smart antennas can be integrated with OFDMA. MIMO systems and space-time coding can be realized on OFDMA and all the benefits of MIMO systems can be obtained easily. Adaptive modulation and tone/power allocation are also realizable on OFDMA.

- OFDM is spectrally efficient; IFFT/FFT operation ensures that sub-carriers do not interfere with each other. OFDM has an inherent robustness against narrowband interference. Narrowband interference will affect at most a couple of subchannels. Information from the affected subchannels can be erased and recovered via the forward error correction (FEC) codes

- WiMAX mobile and point-to-multipoint fixed utilize OFDMA for improved multipath performance in non-line-of-sight environments. OFDMA has multiple closely spaced subcarriers which are also grouped. OFDMA is able to assign a different subset of subcarriers to an individual user depending on the subscriber's capability, profile, and the RF channel bandwidth.

- Additionally mobile WiMAX uses Scalable Orthogonal Frequency-Division Multiple Access (SOFDMA), which was introduced in the IEEE 802.16e amendment to support scalable channel bandwidths from 1.25 to 20 MHz. The scalability is supported by adjusting the FFT size while fixing the subcarrier frequency spacing at 10.94 kHz. In essence, SOFDMA adjusts the size of the number of FFTs while fixing the subcarrier frequency enabling better spectral efficiency through allocating smaller FFT sizes for lower bandwidth channels and larger FFT sizes to wider channels. However, with SOFDMA the capacity of each individual subchannel remains constant, which reduces system complexity for smaller channels and improves performance of wider channels through better spectral efficiency.

- All versions of WiMAX utilize subchannels, and subchannelization techniques are a means to better manage network performance based on coverage and capacity requirements. The subcarriers based on the FFT size can be grouped together forming a subchannel.

- There are a few subchannel techniques that are used in WiMAX and those are adjacent and distributed.

- Distributed subchannels are also called Frequency Diverse Transmission (FDT). The FDT can use the Full Usage of Subchannels (FUSC) and Partial Usage of Subchannels (PUSC) modes. With FDT, the subcarriers assigned to each logical subchannel are pseudorandomly distributed across the available subcarrier set and is meant to adjust for RF channel conditions for coverage and capacity optimization.

- Adjacent subcarriers, also called Frequency Selective Transmission (FST), use both the Band Adaptive Modulation (BAM) and Adaptive Modulation and Coding (AMC) mode.

- BAM and AMC permit subchannel construction and allocation to be adjacent to each other.

- As part of the FST, the scheduler uses closed-loop channel feedback techniques to determine the optimal subchannels to be allocated to each SS based on the individual RF channel conditions.

- However, with fixed WiMAX the OFDM has an FFT of 256 and the amount of FFTs is independent of the bandwidth that it occupies. OFDM bandwidths for WiMAX range from 1.25 MHz to 28 MHz. However, in both FDD and TDD modes there are really 200 usable carriers (FFT 256), of the 256 FFTs, or rather subcarrier, since the number of FFTs determines the amount of subchannels, there are 192 subcarriers for data of which are used for pilot and 56 for guard band.

- However, since the FFT size is fixed, the spacing between subcarriers is variable. Specifically for larger channel bandwidth the subcarrier spacing increases, which decreases the symbol time and is the fundamental tradeoff between spectral efficiency and delay spread that can occur.

- Mobile WiMAX uses a Scalable OFDMA scheme (SOFDMA). The FFT size, however, is not fixed as in the case of fixed WiMAX but is variable ranging from 128 to 2048. The number of FFTs possible is directly related to the size of the channel bandwidth and, unlike fixed WiMAX, the subcarrier spacing in mobile WiMAX is constant.

- The amount of FFTs associated with several typical channel bandwidths in mobile WiMAX is:

  - 1.25 MHz (128 FFT).

  - 5.0 MHz (512 FFT).

  - 10 MHz (1024 FFT).

  - 20 MHz (2048 FFT).

- Subchannels can be used to group a set of carriers together so they can be assigned for different services or frequency reuse schemes.

- The subcarriers are differentiated by use of a subchannel index.

5.8 CHANNEL STRUCTURE

- WiMAX 802.16d, e, and m all have different frame structures and are not compatible with each other. There is legacy support for 802.16e within 802.16m; however, each has its own signaling protocols.

5.8.1 802.16e

- In 802.16e the signaling protocol consists of slots and the frame structure. The slot is the minimum resource that can be allocated where one subchannel can have one, two, or three OFDM symbols. The user's data region is typically a contiguous series of slots that are assigned to the user. The frame, however, in a TDD mode is variable in size ranging from 2 ms to 20 ms.

- The OFDMA frame consists of a DL sub-frame and an UL sub-frame. The flexible frame structure of the TDD signal consists of a movable boundary between the DL and UL sub-frames. A short transition gap is placed between the DL and UL sub-frames and is called the Transmit-receive Transition Gap (TTG). After the completion of the UL subframe, another short gap is added between this sub-frame and the next DL sub-frame. This gap is called the Receiver-Transmit Transition Gap (RTG). The overall structure for DL and UL is shown in Fig. 5.10.

- DL Subframe begins with the preamble, which is used for PHY layer procedures, such as time and frequency synchronization and initial channel estimation. Preamble occupies first symbol of the DL subframe.

- The Fig. 5.10 also shows the relative position of the preamble, Frame Control Header (FCH), which provides frame configuration information, such as the MAP message length, the modulation and coding scheme, and the usable subcarriers.

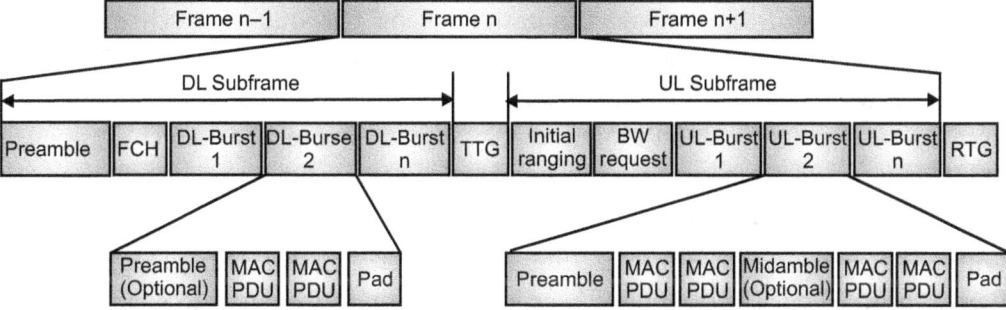

Fig. 5.10 : 802.16e frame layout

- Users are allocated data regions within the frame and these allocations are specified in the MAP messages DL-MAP, downlink, and UL-MAP, uplink. The DL-MAP and UL-MAP messages are broadcast following the FCH in the downlink subframe.

- MAP messages include the burst profile for each user, which defines the modulation and coding scheme used in that burst.

- The UL subframe consists of UL bursts, RNG channel, HARQ ACK channel, and CQI channels. The RNG channel is used for entry, periodic ranging, and bandwidth requests.

- The ACK channel is how the mobile stations provide HARQ acknowledgment messages.

- The CQI channel provides channel-quality indication which enables the scheduler to alter the modulation parameters to maximize system throughput.

5.8.2 802.16m

- The IEEE 802.16m basic frame structure is illustrated in Fig. 5.11. A superframe is defined as a set of four consecutive and equally-sized radio frames.

- Each 20 ms superframe contains a Primary Superframe Header (P-SFH) and a Secondary Superframe Header (S-SFH). The number of subframes per frame varies depending on the cyclic prefix size, the number of available OFDM symbols per frame, and the transmission bandwidth.

- A subframe is assigned to either DL or UL transmissions subject to the duplexing method. The basic frame structure with CP =¼ 1/8Tu, due to backward compatibility with the legacy system, is of higher importance. The CP= ¼ 1/16Tu is used when the sum of

Round Trip Time (RTT) and the RMS delay spread of the channel is less than 5.71 ms, assuming transmission bandwidths of 5, 10, or 20 MHz.

- There are four types of subframes defined in the IEEE 802.16m standard: (1) type-1 subframe consists of six OFDM symbols; (2) type-2 subframe consists of seven OFDM symbols; (3) type-3 subframe consists of five OFDM symbols; and (4) type-4 subframe consists of nine OFDM symbols.

- The basic frame structure is applied to both FDD and TDD duplexing schemes including H-FDD operation. The number of switching points in each radio frame in TDD mode is limited to two, where a switching point is defined as a change of transmission direction from DL to UL or from UL to DL. Note that an excessive number of switching points in a radio frame would result in inefficient use of radio resources due to consumption of radio resources by the switching gaps.

- With 802.16m the frame length is 5 ms where in 802.16e the frame length is variable from 2 ms to 20 ms. The reason for 5 ms frame length in 802.16m is to enable WiMAX to coexist with LTE.

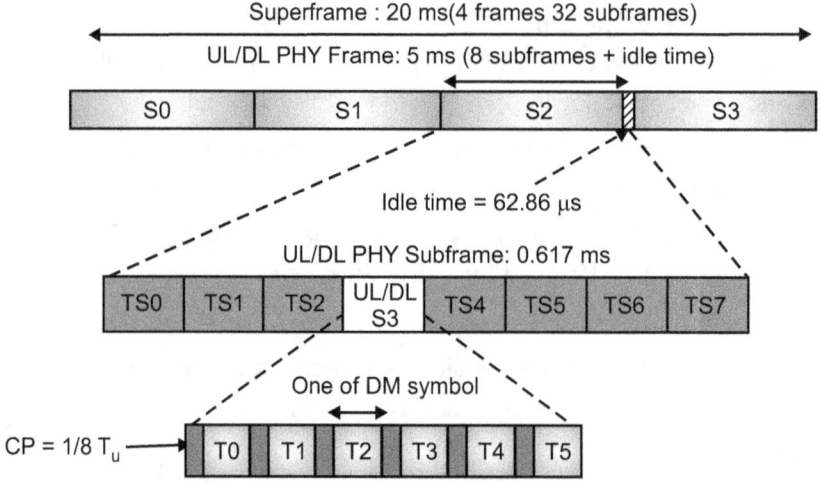

Fig. 5.11 : 802.16m FDD structure either DL or UL

- The fundamental layout of the frame is that there are eight subframes and each subframe can have six symbols associated with it.

- Fig. 5.12 represents the frame structure of a TDD system with 802.16m. With TDD each frame can contain a different number of subframes depending on the edge device as well as the bandwidth requirement needed.

- The subframes can be 5, 6, 7, or 8, additionally the number of symbols can also vary with a subframe leading to many valid perturbations.

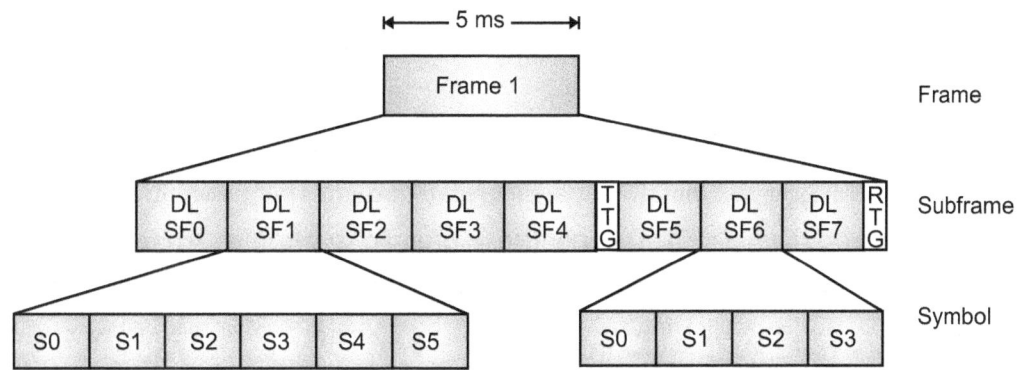

Fig. 5.12 : 802.16m TDD

- TDD, however, is the preferred WiMAX 802.16m configuration largely due to the spectrum allocation it occupies. MMDS, which is the former wireless cable band, is in 6-MHz channel blocks.

- Additionally, in 802.16m the concept of a superframe structure was introduced and is shown in Fig. 5.13. A Superframe consists of four frames for a total period of 20 ms.

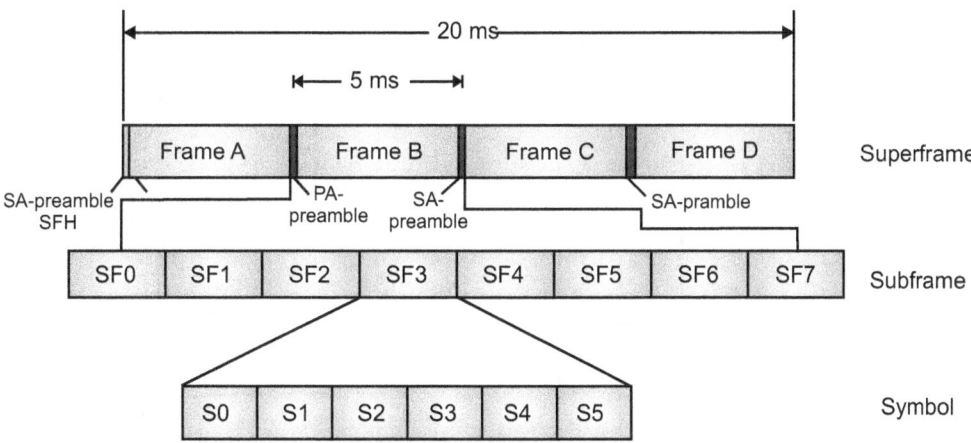

Fig. 5.13 : Superframe

- As expected, 802.16m uses a different method for resource assignments as compared to 802.16e. Specifically, 802.16m uses a Physical Resource Units (PRU) instead of slots and tiles. With 802.16m the PRU is assigned for both UL and DL.

- A Physical Resource Unit (PRU) is the basic physical unit for resource allocation that comprises Psc consecutive sub-carriers by Nsym consecutive OFDM symbols. The default value for Psc is 18 subcarriers, and Nsym can be 6, 7, or 5 OFDM symbols for type-1, type-2, and type-3 subframes, respectively. A Logical Resource Unit (LRU) is the basic logical unit for localized or distributed resource allocations. An LRU comprises Psc x Nsym sub-carriers, inclusive of the pilot sub-carriers that are embedded in a PRU.

- A Distributed Resource Unit (DRU) is defined to achieve frequency diversity gain in multipath fading channels. The DRU contains a group of sub-carriers which are physically spread across the distributed resources within a frequency partition. The size of the DRU is the same size as the PRU. The minimum unit for forming a DRU is equal to one sub-carrier or a pair of subcarriers also known as a tone-pair.

- Logical Resource Unit (LRU or LPRU) is the basic logical unit for localized and distributed resource allocations. An LPRU can have the same number of symbols and carriers as the PRU. As such, an LRU is the fundamental resource allocation in the DL and UL.

- In the UL, the LRU can be either localized (contiguous) or distributed (DRU), as shown in Fig. 5.14. Because PRU and LRU are mapped together, if the distributed LRU is used then the PRU is also distributed in the same fashion.

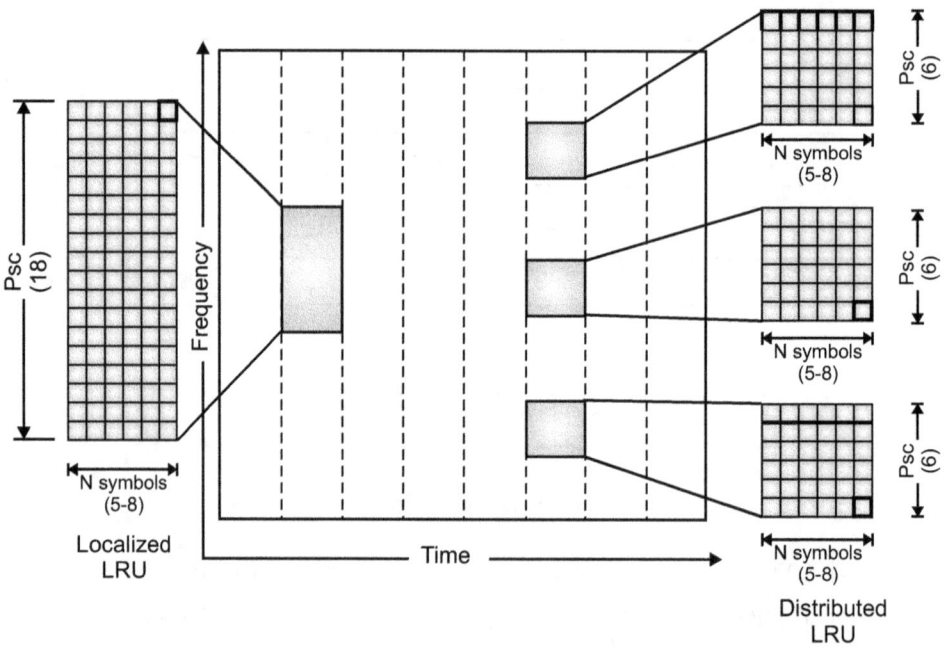

Fig. 5.14 : 802.16m supports MIMO and as a minimum configuration it is a 2 × 2

- 802.16m has one fixed pilot per PRU and how the pilots are distributed in the PRU is dependent upon the amount of antennas deployed at the base stations and are common to all subscribers.

- In the UL side, the pilots are dedicated for each user. For a contiguous LRU the pilots are the same as that for the PRU. However, in the distributed LRU the pilots are replicated in each LRU leading to a higher density of pilots for a distributed LRU scenario.

- As expected 802.16m has channels to increase its functionality over 802.16e. These channels are described in Tables 5.4 and 5.5.

Table 5.4 : DL

Downlink	Name	Description
A-Preamble	Advanced Preamble	Base Station ID, Time reference, frequency and frame synchronization, RSSI and channel sounding estimation.
PA-Preamble	Primary Advanced Preamble	Initial acquisition, BS type, section ID, bandwidth, carrier config, and superframe synch.
SA-Preamble	Secondary Advanced Preamble	Cell/sector ID, channel estimation and synchronization refinement.
SFH	Superframe Header	System parameters as well as P-SFH and S-P-SFH.
P-SFH	Primary	Short-term control info and is sent with every superframe.
S-SFH	Secondary	Contains DUIC.
A-MAP	Advanced MAP	Resource assignment, scheduling info, power control, HARQ.
E-MBS-MAP	Enhanced Multicast Broadcase Services MAP.	Multicast service control info.

Table 5.5 : UL

Uplink	Description
P-FBSCH	Primary fast feedback channel
S-FBSCH	Secondary fast feedback channel
UL HARQ FBCH	UL HARQ feedback channel
Ranging	UL-link synchronization
BW Req	Bandwidth request (3 steps and 5 steps)
CQI	Channel quality indicator regarding channel quality as seen by user
Power control	DL-MAP power control based on UL channel quality

Following table gives major difference between WiMAX (802.16e) and WiMAX Advanced (802.16m) technologies

Table 5.6 : Comparison of WiMAX(802.16e) and WiMAX Advanced(802.16m) Technologies

Specifications	Mobile WiMAX(16e)	WiMAX Advanced (16 m)
Data Rate(Aggregate)	About 60-70 Mbps	100 Mbps(Mobile subscribers) 1GBPS (Fixed subscribers)
RF Frequency	2.3GHz, 2.5 to 2.7GHz, 3.5GHz	<6GHz
Topology	FDD/TDD, H-FDD(in Mobile Subscriber)	FDD/TDD(BS), H-FDD(in Mobile Subscriber)
MIMO (Antennas)	up to 4 streams, no limit on number of antennas	upto 4/8 streams, no limit on number of antennas
Antenna Configurations support	Downlink: 1×1(SISO), $1 \times 2, 2 \times 1, 2 \times 2,$ $2 \times 4, 4 \times 2, 4 \times 4, 8 \times 8, 4 \times 8$ Uplink: 1×1(SISO), $1 \times 2, 1 \times 4, 2 \times 4, 4 \times 4$	Downlink: $2 \times 2, 2 \times 4,$ $4 \times 2, 4 \times 4,$ $8 \times 8, 4 \times 8$ Uplink: $1 \times 2, 1 \times 4,$ $2 \times 4,$ 4×4
Distance coverage	About 10 km	3Km to 100 Km
Carrier Aggregation (multi-carrier) support	Not supported	Supported
Bandwidth	5-20MHz per RF Carrier	5-20MHz per RF carrier, CA(carrier aggregation) feature will help achieve BWs upto 100MHz.
Frame Length	2-20ms without any superframe	Fixed 5ms , With superframes frame duration of 20ms is used including 4 frames

5.9 MIXED MODE

- Mixed mode 802.16m and 802.16e is supported, enabling legacy and new systems to operate on the same RF carrier sharing radio resources dynamically. However, as described previously, both 802.16e and 802.16m have their own protocols and are not compatible with each other.

- Fig. 5.15 shows an example of how 802.16e and 802.16m can share the same RF carrier in a TDD configuration. In all cases for mixed mode operation the legacy protocol precedes the other.

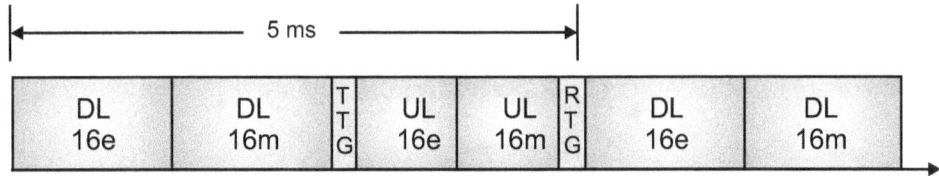

Fig. 5.15 : TDD multimode operation

5.10 INTERFERENCE MITIGATION TECHNIQUES

- Since the wireless systems reuse frequencies, interference mitigation becomes must Proper frequency planning and good cell site optimization is, the primary method of interference mitigation in WiMAX.

- In spite of good frequency planning and excellent optimization some interference remains.

- Smart antennas in the form of beam-forming, spatial multiplexing and MIMO have been widely used in wireless communication networks to mitigate interference.

- In a WiMAX system, various software and hardware techniques are used to minimize interference including

    (a) Smart antenna systems (beam steering on a per-frame basis)

    (b) Subgrouping of transmit and receive frames between adjacent sites (TDD)

- In addition to above methods, WiMAX uses adaptive modulation and coding that is based on the Signal-to-Interference Plus Noise Ratio (SINR). The modulation technique is used to match the link quality and dynamically adjust based on improving or degrading conditions.

- Spatial multiplexing is also used where multiple independent streams are transmitted in parallel over several antennas (MIMO).

- This enables the multipath channels to be somewhat independent by decorrelating them.

- This assists in high multipath environments that are NLOS. Spatial multiplexing also improves the data rates and overall capacity of the network based on the use of multiple antennas.

5.11 FREQUENCY PLANNING

- Frequency spectrum is a limited and increasingly expensive resource. Wireless network operators or WISPs often have to compete in acquiring licenses to operate on frequencies of their choice. Of course, they still have another alternative, that's using free spectrum in license-exempt bands. But then, they have to find the means to control interference from other networks sharing the same band and to limit spillover to other users of the band.
- Mobile WiMAX in mobile mode (remember, Mobile WiMAX also supports fixed mode) will be deployed like a cellular network (2G, 3G), requiring a large number of base stations to have a considerable coverage. So in most cases it will operate in licensed bands. Operation in unlicensed bands may be considered only for greenfield deployment where there are no other users of the same spectrum.

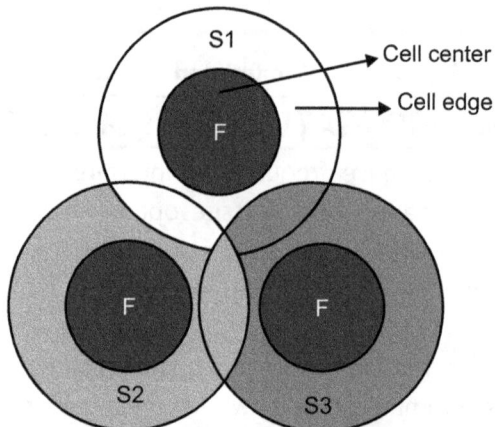

Fig. 5.16 : Picture. Fractional Frequency Reuse

S1, S2, and S3 are different sets of sub-channels, allocated to users at cell edges.

F = S1 + S2 + S3. The whole sub-channels (F) are allocated to users at cell centers.

- Regardless of licensed or unlicensed spectrum, frequencies have to be used efficiently. Therefore, it's crucial to maintain frequency reuse one. Frequency reuse one is achieved when all sectors within a cell and all cells within a network operate on the same frequency channel. However, frequency reuse one in a cellular network implies that users at a cell edge may get degraded signals due to interference from adjacent cells.
- Mobile WiMAX addresses this issue by "tweaking" the frequency reuse one. It works by allowing users at a cell center to operate on all available sub-channels. Cell center is the area closer to a base station (BS) that is particularly immune to co-channel interference. While users at a cell edge are only allowed to operate on a fraction of all available sub-channels. This sub-channels fraction is allocated in such a way that adjacent cells' edges will operate on different sets of sub-channels (see picture above). This is called fractional frequency reuse.

- Fractional frequency reuse takes advantage of the fact that a Mobile WiMAX user transmits on sub-channels (because in OFDMA, a channel is divided into sub-channels) and doesn't occupy an entire channel such as in 3G (CDMA2000 or WCDMA). Fractional frequency reuse maximizes spectral efficiency for users at a cell center and improves signal strength and throughput for users at a cell edge.

5.12 FEATURES AND APPLICATIONS

- WiMAX for mobility has a variety of features that help enhance its ability to provide IP services to a mobile environment. Some of the features involve power management, multicast, and multihop relay.

5.12.1 Power Management

- IEEE 802.16e is an emerging standard for mobile wireless broadband access systems. In any mobile networks, power saving is one of the most important features for the extension of devices' lifetime. To manage power usage in a more efficient way, the IEEE 802.16e standard specifies two mechanisms, sleep mode and idle mode. Idle mode allows the Mobile Station (MS) to conserve power and resources by restricting its activity to scanning at discrete intervals and thus eliminates the active requirement for handover operation and other normal operations.
- On the Base Station (BS) and network side, idle mode provides a simple and timely method for alerting the MS for pending Downlink (DL) traffic directed to the MS and thus eliminates air interface and network handover traffic from essentially inactive MSs.
- In the active mode, the MS is sending and or receiving data, hence the term active.
- When the MS is no longer sending and receiving data for a period of time it enters a sleep mode.
- After a period of time the MS comes back to active mode and is meant to conserve power this way. The ability to enter sleep mode is made by the base station.
- The MS can also enter into an idle mode where it effectively enters a listen-only mode for the DL and does not communicate with the ASN anymore until it reestablishes for an active session.

5.12.2 Multicast and Broadcast Service (MBS)

- Multicast Broadcast Services (MBS) may be required when multiple MSs connected to a BS receive the same information or when multiple BSs transmit the same information. Indeed, this allows resource to be saved by allocating a single radio pipe for all users registered to the same service instead of allocating as many pipes as there are users. This is of particular interest for the broadcast TV type of application where, at the same time, several users under the same coverage area are connected to the same service (in this case, a TV channel).
- This feature for WiMAX mobility enables the same data content to be sent to multiple users at the same time as a broadcast message. MBS has many of the same attributes as DVB-H, MediaFLO, and LTE.

- This is important for delivering the same streaming video to multiple users at the same time, therefore minimizing the resource consumption of the network.

5.12.3 Multihop Relay

- The demand for high speed data service has been increasing dramatically since the Internet has become a part of people's lives. Most broadband wireless service providers have boosted data service rates by adopting recently developed technologies such as OFDM, MIMO, and smart antennas.
- However, in practice there are still problems such as coverage holes due to shadowing, and poor Signal to Interference and Noise Ratio (SINR) for the Subscriber Stations (SSs) that are far away from the Base Station (BS). A simple solution for this problem is to add more BSs, but it is a very inefficient solution especially when there are few SSs to be served (e.g., in rural areas.)
- As an alternative to adding BSs, deploying low-cost Relay Stations (RSs) provides a cost-effective way to overcome the above problem (RSs are a simplified version of a full BS resulting in with lower upfront cost than BS; additionally, RSs do not require backhaul connections, thus reducing operating costs).
- The WiMAX specification was amended (802.16j, 2009) to include multihop relays, an extension which has gained much attention and proved to be an attractive technology for the next-generation of wireless communications.

5.13 SECURITY

- Like any system security is a key element within the overall WiMAX system. WiMAX security has to implemented in a way that provides sufficient protection against intrusion and other forms of unauthorised access without hindering the overall operation.
- Accordingly WiMAX security has been incorporated into the heart of the system to ensure that seamlessly integrated and provides an effective solution.
- WiMAX security utilises a number of advanced techniques including PKMv2 based authentication and over the air encryption. These considerable improve the level of security that is can be attained, but overall end-to-end security is still challenging and requires each network to adopt security within the overall network design and roll out as well as in the ways of working.
- WiMAX security elements are included in the standard and fall under four main headings:
  - Authentication of the user device.
  - Higher level user authentication.
  - Advanced over-the-air encryption.
  - Methods for securing the control and signalling within an IP scenario.
- Each of these WiMAX security areas has been addressed within standards, but even so, it is still necessary for the network operators to use good practice to ensure that security is not compromised. It is quite possible to circumvent the best security technology if the correct operating procedures are not in place.

- WiMAX in all its variants has a robust level of authentication and security. Security in WiMax is done not only at the time of system access but also during the data, session, ensuring all transmitted information is protected.
- Security is handled by a privacy sublayer within the WiMAX MAC and is based on the privacy key management protocol, which is part of the DOCSIS specification.
- WiMAX terminal devices come with built-in X.509 digital certificates that contain their public key and MAC address. WiMAX operators can use the certificates for device authentication and use a username/password or smart card authentication on top of it for user authentication.
- The digital certificates allow the SS to uniquely authenticate itself back to the ASN base station. The ASN base station can then check to see if the SS is authorized to receive service.
- If the SS is authorized the ASN base station sends the SS an encrypted authorization key.
- The authorrization key along with the SS public key is used to encrypt and protect the sessions meeting DES security.

5.14 QoS

- The 802.16 standard includes several QoS mechanisms at the PHY layer, such as Time Division Duplex (TDD), Frequency Division Duplex (FDD) and Orthogonal Frequency Division Multiplexing (OFDM). Each can help in providing QoS. TDD can dynamically allocate uplink and downlink bandwidth, depending on their requirements. For example, when there is more uplink traffic, more bandwidth can be allocated to that, and when there is less uplink traffic it can be taken away. This is illustrated in Figure 1. Each 802.16 TDD frame is one downlink subframe and one uplink subframe, separated by a guard slot. 802.16 adaptiveley allocates the number of slots for each, depending on their bandwidth needs.
- In FDD, base stations transmit on different sub-bands, and thus do not interfere with each other. This allows for even more bandwidth allocation flexibility. And, OFDM provides greater spectral efficiency, and mitigates interference with its tighter beam width and its dispersal of data across different frequencies.
- There are a couple of QoS aspects that are specific to OFDM. Forward Error Correction (FEC) builds redundancy into the transmission by repeating some of the information bits, so bits that are missing or in error can be corrected at the receiving end. Without FEC, error correction would require whole frames to be retransmitted, resulting in latency and lower QoS. The other way OFDM helps with QoS is with interleaving. Since OFDM uses multiple subcarriers, a portion of each information bit can be carried on a number of subcarriers, so that if any of the subcarriers is weakened, the information bit can still be received at the destination. And, interleaving means that bits that were close together in time are transmitted on subcarriers that are spaced out in frequency. Thus, errors created on weakened subcarriers are broken up into small bursts and spread out. And these small errors can more easily be corrected with FEC.

- OFDM also uses Fast Fourier Transforms (FFT), which in mathematical terms makes evaluating complex numbers more efficient by greatly reducing the number of arithmetical operations required. In radio technology, digital data signals in the form of square waves can be expressed as the sum of a series of sine waves in Fourier's Theorem. OFDM converts a single data stream into M streams and modulates them onto M subcarriers using FFT. In general, FFT can make the transmission of digital signals over the airlink more efficient, which also helps in providing QoS.

- The QoS mechanisms described above are some of the general mechanisms that 802.16 uses to ensure good QoS. These mechanisms are already well established in the wireless technology industry, and they have been proven to reduce latency, jitter, and packet loss, which are all goals of QoS.

- The 802.16 standard also provides adaptive modulation, which enables dynamic bandwidth allocation to match the current channel conditions. The three modulation schemes used in 802.16 are (from high to low modulation order): 64-QAM, 16-QAM, and QPSK. A higher order modulation scheme can deliver higher throughput, but a higher number of bits per symbol makes it more susceptible to interference and noise. There is a tradeoff between throughput and range. The modulation order can be based on the distance from BS to SS. With adaptive modulation, the BS can adaptively change the code if the distance and atmospheric conditions require it. For example, if the BS cannot establish a robust link to a distant SS using 64-QAM, the modulation order can be reduced to 16-QAM or QPSK. The greater the distance, the lower the QoS guarantee].

- To summarize, the 802.16 standard incorporates a number of mechanisms to provide QoS as follows:
  - Adaptive Modulation (QPSK to QAM 16 to QAM 64)
  - Frequency Division Duplex (FDD)
  - Time Division Duplex (TDD)
  - Orthogonal Frequency Division Multiplexing (OFDM)
  - Fast Fourier Transform (FFT)
  - Forward Error Correction (FEC)

- In addition to the above, WiMAX also utilizes another mechanism for QoS in the PHY level called adaptive burst profiles. Both TDD and FDD configurations are able to support adaptive burst profiling.

- With adaptive burst, the modulation and coding schemes are defined in the actual burst profile and the burst profile can be modified for each SS on a frame-by-frame basis based on the actual link conditions and are done for the UL and DL individually.

- The 802.16 standard has three main methods for QoS provisioning:
  - Service Flow Classification
  - Dynamic Service Establishment
  - Two-Phase Activation Model

5.14.1 Service Flow Classification

- The main feature of 802.16 QoS provisioning, and what distinguishes it from its competitors (i.e. 802.11 and 3G), is that it associates each packet with a service flow. 802.16 is a connection-oriented MAC. Each connection is assigned a unique Connection ID (CID) and a Service Flow ID (SFID) with an associated service class. The upper part of the MAC maps data into a QoS service class. Also, external applications can request service flows with desired QoS parameters using a named service class.
- WiMAX has three main methods for QoS provisioning:
  1. Service flow classification,
  2. Dynamic service establishment,
  3. Two-phase activation model.
- In order to categorise the different types of quality of service, there are five WiMAX QoS classes that have been defined. 802.16 provides four scheduling services for 802.16e and an additional one for 802.16m. These are referenced in Table 5.7.

Table 5.7 : QoS

WiMAX QOS Class	WiMAX QOS CLASS DETAILS
Unsolicited Grant Service	The Unsolicited Grant Service, UGS is used for real-time services such as Voice over IP, VoIP of for applications where WiMAX is used to replace fixed lines such as E1 and T1.
Real-time Packet Services	This WiMAX QoS class is used for real-time services including video streaming. It is also used for enterprise access services where guaranteed E1/T1 rates are needed but with the possibility of higher bursts if network capacity is available. This WiMAX QoS class offers a variable bit rate but with guaranteed minimums for data rate and delay.
Extended Real Time Packet Services	This WiMAX QoS class is referred to as the Enhanced Real Time Variable Rate, or Extended Real Time Packet Services. This WiMAX QoS class is used for applications where variable packet sizes are used - often where silence suppression is implemented in VoIP. One typical system is Skype.
Non-real time Packet Services	This WiMAX QoS class is used for services where a guaranteed bit rate is required but the latency is not critical. It might be used for various forms of file transfer.
Best Effort	This WiMAX QoS is that used for Internet services such as email and browsing. Data packets are carried as space becomes available. Delays may be incurred and jitter is not a problem.

5.14.2 Dynamic Service Establishment

The 802.16 standard provides a signaling function for dynamically establishing service flows and requesting QoS parameters. There are three types of control messages for service flows:

- Dynamic Service Activate (DSA): Activate a service flow.
- Dynamic Service Change (DSC): Change an existing service flow.
- Dynamic Service Delete (DSD): Delete a service flow.

New connections may be established when a customer's needs change. This may be initiated by the BS. The BS sends a control message called a DSA-REQ, which can contain the SFID, CID, and a QoS parameter set. The SS then sends a DSA-RSP message to accept or reject the service flow.

This mechanism allows an application to acquire more resources when required. Multiple service flows can be allocated to the same application, so more service flows can be added if needed to provide good QoS.

5.14.3 Two-Phase Activation

- Activation of a service flow proceeds in two phases: Admit first, then activate. An Authorization Module in the BS provides this function. It approves or rejects a request regarding a service flow. The Authorization Module can activate a service flow immediately or defer activation to a later time.

- Once the service flow has been admitted, both the BS and SS can reserve resources for it. Resources reserved by the BS and SS are not limited to bandwidth. They can include other resources, such as memory. Dynamic changes to the QoS parameters of an existing service flow are also approved by the Authorization Module. QoS parameter changes are requested with Dynamic Service Flow messages sent between the BS and SS. All requests are in the form described above (i.e. DSA, DSC, DSD).

5.15 PROFILES

- A WiMAX system certification profile is a set of features of the 802.16 standard, selected by the WiMAX Forum, that is required or mandatory for these specific profiles. This list sets, for each of the certification profiles of a system profiles release, the features to be used in typical implementation cases. System certification profiles are defined by the TWG in the WiMAX Forum. The 802.16 standard indicates that a system (certification) profile consists of five components: MAC profile, PHY profile, RF profile, duplexing selection (TDD or FDD) and power class. The frequency bands and channel bandwidths are chosen such that they cover as much as possible of the worldwide spectra allocations expected for WiMAX.

- Table 5.8 shows the fixed WiMAX profiles. These system profiles are based on the OFDM PHYsical Layer IEEE 802.16-2004 (in fact, this PHY Layer did not change very much with 802.16e). All of the profiles use the PMP mode. The profiles for fixed WiMAX have channel sizes of 3.5 MHz, 5 MHz, 7 MHz, and 10 MHz, while those for mobile are 5 MHz,

8.75 MHz, and 10 MHz. The current fixed profiles are defined for both TDD and FDD profiles. Presently, all the mobile profiles are TDD only; however, this is possible to change in the near future.

- Table 5.8 (a) and (b) shows some of the WiMAX system profiles presently available; there are other profiles while new profiles can be and are added.

Table 5.8 (a) : Fixed WiMAX System Profiles

Frequency Band (GHz)	Duplexing Mode	Channel Bandwidth (MHz)	Profile Name
3.5	TDD	7	3.5T1
3.5	TDD	3.5	3.5T2
3.5	FDD	3.5	3.5F1
3.5	FDD	7	3.5F2
3.5	TDD	10	5.8T

Table 5.8(b) : Mobile WiMAX System Profiles

Frequency Band (GHz)	Duplexing Mode	Channel Bandwidth and FFT size (Number of OFDMA subcarriers)
2.3–2.4	TDD	5 MHz, 512; 8.75 MHz, 1024; 10 MHz, 1024
2.305–2.320	TDD	3.5 MHz, 512; 5 MHz, 512; 10 MHz, 1024
2.496–2.690	TDD	5 MHz, 512; 10 MHz, 1024
3.3–3.4	TDD	5 MHz, 512; 7 MHz, 1024; 10 MHz, 1024
3.4–3.8	TDD	5 MHz, 512; 7 MHz, 1024; 10 MHz, 1024

5.16 ORIGINATION

- For a subscriber to gain access to the WiMAX network it needs to request a connection, or rather an attachment, to the network. As part of the process, the MS needs to communicate its capabilities to the base station and if compatible based on its profile keys are exchanged as part of the authentication process. Fig. 5.17 is a high-level depiction of the basic origination/access request to a WiMAX network.

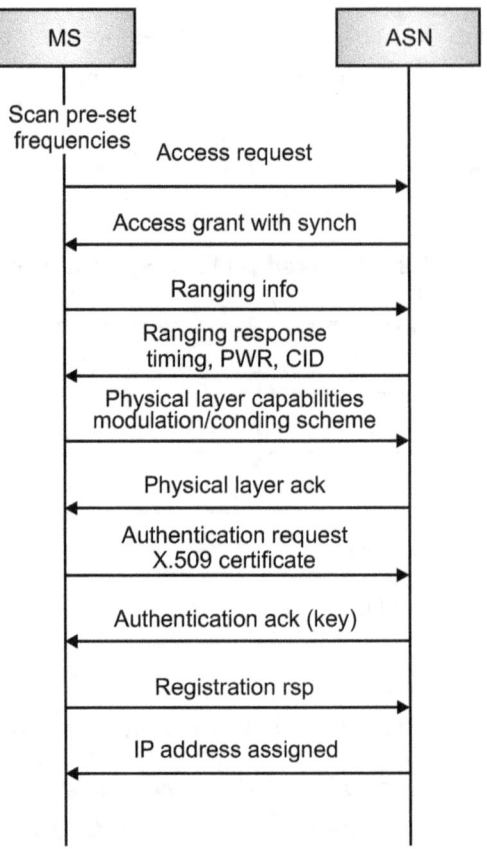

Fig. 5.17 : Access request

- More details regarding the origination and access request process can be found in the specifications for WiMAX.

5.17 HANDOVER/HANDOFF

- For implementing a mobile network, a handoff mechanism must be defined to maintain uninterrupted user communication session during his/her movement from one location to another. Handoff mechanism handles Subscriber Station (SS) switching from one Base Station (BS) to another. Different handoff techniques have been developed. In general, they can be divided into soft handoff and hard handoff.

- Soft handoff is used in voice-centric cellular networks such as GSM or CDMA. It uses a *make-before-break*approach whereas a connection to the next BS is established before a SS leaves an ongoing connection to a BS. This technique is suitable to handle voice and other latency-sensitive services such as Internet multiplayer game and video conference. When used for delivering data traffic (such as web browsing and e-mail), soft handoff will result in lower spectral efficiency because this type of traffic is bursty and does not require continues handover from one BS to another.

- Mobile WiMAX has been designed from the outset as a broadband technology capable of delivering triple play services (voice, data, video). However, a typical Mobile WiMAX network is supposedly dominated by delay-tolerant data traffic. Voice in Mobile WiMAX is packetized (what is called VoIP) and treated as other types of IP packets except it is prioritized. Hard Handoff (HHO) is therefore used in Mobile WiMAX. In hard handoff, a connection with a BS is ended first before a SS switches to another BS. This is known as abreak-before-make approach. Hard handoff is more bandwidth-efficient than soft handoff, but it causes longer delay. A network-optimized hard handoff mechanism was developed for Mobile WiMAX to keep a handoff delay under 50 ms.

- As with all handoff/handover scenarios the process and procedures vary based on if the subscriber is handing off between base stations that are connected to the same ASN-GW or if an ASN-GW needs to be changed since the new base station has a different ASN-GW. Additionally, the handover process has some unique characteristics when handing over via InterRAT to another network. The various details of the process are included in great detail within the 802.16 specification.

- With hard handover, the MS only communicates with one BS at a time (each time) and the connection with the old, or rather source, BS is broken before the new connection is established with the target BS.

- The handover is requested when the signal strength from the neighbor's cell exceeds the signal strength from the current cell site.

- Fig. 5.18 is a high-level depiction of the handover process with WiMAX.

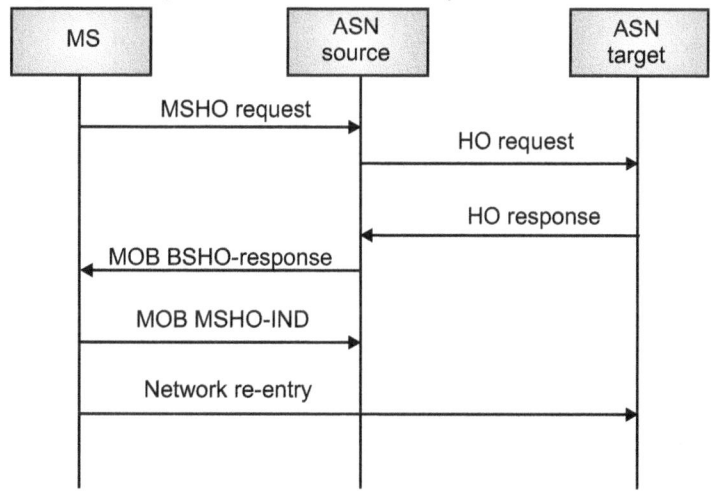

Fig. 5.18 : Handover process

5.18 FEMTO AND SON

- Femtocells are low-power wireless access points that operate in licensed spectrum to connect standard mobile devices to a mobile operator's network using residential DSL or cable broadband connections

- Mobile WiMAX supports both femto cells and Self-Organization Networks (SONs). Femto cells are covered elsewhere in this book; however, they are low-powered cellular base stations typically deployed in residences or small offices using another broadband provider for the backhaul.

- SONs are also part of 802.16m where the various network nodes and cells are self-aware and can adapt to the network configuration as it changes, including the update of neighbor nodes and neighbor cells for fast reconfiguration either because of a new node or loss of a node.

5.19 COMPARISON OF 3G, WiMAX, LTE, WIFI

Parameter	3G	3.5G	WiMAX	LTE
Standard	3GPP(UMTS)	3GPP (HSDPA)	IEEE 802.16e-2005	3GPP (GSM/EDGE and UMTS/HSDPA)
Data rate (Bandwidth)	5MHz	5MHz	3.5MHz, 7MHz, 5MHz, 10MHz, and 8.75MHz initially	1.4 MHz, 3 MHz, 5MHz, 10MHz, 15MHz, 20MHz
Frequency	700/800/900/1500 /1700/1900/2100 MHz	800/900/1,800 /1,900/2,100M Hz	2.3GHz, 2.5GHz, and 3.5GHz	2.6GHz,1.8GHz,Advanced Wireless Service (1.7GHz in the uplink and 2.1GHz in the downlink), 700MHz, and 2.1GHz.
Coverage	1-3miles	1–3 miles	< 2 miles	3 miles-60 miles
Mobility	High	High	Medium	Up to 500kmph but optimized for low speeds from 0 to 15kmph

...Conti.

Download rate (bit/sec)	384 kbit/s	13.98 Mbit/s	128 Mbit/s (in 20MHz bandwidth FDD)	100 Mbit/s for Category3 150 Mbit/s for Category4 300 Mbit/s for Category5 (in 20MHz FDD)
Upload rate (bit/sec)	384 kbit/s	5.760 Mbit/s	56 Mbit/s (in 20MHz bandwidth FDD)	50 Mbit/s for Category3/4 75 Mbit/s for Category5 (in 20 MHz FDD)

Parameter	WiMAX (802.16a)	Wi-Fi (802.11b)	Wi-Fi (802.11a/g)
Primary Application	Broadband Wireless Access	Wireless LAN	Wireless LAN
Frequency Band	Licensed/Unlicensed 2 G to 11 GHz	2.4 GHz ISM	2.4 GHz ISM (g) 5 GHz U-NII (a)
Channel Bandwidth	Adjustable 1.25 M to 20 MHz	25 MHz	20 MHz
Half/Full Duplex	Full	Half	Half
Radio Technology	OFDM (256-channels)	Direct Sequence Spread Spectrum	OFDM (64-channels)
Bandwidth Efficiency	<=5 bps/Hz	<=0.44 bps/Hz	<=2.7 bps/Hz
Modulation	BPSK, QPSK, 16-, 64-, 256-QAM	QPSK	BPSK, QPSK, 16-, 64-QAM

...Conti.

FEC	Convolutional Code Reed-Solomon	None	Convolutional Code
Encryption	Mandatory- 3DES Optional- AES	Optional- RC4 (AES in 802.11i)	Optional- RC4 (AES in 802.11i)
Mobility	Mobile WiMax (802.16e)	In development	In development
Mesh	Yes	Vendor Proprietary	Vendor Proprietary
Access Protocol	Request/Grant	CSMA/CA	CSMA/CA

QUESTIONS

1. Write a short note on WiMAX.
2. What is IEEE standards ? and Explain the IEEE 802.16 variants.
3. Draw and explain the generic architecture of WiMAX.
4. Explain following terms :
   (i) Fixed   (ii) Point to multipoint (PMP)   (iii) Mesh   (iv) Mobility
5. Explain the core network of WiMAX.
6. Describe the radio network.
7. Explain the WiMAX spectrum.
8. What are the modulation techniques used in WiMAX.
9. Describe the 802.162 e and 802.16 m frame layout.
10. Differentiate between Mobile WiMAX (16e) and WiMAX advanced (16m).
11. Explain the interference mitigation techniques.
12. Write a short note on Frequency Planning.
13. Write a short note on :
    (i) Power management (ii) Multicast and Broadcast service (iii) Multihop relay (iv) Security (v) QoS (Quality of Services).
14. Explain following terms :
    (i) Profiles (ii) Orgination (iii) Hand over / Handoff (iv) Fem to and SON.
15. Compare the 3G, 3.5 G, LTE and WiMAX.

Unit - VI

VOICE OVER IP (VoIP) TECHNOLOGY

6.1 INTRODUCTION

- Voice can be digitalized. The digitalize voice can be transmitted in packets over the network. Voice transmission comes in different flavors. In the past, telecommunication through fixed circuit switched network has dominated. In recent years, we see data communication networks, especially voice over IP.

- Voice over IP is the transmission of voice traffic in packets using the Internet as the transmission medium. IP is used rather than the traditional circuit transmission.

- Telephony service today is provided for the most part over circuit-switched networks, which are referred to as Public Switched Telephone Networks (PSTN). This service is known as Plain Old Telephone Service (POTS).

- A new trend that is beginning to emerge in recent years is to provide telephony service over IP networks, known as IP telephony, or Voice over IP. An important driving force behind IP Telephony is cost savings, especially for corporations with large data networks.

- Two standards compete for IP Telephony signaling. The older and currently more widely accepted standard is the ITUT recommendation H.323, which defines a multimedia communications system over packet-switched networks, including IP networks.

- The other standard, Session Initiation Protocol (SIP), comes from the IETF MMUSIC working group

6.2 WHY VoIP?

- The Internet Protocol (IP) is used to deliver packets carrying digitized voice. However, IP was not designed for real time traffic such as voice and video communication. IP is a connectionless protocol meaning a virtual connection is not established through a network prior to transmission.

- IP makes no guarantees concerning reliability, flow control, error detection or error correction. Potential errors include out of sequence packets or even loss of packets. Voice transmission requires guaranteed connection and a reasonable delay.

- Nevertheless, IP succeeds partly due to the high cost associated with the traditional circuit switched TDM network.

- VoIP uses packet switched network. It makes the network transparent to the upper layers that are involved in voice transmission through an IP based network.

- The existing use of IP network also allows the integration of voice and data integration.

- To leverage the connectionless nature of IP, vendors have developed higher layer protocols to address the guaranteed connection and transmission issue.
- Voice over Internet Protocol (VoIP) is the technology used to transmit voice conversation over a network using the Internet Protocol (IP). It has many advantages over the traditional Public Switched Telephone Networks (PSTNs):
- IP networks are more cost-efficient. Service providers can effectually reduce their operating cost from the standard equipment and cheap communication carrier. So service subscribers can get a lower price for the better or same services supplied by PSTNs.
- IP networks can provide integrative data and voice services. VoIP can handle data packets as well as voice packets. So it can provide new interesting services.
- IP networks are more bandwidth-efficient. Bandwidth of the communication channel is very limited. In some sense, it is a priceless source. PSTNs mainly use International Telecommunication Union (ITU) Recommendation G.711 coding scheme, which samples the analog voice signals at a rate of 8,000 Hz, encodes one sample with 8 bits and take up 64 kbps bandwidth. IP networks can use more advanced voice coding schemes and take up less bandwidth. Besides G.711, IP networks can also implement G.726, G.728, G.729 and G.723 coding schemes, which only take up 32 kbps, 16 kbps, 8 kbps, and 6.3 kbps bandwidth respectively.

6.2 THE BASICS OF IP TRANSPORT

- Internet Protocol (IP) version 4 (IPv4) is the current standard "IP" protocol used with TCP/IP Transmission Control Protocol/Internet Protocol which is the protocol for Internet addressing. Like the Open System Interconnection (OSI) model, TCP/IP has its own model.
- The OSI model and the TCP/IP models were both created independently. The TCP/IP network model represents reality in the world, whereas the OSI model represents an ideal. With that said, the TCP/IP network model matches the standard layered network model as it should.
- Fig. 6.1 shows correspondence between OSI model and TCP/IP model.
- The IP layer creates a packet with IP header. Based on this header information the packet is forwarded to the next router so that finally it reaches the appropriate destination. This protocol is unreliable in the sense that it does not guarantee delivery of packet.
- The packet may be lost due to congestion. It may go through any available route to the final destination.
- Thus packets belonging to the same source may be delivered through different routes and may reach destination out of sequence.

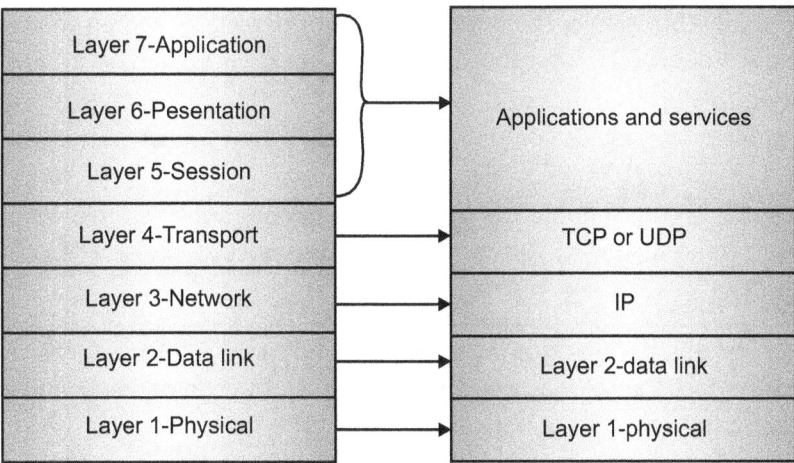

Fig. 6.1 : OSI and IP protocol stacks

- Since IP provides unreliable service, It is the responsibility of the upper layer i.e. transport layer to ensure to ensure an error-free in-sequence delivery of packets to the destination.

- The transport layer does this using Transmission Control Protocol (TCP). It is connection oriented and reliable protocol.

- The TCP header consists of source and destination port numbers, which identify the applications at each end; sequence numbers and acknowledgment numbers, which enable the detection of lost packets; and a checksum, which enables the detection of corrupted packets.

- TCP uses these information elements to request retransmission of lost or corrupted packets and to deliver packets to the destination application in the correct order.

- The stream of data is sent from the process to the transport layer. TCP establishes a connection between the transport layers of the transmitter and receiver stations. It then divides the stream of data into units called segments. Segments are numbered and transmitted one by one.

- The TCP protocol at the receiver side checks the arriving segments for error, loss, and duplication. It orders the segments, makes a stream, and transfers the stream to the receiver side process.

- TCP provides stream delivery service. Both the sender and the receiver processes deal with the stream of bytes and are not aware of stream segmentation in the lower layers. After all segments are transmitted, TCP at the transmitter side closes the connection.

- Another transport layer protocol used at transport layer is User Datagram Protocol (UDP) UDP sender transmits the data unit of the upper layer process and does not care if the transmission is reliable.

- In other words, if the data unit get lost due to the congestion or duplicated in the path, UDP does not recognize it. UDP does not deploy ACK, flow and congestion control.

That's why UDP is unreliable. There is minimal error detection, and erroneous packets will be simply discarded.

- The beauty of UDP is its simplicity. The only overhead that UDP adds to the packet is to establish process to process communication, rather than a host to host communication of IP layer.

- Therefore, UDP is very suitable for small message communications or applications that do not need strong reliability, such as client/server request/reply or video conferencing.

6.3 VoIP CHALLENGES

- For VoIP to become popular, some key issues need to be resolved. Some of these issues stem from the fact that IP was designed for transporting data while some issues have arisen because the vendors are not conforming to the standards.

Quality of Voice

- As IP was designed for carrying data, so it does not provide real time guarantees but only provides best effort service. For voice communications over IP to become acceptable to the users, the delay needs to be less than a threshold value and the IETF (Internet Engineering Task Force) is working on this aspect.

- To ensure good quality of voice, there should be minimum loss of information.

- We can use Echo Cancellation, Packet Prioritization (giving higher priority to voice packets) or Forward Error Correction for this. But this will increase delay.

- Thus these requirements of low delay and low loss are contradictory. Use of TCP will ensure low loss but will increase delay whereas use of UDP will reduce delay but increase the loss.

- In case of speech the excessive delay or excessive jitter is disturbing than the loss of packets hence UDP is preferred over TCP.

- A Real Time Protocol(RTP) is used which is better than UDP. Whenever a packet of coded voice is to be sent, it is sent as the payload of an RTP packet.

- This packet contains an RTP header, which provides information such as the voice coding scheme being used, a sequence number, a time stamp for the instant at which the voice packet was sampled, and an identification for the source of the voice packet.

- Another protocol called Real Time Control Protocol (RTCP) is used to improve the performance of RTP. To ensure the quality of service during the call, another IETF protocol Real Time Control Protocol (RTCP) is used. RTCP transmits periodical control packets to both the caller and the receiver.

- The control packets provide information to allow the participants to optimize the quality of voice transmission during the call. Usually it uses a separate port number with UDP as the underlying transport layer protocol.

- An IETF protocol is used for providing statistics about a RTP (Real Time Protocol) transmission to participants in the transmission. The information provided in the RTCP packets enable participants to take proactive measures in optimizing the quality of the RTP transmission.

- The TCP/IP protocol stack with these protocols is shown in Fig. 6.2
- It should be noted that RTP and RTCP do not guarantee minimal delays, low jitter, or low packet loss. In order to do this, other protocols are required.
- RTP and RTCP simply provide information to the applications at either end so that those applications can deal with loss, delay, or jitter with the least possible impact to the user.

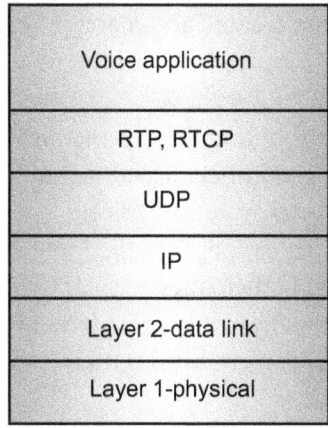

Fig. 6.2 : VoIP protocol layers

Interoperability

- In a public network environment, products from different vendors need to operate with each other if voice over IP is to become common among users.
- To achieve interoperability, standards are being devised and the most communication standard for VoIP is the H.323 standard, which is described in the next section.

Security

- This problem exists because in the Internet, anyone can capture the packets meant for someone else.
- Some security can be provided by using encryption and tunneling. The common tunneling protocol used is Layer 2 Tunneling protocol and the common encryption mechanism used is Secure Sockets Layer (SSL).
- Integration with Public Switched Telephone Network (PSTN).
- While Internet telephony is being introduced, it will need to work in conjunction with PSTN for a few years. We need to make the PSTN and IP telephony network appear as a single network to the users of this service.

Scalability

- As researchers are working to provide the same quality over IP as normal telephone calls but at a much lower cost, so there is a great potential for high growth rates in VoIP systems. VoIP systems needs to be flexible enough to grow to large user market and allow a mix of private and public services.

6.4 H.323

- VoIP requires a means for prospective communications partners to find each other and to signal to the other party their desire to communicate.
- This functionality is referred to as Call Signaling. The need for signaling functionality distinguishes Internet telephony from other Internet multimedia services such as broadcast and media-on demand services.
- VoIP, when used for synchronous voice or multimedia communication between two or more parties, uses signaling that creates and manages calls.
- The called can define a call as a named association between applications that is explicitly set up and torn down.
- Examples of calls are two-party phone calls, a multimedia conference or a multi-player game. A call may encompass a number of connections, where a connection is a logical relationship between a pair of end systems in a call.
- For example, a non-bridged three party audio only call will have three connections, creating a full mesh among the participants.
- A media stream or session is the flow of a single type of media among a set of users. This flow can either be unicast (in which case it is between two users), or multicast (more than two users).
- A media session is associated with one or more connections. In the above three party call example, if the media is distributed using unicast, there will be one audio session per connection.
- If the audio is distributed via multicast, there will be one audio session associated with all three connections. It is not required that calls have media streams associated with them, but this is likely to be the common case.
- Internet telephony signaling may encompass a number of functions: name translation and user location involves the mapping between names of different levels of abstraction, feature negotiation allows a group of end systems to agree on what media to exchange and their respective parameters such as encoding, call participant management for participants to invite others on an existing call or terminate connections with them, feature changes that make it possible to adjust the composition of media sessions during the course of a call, either because the participants require additional or reduced functionality or because of constraints imposed or removed by the addition or removal of call participants.
- There are several VoIP call signaling protocols. We shall discuss and compare the characteristics of the H.323 protocol suite, Session Initiation Protocol (SIP), Media Gateway Control Protocol (MGCP), and Megaco/H.248.
- H.323 and SIP are peer-to-peer control-signaling protocols, while MGCP and Megaco are master–slave control-signaling protocols. MGCP is based on the PSTN model of telephony.

- H.323 and Megaco are designed to accommodate video conferencing as well as basic telephony, but they are still based on a connection-oriented paradigm similar to circuit-switching, despite their use for packet communications systems.
- H.323 gateways have more call control function than the media gateways using MGCP, which assumes that more of the intelligence resides in a separate media gateway controller. SIP was designed from scratch for IP networks, and accommodates intelligent terminals engaged in not only voice sessions, but other applications as well.

6.4.1 H.323 Network Architecture

- The ITU-T recommended H.323 protocol suite has evolved out of a video telephony standard. When early IP telephony pioneers developed proprietary products2, there was an industry call to develop a VoIP call control standard quickly so that users and service providers would be able to have a choice of vendors and products that would interoperate.
- The Voice-over-IP Activity Group of the International Multimedia Telecommunications Consortium (IMTC) recommended H.323, which had been developed for multimedia communications over packet data networks.
- These packet networks might include LANs or WANs. The IMTC held the view that VoIP was a special case of IP Video Telephony.
- Although not all VoIP pioneers agreed that video telephony would quickly become popular, the H.323 protocol suite became the early leading standard for VoIP implementations. Versions 2-4 of the standard include modifications to make H.323 more amenable to VoIP needs.
- H.323 defines four logical components viz., Terminals, Gateways, Gatekeepers and Multipoint Control Units (MCUs) as shown in Fig. 6.3. Terminals, gateways and MCUs are known as end points.

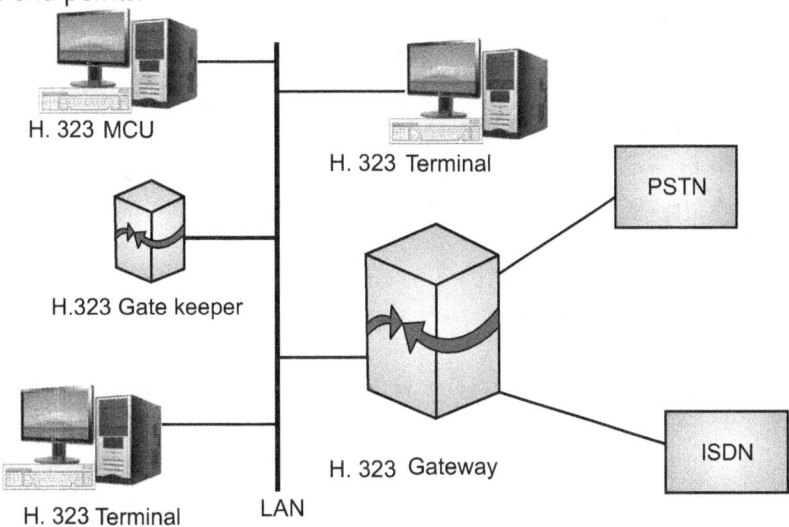

Fig. 6.3 : H.323 network architecture

- H.323 entities may be integrated into personal computers or routers or implemented in stand-alone devices. For VoIP, the important H.323 entities are terminals, gateways, and gatekeepers.
- An H.323 gateway provides protocol translation and media transcoding between an H.323 endpoint and a non-H.323 endpoint.
- For example, a VoIP gateway provides translation of transmission formats and signaling procedures between a circuit switched telephone and a packet network. In addition, the VoIP gateway may perform speech transcoding and compression, and it is usually capable of generating and detecting Dual Tone Multiple Frequencies (DTMF) (i.e.touch tone) signals.

Terminals
- These are the LAN client endpoints that provide real time, two way communications. All H.323 terminals have to support H.245, Q.931, Registration Admission Status (RAS) and Real Time Transport Protocol (RTP).
- H.245 is used for allowing the usage of the channels, Q.931 is required for call signaling and setting up the call, RTP is the real time transport protocol that carries voice packets while RAS is used for interacting with the gatekeeper.
- H.323 terminals may also include T.120 data conferencing protocols, video codecs and support for MCU.
- A H.323 terminal can communicate with either another H.323 terminal, a H.323 gateway or a MCU.

Gateways
- An H.323 gateway is an endpoint on the network which provides for real-time, two-way communications between H.323 terminals on the IP network and other ITU terminals on a switched based network, or to another H.323 gateway.
- They perform the function of a "translator" i.e. they perform the translation between different transmission formats, e.g from H.225 to H.221.
- They are also capable of translating between audio and video codecs. The gateway is the interface between the PSTN and the Internet.
- They take voice from circuit switched PSTN and place it on the public Internet and vice versa. Gateways are optional in that terminals in a single LAN can communicate with each other directly.
- When the terminals on a network need to communicate with an endpoint in some other network, then they communicate via gateways using the H.245 and Q.931 protocols.

Gatekeepers
- It is the most vital component of the H.323 system and dispatches the duties of a "manager".
- It acts as the central point for all calls within its zone (A zone is the aggregation of the gatekeeper and the endpoints registered with it) and provides services to the registered endpoints.

- Some of the functionalities that gatekeepers provide are listed below:

Address Translation: Translation of an alias address to the transport address. This is done using the translation table which is updated using the Registration messages.

Admissions Control: Gatekeepers can either grant or deny access based on call authorization, source and destination addresses or some other criteria.

Call Signaling: The Gatekeeper may choose to complete the call signaling with the endpoints and may process the call signaling itself. Alternatively, the Gatekeeper may direct the endpoints to connect the Call Signaling Channel directly to each other.

Call Authorization: The Gatekeeper may reject calls from a terminal due to authorization failure through the use of H.225 signaling. The reasons for rejection could be restricted access during some time periods or restricted access to/from particular terminals or Gateways.

Bandwidth Management: Control of the number of H.323 terminals permitted simultaneously access to the network. Through the use of H.225 signaling, the Gatekeeper may reject calls from a terminal due to bandwidth limitations.

Call Management: The gatekeeper may maintain a list of ongoing H.323 calls. This information may be neccesary to indicate that a called terminal is busy, and to provide information for the Bandwidth Management function.

Multipoint Control Units (MCU)

- The MCU is an endpoint on the network that provides the capability for three or more terminals and gateways to participate in a multipoint conference.
- The MCU consists of a mandatory Multipoint Controller (MC) and optional Multipoint Processors (MP).
- The MC determines the common capabilities of the terminals by using H.245 but it does not perform the multiplexing of audio, video and data.
- The multiplexing of media streams is handled by the MP under the control of the MC. The following Fig. 6.4 shows the interaction between all the H.323 components

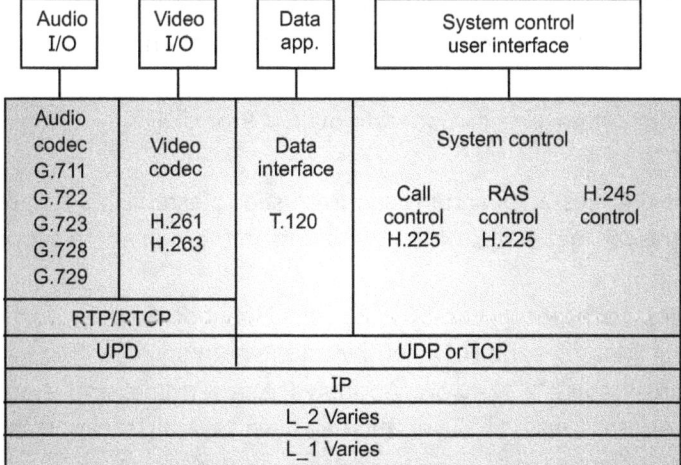

Fig. 6.4: H.323 Protocol Stack

6.4.2 Overview of H.323 Protocols

- H.323 suite consists of a set of standards. H.323 cites the use of the audio codes shown in Fig. 6.4 For audio applications, the minimum requirement is the support of recommendation G.711 (64 kbps channel).

- Other voice codec standards cited by H.323 are G.722 (48, 56, and 64 kbps channels), G.723 (5.3 and 6.3 kbps channels), G.728 (16 kbps channel), G.729 (8 kbps channel). The H.245, control protocol for multimedia communication, is used during an initial handshake between the machines to determine the audio encoding algorithm, terminal capabilities, and media channels.

- The terminals should be capable of sending and receiving different audio streams. After H.245 has completed the agreements on the terminals' capabilities and media channels, the H.225, call signaling and setup protocol, is used to format the audio stream. H.261 is video coding standard. It was designed for data rates which are multiples of 64kpbs. H.261 supports two resolutions, QCIF (Quarter Common Interchange format) and CIF (Common Interchange format).

- If video is supported, the H.323 terminals must code and decode the video streams in accordance with H.261 QCIF.

- Options are available, but they must use the H.261 orH.263 specifications. The coding algorithm of H.263 is similar to that used by H.261, however with some improvements and changes to improve performance and error recovery. H.263 supports five resolutions, QCIF, CIF, SQCIF (Sub-QCIF), 4CIF, and 16CIF.

- Data support is through T.120, and the various control, signaling, and maintenance operations which are provided by H.245, Q.931, and the Gatekeeper specification. The audio and video packets must be encapsulated into the Real Time Protocol (RTP) and carried on a UDP socket pair between the sender and the receiver.

- The Real-Time Control Protocol (RTCP) is used to assess the quality of the sessions and connections as well as to provide feedback information among the communication parties.

- The data and support packets can operate over TCP or UDP.

Call Signaling

- Call signaling is the messages and procedures used to establish a call, request changes in bandwidth of the call, get status of the endpoints in the call, and disconnect the call.

Addresses

- In H.323 system, each entity has at least one Network Address (e.g. IP address). This address uniquely identifies the H.323 entity on the network.

- Some entities may share a Network Address (i.e. a terminal and a collocated MC). For each Network Address, each H.323 entity may have several Transport layer Service Access Point (TSAP) identifiers.

- These TSAP Identifiers allow multiplexing of several channels sharing the same Network Address. An endpoint may also have one or more alias addresses associated with it.
- An alias address may represent the endpoint or it may represent conferences that the endpoint is hosting.
- The alias addresses provide an alternate method of addressing the endpoint
- Registration, Admission and Status (RAS). The RAS channel is used between H.323 endpoints and gatekeepers for Gatekeeper discovery, endpoint registration, endpoint location, admission control, and access token. The RAS messages are carried on a RAS channel that is unreliable. Hence, RAS message exchange may be associated with timeouts and retry counts.

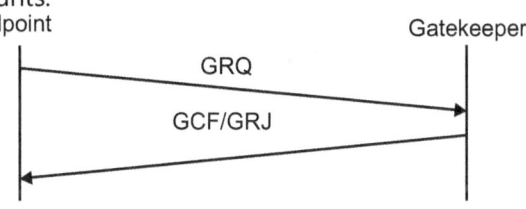

Fig. 6.5 : Gatekeeper Discovery

Gatekeeper Discovery

- Gatekeeper discovery is the process an endpoint uses to determine which Gatekeeper to register with.
- The gatekeeper discovery can be done statically ordynamically. In static discovery, the endpoint knows the transport address of its gatekeeper a priori. In the dynamic method of gatekeeper discovery, the endpoint multicast GRQ message on the gatekeeper's discovery multicast address. One or more gatekeepers may respond with GCF message.

Endpoint Registration

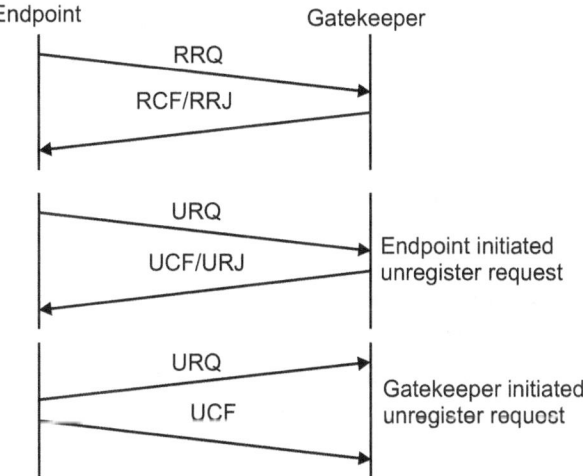

Fig. 6.6: Endpoint registration

- Endpoint registration is the process by which an endpoint joins a Zone, and informs the Gatekeeper of its Transport Address and alias address.

- All endpoints register with a gatekeeper as part of their configuration process. Registration occurs before any calls are attempted and occurs periodically as necessary.

Endpoint Location

- Endpoint location is a process by which the transport address of an endpoint is determined and given its alias name or E.164 address.

Other Controls

- Other controls such as admission control, to restrict the entry of an endpoint into a zone; bandwidth change, to modify the call bandwidth during a call; and disengagement control, to disassociate an endpoint froma gatekeeper and its zone.

H.225 Call Signaling and H.245 Control Signaling

- H.225 Call signaling H.225 call signaling is used to set up connections between H.323 endpoints, over which the real-time data can be transported. The call signaling channel is are liable channel, which is used to carry H.225.0 call control messages. For example, H.225 protocol messages are carried over TCP in an IP based H.323 network.

- In networks that do not contain a Gatekeeper, call signaling messages are passed directly between the calling and called endpoints. It is called direct call signaling. In networks that do contain a Gatekeeper, theH.225 messages are exchanged either directly between the endpoints or between the endpoints after being routed through the gatekeeper. It is called gatekeeper routed signaling. The method chosen is decided by the gatekeeper during RAS-admission message exchange.

Gatekeeper-Routed Call Signaling

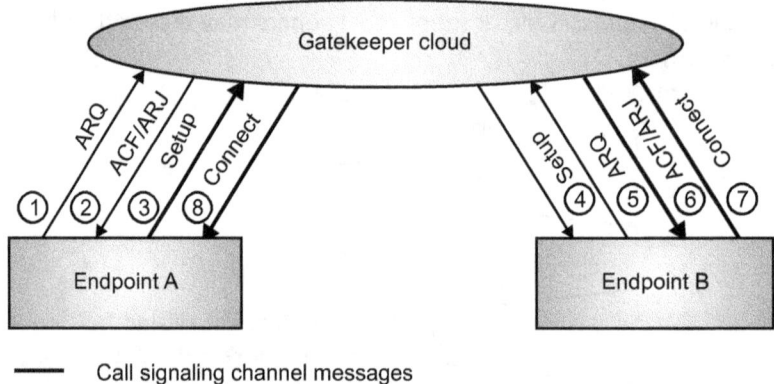

Fig. 6.7: Gatekeeper routed call signaling

- The admission messages are exchanged between endpoints and the gatekeeper on RAS channels.

- The gatekeeper receives the call-signaling messages on the call-signaling channel from one endpoint and routes them to the other endpoint on the call-signaling channel of the other endpoint.

Direct Call Signaling

- During the admission confirmation, the gatekeeper indicates that the endpoints can exchange call-signaling messages directly. The endpoints exchange the call signaling on the call-signaling channel.

H.245 Control Signaling

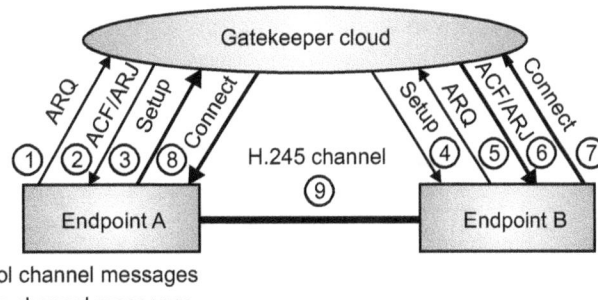

H.245 Control channel messages
Call signaling channel messages
RAS channel messages

Fig. 6.8: H.323-H.245 control channel connection between endpoints

- When Gatekeeper routed call signaling is used, there two methods to route the H.245 Channel. In the first method, the H.245 Control Channel is established directly between the endpoints (see Fig. 6.8).
- In the second method, the H.245 Control Channel is routed between the endpoints through the Gatekeeper.
- This method allows the Gatekeeper to redirect the endpoints through the Gatekeeper. This method allows the Gatekeeper to redirect the H.245 Control channel to an MC when an ad hoc multipoint conference switches from a point-to-point conference to a multipoint conference.
- This choice is made by the Gatekeeper. When Direct Endpoint call signaling is used, the H.245Control Channel can only be connected directly between the endpoints.

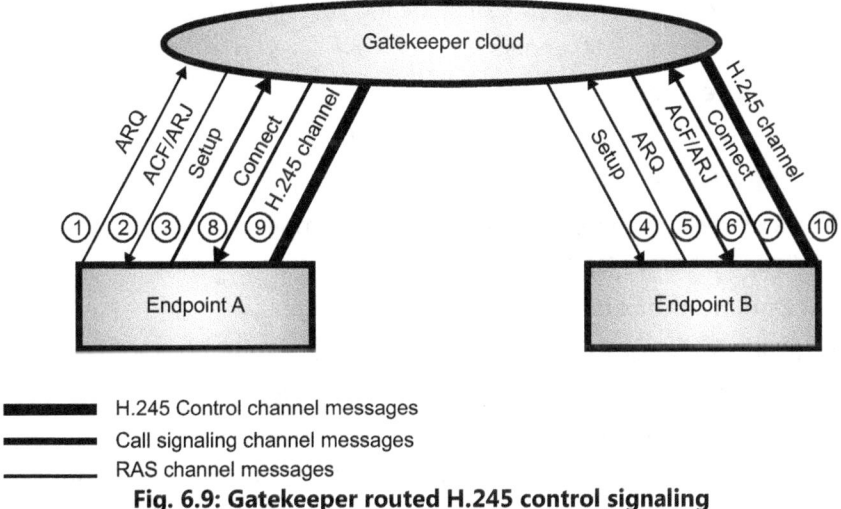

H.245 Control channel messages
Call signaling channel messages
RAS channel messages

Fig. 6.9: Gatekeeper routed H.245 control signaling

Connection Procedures

- The connection procedures of the H.323 systems communication are made in the steps of Call setup, Initial communication and capability exchange, Establishment of audio visual communication, Call services, and Call termination.
- This section uses the example network, which contains two endpoints connecting to a gatekeeper to illustrate to whole connection steps.

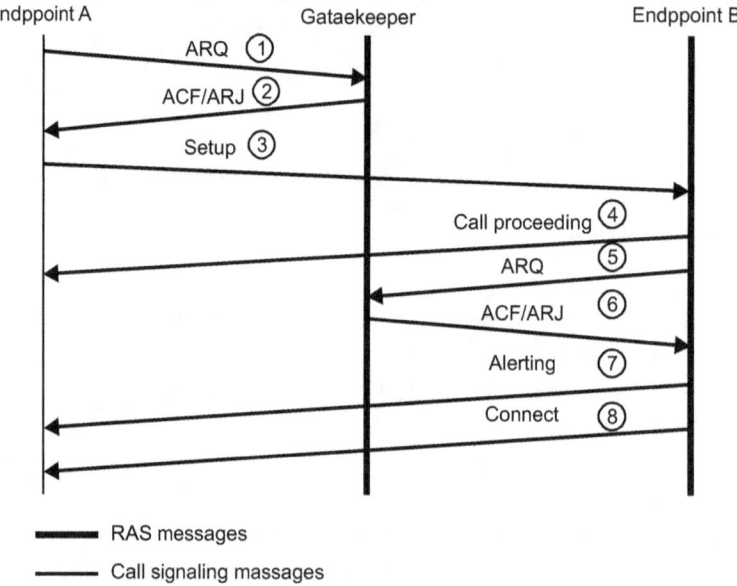

Fig. 6.10: Call setup

Step A: Call Setup

Call setup can be in all following cases:

- All combinations of Direct Routed Call signaling (DRC)/Gatekeeper Routed Call signaling (GRC), same or different Gatekeepers;
- Fast connect procedures;
- Call forwarding using facility (restarts the procedure);
- Setting up conferences

Fig. 6.10 illustrates the call setup process with the example of both endpoints registered to the same Gatekeeper. It assumes direct call signaling

Step B: Initial Communication and Capability Exchange

- This step includes the procedures of Capability exchange, Master/Slave determination, and H.245 tunneling. Once both sides have exchanged call setup messages from step A, the endpoints shall establish the H.245 Control Channel.
- The procedures of H.245 are used over the H.245 Control Channel for the capability exchange and to open the media channels.

- The H.245 Master-slave determination procedures are used to resolve conflicts between two endpoints which can both be the MC for a conference, or between two end points which are attempting to open a bidirectional channel. Fig. 6.10 is an example H.323 control signaling flows.

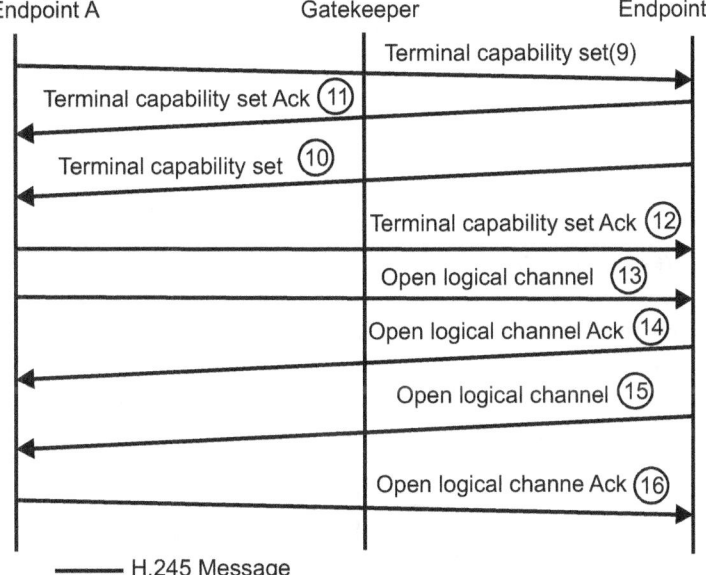

—— H.245 Message

Fig. 6.11 : H.323 control signaling flows

Step C: Establishment of Audio Visual Communication

- Following the exchange of capabilities, master-slave determination, and opening of the logical channels for the various information streams, the audio and video streams, which are transmitted in the logical channels setup in H.245, are transported over dynamic Transport layer Service Access Point (TSAP) Identifiers using an unreliable protocol.
- Data communications, which are transmitted in the logical channels setup in H.245, are transported using a reliable protocol. Fig. 6.12 is an example of illustrating the H.323 media stream and media control flows

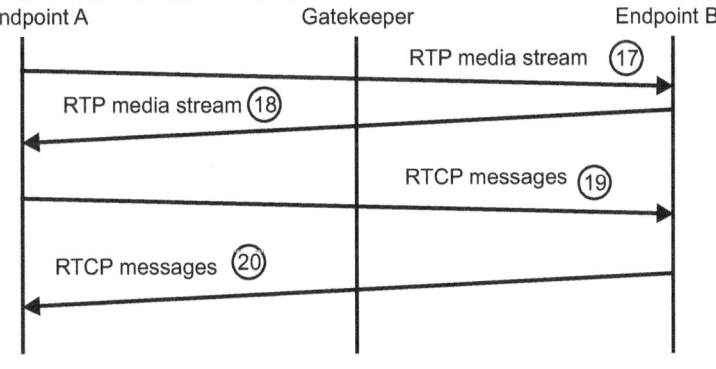

—— RTP media stream and RTCP messages

Fig. 6.12: Media stream and media control flows

Step D: Call services

- Call services include Bandwidth changes, Status Information request for management, Conference expansion, Multicast cascading, and H.450 Supplementary Services.

Bandwidth Changes

Call bandwidth is initially established and approved by the Gatekeeper during the admission exchange. At any time during a conference, the endpoints or Gatekeeper may request an increase or decrease in the call bandwidth. An example of Bandwidth changes is given in Fig. 16.

Status

Status is procedures of gatekeeper determining the work status, on/off or failure, of the endpoints. The Gatekeeper may use the H.225 Information Request (IRQ)/Information Request Response (IRR) messages to poll the endpoints periodically.

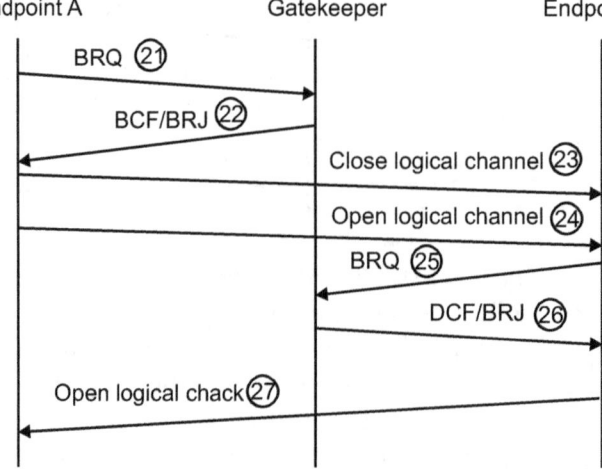

Fig. 6.13: Bandwidth change

Conference Expansion

- Conference expansion is the procedure for expanding a point-to-point conference involving an MC to a multipoint conference. First, a point-to-point conference is created between two endpoints. At least one endpoint or the Gatekeeper, must contain an MC. Once the conference has been created, the conference may be expanded to multipoint conference by any endpoint in conference inviting another endpoint into the conference through the MC, or an endpoint joins an existing conference by calling an endpoint in the conference. Fig. 6.14 (a) illustrate the H.245 Control Channel topology for the Direct Call Signaling model, and the Gatekeeper routed Call Signaling model.

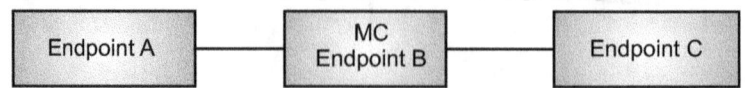

Fig. 6.14 (a): Direct call signaling model

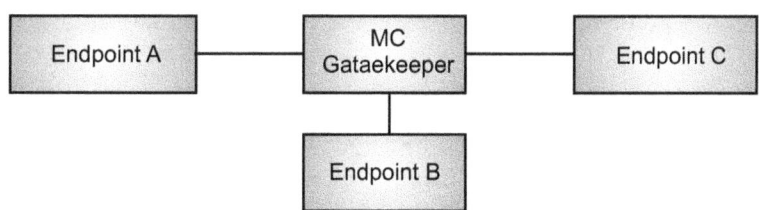

Fig. 6.14 (b) : Gatekeeper routed call signaling model

Multicast Cascading

Multicast cascading is the case when a call is established between the entities containing the MCs, and the H.245. Control Channel is opened, the active MC (Master/Slave procedure) may active the MC in a connected entity. Once the cascade conference is established, either the master or slave MCs may invite other endpoints into the conference. There is only one master MC in a conference. A slave MC can only be cascaded to a master MC.

H.450 Supplementary Services

The H.450 supplementary services are optional to H.323 systems. These services include call forward, call hold, call waiting, message waiting indication, and name identification etc.

Step E: Call Termination

Call termination can be made by any endpoint when video, audio, or data transmissions are at end. Correspondingly all logical channels for video, audio, or data are closed. Terminating a call may not terminate a conference. It can be done by MC that the terminating of a conference. Fig. 6.15 illustrates the call release procedure.

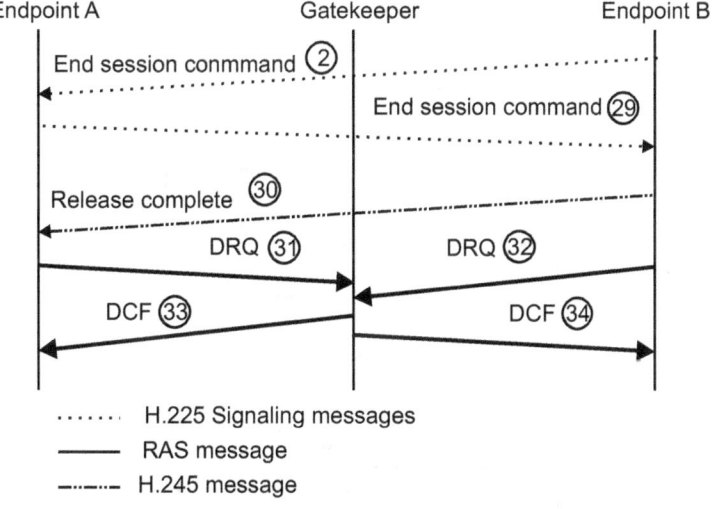

Fig. 6.15: Call release

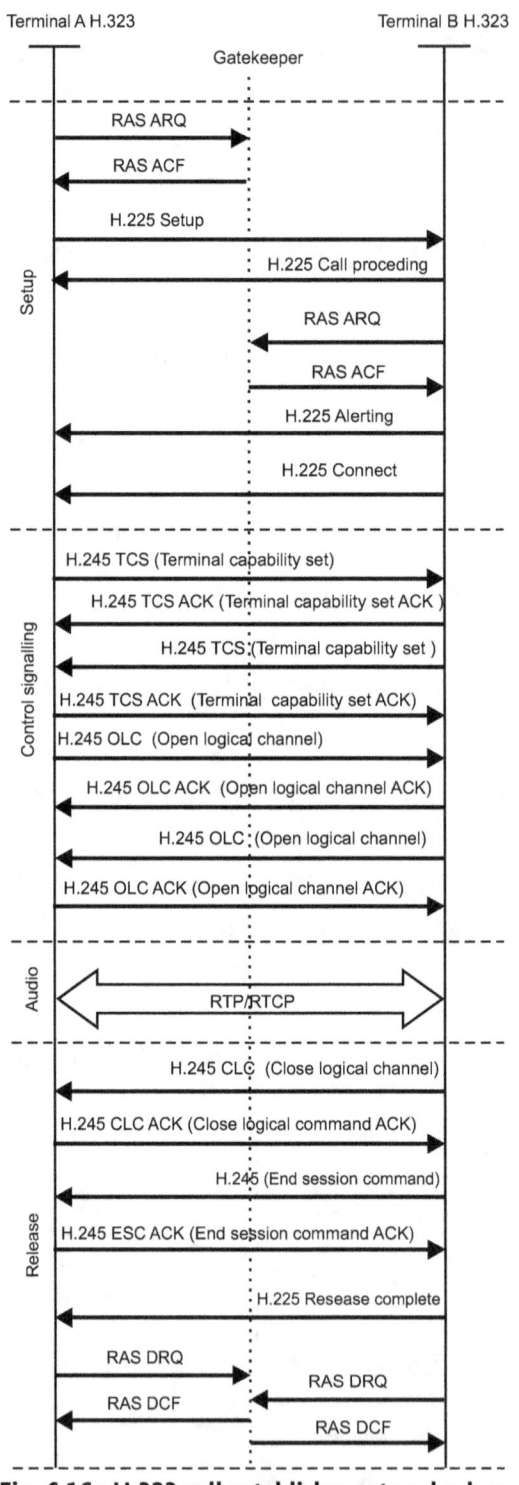

Fig. 6.16 : H.323 call establishment and release

A H.323 Call has 4 Different Processes:

1. Setup

- Terminal 1 register itself with the gatekeeper using the RAS protocol (Register, admission, status) sending an ARQ message and receiving an ACF message.

- Using H.225 protocol (used for setup and release of the call) terminal T1 sends a SETUP message to T2 requesting a connection. This message contains the IP address, port and alias of the calling user or the IP address and port of the called user.

- T2 sends a CALL PROCEEDING message warning on the attempt to establish a call

- Now, T2 terminal must register itself in the gatekeeper as T1 previously do.

- Alerting message indicates the beginning of tone generation phase.

- And finally, CONNECT message shows the beginning of the connection.

2. Control Signalling

In this phase a negotiation using H.245 protocol is opened (conference control), the interchange of the messages (request and answer) between both terminals establishes who will be the master and who the slave, the capacities of the participants and the audio and video codecs to be used. When the negotiation finishes the communication channel is opened (IP addresses, port).

The main H.245 messages used in this step are:

- TerminalCapabilitySet (TCS). Message capabilities supported by the terminals that take part in a call

- Open Logical Channel (OLC). Message to open the logical channel which contains information to allow the reception and codification of the data. It contains information of the data type that will be sent.

3. Audio

Terminals start the communication using the RTP/RTCP protocol.

4. Call Release

- The calling or the called terminal can initiate the ending process using the Close Logical Channel and End Session Comand messages to finish the call using again H.245.

- Then using H.225 the connection is closed with the RELEASE COMPLETE message.

- And finally the registration of the terminals in the gatekeeper are cleared using RAS protocol.

6.4.3 The H.323 Fast Connect Procedure

- Fast Start, also known as Fast Connect, allows two H.323 endpoints the ability to establish two media DS-0's before the H.245 CONNECT message is sent.

- Fast Connect bypasses some call setup steps in order to make it faster and allows the media channels to be operational before the CONNECT message is sent, which is a requirement for certain billing procedures.

The Fast Connect functionality operates as follows:

- A SETUP message is transmitted from the originating endpoint. This SETUP message has the fastStart component in it which is a series of encoded logical channel patterns, each having their own capability media type for both send and receive directions.

- The Called endpoint selects one or more of the media types offered and returns its selection in a fastStart component in any H.225 message up to and including connect. At this point, the called endpoint must be prepared to receive media along any of the channels it selected.

- The Fast Start procedure is optional in the H.323 Version 2 network, but the 2020 IMG will always attempt it. If Fast Start fails due to unmatched preferred capabilities or because the remote end does not support Fast Start, then the 2020 IMG will fall back to the TermCaps procedure. For more information regarding the Fast Start procedure, refer to Version 2 of the ITU H.323 Specification. Below is a call flow diagram displaying the Fast Start setup procedure for 2020 IMG in H.323 Version 2 as shown Fig. 6.17.

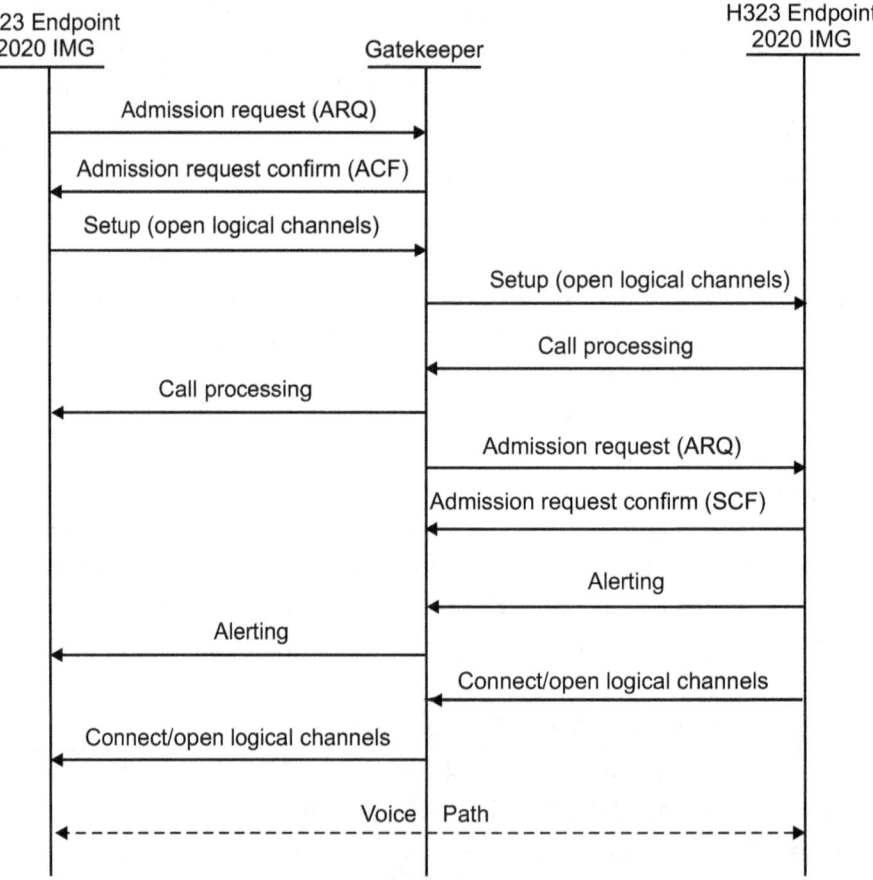

Fig. 6.17 : H.323 fast connect procedure

6.5 THE SESSION INITIATION PROTOCOL (SIP)

- SIP (Session Initiation Protocol) is a signaling protocol used to create, manage and terminate sessions in an IP based network. A session could be a simple two-way telephone call or it could be a collaborative multi-media conference session.

- This makes possible to implement services like voice-enriched e-commerce, web page click-to-dial or Instant Messaging with buddy lists in an IP based environment. Don't worry if you don't know about these services. You don't need to know them before you learn about SIP.

- The SIP is better and simpler than H.323. It is easier to implement, better suited to the support of intelligent user devices, and better suited to the implementation of advanced features such as IMS. Even though, H.323has large installation base, SIP will soon take over as a signaling protocol of VoIP. 3GPP has endorsed SIP as the session management protocol. SIP is simply a signaling protocol and uses services of RTP for the transport of the voice packets.

- SIP is limited to only the setup, modification and termination of sessions. It serves four major purposes SIP allows for the establishment of user location (i.e. translating from a user's name to their current network address).

- SIP provides for feature negotiation so that all of the participants in a session can agree on the features to be supported among them. SIP is a mechanism for call management for example adding, dropping, or transferring participants. SIP allows for changing features of a session while it is in progress.

6.5.1 The SIP Network Architecture

- SIP uses a client–server model. Entities interacting in a SIP scenario are called User Agents (UA).

User Agents may operate in two fashions:

- **User Agent Client (UAC) :** It generates requests and send those to servers.
- **User Agent Server (UAS) :** It gets requests, processes those requests and generate responses.

Clients:

- In general we associate the notion of clients to the end users i.e. the applications running on the systems used by people. It may be a softphone application running on your PC or a messaging device in your IP phone.

- It generates a request when you try to call another person over the network and sends the request to a server (generally a proxy server).

- We will go through the format of requests and proxy servers in more detail later.

Servers:

Servers are in general part of the network. They possess a predefined set of rules to handle the requests sent by clients.

Servers can be of several types :

Proxy Server: These are the most common type of server in a SIP environment. When a request is generated, the exact address of the recipient is not known in advance. So the client sends the request to a proxy server. The server on behalf of the client (as if giving a proxy for it) forwards the request to another proxy server or the recipient itself.

Redirect Server: A redirect server redirects the request back to the client indicating that the client needs to try a different route to get to the recipient. It generally happens when a recipient has moved from its original position either temporarily or permanently.

Registrar: As you might have guessed already, one of the prime jobs of the servers is to detect the location of an user in a network. How do they know the location? If you are thinking that users have to register their locations to a Registrar server, you are absolutely right. Users from time to time refreshes their locations by registering (sending a special type of message) to a Registrar server.

Location Server: The addresses registered to a Registrar are stored in a Location Server.

The SIP specification defines following request methods(commands):

Invite : Invites a user to a call

ACK : Acknowledgement is used to facilitate reliable message exchange for invites.

BYE : Terminates a connection between users

Cancel : Terminates a request, or search, for a user. It is used if a client sends an INVITE and then changes its decision to call the recipient.

Options : Solicits information about a server's capabilities.

Register : Registers a user's current location

Info : Used for mid-session signaling

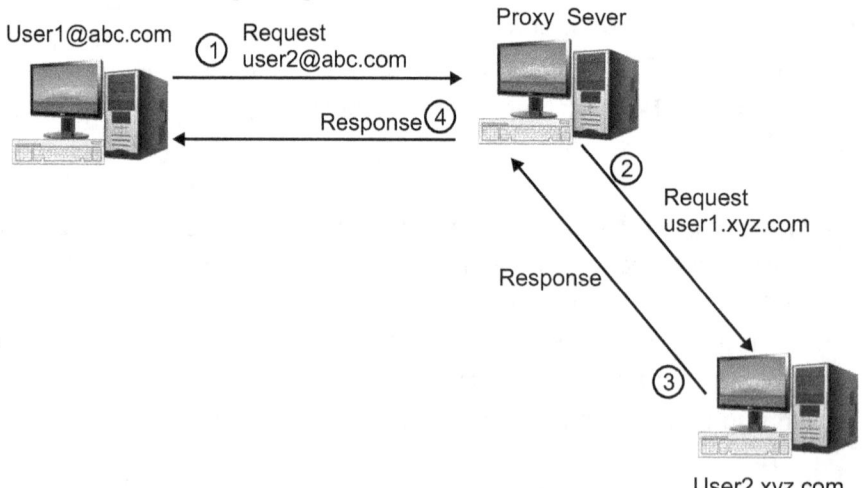

Fig. 6.18 : SIP proxy server

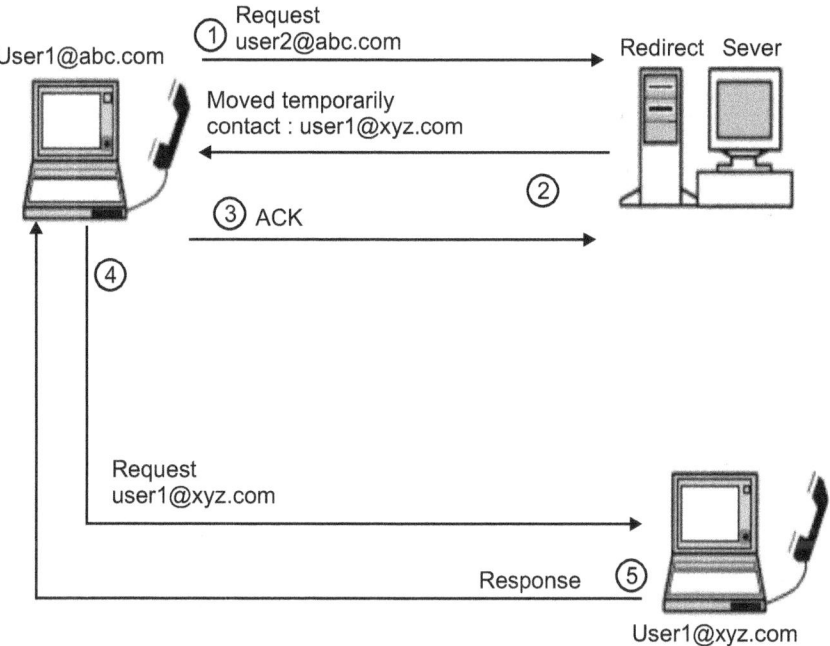

Fig. 6.19 : SIP redirect server

6.5.2 A Basic SIP Call Flow

- There are many different SIP scenarios and call flows in a VoIP environment. This post describes a very basic SIP call flow case where A is the caller and B is the recipient. Users A and B probably have a SIP proxy server each handling the signaling on behalf of them.

- When A wants to initiate a new call, it sends an initial invite to B. This invite contains various headers with signaling information such as A's and B's addresses/phone numbers, SIP path information, etc. The invite also carriers a Session Description Protocol (SDP) body with information regarding the media settings that A supports/prefers e.g. codecs and media addresses.

- When B's SIP proxy receives the invite, it sends back an "100 Trying" SIP response which means that it has accepted the invite and it processes it. When B's phone starts ringing, a "180 Ringing" is sent back to notify A.

- When B answers the phone, a "200 OK" SIP message is sent back to A. This message usually contains a SDP body with the media settings that B supports/prefers.

- The point here is that A and B -via SDP- are negotiating the media parameters that will be used during the call.

- Finally A replies with an ACK in order to confirm that the "200 OK" has been received.

- From that moment, the two parties can start speaking with each other using the negotiated media parameters. When one of the parties releases the call, a BYE message is sent to the other party who in turn sends back a "200 OK" to confirm the call release.

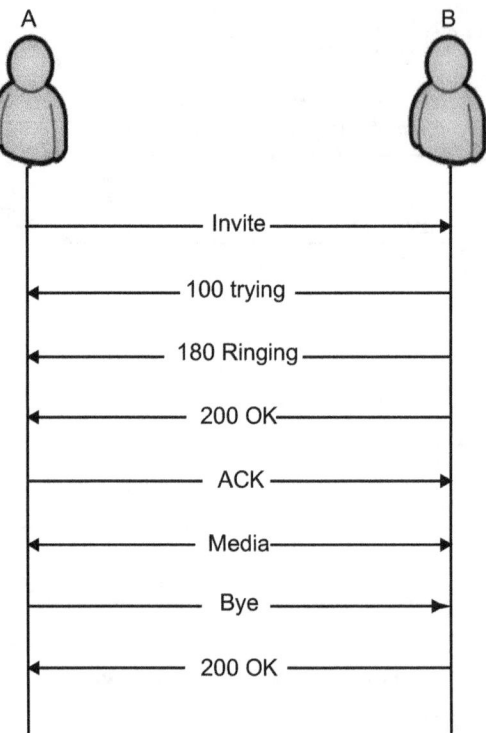

Fig. 6.20 : SIP Call Flow

6.5.3 Information in SIP Messages

- Every SIP request or respon semessage contains addresses for the calling and called parties. This address is called SIP Uniform Resource Locator (URL). Its format is SIP: user@domain. It is similar to email ID. Hence it is easy to remember instead of a number.

- When the called user is not available, then the response Temporarily Unavailable (status code 480) is sent instead of OK.

- Number of information elements also can be contained in those requests and responses in the form of header fields. For example, when sending an Invite, the message can contains a session description, the to and from addresses and also a Subject header field.

- The subject field can be used to indicate purpose of the call so that the called party knows about it.

- Some more header fields are Call ID, Date, Timestamp, In-reply-to, Retry-after, and Priority. For example The Retry-after header is useful to respond to the caller to try again later.

- The Content-type header field indicates the type of additional information included in the message. For example, a session description, which tells receiver the type of session, is included when Invite message is sent.

6.5.4 The Session Description Protocol (SDP)

- The purpose of SDP is to convey information about media streams in multimedia sessions to help participants join or gather info of a particular session.

SDP is a Short Structured Textual Description :

- SDP contains information about Parties to be involved in the session, the date and time when the session is to take place, the types of media streams to be shared, addresses and port numbers to be used.
- It conveys the name and purpose of the session, the media, protocols, codec formats, timing and transport information.
- A tentative participant checks these information and decides whether to join a session and how and when to join a session if it decides to do so.
- The format has entries in the form of <type> = <value>, where the <type> defines a unique session parameter and the <value> provides a specific value for that parameter.
- The general form of a SDP message is: x = parameter1 parameter2 ... parameterN
- The line begins with a single lower-case letter, for example, x. There are never any spaces between the letter and the =, and there is exactly one space between each parameter. Each field has a defined number of parameters.
- A session description can indicate multiple media streams. For example, in a video conference a coded voice and coded video are to be used. Consequently, SDP is structured so that it can describe information related to the session as a whole (e.g., the name of the session) plus information associated with each individual stream (e.g., the media format and the applicable port number).
- Some of the information included in an SDP session description also will be included in the SIP message that carries the SDP description. It is due to the fact that SDP is designed to be used not only by SIP but also by other protocols.

6.6 DISTRIBUTED ARCHITECTURE AND MEDIA GATEWAY CONTROL

- SIP and H.323, that are primarily deployed to control end stations, such as multimedia terminals or video-conferencing systems. These protocols may be resident within the applications or operating systems of these end stations, enabling the end stations to initiate, control, and terminate a call.
- However, when dissimilar networks are involved in the communication path, such as a workstation attached to an IP network calling an analog telephone connected to the PSTN, gateways between those networks must get involved.
- A second category of signaling protocols is thus required between the telephone gateway to control their operation and establish paths between those dissimilar networking environments.

- The Media Gateway Protocol (MGCP) was developed by the IETF (7). The MGCP specification details the commands and parameters that are passed between the MGC (call Agent) and the telephone gateway to be controlled.

- The call control element is referred to as a Call Agent in MGCP. Thus, the purpose of MGCP is to send commands from the Call Agent to one of the above types of gateways in a master/slave fashion. MGCP does not define any communication mechanism for synchronization between Call Agents.

- MGCP further assumes a connection model and defines both endpoints and connections. Endpoints are sources or sinks of data and can be either physical or virtual. Endpoints identifiers have two components: the domain name of the gateway that is managing the endpoint, and a local name within that gateway.

- Connections can be either point-to-point or multipoint in nature. Further connections are grouped into calls, where one or more connections can belong to one call. The connections and calls are established by the actions of one or more Call Agents.

- The information communicated between Call Agents and endpoints is either events or signals. An example of an event would be a telephone going off hook, while a signal may be the application of dial tome to an endpoint.

- These events and signals are grouped into packages, which are supported by a particular type of endpoint.

- One package may support events and signals for analog lines, while another package may support a group of events and signals for video lines.

- Some of these packages are, generic media, DTMF, MF, Trunk, Line, Handset, RTP, Network Access Server, Announcement Server, and Script. Each on these had specific functions and parameters.

- Though IP telephony may well be the springboard for the kinds of new, enhanced voice and data services that carriers crave, deployment has been slowed by lack of (or too many!) Voice over IP (VoIP) standards.

- The latest call control protocol, Megaco (an evolution of Media Gateway Control), adds to the problem while seeking to reduce the number of protocols in use.

- Megaco addresses the relationship between the Media Gateway (MG), which converts circuit-switched voice to packet-based traffic, and the Media Gateway Controller (MGC), sometimes called a call agent or softswitch, which dictates the service logic of that traffic (see Fig. 6.21).

- Put another way, Megaco is designed for intradomain remote control of connection-aware or session-aware devices, such as VoIP gateways, remote access servers, Digital Subscriber Line Access Multiplexers (DSLAMs), Multiprotocol Label Switching (MPLS) routers, optical cross-connects, PPP session aggregation boxes, and so on.

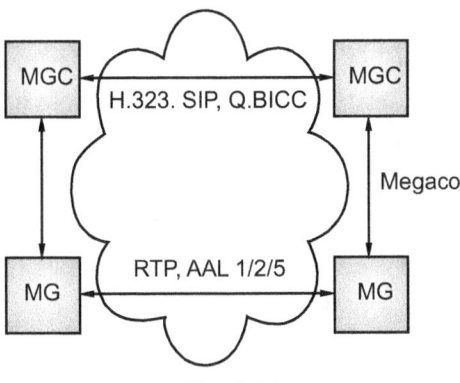

Fig. 6.21

- For carriers and vendors, the decision to implement Megaco means answering the question "How much signaling-the protocols that make connections between endpoints (such as telephones, PBX uplinks, and videoconference stations)-should be in the gateway?" From time to time, this debate has swung from "Endpoints are where the action is; they should be smart," to "Interaction is king; best to centralize."

- For those who believe that end devices should be intelligent, signaling terminates in the MG itself.

- An example is a Session Initiation Protocol (SIP) phone, as the call control signaling runs directly on the end device. For those who believe there is merit in leaving the signaling on a general-purpose computer, leaving adaptation of media on and off the network to a specialized device, there is need for a protocol between the media handling part (the MG) and the signaling part (the MGC).

- That's where MGCP and the newest kid on the block, Megaco, (also known by its ITU designation, H.248) come in.

- These are relatively low-level device-control protocols that instruct an MG to connect streams coming from outside a packet or cell data network onto a packet or cell stream such as the Real-Time Transport Protocol (RTP).

- Megaco is essentially quite similar to MGCP from an architectural standpoint and the controller-to-gateway relationship, but Megaco supports a broader range of networks, such as ATM.

- For example, MGCP typically conditions the endpoint to look for an off-hook indication (when a person lifts the receiver to make a call).

- When the MG detects the off hook, it tells the MGC, which might respond with a command to instruct the MG to put dial tone on the line and listen for DTMF tones indicating the dialed number.

- After detecting the number, the MGC determines how to route the call and, using an inter-MGC signaling protocol such as H.323, SIP, or Q.BICC, contacts the terminating MGC.

- The terminating MGC might instruct the appropriate gateway to ring the dialed line. When the MG detects the dialed line is off hook, both MGs might be instructed by their respective MGCs to establish two-way voice across the data network.

- Thus, these protocols have ways to detect conditions on endpoints and notify the MGC of their occurrence; place signals (such as dial tone) on the line; and create media streams between endpoints on the MG and the data network, such as RTP streams.

- Right now, many vendors consider it more practical to build large gateways that separate the signaling from the media-handling because of the density of the interconnections (which may have OC-3 or even OC-12 connections).

- Removing the signaling to a fast server is more practical than trying to integrate it into the MG.

- Also, by removing the signaling from a residential gateway, network operators retain a higher degree of control, which many believe will result in more reliable networks-vital if VoIP systems support lifeline/emergency services.

6.6.1 Concept of Megaco

- There are two basic constructs in Megaco: terminations and contexts as shown in Fig. 6.22.

- Terminations represent streams entering or leaving the MG (for example, analog telephone lines, RTP streams, or MP3 streams).

- Terminations have properties, such as the maximum size of a jitter buffer, which can be inspected and modified by the MGC. A termination is given a name, or Termination ID, by the MG. Some terminations, which typically represent ports on the gateway, such as analog loops or DS0s, are instantiated by the MG when it boots and remain active all the time.

- Other terminations are created when they are needed, get used, and then are released. Such terminations are called "ephemerals" and are used to represent flows on the packet network, such as an RTP stream.

- Terminations may be placed into contexts, which are defined as when two or more termination streams are mixed and connected together.

- The normal, "active" context might have a physical termination (say, one DS0 in a DS3) and one ephemeral one (the RTP stream connecting the gateway to the network).

- Contexts are created and released by the MG under command of the MGC. Once created, a context is given a name (Context ID), and can have terminations added and removed from it.

- A context is created by adding the first termination, and it is released by removing (subtracting) the last termination.

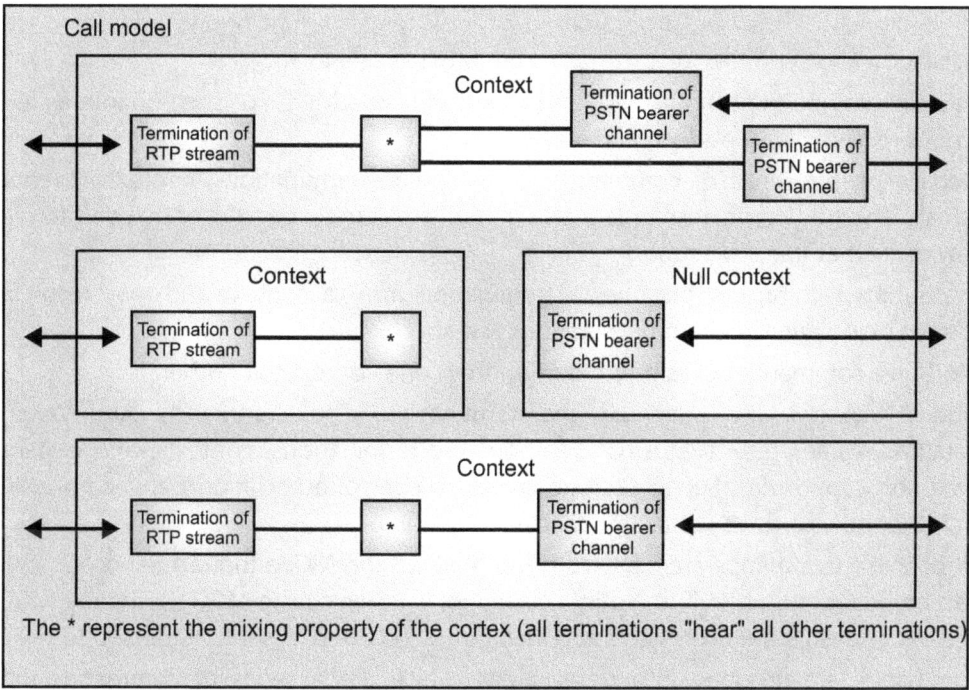

Fig. 6.22

- While a simple call may have two terminations per context (the termination representing the end device, such as the telephone, and the termination representing the RTP connection to the network), a conference call might have dozens, each one representing one leg of the conference.

- It's also possible to have a context with only one termination (say, in a three-way call).

- At any one time, two of the terminations are in one context (and are therefore connected together), while the third termination is in a context all by itself.

- When the user indicates that he or she wants to switch from the active to the standby caller (by using "flash," for instance), one of the terminations is moved to the other context.

- A termination may have more than one stream, and therefore a context may be a multistream context. Audio, video, and data (for example, T-120 shared whiteboard) streams may exist in a context among several terminations.

- Besides making basic connections by placing terminations in contexts, MGs may also be able to generate tones, announcements, ringing, and other signals that the user can hear. Megaco includes facilities to apply signals to terminations and control them.

- This enables gateways that have Interactive Voice Response (IVR) functionality to be controlled with Megaco, and also provides normal call-progress indications.

- Asynchronous events, such as the took switch on a phone or a DTMF key press, can be detected on the MG and reported to the MGC. By using a shorthand notation called a "digitmap," MGs may be programmed to look for an entire phone number or feature invocation and send the "dial string" to the MGC as one event.

- Statistics may be kept by the MG, and reported to the MGC, for such quantities as bytes sent or received, packets lost, and so on.

- Megaco uses a series of commands to manipulate terminations, contexts, events, and signals. The Add command adds a termination to a context and may be used to create a new context at the same time.

- The Subtract command removes a termination from a context and may result in the context being released if no terminations remain.

- The Move command moves a termination from one context to another.

- Modify changes the state of the termination. The commands AuditValue and AuditCapabilities return information about the terminations, contexts, and general MG state and capabilities. ServiceChange creates a control association between an MG and an MGC and also deals with some failover situations.

- All of these commands are sent from the MGC to the MG, although ServiceChange can also be sent by the MG. The Notify command, with which the MG informs the MGC that one of the events the MGC was interested in has occurred, is sent by the MG to the MGC.

- Commands are grouped into transactions, which are a series of commands that are executed in order, acting as the unit of transfer from the MG to the MGC and back again. Transactions are sent by a variety of transports between MGs and MGCs, including UDP and TCP (other transport options are coming). The MGC then sends an acknowledgement, along with replies for each command, back to the MG.

- Commands are grouped into transactions, which are a series of commands that are executed in order, acting as the unit of transfer from the MG to the MGC and back again. Transactions are sent by a variety of transports between MGs and MGCs, including UDP and TCP (other transport options are coming).

- The MGC then sends an acknowledgement, along with replies for each command, back to the MG.

- A package is a set of properties, events, signals, and statistics that are defined in a document and realized on a set of terminations in a gateway.

- Megaco defines a base set of packages for very common capabilities, such as analog and digital loops, DTMF detection and generation, and RTP.

- Both the IETF and ITU are working on additional package definitions. By defining a package, all the specific characteristics of a termination that realizes how that package is defined, and all gateways that implement that package can be controlled by an MGC that understands the package.

- The analog loop package has events for hookstate, signals for ring, and statistics for bytes sent and received, for example. A termination can have more than one package implemented on it. Packages can also be defined by any organization; a vendor could even define its own package.

6.7 VoIP AND SS7

- SS7 has been the tried and true signaling mechanism for providing signaling in traditional PSTN networks. But, with Voice-over-IP (VoIP) becoming a more important technology for carriers, carriers are starting to look for more IP friendly signaling schemes to use in their network architectures.

- Enter Sigtran. Developed by the Internet Engineering Task Force (IETF), the Sigtran protocol suite lets operators carry SS7 signaling traffic between a signaling gateway (SG) and a media gateway controller (MGC) or IP-enabled signaling control point (IP-SCP), thus allowing carriers to maintain their SS7 signaling schemes while being able to tap into the IP network for transport.

- Sigtran is a suite of networking protocols consisting of the stream control transport protocol (SCTP) and a set of user adaptation (UA) layers (which transform the look and feel of SCTP into the lower layers of SS7). The Sigtran architecture is shown in Fig. 6.23.

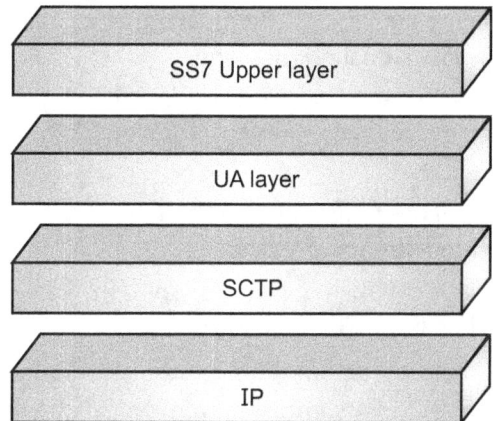

Fig. 6.23: Diagram illustrating the Sigtran layers

6.7.1 Stream Control Transmission Protocol (SCTP)

- The stream control transport protocol (SCTP) is a new transport protocol defined by the Sigtran specification as aa replacement for TCP.

- SCTP is designed to cope with time-sensitive signaling data while remaining flexible enough for general use.

- SCTP has been designed to counter some features of TCP that make it unsuitable for transporting real-time signaling data, such as:

- TCP is byte-streamed TCP provides a single stream of data and guarantees that data to be delivered in byte-sequence order.

- This makes it ideal for delivery of large, unstructured pieces of data, such as a file or email message.

- TCP is particularly sensitive to delays caused by network errors cause by loss of bytes, messages or sequence violation. When this occurs, TCP will hold up delivery of all data (for all applications) until the correct sequence is restored. Because of this, data for one application may be delayed due to problems in transporting data from an unrelated application.

- TCP timers are defined in terms of many seconds. In particular, the length of the connection, keep alive, and retransmission timers may result in excessive delays.

There are no Inherent Security Features in TCP itself

- SCTP is very similar to TCP, but has a number of features which aim to overcome the limitations listed above. These include:
- It defines timers of much shorter duration than TCP.
- It supports multi-homing. Each SCTP endpoint may be known by multiple IP addresses. Routing to one address is independent of all others and, if one route becomes unavailable, another will be used.
- It uses an initialization procedure, based on cookies, to prevent denial of service attacks.
- It supports bundling, where a single SCTP message may contain multiple 'chunks' of data. Each chunk contains a whole signaling message.
- It supports fragmentation, where a single signaling message may be split into multiple SCTP messages in order to be accommodated within the underlying Packet Data Unit (PDU).
- It is message-oriented, defining structured frames of data. TCP, conversely, imposes no structure on the transmitted stream of bytes.
- It has a multi streaming capability. Data is split into multiple streams, each with independent sequenced delivery. TCP has no such feature.
- Multi-streaming is the main attraction. This feature allows users to partition a single IP connection between two endpoints into separate logical streams of data, assigning each stream to a particular application or resource. The principle is that errors or delays on one stream will not interfere with normal delivery on another.

6.8 VoIP QUALITY OF SERVICE

- Perhaps the biggest issue with VoIP is ensuring that the Quality of Service (QoS) is comparable with the QoS achieved in traditional circuit-switched telephony. As we have seen, IP and UDP provide no quality guarantees whatsoever.

- Although RTP and RTCP provide QoS-related information (such as jitter, number of lost packets, and so on), they do not provide any assurance of quality. In order to ensure that VoIP is not a low-quality service, specific solutions must be implemented in the network.

- One way to help ensure that VoIP offers high quality is to ensure that more than enough bandwidth is available in terms of both throughput on transmission facilities and processing power within routers. By over provisioning the network, one can reduce the likelihood of congestion and thereby improve quality.

- This, however, is an expensive option that leaves much of the network capacity unused much of the time. Moreover, it does not guarantee quality.
- Thus one needs technical solutions within the network. Additionally, LTE has unique QoS capabilities that can be leveraged to support VoIP.
- The LTE QoS parameters can be used in place of the traditional method of over provisioning.
- The following subsections provide a brief overview of some QoS techniques. For more detailed explanations, the reader is referred to the applicable IETF specifications.

6.8.1 The Resource Reservation Protocol

- The Resource Reservation Protocol (RSVP) is a network-control protocol that enables Internet applications to obtain differing Qualities of Service (QoS) for their data flows.
- Such a capability recognizes that different applications have different network performance requirements. Some applications, including the more traditional interactive and batch applications, require reliable delivery of data but do not impose any stringent requirements for the timeliness of delivery.
- Newer application types, including videoconferencing, IP telephony, and other forms of multimedia communications require almost the exact opposite: Data delivery must be timely but not necessarily reliable. Thus, RSVP was intended to provide IP networks with the capability to support the divergent performance requirements of differing application types.
- A host uses RSVP to request a specific Quality of Service (QoS) from the network, on behalf of an application data stream. RSVP carries the request through the network, visiting each node the network uses to carry the stream. At each node, RSVP attempts to make a resource reservation for the stream.
- To make a resource reservation at a node, the RSVP daemon communicates with two local decision modules, admission control and policy control.
- Admission control determines whether the node has sufficient available resources to supply the requested QoS.
- Policy control determines whether the user has administrative permission to make the reservation. If either check fails, the RSVP program returns an error notification to the application process that originated the request.
- If both checks succeed, the RSVP daemon sets parameters in a packet classifier and packet scheduler to obtain the desired QoS.
- The packet classifier determines the QoS class for each packet and the scheduler orders packet transmission to achieve the promised QoS for each stream.
- A primary feature of RSVP is its scalability. RSVP scales to very large multicast groups because it uses receiver-oriented reservation requests that merge as they progress up the multicast tree.

- The reservation for a single receiver does not need to travel to the source of a multicast tree; rather it travels only until it reaches a reserved branch of the tree. While the RSVP protocol is designed specifically for multicast applications, it may also make unicast reservations.

- RSVP is also designed to utilize the robustness of current Internet routing algorithms. RSVP does not perform its own routing; instead it uses underlying routing protocols to determine where it should carry reservation requests.

- As routing changes paths to adapt to topology changes, RSVP adapts its reservation to the new paths wherever reservations are in place. This modularity does not rule out RSVP from using other routing services.

- Current research within the RSVP project is focusing on designing RSVP to use routing services that provide alternate paths and fixed paths.

- RSVP runs over IP, both IPv4 and IPv6. Among RSVP's other features, it provides opaque transport of traffic control and policy control messages, and provides transparent operation through non-supporting regions.

- RSVP is not a routing protocol, it is a signaling protocol; it is merely used to reserve resources along the existing route set up by whichever underlying routing protocol is in place. Fig. 6.24 shows an example of RSVP for a multicast Session involving one sender, S1 and three receivers, RCV1 - RCV3.

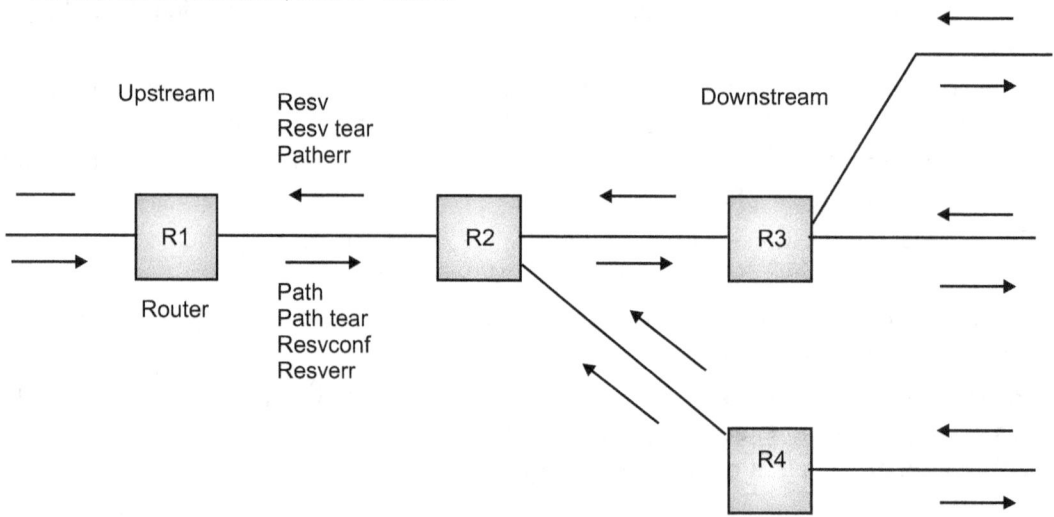

Fig. 6.24 : Resource reservation

- The primary messages used by RSVP are the Path message which originates from the traffic sender and the Resv message which originates from the traffic receivers.

- The primary roles of the Path message are firstly, to install reverse routing state in each router along the path and secondly, to provide receivers with information about the characteristics of the sender traffic and end-to-end path so that they can make appropriate reservation requests.

- The primary role of the Resv message is to carry reservation requests to the routers along the distribution tree between receivers and senders.

- Returning now to Fig. 6.25 as soon as S1 has data to send it begins periodically forwarding RSVP Path messages to the next hop, R1 down the distribution tree. RSVP messages can be transported raw within IP datagrams using protocol number 46 although hosts without this raw input / output capability may first encapsulate the RSVP messages within a UDP header.

6.8.2 Differentiated Service

- Differentiated Services describes a set of end-to-end Quality of Service (QoS) capabilities. End-to-end QoS is the ability of a network to deliver service required by specific network traffic from one end of the network to another.

- By configuring differentiated services, you configure your network to deliver particular levels of service for different packets based on the QoS specified by each packet.

- Differentiated Services (also called DiffServ) is defined by RFC 2474 and 2475 as enhancements to IP networking to enable scalable service discrimination in the IP network without the need for per-flow state and signaling at every hop.

- Routers that can understand differentiated services sort IP traffic into classes by inspecting the DS field in IPv4 header or the Traffic Class field in the IPv6 header.

- The differentiated services architecture consists of two sets of functional elements:

- **Edge Functions:** Packet classification and traffic conditioning. At the incoming "edge" of the network (i.e., at either a differentiated services capable host that generates traffic or at the first DS-capable router that the traffic passes through), arriving packets are marked. More specifically, the Differentiated Service (DS) field of the packet header is set to some value.

- **Core Function:** Forwarding. When a DS-marked packet arrives at a DS-capable router, the packet is forwarded onto its next hop according to the so-called per-hop behavior associated with that packet's class. The per-hop behavior influences how a router's buffers and link bandwidth are shared among the competing classes of traffic.

- The second key component of the DS architecture involves the per hop behavior (i.e., packet forwarding function) performed by DS-capable routers.

- The per-hop behavior (PHB) is rather cryptically, but carefully, defined as "a description of the externally observable forwarding behavior of a DS node applied to a particular DS behavior aggregate."

- There are two types of PHBs. The Expedited Forwarding (EF) PHB specifies that the departure rate of a class of traffic from a router must equal or exceed a configured rate.

That is, during any interval of time, the class of traffic can be guaranteed to receive enough bandwidth so that the output rate of the traffic equals or exceeds this minimum configured rate.

- The Assured Forwarding (AF) PHB is more complex. AF divides traffic into four classes, where each AF class is guaranteed to be provided with some minimum amount of bandwidth and buffering.

- Within each class, packets are further partitioned into one of three "drop preference" categories. When congestion occurs within an AF class, a router can then discard (drop) packets based on their drop preference values.

6.8.3 Multi-Protocol Label Switching

- MPLS is a famous networking technology that uses labels which are attached to packets to forward them through the network. MPLS is standard from IETF for including routing information in the packets of an IP networks.

- MPLS is used to ensure that all packets in particular flow take the same route over a backbone. MPLS can deliver the quality of service (QoS) required to support real time voice and video as well as service level agreements (SLAs) that guarantees bandwidth.

- In computer networking and telecommunications is data carrying mechanism related to packet switched networks. MPLS operates between that OSI layer 2 and the layer 3, so it can be considered as layer 2.5 protocol.

- It can be used to carry many different types of traffics including IP packets, ATM, SONET and ETHERNET frames.

- Multi Protocol Label Switching is a technology for delivering IP services. MPLS technology switches packet (IP packets, AAL5 frames) instead of routing packets to transport the data. MPLS packets can run on other Layer 2 technologies such as ATM, Frame Relay, PPP, POS, and Ethernet. Other Layer 2 technologies can be run over an MPLS network.

- Multiprotocol Label Switching (MPLS) is a protocol framework used to prioritize Internet traffic and improve bandwidth utilization.

- Those functions are accomplished by inserting a label between OSI layer 2 and OSI layer 3 in a packet and forwarding the packet based on the label contents alone as in ATM networks.

- Performance and efficiency are increased by this approach because less time is required to process a label than to process routing information like source and destination IP addresses.

- Errors are also detected more quickly they can only occur with a single label than with potentially several data types in different protocols. Figure describes a packet that has been modified for MPLS.

- Protocol data which is above layer 3 is unused in MPLS while layer 2 data appears transparent.

- Since the Internet is a collection of numerous networks using various communications technologies MPLS can be used without any changes to those existing mechanisms.

- Multiprotocol Label Switching (MPLS) is a versatile solution to address the problems faced by present day networks. Some of the benefits are given below:

  1. Speed
  2. Scalability
  3. QOS (Quality of Service) management
  4. Traffic Engineering

- MPLS has emerged as an elegant solution to meet the bandwidth-management and service requirements for next generation Internet Protocol (IP) based backbone networks.

- MPLS addresses issues related to scalability and routing (based on QoS and service quality metrics and can exist over existing Asynchronous Transfer Mode (ATM) and Frame Relay networks.

QUESTIONS

1. What are advantages of VoIP over traditional circuit switched TDM network ?

2. What are challenges for implementation of VoIP ?

3. What is H.323 ? Explain in brief.

4. Draw the basic H.323 network architecture. Explain any one of the components in the architecture.

5. What are terminals in in H.323 ?

6. What are Gatekeepers in H.323 ?

7. What are Gateways in H.323 ?

8. What are multipoint control units in H.323 ?

9. Draw the H.323 protocol stack. Explain in brief the services provided by each layer.

10. What is Gatekeeper discovery in H.323 ?

11. What is Endpoint Registration in H.323 ?

12. Explain the connection procedure in H.323.

13. Explain the call termination procedure in H.323.

14. What is SIP protocol? Explain in brief.

15. Explain in brief the SIP network architecture.

16. Explain with suitable diagram the SIP call flow.

17. Explain with suitable diagram the SIP call flow.

18. What is session description protocol ? Explain.

19. Explain in brief media gateway control protocol for VoIP.

20. Explain in brief the concept megaco protocol.

21. What is SCTP protocol?

22. What is Resource Reservation Protocol?

Sample Question Paper for
In-Semester Examination (30 Marks)

Time: 1 Hour   **Marks: 30**

1. (a) What is spread spectrum system? Draw block diagram of the DSSS transmitter and receiver. **(6)**

    (b) What are the features of 3G mobile systems which made it data centric ? **(4)**

OR

2. (a) Compare FDD and TDD. **(6)**

    (b) What are advantages of cell structures in cellular systems ? **(4)**

3. (a) What are key issues to be addressed for implement of Wi-Fi. **(6)**

    (b) What is Adhoc Wi-Fi network ? Explain **(4)**

OR

4. (a) What are various Wi-Fi protocols ? Explain features of any one of them. **(6)**

    (b) What is WEP ? Explain **(4)**

5. (a) What different QoS Classes in UMTS? Explain any one of them **(6)**

    (b) Draw System architecture of TD-CDMA **(4)**

OR

6. (a) What is WCDMA? Explain in brief. **(6)**

    (b) Write any four characteristics of IMT-2000 **(4)**

Sample Question Paper for
End-Semester Examination (70 Marks)

Paper - I

Time: 2:30 Hour   **Marks: 70**

1. (a) Explain following terms w.r.t. Wi-Fi. (i) Access point (ii) Basic service set (iii) Extended service set (iv) Distributed system   **(8)**
   (b) Draw the block diagram of OFDM system to explain how it works.   **(6)**
   (c) Write a shot note on Project 3GPP.   **(6)**

OR

2. (a) What are alternatives for WEP ? Explain any one of them   **(8)**
   (b) What are features of Next Generation Wireless (NGW) systems ?   **(6)**
   (c) Draw UMTS architecture as specified in 3GPP Release 99.   **(6)**

3. (a) Explain the System Information messages (SIB) in LTE   **(8)**
   (b) Draw and Explain the LTE architecture.   **(10)**

OR

4. (a) Draw and Explain the uplink logical channel structure in LTE   **(10)**
   (b) Draw and Explain the X2 handover in LTE   **(8)**

5. (a) What are various standards in WiMAX? Explain in brief features of 802.16m   **(8)**
   (b) Write about Modulation schemes used in WiMAX   **(8)**

OR

6. (a) Explain Handover process in WiMAX   **(8)**
   (b) Write about interference mitigation schemesused in WiMAX   **(8)**

7. (a) What are advantages of VoIP over traditional circuit switched TDM network?   **(6)**
   (b) What are terminals in in H.323 ?   **(4)**
   (c) What is Resource Reservation Protocol?   **(6)**

OR

8. (a) What is SIP protocol? Explain in brief.   **(8)**
   (b) What is SCTP protocol? Explain in brief   **(8)**

Time : 1 Hour   **Max. Marks : 30**

1. (a) With the help of suitable diagram, explain the evolution of wireless technologies from 1G to 4G.   **[7]**

Ans.: Please Refer Section 1.3. on Page No. 1.2.

    (b) Differentiate FDD and TDD techniques used in wireless networks.   **[3]**

Ans.: Please Refer Section 1.4.2. on Page No. 1.19, 1.20.   **OR**

2. (a) With the help of suitable diagram, explain and compare FDMA, TDMA and CDMA techniques.   **[7]**

Ans.: Please Refer Section 1.4.3. on Page No. 1.4.3.

    (b) Enlist the objectives of next generation wireless technologies.   **[3]**

Ans.: Please Refer Section 1.3.6. on Page No. 1.14.

3. (a) Compare the performance of various IEEE 802.11 standards.   **[7]**

Ans.: Please Refer Section 2.4. on Page No. 2.8.

    (b) Enlist various communication technologies deployed in ISM band.   **[3]**

Ans.: (i) WLAN   (ii) Wifi   (iii) Bluetooth   (iv) 2 gbee   **OR**

4. (a) Discuss various issues and challenges in the design of WiFi networks.   **[7]**

Ans.: Please Refer Section 2.8.3. on Page No. 2.26.

    (b) Explain the WEP in brief. What are the alternatives to that?   **[3]**

Ans.: Please Refer Section 2.9.1, 2.9.3. on Page No. 2.28, 2.30.

5. (a) Enlist the 3G proposals standardized by IMT2000. Explain the architecture of WCDMA - FDD networks.   **[7]**

Ans.: Please Refer Section 3.2, 3.4.1. on Page No. 3.7, 3.13.

    (b) Compare the performance of UMTS, CDMA2000 and TD-SCDMA in terms of spectrum requirements and modulation used.   **[3]**

Ans.: Please Refer Section 3.11. on Page No. 3.38.   **OR**

6. (a) What is the importance of IMS for all IP architecture? Draw architectural diagram of IMS based 3G network.   **[7]**

Ans.: Please Refer Section 3.5. on Page No. 3.18.

    (b) Explain the difference between1 XEVDO and 1 XEVDV.   **[3]**

Ans.: Please Refer Section 3.8. on Page No. 3.25.

MAY 2016

Time : $2\frac{1}{2}$ Hours   Max. Marks : 70

1. **(a)** What are the reasons for adopting All IP architectures in all the advanced wireless technologies ? With the help of suitable schematic, describe 3GPP Release 5 All IP network architecture.   **[7]**

Ans.: Please Refer Section 3.1 and 3.2. on Page No. 3.1, 3.7.

   (b) What is the importance Virtual Private Network (VPN)? Describe various types of mobile VPNs.   **[7]**

Ans.: Please Refer Section 2.12, 2.13, 2.14. on Page No. 2.34, 2.35, 2.37.

   (c) Describe the various types of hand-offs in used 3G networks.   **[6]**

Ans.: Please Refer Section 3.9.4. on Page No. 3.33.   **OR**

2. **(a)** What are the advantages of using CDMA air interface in 3G technologies ? With the help of suitable diagram, describe 3GPP Release 4 distributed network architecture.**[7]**

Ans.: Please Refer Section 3.1 and 3.6. on Page No. 3.1, 3.20.

   (b) Describe various type of services used in IEE 802.11 for delivering protocol data units, accessing the network and for maintaining privacy.   **[7]**

Ans.: Please Refer Section 2.10. on Page No. 2.32.

   (c) Discuss the evolution of 3GPP2 wireless technologies.   **[6]**

Ans.: Please Refer Section 3.2.1. on Page No. 3.8.

3. **(a)** Enlist the important features of LTE systems. With the help of block schematic, describe various components required in LTE architecture.   **[9]**

Ans.: Please Refer Section 4.1 and 4.5. on Page No. 4.1, 4.9.

   (b) How is MIMO used to enhance the performance of LTE ? Draw and explain eNodeB 4×4 MIMO.   **[9]**

Ans.: Please Refer Section 4.11. on Page No. 4.32.   **OR**

4. **(a)** Explain the importance of using HARQ. QCI and ARP in LTE systems.   **[9]**

Ans.: Please Refer Section 4.9.1.3, 4.9.1.4. on Page No. 4.20, 4.22.

   (b) What are advantages of using TDD in wireless networks? Draw and explain TDD frame structure used in LTE.   **[9]**

Ans.: Please Refer Section 4.10. on Page No. 4.30.

5. **(a)** Why do we use d OFDM and its different flavors in WiMAX technology? With the help of suitable diagrams, explain the detailed working of OFDM.   **[8]**

Ans.: Please Refer Section 5.7, 1.4.3. on Page No. 1.22, 5.16.

(b) Write short note on: **[8]**

    (i) Specturem used for WiMAX Technology

    (ii) Frequency Planning in WiMAX Networks.

Ans.: (i) **Specturem used for WiMAX Technology :** Please Refer Section 5.6. on Page No. 5.14.

    (ii) **Frequency Planning in WiMAX Networks :** Please Refer Section 5.11. on Pager No. 5.26.   **OR**

6. (a) With the help of suitable schematic, explain the generic architecture of WiMAX technology.   **[8]**

Ans.: Please Refer Section 5.3. on Page No. 5.6.

    (b) Describe the evolution of WiMAX. Compare different variations of IEEE 802.16?   **[8]**

Ans.: Please Refer Section 5.2. on Page No. 5.3.

7. (a) What is the significance of using SIGTRAN? With the help of sutiable diagram. Explain in brief various protocols used in its stack.   **[8]**

Ans.: Please Refer Section 6.1. on Page No. 6.1.

    (b) What are advantages of using SIP in VoIP ? Explain the complete functionalities of SIP for VoIP calls.   **[8]**

Ans.: Please Refer Section 6.5. on Page No. 6.21.   **OR**

8. (a) Compare in detail the various protocols such as H.323, SIP and MEGACO used for VoIP.   **[8]**

Ans.: Please Refer Section 6.4.2, 6.5 on Page No. 6.10, 6.21.

    (b) How do we differentiate QoS requirements for data and audio? Explain various mechanisms used to maintain QoS in VoIP.   **[8]**

Ans.: Please Refer Section 6.8. on Page No. 6.32.

NOVEMBER 2016

Time : $2\frac{1}{2}$ Hours   **Max. Marks : 70**

1. (a) What is OFDM? Discuss advantages and disadvantages of OFDM for wireless networks.   **[7]**

Ans.: Please Refer Section 1.4.3. on Page No. 1.22.

    (b) Explain in detail different protocols for WiFi.   **[7]**

Ans.: Please Refer Section 2.4. On Page No. 2.8.

    (c) With the help of suitable diagram explain in detail 3GPP release 4 network architecture.   **[6]**

Ans.: Please Refer Section 3.6. on Page No. 3.20.   **OR**

2. (a) List in tabular form mobile data supported by 2G and 3G technologies   **[6]**

Ans.: Please Refer Section Table No. 3.2. on Page No. 3.7.

     (b) Describe with neat diagram basic components of WLAN with their characteristics. **[7]**

Ans.: Please Refer Section 2.7. on Page No. 2.17.

     (c) Explain speech and data services supported by UMTS.   **[7]**

Ans.: Please Refer Section 3.3.1 and 3.3.2. on Page No. 3.11, 3.12.

3. (a) Describe downlink and uplink LTE channels.   **[9]**

Ans.: Please Refer Section 4.9.1. on Page No. 4.16.

     (b) What is Handover? With suitable diagram explain X2 Handover mechanism.   **[9]**

Ans.: Please Refer Section 4.17.1. on Page No. 4.41.   **OR**

4. (a) Explain the function of LTE scheduler.   **[9]**

Ans.: Please Refer Section 4.12. on Page No. 4.34.

     (b) Write notes on :   **[9]**

         (i)   Self Organizing Networks (SONs)

         (ii) Hetrogeneous Networks (HetNET)

Ans.: (i) **Self Organizing Networks (SONs):** Please Refer Section 4.18. on Page No. 4.46.

       (ii) **Hetrogeneous Networks (HetNET):** Please Refer Section 4.20. on Page No. 4.47.

5. (a) Give the functions of ASN, ASN-GW, CSN and different interfaces used in WiMAX. **[8]**

Ans.: Please Refer Section 5.3. on Page No. 5.6.

     (b) Explain 802.16m FDD and TDD frame formats.   **[8]**

Ans.: Please Refer Section 5.8.2. on Page No. 5.19.   **OR**

6. (a) What is meant by Interface mitigation? With suitable diagram explain frequency planning with fractional frequency Reuse (FFR).   **[8]**

Ans.:   Please Refer Section 5.10. on Page No. 5.25.

     (b) Explain Mesh network for WiMAX technology.   **[8]**

Ans.: Please Refer Section 5.3.3. on Page No. 5.11

7. (a) What are challenges of VoIP? Explain VoIP protocol layers.   **[8]**

Ans.: Please Refer Section 6.3. on Page No. 6.4.

     (b) Explain the process of SIP call establishment and release.   **[8]**

Ans.: Please Refer Section 6.5.2. on Page No. 6.23.   **OR**

8. (a) With neat diagram describe H.323 network architecture.   **[8]**

Ans.: Please Refer Section 6.4.1. on Page No. 6.7.

     (b) Write short note on SS7 protocol stack.   **[8]**

Ans.: Please Refer Section 6.7. on Page No. 6.31.